The AdderStane

Avalina Kreska

Broken Spectacle Publishing

First Published in 2017
by Broken Spectacle Publishing
Printed by CreateSpace
Copyright © Avalina Kreska 2017
The moral right of the author has been asserted.
All rights reserved.

Front Cover:
Papil Stone illustration &
Cover Design by Avalina Kreska

Back Cover Photo:
© Fetlar Aerial (public domain)

ISBN 978-0-9956995-0-2

From an idea by Avalina & Shraga Kreska

www.avalinakreska.uk

It's a rare thing these days, most people don't
have time to stop, to allow themselves to be moulded
and shaped by the Creation. A feather falls from
a bird and starts its journey alone; once it
was attached, part of the whole, then
it becomes an uncomplaining hobo,
drifting with no agenda, changed
by its separation—who knows
where it ends up or
what it becomes?

The AdderStane

> *"There comes a time in every rightly constructed boy's life that he has a raging desire to go somewhere and dig for hidden treasure."*
>
> *-Mark Twain-*

CHAPTER ONE

Metal ring-pulls, rusty nails, spent rifle cartridges and driving rain; that was all Liam found the last time he went treasure hunting in Morcambe Bay. Like ferreting—it was something he swore he'd never do again. But his desire had grown exponentially over the last two weeks, he felt sure that somewhere as remote and untouched as Fetlar would turn up all sorts of Viking treasure. He checked the level of his mobile phone before sneaking out of the back door; his father's 'borrowed' metal detector hanging from his rucksack. After walking for a mile along the island's only main road, he turned right at the grit storage area, and followed the dirt track up the hill to the unused, somewhat abandoned airstrip. Opportunist weeds and loose grit plagued the runway, and grasses had begun to encroach on the airstrip boundary. Fetlar once saw regular Loganair flights to neighbouring islands and mainland Shetland, but these were in the affluent, oil boom days of the 1970's. Now the only incoming flights were in extremis; from an air ambulance or coast guard helicopter. Following the airstrip to the end, he reached the RSPB Nature Reserve. He looked out over Vord Hill, the highest vantage point on Fetlar; a bleak looking, blank canvas in the north of the island. Due to the underlying noxious and inhospitable ferruginous deposits, the hill was perennially covered with sparse vegetation, so no tender plants could lay down roots. At the foot of the hill, the landscape merged into heather and grass fields, dotted with mires, and a kind of hummocky heath. Hidden underneath is a strip of green rock called Serpentine—this snakes north from the lower Houbie Valley (the centre of Fetlar), widening to encompass Vord Hill. Some believe this is what makes Fetlar special; that Serpentine helps people to see—to tune into past lives and heal imbalances. But for the modern 'Fetlarian', this was just an old wives' tale. Liam often spent hours with an Elder: Da Anderson, who told him all the ancient stories; Da still believed the trows, and other supernatural creatures held sway over the island.

But Vord Hill held no fascination for Liam—he was searching for the elusive Hjaltadans Stone Circle. He remembered the first time he tried to find it. It was not uncommon (the stone circle being smaller than most envisaged), for people to trek all the way out to the Reserve and come away disappointed. Sitting cross-legged on the heather, he reflected on how different the atmosphere felt, considering it was only a couple of miles away from the small council estate where he lived. The silence was sometimes accompanied by a tinge of loneliness, reminding him of a forgotten attic. He wondered if this was due to the Clearances. Da had told him about these practices—in the 1800's, landlords had favoured sheep farming over tenants, and many families had been turfed unceremoniously out of their homes, often with nowhere to go. He had never lived in a place where there was no traffic or 'people' noise—this is what he liked about Fetlar—not having to walk too far to be totally and utterly alone. The possibility that no-one would find him if something happened, excited him in a ghoulish sort of way. He seriously contemplated camping somewhere remote, possibly on the furthest reaches of the Lamb Hoga peninsula. He could take the dogs. He imagined himself a Shackleton-like figure pushing the unexplored boundaries of the island—not forgetting the hidden cave network.

He walked gingerly across the marshy parts of the grassland, heading in the general direction of the stone circle, walking slowly so he didn't miss them in the grass. His wellington boots squelched and sucked at the earth, and at times he ran quickly, so the island didn't consume him; he thought it more than capable of doing so. Walking further along, he looked back, only to realise he'd walked right past them again. He doubled back, and hastily took some pictures, just in case the stones did another disappearing trick. He zoomed in on the two stones in the centre of the ring. These were reported to be the remains of a fiddler and his wife, who had danced and fiddled all night, before being caught by the light of the rising sun that turned them to pillars of stone. The outer ring was supposedly the remains of the immortalised 'Trow Guardians' of the north. Like Da, he truly believed that such creatures could exist; like ghosts and fairies.

Many of the stones were well hidden in the grass, covered with rosettes of grey foliose lichens and mustard coloured patches of crustose lichen. He thought the lichen looked like tiny collections of islands, or volcano craters, as seen from a great height. The Hjaltadans were not the only circle of stones in the area; he looked to the left, in the direction of the Fiddlers Crus, reportedly made of three rings of stone. Da told him, that in the past, they held trials for men there, but he hadn't visited the site—apparently it was even harder to find than the Hjaltadans. Finely formed, companionless clouds dotted the blue sky; it was a fine Shetland day, but strangely quiet. He thought this odd, because the last time he visited, the place was alive with nesting birds, particularly the barrel-chested 'Bonxies' (the Great Skua) that zealously guard the area. It wasn't just the lack of birds; he noticed the air seemed bereft of any sound at all; as if the island was holding its breath—or maybe he was.

'Time to take out the beast,' he whispered. He assembled the metal detector and switched it to 'metal mode' and started swinging it slowly, side to side; or 'Slow and Lo' so he was told by his father. He dreamed of finding a Viking boat and camping out for the entire summer holiday, meticulously digging, until finally it was uncovered, complete with its hoard of treasure. He envisaged camera crews, flash photography, and his father speaking eulogies. Sweeping an area just past the stone circle, a small beep rang out, disturbing some small nesting birds who took flight. Excited, he pulled out the hand spade and carefully started digging. He ran the detector over it again—another beep. He looked around, not wanting to be discovered, as he didn't have permission to dig near a national monument. He fished out what appeared to be a small hook. He wondered if it was ancient, either way, he was glad it wasn't a metal ring-pull.

He swept the area again, but the metal detector remained silent. Investigating further to the right, he found a small fragment of metal. One edge was curved; as if fashioned from a larger piece. He retrieved the water bottle from his rucksack and spilled some water over it, rubbing it gently with his sleeve. His heart thudded like a boom box, as it looked like it could be silver, and bore tiny markings. Elated, he moved further right, the detector emitted a different, stronger signal this time. He switched off the detector, sure he was going to find another part of the fragment. It didn't take him long to dig a deep hole with the peaty soil being so waterlogged. He then hit something of a different substance to the soil. The material was velutinous; like soft, supple leather. Holding his breath, he carefully dug around the material, sweating with excitement. He attempted to lift it out, wondering if it was strong enough to withstand hard tugging without tearing it. Exhilarated, he pulled gently, changed position, tugged harder—then made a decision to give it one good yank. Before doing so, he savoured the moment, wishing he could share his good fortune with another soul; even his dog Rufus would have been better than nothing.

The wind picked up. Grateful, he turned to face the cooling breeze, and scanned the horizon. It yielded the same result: he was still alone. He knelt down and momentarily raised his eyes to Vord Hill. He felt the atmosphere change to one of solemnity; as if a teacher had entered a classroom full of unruly children. He turned back, eager to reach in and grab the material, but it seemed there was no longer any 'down'. The entire scene had lifted itself up in front of him like a massive picture—a vertical landscape towering over him. He gasped and almost choked on his saliva. He tried to resist screaming. Something compelled him forward—he felt an aching desire to immerse himself into this undeniably ominous spectacle. He made an involuntary noise; a half-cry, half-whimper, and struggled against the rising panic. His arm moved seemingly of its own volition. As soon as his fingers touched the scene, the upright landscape metamorphosed into a black, mirror-like surface of still water, enabling him to see his own timorous reflection. He thought he heard sounds. He strained to hear. He closed his eyes and held his breath (the only movements he seemed able to control) and reaching further in, he felt something cold metal. The sensation made him jump. He attempted to get a grip on it, something within him anxious to claim it. One hand made contact, then both hands closed around it. He pulled it back towards him in a rush; as if taking, rather than giving birth. Exhausted, and seemingly on firm ground, he lay quietly. He hugged the item closely to his chest, wondering what had happened—too frightened to open his eyes. He listened with such attentiveness, he fancied he heard the earth revolving around the sun. Opening one eye, just a crack, revealed a familiar scene. Relieved, he allowed himself to sit up and pant with impunity, desperate to look down at what he was holding, but was afraid—afraid of what it meant, and the fact that he was alone with it. He looked down. In his hands was an ornately engraved golden cup. Holding it carefully, as if it were a newborn babe, he gently turned the cup around, chuckling to himself and muttering about his good fortune.

In the centre was a lion. Encircling the lion; vine leaves, with long, curly tendrils that merged with the lions mane. Grapes hung in clumps from the vine, and he couldn't resist running a forefinger over the tiny bumps. Looking into the cup, he saw coins and other items. The cup was quite a size and heavy, and needed two hands to hold it comfortably. He lay back on the grass and thrust the cup upwards so it blocked the sun, intoxicated at finding something so special. He noticed his hands were muddy, so he sat up and wiped them on his t-shirt. He picked up the cup again and turned it around, grinning stupidly. Thinking he'd heard something, he instinctively covered the top of the cup with his hand and hugged it to his chest. Fully expecting someone to discover him, he sat still, and wondered if it was too late to hide it under his t-shirt;

but no-one came. He figured it must've been birds; maybe the ones with the long beaks, or the Bonxies had returned.

The enormity of the discovery left him feeling a sense of vulnerability, so he packed away his gear and decided to enjoy the cup in the confines of his bedroom. Wrapping an old t-shirt carefully around the cup, he placed it in a carrier bag, and then inside the rucksack. Scooping as much soil as he could back into the hole, he stamped it down before carefully replacing the divots. He walked heavily on them, squishing them down hard, and then stood back; certain no-one would notice he'd been digging. He was about to leave when he suddenly felt spooked—as if an unknown force were observing his actions. He swung around, not wanting to see a tangible reason for feeling unnerved—yet a part of him needed confirmation.

Checking his direction, he marched back to the airstrip, and then ran down the track to the road. He was relieved to be standing on hard tarmac again; as if it placed him back into civilisation, away from the mucky soil and creepiness. Normally, he would have dropped into the cafe for a can of coke, but he was desperate to get home, unable to shake the inexorable feeling that something was following him. Whatever it was, it was as tangible as a faint shadow—a mere suggestion. He tried to remember what had happened; but his mind, being overwhelmed by the experience, had somehow blanked out all memory of the vertical landscape; or maybe that's what the power behind this whole event required of him. With salient thoughts of returning home and admiring his treasure in private, he hurried back, breaking into a grateful run when the house came into view.

Like all guilty people, he tried to avoid being noticed. He sneaked through the back door and flew upstairs. His sister Holly saw him disappearing into his bedroom.

'Liam's home, Mum!' she screeched; not dissimilar to the alarm call of a prey animal. In a mad panic, he wrenched off the rucksack and hid it under his bed. Liam's mother, Sue, gently tapped on the door, and without waiting for an answer walked into his bedroom.

'Had a good day?' she enquired with a wry smile, scanning the room like all observant mothers do.

'Yeah—not bad. Oh yeah Mum, guess what? I finally found the stone circle, I photographed it. Look.' He stopped, remembering his mobile phone was in his rucksack.

'Oh—I'll show you later, it's hidden amongst all the bits in my rucksack, don't want to get it all out now.' He fake yawned. Sue narrowed her eyes.

'You realise you've been gone for seven hours?' she remarked, folding her arms. A jolt ran through his body; then a fleeting moment of uncertainty that she might be teasing him.

'Seven hours?' He figured he'd been gone two hours at the most. She nodded, her mouth set in a straight line with a fixed 'tell me' everything gaze.

'Well—of course—I did drop in on Simon, we played some music and computer games. I must've forgot the time,' he countered, amazed at how quickly a lie came to him. She backed off, realising she was being overly protective. She wanted her children to feel unfettered and free; it was one of the reasons Trevor and herself had decided to make Fetlar their home.

'Dinner will be ready in about three-quarters of an hour, might be worth you having a quick bath by the looks of you. Have you been digging or something?' He looked down at himself.

'You get dirty just playing around—you know how wet the ground is around here,' he murmured, smiling awkwardly.

'Well, get cleaned up. I'm glad you're having fun. So it wasn't a mistake to move here after all then?' She pulled a stray clump of hair away from his eyes.

'MUM!' He was certain that close proximity would enhance her maternal mind-reading powers.

'Three-quarters of an hour—then I want to see you downstairs . . . clean.' She studied him again before leaving, knowing in her heart he wasn't telling the truth; as all mothers know this instinctively about their offspring. Glad to be out of his dirty clothes, he floated away his felonious deed. Feeling a stinging sensation on his wrist, he lifted his arm to investigate; it was a shallow cut, at least 4cm long, red and angry, but not bleeding. He peered closely at it, having no memory of injuring himself. He was glad he'd worn a long sleeved t-shirt or his mother might've dragged him off to see the nurse. Not wanting his parents to ask any awkward questions, he decided to wear an old tennis wristband over it until it healed. He thought about the treasure and planned to take a closer look when everyone was asleep.

To avoid the risk of anyone walking in, he catnapped with the TV on low, and woke in a semi-panic at 1am in the morning. At first he thought he'd dreamt the whole thing, until he slid the rucksack out and retrieved the plastic bag. So as not to make noise, he extracted the cup under his duvet. Bringing the cup to the surface, he carefully peeled back the t-shirt; the gold cup stared back, its sheer size startling him. He thought it looked bigger than before—or maybe the four walls made it seem smaller. He tipped out the contents of the cup and searched for a sock. Pulling the computer chair up to his bed, he sat and patiently polished the cup. He was amazed that it wasn't tarnished, and it didn't take much effort to bring a real shine to it. On closer inspection, the lion looked sleek, almost stylized, with its tail arched over its back. It appeared to rear up in an almost indignant manner, with its tongue poking out. He admired the exquisitely carved grapes and vines that were connected to the long ringlets extending from the lion's mane. Lifting the cup, he attempted to calculate its weight, he figured it weighed at least 4lbs. He was desperate to run into his parent's room and show them, knowing they would be awestruck. He imagined laying the treasure out on their bed; his Dad would carefully turn the cup around and around with a stupid grin on his face, occasionally breaking into laughter at how truly amazing it was. His mother would just sit there with that proud son look on her face. He wondered whether it was a cup, a goblet, or maybe a chalice? Would they have used it for rituals, or special occasions? Or was it just a gift to an honorary member of the clan?

Investigating the contents of the cup, he found twenty-six silver coins, all about the size of a one pound coin. Some of them had been cut into, some were slightly bent, but all had the same cross in the middle and lettering around the circumference. He picked up what appeared to be a flattened metal band, maybe once a type of arm band or bracelet. There was writing on it; he figured it was some sort of ancient Viking language. Spitting on the bed cover, he rubbed the edge of the band, it had the lustre of silver, and was further engraved with a figure of eight design. If it hadn't been squashed, he might have tried it on—just to see how it felt—and imagine he was a noble Viking, with a weapon of some kind, and a wench. He laughed out loud at the thought and then realised he might wake someone. He listened intently, thinking of ways to hide it at a moment's notice. All that remained to be investigated was a piece of black wood about the size of a matchbox; it had no markings. Curious, he tried to find an opening; a latch or lock hole, but it appeared to be a single, uncut piece of wood. Upon doing this, he felt a sharp pain in the cut on his arm. He peeled back the wristband, his cut was still red, but now throbbed. Thinking he'd heard the sound of muffled feet on the landing, he quickly grabbed the coins and extras, placed them in the cup, and hid them in the chest of drawers next to his bed. He scooted under the duvet. There was movement outside, the door opened, there was a pause, and then somebody turned out the light. Liam was sure they'd hear his thumping heart. He closed his eyes for a second, but fell straight to sleep.

Fruma tried to ignore her rising annoyance as a passenger offered a fusillade of information about a distant Australian relative who'd just won the lottery.
The man continued, and as much as she felt pleased
for the stranger's distant cousin who'd just installed a
new luxury swimming pool with automatic pool covers, she felt as if she was giving away something very
precious: her time. With rising anxiety, and in a half
hysterical and abrupt manner, she cut the man off in
mid-sentence, offering some barefaced lie about needing to check on her dog; although she owned no such
creature. She felt she'd spent enough of her life listening patiently with things that didn't concern her. Only
last week, her neighbour had bitterly complained that
his neighbour was planning to poison his roses while
creosoting the fence. She wondered why she got
involved with other people's problems, and at what
point did everyone else's lives become more important
than finding out what she wanted in her dotage?

Recently retired from a lifetime of teaching, she
yearned for meaning in life; for peace and content-
ment. For a long time she believed that such things
didn't exist, that it was just words that one assumes
ought to exist, bandied around among religious types,
and New Age propaganda. Like the illusive notion of
love and happiness; neither of which she'd ever experienced. Either way—she was convinced, that by
spending three weeks on a remote island in the middle of the North Sea, a revelation would be forthcoming. Failing that, she'd enjoy endless, halcyon days
with nothing to do but observe the innocent wildlife
and remarkable scenery.

To the left, the Fetlar shoreline was clearly visible,
with seaweed strewn rocky shores that led to acres of
rough grazing land, rising further upward to the
northern cliffs. Further to the left, in the distance, she

spotted ruins on a flat stretch of shingle inlets hardly out of the water. She checked her map: Urie Ness— she imagined them to be old, abandoned fishing stations. She remembered seeing old photos of similar fishing stations; with fish drying on lines outside. Split open—then cured, salted and dried, their caudal fins reminding her of Swallow's tails. With loose twine wrapped around the base of the caudal peduncle; a pair would hang together—as if married in death.

She observed the ferry patiently swing itself into position, its huge, blue jaws slowly opening. Everything seemed measured—as if expending only the *exact* amount of energy to achieve its goal. She juxtaposed this against the yellow jacketed ferrymen, who seemed anxious to liberate the cargo. She watched as they rushed to push buttons and pull levers, then they would stare down over the lip of the ramp, as if wary of a 'Herald of Free Enterprise' moment catching them unawares. As the ferry butted the rubber tyres that lined the docking bay, it reminded her of the singular time she was taken to a fun fair as a girl. She'd insisted on riding the Dodgems and then spent an anxious ten minutes avoiding getting 'bumped' by maniacal teenagers—as if the cars gave them licence to use whatever force needed to *take out* the young Fruma. She knew curiosity laced with tenacity would be her biggest nemesis.

With the ferry finally ensconced, she set off. The vast expanse of empty grassland appeared to stretch for miles, dotted with foraging ruminants, the occasional roofless, abandoned stone croft houses, and dumpy Shetland ponies. A herd of brown spotted cows seemed strangely out of place to her; as if someone had swapped the hardy, Highland cows with ape hanger, handlebar horns, for a weedy bunch of bovines that probably needed shelter, and Shetland sweaters in the winter. In fact, if it hadn't been for the 'Welcome to Fetlar' sign she passed by the ferry terminal, she could've been forgiven for thinking the island was uninhabited by humans. A few brightly coloured storage containers stood resolutely on the side of the road—like a modern Stonehenge art installation. To the right of the containers, a new red van rested in a field as if delicately deposited by helicopter. To the left, by the road, wooden sheep pens seemed left to rot, ravaged by the ghastly winds that hardly ever left the island in peace. Today there was no wind; the sun had burned away the low cloud cover and heralded another promising summer day. She pulled over into a passing place, emerged from the car and scanned the horizon for houses. In the distance stood a dominant abode; obviously once of great importance. Nearby, incongruous to its surroundings, perched on a higher mound, stood a round castle-like folly complete with turrets. She stood quietly for a moment, absorbing the silence punctuated by the occasional clarion bird-call.

'So this is what a remote island feels like,' she whispered. Feeling it utterly peaceful, she could've set up camp right where she was, and lived happily ever after. But knowing her hosts were waiting for her, she returned to the car. 'Da Ty Rigg'—the place she would call home for the next three weeks, a small bed and breakfast run by a retired couple: Mary and Peter Smith. Turning right at the Tresta sign, she drove slowly past a dilapidated croft house with a sagging roof, aptly named 'Tiptoby'. Out the corner of her eye, she espied a ginger cat that leapt onto the windowsill before disappearing through a missing pane into the eldritch interior. Opposite, stood a bolder, modern dwelling. It was half-erected with no roof, but promised new life. A worker's radio blared out a golden-oldie; the men whistling and unintentionally hammering in time. Turning a corner, set in a valley, was Tresta Bay, a magnificent vista, and only a stone's throw from where she was staying. She decided to make it her first port of call after she'd checked in.

Mary Smith was in the garden excavating rogue dandelions when she arrived. Mary shouted to her husband who was in the kitchen.

'Guest is here—pop the kettle on!'

'I-i,' Peter replied, fumbling with the water filter. From the window, he noticed that Fruma had difficulty extricating her luggage from the boot of the car, so he decided to relieve her of her encumbrance.

'I-i, lovely day,' he commented.

'Oh, it's just beautiful and so, so—' Fruma struggled to find the right word, 'salubriously quiet too!' she replied melodramatically, with an upward flourish of hands. He raised his eyebrows and smiled, thrusting an unlit pipe into his mouth like a pacifier. He lifted the two suitcases with ease, surprised at their lightness. Mary came to the gate.

'Hello there! How's du? Glad you both made it in one-piece. Good journey?'

'Good. Yes—thank-you,' Fruma said, then realising Mary's error,

'Both?' she replied quizzically. Puzzled, Mary leant heavily against the gate, glancing in all directions.

'I was sure you mentioned you had a dog.'

'No, I've never owned a pet.'

'Sorry, my mistake—but hang on—isn't that *Laura Harrison* luggage you have there?' Mary asked breezily, hoping to change the subject away from her faux pas. She stopped her husband by bending down to investigate.

'An impulse purchase many years ago—I know—it's a bit high-class,' Fruma countered, embarrassed at the brash countenance of the shiny, aluminium suitcases against the humility and simplicity of the natural surroundings.

'I've seen it advertised, but it's even better in the flesh as it were,' Mary cooed, touching the classic, brushed stainless steel *L.H.* emblem. Peter coughed through his pipe at Mary, who straightened up and in a serious tone announced:

'Peter will show you to your room.' Then, in a more welcoming manner, 'Come downstairs for a cup of tea and a slice of cake—you can tell us about your journey.'

Like most travellers upon checking in, she scrutinised the bathroom for cleanliness before relieving herself, and reflected upon Mary's comment. She wondered what had given her the impression that she owned a dog. Deciding that Mary must have mistaken her for another guest, she wearily unpacked her belongings, glancing occasionally into the back garden whilst distributing underwear into a drawer. Recently watered tiers of potted pansies, and Sweet Williams graced the patio, and white plastic chairs clung to a matching plastic table like a mother guarding wayward children. Further out, the occasional low shrub skulked around the wire fencing. The remainder of the back garden was a recently mowed field that faded to distant boundaries. The long arm of Lamb Hoga, and Tresta Bay provided the perfect backdrop; it was impressive, and she figured it must be the most photographed part of the island. Stretching out on the ample bed she was relieved to have finally arrived, but was left with the inexorable feeling that she was still moving. She worked out that she'd been travelling for almost eighteen hours, if she included the overnight mainland ferry journey from Aberdeen to Lerwick. Then it took a further two hours to reach Fetlar by road; and two more ferry rides. She sighed, remembering it took less time and hassle to fly to America. The room was nothing special. A vast expanse of lemon wall stared back at her, punctuated by natural, wooden skirting boards and window sills. On the wall opposite hung a hand painted acrylic of what she presumed was a Fetlar scene; the picture far too small to be appreciated from the bed, and then on closer inspection wasn't worth the intrigue. On the windowsill stood a miniature, wooden spinning wheel, and a small, blue bottle stuffed with an assortment of dried flowers. 'Dust-catchers,' she muttered under her breath. She investigated the bedside cabinet drawers, expecting to find the ubiquitous Gideon Bible, but found instead an old book of prose. Flicking through, she found a Fetlar entry written in 1768 by a visiting Englishman: Thomas Letterton.

"Flickering light in pale, sparse yellow punctures loneliness with stars of warmth. Simmer Dim on Shetland traces eerie twilight at midnights across stark beauty precariously formed of light. The wisps of mist cling vaporously to the shores of Papil Water; inky blackness transformed to abyssal, polarized depths—no foot has passed this way this year—no voice has pierced the cloying silence of this shore—not this year—but waiting is the stones expertise that is shared by water, tied in serpentine stoicism that bakes a waiting birth."

'Tied in serpentine stoicism . . . . ' She retrieved

her map from the side table, noting that Papil Water was right next to Tresta Beach. Aware her hosts were waiting she went downstairs, finding them both sitting at an oak table that would comfortably seat six people. Long, heavy drapes were drawn one side to provide half of the room with shade. A tall Welsh dresser packed with blue, ceramic cutlery loomed over the seated Mary, who was pouring from a blue teapot that had a knitted puffin cover. She looked up and smiled at Fruma, motioning her to a spare seat at the table.

'Let us know if there's anything you want—evening meal is usually around six thirty; we can provide you with a packed lunch if you need one—just come down and ask. The back garden is at your disposal for those days when you want to lounge around and take it easy. So, how was the journey?' Mary enquired, tipping the milk jug at an oblique angle towards Fruma, indicating a question mark. Fruma nodded, and helped herself to a piece of dark, squidgy fruit cake that had an unusual short crust pastry surround.

'Long, but pleasant. I was glad it was a calm crossing—it's certainly a major expedition to get here.'

'It is. We try to avoid making the trip to Lerwick too often, that's a hundred mile round trip on its own, but coming up from England—that's a different story. Where do you bide again? Gateshead was it?' Mary queried.

'Yes.' She paused. 'I've been planning to get here since 2007—it's only taken me seven years!' she explained with levity.

'Time does seem to fly doesn't it Fruma? I mean, we've lived on the island for almost . . . must be close to thirty years now.' She turned to Peter for confirmation who nodded sagely.

'Has much changed?'

'Yes, seen a fair few folk come and go. When we first came here—that was in the seventies—they'd only just had running water and electricity put on. We came for a holiday, fell in love with the place and decided to buy a property here, then over the years we extended the building. Bed and breakfast accommodation is few and far between on the island, it doesn't make a huge amount, but enough to get us through winter, and it's nice to have folk visiting.' Fruma felt the shadow of a large bird fly past the window.

'Fruma, that's an interesting name, it's not English is it?' Peter probed. He seemed undecided about eating the cake, then snatched at a slice; the crust fell away in pieces on the table which he picked away at.

'It's not, no . . . . '

'We've got our own share of unusual names on Fetlar too—reminds me of—what was his name? Harpy?' Mary asked Peter, who barked back,

'Not Harpy—Harby.'

'Harby? It's not Harby—Haby—HABY—that's it! We'll get there in the end. Haby—that's right. He disappeared one night, his son had a strange name too,' Mary remembered. Peter quipped in.

'Heed.'

'That's it—Heed,' Mary confirmed.

'That *is* unusual,' Fruma said. Briefly, they sat in silence, Fruma yawned.

'This is a wonderful place to get away from it all. I tell you—you'll sleep soundly tonight, most folks do!' Peter said proudly, winking at Fruma.

'I'm sure you're right. That big house on the hill as you drive in, what's that called?'

'Brough Lodge. And it's odd little folly—it used to be an observatory.' Peter stated. There was a pause.

'Yes, I was beginning to wonder if I was on the right island—didn't see any houses until quite a way in.'

'I know, there's only forty of us presently. We had a drive for more people, but not many came; and then some of those left too. That estate on the hill—Brough Lodge, it's under repair at the moment, it used to belong to the Nicholson family, but their reputation is not very good with the local folk—not after all the clearances . . . . '

'Now, that's all for another time,' Mary stated authoritatively, knowing he'd keep Fruma talking for hours if she let him.

'I'm sure Fruma is tired, don't let us keep you, it's been a long day and I'm sure you want to settle in. As I said, just ask if you need anything,' Mary advised.

'Yes, I am feeling a bit travel weary, but I think I'll stretch my legs before dinner, get some fresh air. Tresta Bay seems a good place to start.'

'It is. See you at six-thirty for dinner.' Mary started, clearing away cups and plates.

'Thanks. I should be fine until then . . . with your lovely cake,' Fruma intimated. Mary beamed with pride, having no doubt in her mind that her home cooking always hit the mark.

Slipping her room key into her jacket pocket, she head out to explore Tresta Bay. She sauntered by an old 18th century manse, its walled garden completely filled with sycamores, all bent over by decades of punishing winds. Further on, she passed a featureless, grey, boxlike kirk on her right, surrounded by a cemetery wall that enclosed the resting inhabitants of the graveyard. A wind-worn, wooden notice board stood as a monument to a once active, bustling community; the notices inside had faded and yellowed with age.

Next to the car-park, it was obvious the graveyard had recently been extended. A rather elaborate, dry-stone wall had been installed; this made her wonder if the Shetland Island Council knew something the residents didn't. Standing between her and the beach was an unpretentious, metal five-bar gate. Opening it, she slipped through, obeying the warning notice about closing gates.

She faced the impressive Lamb Hoga peninsula; a jutting piece of sphinx-like headland made primarily of ancient gneiss. Old peat trails could be seen following the contours of the hill, disappearing over the ridge. Lamb Hoga guarded a crescent-shaped beach with scintillating, pearly sand, packed like compact powder; while natural polished pebbles of all different types and colours mingled at the sandy border.

To the right was Papil Water—it stood in stark contrast to the sea; a body of dark, peaty, motionless fresh water, separated by a short stretch of rough, machair grassland. Further round, the flanks of Lamb Hoga became steeper, curling cliffs over Papil Water— she likened it to a frozen tidal wave poised to engulf. The tide was out midway, so she decided to walk along the beach, enjoying the chattering and squabbling noises of a community of nesting Fulmars; their bodies snuggled into ledges and pockets on the cliff edge. She thought the translucent, turquoise sea wouldn't have looked out of place in Greece, but probably would take much more courage (and a dry suit) before immersing oneself in the chilly, single digit temperature of the sea. Because of the clarity of the water, she could make out the darker area of the kelp forests in the distance.

The sense of isolation gave her the feeling of being in a state of suspension. It was more raw and honest than she was used to—as if hope for the future wasn't required; just a faith in nature, and the will to merely exist. This was real freedom—with no obligations. The grass doesn't ask anything, the birds do what they always do, and a person is able to live in the moment.

Walking back up the beach she perched on a grass ledge and faced the north sea. The warm sun and stroboscopic light on the water sent her into a trance-like state. The area became misty; metamorphosing from summer to winter. Surprised, she turned towards Papil Water, the ground now covered with a light crust of snow. She watched as a group of men walked solemnly with heads bowed. They wore long, white robes that hung on malnourished frames. The loose belts tied around their waists accentuated their condition, and they each clutched books like talismans. They were dark skinned; their colour emphasised by the lightness of their garments. The only sound she heard was their sandalled feet crunching on the snowbound grass. Shivering from the sudden drop in temperature, she felt as if something had brushed past her, thereby throwing her back into reality—back into a summer setting. Alarmed, she stood up and looked around. Putting the strange vision down to tiredness, she decided to take a short walk around Papil Water before heading back, remembering the evocative words of the Shetland prose:

'. . . *inky blackness transformed to abyssal, polarized depth . . .*'

She noticed the atmosphere at Papil Water was different to Tresta Beach; the latter feeling more optimistic. As she walked towards the back of the body of water, a foreboding, almost sinister feeling intruded. Feeling uneasy, she decided to turn back, occasionally glancing back at the glossy, dark water, as if something were about to leap out and drag her in. She castigated herself for getting carried away. The ominous mood gradually lifted as she approached the beach, so she sat down again and looked out to sea. Feeling her thoughts drifting, she mindfully snatched them back. Acrobatic Fulmars flew to and fro. A Fulmar scout decided she was a possible threat, and made a few low, sweeping passes, scrutinising her. Standing up, she fiercely stretched her limbs, still taken aback that she was the only person inhabiting the beach. As she walked back to the guesthouse, she wondered about the robed men from her vision.

CHAPTER TWO

Christine laid the butterfly needle gently against Malcum's arm, it slid effortlessly into the vein; Malcum looked away, being squeamish about blood. She withdrew the needle, pressing down with a wad of cotton.

'There you go Malcum.'

'That's almost an armful that is. Nicely done, I hardly felt a thing,' he said, relieved it was over.

'Old Da knows just the thing for my arthritis—he's very good with the herbs you know.'

'This could take more than a few herbs to sort out —we need to do some tests, just to be sure. The trouble is, if you rely on only fixing the surface things and don't check these symptoms out properly, then you could miss an underlying health problem. Da can't fix cancer, or diabetes, or a genetic problem with chamomile tea,' she replied with a hint of sarcasm. She thought about Da Anderson's herbal concoctions, wondering how many other people's medical problems he'd attempted to fix. Seeing Malcum's worried expression she added:

'I'm not saying it's anything serious, but you need to be sure with these things. The Government has spent a lot of money on research; its proper medicine and we know it works—you were right to not leave it too long. So, just take it easy, no strenuous work, maybe take a few days off your postie rounds, drink plenty of fluids and avoid alcohol . . . . ' She carefully placed a small, round plaster over the puncture.

'Cut off my own arms you mean? How would I

deliver the mail?' he added, pressing down on the plaster. 'A man needs a wee tipple every now and then, surely you're not—'

'There's a great difference between a little tipple and a whole bottle Malcum. Who knows? You might be suddenly intolerant to alcohol. It is a poison after all.' She crossed her arms defensively. People drinking to excess was the bane of most nurses lives. Fetlar was no different to any other remote island—or Scotland for that matter—and it was more prevalent in England than most would admit; they were just more skilled at hiding it.

'Poison. Pshhhh! My father lived 'til he was 101. He smoked and drank heavily right up 'til he died. In fact, I reckon he died when he was told to cut back on the smoking. Nah—can't see me giving up on it,' then seeing her expression he mumbled, 'but I'll try and cut down.' He stood up to put his coat on. He didn't mind nurses, but he didn't trust doctors. Over the course of six years, various doctors had attempted to find a solution to his high blood pressure. He tried tablet after tablet, each with different side effects: aching joints, tiredness, backache, sore kidneys—he felt like a guinea pig. The worst side effect was erectile dysfunction; it made him and his wife miserable for months. He hoped that the headaches and nausea were just caused by 'overdoing things'.

'You'll let me know when the results come in,' he said; more of a statement than a question. She nodded and returned to her paperwork. This was her fourth year on the island, coming from a busy Sussex practice with a team of nurses. It was a very different experience being the only nurse in charge of forty people. One of the drawbacks, she noted, was dealing with fewer unusual or varied medical problems, but the Islanders kept her occupied—many just wanting a willing ear. She recalled a saying from one of the older residents:

'People shouldn't come to a remote island if they want to stay anonymous.'

In a small community like Fetlar, gossip was a common dish served daily; often several times. For Christine, it was a fine line to tread between being professional and antisocial. In a busy town practice, there was hardly enough time to treat people, let alone gossip about them. On Fetlar, she preferred to see patients in the surgery; the 'white coat syndrome' made the inquisitive ones behave themselves. But she enjoyed the continuity, of knowing everyone's name, and medical history—and it made her job less laborious.

'Cup of tea love?' William offered, his six foot two frame dwarfed the surgery door.

'That'd just hit the spot that would. Lovely. I'm hopefully done here for today.'

She closed the computer down and locked up. Living next door to the surgery was a blessing and a curse. Although she enjoyed being her own boss, she often felt her time wasn't her own, being on call twenty-four hours a day. The doctor from a neighbouring island visited every two weeks and was always available by telephone, which she was thankful for; but most of the time, she enjoyed Fetlar's slow pace. She recognised the greatest change in William. No longer overworked and stressed, he'd taken early retirement from a managerial post and was happy to potter around in the garden, tinkering with pubescent plants and harvesting the rhubarb forest at the bottom of the garden. He became fond of the resident minister, Reverend Mackey, and had surprised Christine by going back to Church on a Sunday—something he swore he'd never do again. William and Mackey often spent time together playing chess and going for long walks with a gaggle of dogs in tow.

She befriended Barbara, a newcomer who had arrived on the island about the same time. Barbara, and her husband, Lawrence, owned the only shop on Fetlar. Barbara had encouraged Christine to take up spinning, but Christine never showed any real talent for the art, preferring to curl up with a good crime thriller instead. Often, when arriving on Fetlar, there would be a time of frenetic activity for newcomers. Ideas would burst forth from those who thought they could 'civilise' the island, but the Fetlarians would patiently sit back and wait for the commotion to die down.

Other newcomers embraced Shetland tradition through osmosis. Trying their hand at knitting, spinning, weaving, fishing, crafting or dancing, until the novelty wore off, and each found their place and true calling. The island rhythm took over—and all responded: *poco a poco*. But many left the island, preferring to return to the anonymity of nimble motorways, and the ever expanding city sprawl. The call of an unusual, vagrant bird exchanged for corporate quorum, yet the city had its own share of nameless and homeless—no less unique. And thus 'The Leavers' only remembered the freedom Fetlar gave them in their dreams, where the subconscious could explore on a soul level, without the island tightening its isolationist noose around their necks.

'So, where are you off to today?' Peter enquired, generously buttering a piece of Mary's homemade bread.

'I thought I'd explore Yell. At the café I overheard someone say it's just a lot of peat bogs—I didn't have time to stop and look coming through.' Fruma was unsure if her comment would offend her hosts.

'I don't know about that! Mary's very keen on Cullivoe. Like all these islands, each has its own charm. The Old Haa Museum is worth a look around and you can have lunch at the Wind Dog Cafe or the Hillside Inn. West Sandwick beach is very pretty too isn't it Mary?' Mary nodded in agreement.

'It's been a while since we did any exploring, I guess one way or another we've been too busy here, if we have any spare time we visit relatives in England. But I've always liked Yell, and the folk are very friendly. All the islands have something special to offer and plenty of wildlife; though I'd still say that Fetlar is my favourite. What's that saying Peter?'

'There's an island for every person and a person for every island—or something like that—oh, I forgot to say—careful down the beach if you go today, you might find a different view,' he declared, before attacking a sausage.

'Don't tell me trees have decided to take root after all?' Fruma teased. He simply pointed to the window. She stood up and peered through.

'What am I looking at?' Her eyes darted across the horizon.

'You've not noticed the black water then?' he replied with amusement. Fruma looked again in earnest.

'Skittles! How could I have missed that? The sea is black!' he nodded, bemused. He made muffled, sucking noises as he lit his pipe, his head wrapped with a smoky voile. Fruma hadn't looked at the view that morning, being preoccupied with a vivid dream she'd had. She'd dreamt of dripping, dark water, that became increasingly viscous, a golden chalice was raised in the air, a black tar-like substance spilled over the edge, running over the fingers of the person holding it, before pooling into a lake of black water. Then the dream switched to Tresta beach in full, glorious sunshine, with a scruffy, brown dog holding a piece of driftwood in its mouth, and the number *237* being repeated over and over again. She'd woken with a start because a voice had shouted, or announced something to her—all she remembered was the final question: 'Who is your Master?' It was a male voice she felt she recognised; it was the truth of the voice—it reverberated throughout her whole life. It was *someone* or *something* that couldn't be constrained by the physicality of this world, or the Universe. The voice stayed with her, filling her, as if she were once so very empty. It was the reason she stayed in bed half an hour longer than usual, mulling over the dream and her vision at Tresta.

But she had no intention of sharing her experiences with Mary and Peter, not knowing how they would take it. She had always been wary of spiritual ideas, ever since a young woman tried to foist some lavender on her for good luck. That was the day she crashed her car. Only a minor crash, but it scared her into thinking the woman had cursed her, so she steered clear of anything that smacked of voodoo, witchery or spiritualism. She put vivid dreams and visions into the first category.

'That black water happened before—just before we arrived, it wasn't a particularly good omen, that young lad Heed died not long after—such a terrible business,' Peter stated. Mary fixed a glare at her husband before disappearing into the kitchen. She didn't want to talk about strange things as she'd also experienced unusual dreams the previous night; nothing but whisperings, shadows and hidden threats.

'I might just go and take a look before I go to Yell, I've got time,' Fruma declared, marvelling at such a phenomenon. Peter smiled to himself, knowing she'd be curious.

The sky was uniform in colour: battleship grey, a stark contrast to when she arrived, making the island somewhat cooler and darker. Even the atmosphere seemed to have changed. She sensed the rising tension and anxiety and was glad she'd worn a coat; something to wrap around her—psychically and physically. The entire coastline was black; as if someone had forgotten to place the stopper on an industrial inkwell. It was blacker even than the peaty Papil Water, and extended as far as the end of Lamb Hoga which was approximately two miles out. Dotted along the shore were dead fish of varying shapes and sizes; traces of black stained their scales. She watched the local men fill up buckets with fish, silently excogitating the black water as they moved along.

A couple with two young children observed from a safe distance; the curious children attempting to pull away from their parents' grip. The father lowered himself and whispered something to them. Their expressions changed. Shocked, they made no further attempt to escape. Fruma walked tentatively down to the shore. Standing in close proximity to the water was very different to observing it from Mary's window, and she decided to keep a safe distance. It was almost as if the dark, fathomless deep had come ashore; the part you're not supposed to see on land.

All the men had now gathered together and talked quietly among themselves—all wore a gloomy countenance. Every now and then, they picked up a fish and commented on it, before dropping it back in the bucket. Walking along the shore, she remembered the viscous, black water from her dream, and couldn't help wonder about the dream's prophetic nature. In the distance, a figure walked toward her, accompanied by two black Labradors and a scruffy, brown Lurcher. She did a double-take, staggered at the similarity between the brown dog that hung around the stranger, and the dog that had appeared in her dream. She recognised the same hoary muzzle, long nose and matted coat. Reeling from the seeming coincidence, her mind attempted to blank it out, cushioning her with a kind of seesaw effect; between belief and non-belief. The figure waved as it came closer. She hesitated, not at all sure the waving was directed at her— then remembering it was a local custom, she reciprocated.

'Morning!' the man shouted.

'Morning!' she replied, puzzled as to his breezy attitude considering the alarming scene. He was a tall man of some girth who walked with a slight hunch, as if used to bending over a thought, or ducking into croft house doorways. He appeared to be in his early seventies. He wore a long, green wax coat and a matching wide brimmed hat from which sprongs of unruly, white curls of hair attempted to escape. He purposely strode toward her, his hand held out in advance, a ready smile on his face. His confidence gave her a feeling of hope.

'Mine are friendly, they'll be no trouble,' he stated loudly. 'Mackey—Reverend Mackey—but everyone knows me as Mackey,' he said confidently. She shook his hand. It was a strong handshake; one that could snap bony fingers such as hers. She was taken with his sonorous Scottish accent.

'Fruma.'

In silence, they both watched as the men picked up additional dead fish further along the shore. She noticed the birds seemed subdued; there was the occasional cry, but not the general hubbub that once filled the air.

'Black water .... '

'Sorry?'

'Oh, sorry—I was thinking—it's strange, I dreamt about black water—last night,' she paused, 'didn't really mean for it to come out.'

'No need to apologise. You know, many folk say that their dreams are more vivid on Fetlar.' She decided to ignore his remark, not wanting to appear as someone who puts credence in such things.

'I was told this has happened before—the black water.' She wanted to appear totally rational about it all.

'That's right, in the 1970's—but it first happened in 1768.' *1768?* The date rang a bell for her. Then she remembered, it was the date from the prose she'd read in the bedroom. She tried to remain in control of her emotions at yet another coincidence and purposely ignored his brown dog who was looking more like her dream dog every time she looked.

'Do they know what caused it?'

'It was said to be a sub-marine shock or underwater volcano—but that's according to Mr Gordan, he was the minister here in the 1700's. But no-one really knows. It's fair shaken most folk; especially the older ones who remember the last time it happened.'

More people were arriving. Some were taking photos, some were pointing and talking excitedly, while others joined the group of local men in their discussion.

'You look like you could do with a drink. Fancy a cuppa to calm the nerves, or something stronger, perhaps?' he grinned impishly.

'I'll tell you more about it . . . . ' She considered his offer.

'Sure, why not—did you say you were a Reverend?'

'Yes, I'm the resident minister, been here for seven years now. Shall we?'

She was happy to be led away from the disturbing scene. Mackey's house was a short walk from the parish church; it was a croft house with a rambling, pretty garden about a quarter of an acre in size. Neat squares of flower beds and tall bean poles covered with racing pea shoots stood near the house, the rest of the garden consisted of a mixture of vegetable patches, herb beds and an unfinished stone path with grass growing through the cracks. A rickety, wooden bench sat in the only sun trap in the garden. One side of the garden was lined with fuchsia hedgerows. At the bottom of the garden, a mixture of sycamores and willows acted as a wind barrier from the 'southerlys'. A small greenhouse attached to a garage overflowed with half-ripened tomato tresses, like Mackey, they were bent over by the boundary of their world. Other greenery competed for space, but lost. A rusty spade leaned nonchalantly against the greenhouse frame, as if boasting of all the room in the world. Mackey released his dogs into the garden where they immediately started fighting. He grabbed the Lurcher by the collar and frogmarched it into the house shouting apologies to Fruma on the way.

'Just go in!' he shouted. Stepping into the small porch, she noticed a small cross and a motif over the door: *Man shall not live by bread alone, but by every word that proceeds from the mouth of God.*

'Come in, come in, let me take your jacket—sorry about that—Quincy is becoming quite unmanageable these days, I don't know why,' he asserted, still openly annoyed at the dog, whilst clearing up dirty plates that had been left on the floor.

'It's amazing how you still need to wear a coat in July on these islands,' she mentioned, still trying to ignore how similar Quincy looked to her dream dog. Apart from his colour and matted coat, there were two other recognisable features: a *Fu Manchu* moustache of fur, and prominent double spiral chest whorls that seemed to run counterclockwise. As if sensing her scrutiny, Quincy walked over to her and nudged her hand. Holding a hand under his chin, she looked into his eyes. She wondered how it was possible to dream in such a way, refusing to believe in anything of a supernatural, prophetic or spiritual nature that involved her. Deciding that she must have seen a similar dog elsewhere, she recalled Mackey's comment:

"Many folk say that their dreams are more vivid on Fetlar"

'It just shows how much colder it is compared to mainland England,' she continued.

'Yes, luckily I'm a bit of a cryophilic. I prefer it to the sweltering heat—please—have a seat.' He turned to Quincy who looked at him, defeated.

'Behave yourself!' he hissed. She decided to remove her walking boots.

'No need to worry if they're clean,' he insisted.

'Cryophilic?'

'I purloined it really, it's used in biology—means to

prefer to dwell in lower temperatures.'

'Oh, Cryo, from Cryogenics I guess?'

'Something like that,' he explained weakly. He showed her to a single armchair, the two other armchairs had paperwork stacked high on them.

'Sorry about the clutter, I'm working on something at the mo.' He cleared off the messy papers to a similarly messy desk.

'I'm a closet historian-psychologist-archaeologist given the chance, when I'm not being a minister.' She laughed at the notion while he went into the kitchen to start the tea. All along the back of the room, messy bookcases of varying types and sizes were packed with books; none of them were height matched. She was tempted to check out the titles, but considered that impolite at their first meeting. Her eyes rested upon a large chess set in the far corner of the room. The game appeared to be in full swing although some of the pieces seemed unconventional; or at least that's how she perceived it from a distance. He came back with a laden tray.

'Sugar?'

'One please. Is this a big parish then Mackey?'

'No, not really, we have the regulars, about six folks and then I see the rest of the islanders at births, baptisms and deaths—not many births or baptisms either —mainly deaths actually,' he chuckled. She was tickled by his sense of humour.

'Some folk come to me when they've got problems. As you may, or may not know, there's no Police on Fetlar, and the community council doesn't deal with gossip or petty squabbles—well, not gossip—I mean personal problems, so my role is fleshed out more often than not by just being an unofficial ear for everyone, which I don't mind at all. It's all God's work.'

'You live alone?' she probed, sipping her tea appreciatively.

'Yes, I came here after my wife died. I felt drawn to the place, and then came for a holiday. It just so happened that the Minister at the time mentioned he was thinking of going, and the next thing I knew, I was being offered a job. I snapped it up. My two children visit every year—I have one grandchild—I spoil her terribly given the chance.'

'How about you may I ask?' He studied her closely.

'Retired from teaching—junior children mainly. I never married, I never found the right person, and then suddenly—the years had all . . . anyway, my pupils were very much like having my own children.' He smiled in agreement.

'Just like my dogs,' he paused, 'about marriage . . . well—there's still time yet.' He jokingly tapped his watch. Momentarily, she lowered her eyes and gave him a sheepish grin.

'Let's just say I'm not particularly seeking it. So, tell me more about this strange black water, I've never seen anything like it,' she asserted, feeling a faint ripple of excitement, then reminded herself she'd only just met him.

'Yes, it happened two times before as far as I know. As I said, 1768 it was first recorded, and then again in 1975. Both times the islanders saw it as a bad omen and the one in 1975 happened to coincide with the strange demise of a local lad named Heed.'

'Mary mentioned him when I first arrived, she said something about his father having a strange name too . . . .'

'Haby and Heed—yes—not native Shetland names of course. It was a very sad state of affairs. Haby disappeared one night and was never found, then his son Heed died ten years later—seemingly of old age—but he was only fourteen.' He noticed she frowned in disbelief.

'No—it was true. Almost overnight he became white-haired and he eventually faded away—this was over the course of a couple of weeks. It was said he found something, although over time it has been forgotten or misplaced, anyway, it's fair shaken the islanders up. Of course, the one that happened in 1975 didn't produce quite the level of superstition as the one in 1768. In those days the islanders blamed everything on the trows or witches, and all manner of superstitions arose, a ritual for everything, for milking the cows, hanging out the washing . . . some of the old rituals still hold, usually on big occasions like weddings where the bride visits every house before she goes to the Church to get married. She accepts a peerie nip, and then leaves something small for the trows so they don't take an interest in her wedded life to come—well—her babies to be more precise. There's still folklore about babies being swapped or taken, at least the myth is always in the back of their minds. Either way, this black water will be the talk of the island for many weeks to come—don't be surprised if folks seem withdrawn.' He picked up the teapot and swirled the contents around.

'I can imagine. Did Haby turn up?'

'No, he was never seen again. His wife Lily was a wreck and it hit her even harder when Heed died of course. She became a recluse. She still lives here by the way, up at Baela, the croft house on the road to the school. It's very sad, most folks only see her briefly in the shop, and then she doesn't speak to people much.' Fruma suddenly sat upright.

'Skittles! I missed the 10:50 ferry!' Half rising out of the chair, she looked at her watch. Concerned, he leaned forward.

'I was supposed to go to Yell today. Oh well, I guess I forgot with everything else going on.' She sat back down, looking disappointed.

'Is it urgent?'

'No—no—I just planned to visit, to do some exploring, no reason why it can't wait for another day. I keep forgetting there's no *real* schedule to stick to,' she said, calming down, 'I sometimes forget I'm retired, I still think timetables rule my life.' He nodded.

'I know what you mean. But you have to remember, Shetland time is slower. There's a saying, that Shetland watches don't show minutes or hours—only years!' They both laughed. She enjoyed his ability to make her feel totally at ease.

'So, are you enjoying your stay on Fetlar—any particular reason for visiting?'

'I only arrived two days ago. I'm not visiting anyone, Shetland's been on my agenda for a few years now, I hope to visit some of the islands—well, that's the plan—if I don't forget that is! I wanted somewhere fairly remote as a base, to feel what it's like, you know?' he nodded.

'I haven't visited all of the islands yet. Obviously, I've been to Unst and Yell and I did take a trip to Noss for the birds, but I always wanted to see more—I guess I just never got round to it.' Puzzled, he realised his own exploration of Shetland had been extremely limited. They both sipped their tea in silence. The clock thudded its seconds into the wooden mantelpiece, and they could hear the two Labradors playing in the garden. Quincy was asleep on Fruma's feet and gently snoring.

'Talking of unusual names Fruma—you did say Fruma didn't you?'

'Yes.'

'Where does the name originate from?'

'Oh, I've been told different things,' she said flippantly. 'Apparently, in Icelandic it means cell—but I can't be certain of anything—you see—my early life was spent in an orphanage.' He made a noise that sounded like a mixture of recognition and sorrow; then expertly changed the subject.

'So what made you choose Fetlar?'

'It seemed to stand out on the map,' she said meekly, realising for the first time that she'd felt particularly drawn to Fetlar. Not wanting to appear as someone who sees signs and wonders in everything, she added curtly,

'I think it was because Fetlar is remote enough, but has a shop—that's quite useful isn't it?' For a brief moment Mackey looked at her quizzically for saying the word 'think' and then nodded in agreement.

'At one point driving through, I did wonder if anyone lived here!' she stated with upturned palms; then had a sudden realisation that she'd repeated herself.

'I know. In fact, there are more sheep than humans,' he chuckled, 'they did have a drive for more folk, but many have come and gone. I always look at it this way, if a person comes and stays five years, there's a good chance they'll stay for good, up until then, they're just a question mark for the community. I think folk have resigned themselves to the fact that we'll never have the population we once had.'

'How many was that?'

'Over a thousand at one time, but that was a very long time . . . centuries ago.' He gulped down the last of his tea. She felt it was time to leave.

'Well, I must be going . . . . '

'It's worth taking a look round the Interpretive Centre, there's a picture of Heed there if you're interested, many of the other exhibits are just bits and pieces—items from Brough Lodge and Leagarth

House, the two big estates on the island. Jamesie Laurenson was quite a character and the storyteller of the island; he died in the 1980's, ironically a week before they installed an indoor toilet for him. According to Da Anderson, he was really looking forward to the indoor toilet!' He chuckled again. 'If it wasn't for old Jamesie, we would've lost most of the old stories and folklore of the island—anyway—you'll find something of interest there I'm sure.' He rose from his seat awkwardly. She looked at him, concerned.

'Hip's playing up, not getting any younger—could be worse thanks be to God!'

'I've been lucky—touch wood—I'm in reasonably good health for sixty-nine. Hope it stays that way. I try to keep walking as often as I can. Thanks for the tea Mackey, it was all very interesting,' she said warmly, and held out her hand. He enclosed it with both of his large, pudgy hands, but this time he was gentler.

'Wonderful to meet you Fruma. If you want company at any time, just pop in—the island can be a lonely place sometimes.'

'Thank-you, that's very kind. Can I ask you, have you always been a Minister?' She was curious at how anyone decided on such a vocation.

'No. I finished my teacher training and was in a school for a year when God called me. That was a while ago now—twenty years ago. And Fruma, do you have any spiritual leanings?' he asked tactfully.

'No. I have to say, I'm not religious. I believe in *something* I guess, but I'm not a spiritual person, I wasn't brought up thinking about it—still—room for everybody eh? Wouldn't it be boring if we were all the same!' she half joked while putting on her coat.

'Well, I don't know . . . us Christians—we have all the answers . . . . ' She pretended to swipe him with the back of her hand, and decided that he was someone she'd be happy spending more time with. He touched her arm gently making her pause.

'Dreams are important you know,' he said, with a seriousness that jolted her. She struggled to reply.

'You mentioned you'd had a dream—at the beach— remember?' She nodded glumly, still worried that he might think she was into spooky things, like fortune telling and dream interpretation.

'You don't have to tell me . . . .'

'It was a bit shocking that's all, maybe another time?'

'My door is always open Fruma,' he said, in a deeper, authoritative tone of voice that she thought was the most beautiful intonation she'd ever heard. Realising she was staring, she hurriedly left.

'Lovely to meet you—as I say—my door is always open,' he shouted. She turned and waved. Quincy attempted to follow Fruma, which caused a volley of expletives to erupt from Mackey, who then apologised profusely to her. She waved again, more than a little unnerved at the events of the last two days. On the garden gate she spotted a worn symbol, consisting of wooden concentric circles. Absent-mindedly, she traced the circles with her fingers. She decided to take a walk to Funzie after she'd dropped into the cafe for lunch. For now, she attempted to push all the weird goings-on out of her mind. Her thoughts drifted instead to Mackey, until an image of Quincy crept in, and she couldn't help but think about her dream again.

CHAPTER THREE

The newel cap on top of the post was a polished wooden ball made of oak; it was smooth, cool and tactile. Fruma circled it with her palm while gazing out of the landing window. The tide was out and a few people milled around on the beach, making it appear to be business as usual, but she could tell the island was in shock; the birds had remained subdued. With hunger pulling her to the dinner table, she almost bumped into Peter at the foot of the stairs.

'Didn't see you there. Dinner ready?'
He nodded, but seemed preoccupied, as if eating was suddenly an inconvenience. She followed him into the dining room. Juicy, mutton rib chops shaped like commas were piled high on a platter. A broccoli forest, baby carrots, roast potatoes—and giant Yorkshire puddings waited patiently to be consumed. Thick gravy brooded in a heavy ceramic, Denby gravy boat. Mint sauce provided the top note of aromas.

'Had a good day? I take it you saw the black water?' Mary said, in an overly cheerful manner whilst handing round the warmed plates. The returning black water had made her feel depressed all day, and she had to work hard to shake it off.

'Yes, I went down there this morning, quite eerie really with all those dead fish,' Fruma said, toying with the idea of telling them about her dream and the strange coincidences. Peter grunted something which Mary translated.

'Peter thinks it was a waste of fish—' then she

shouted at him as if he were hard of hearing, 'we don't know what they died of—might poison us. No-one in their right mind would eat those fish.' She passed the potatoes around.

'Did you go Mary?' Fruma asked, spooning out a large Yorkshire pudding, gasping at its size. Mary blushed, remembering one Yorkshire pudding that turned out so big that Peter fancied he could fit a 5kg turkey in it.

'We did indeed—just briefly. Couldn't believe how black the water was, almost silky, unreal—we didn't stay long.' In a moment of impulsive folly, Fruma decided to mention her dream; the thought had almost reached her vocal chords.

'No-one ever thought this would happen again, I wonder why? I mean, what could've sparked it off?' Mary asked no-one in particular, then looked to Fruma as if she'd have the answer. Peter cut in.

'Folk are very twitchy about it—maybe it's best not to discuss it, let's say that's the end of it.' Mary smiled weakly at Fruma who'd decided to ground her thought; she made a decision to pay Mackey a visit— maybe it was time to mention the 'coincidences'. The silence was punctuated with the sound of chewing and busy cutlery.

'I missed the ferry today.'

'What? Was everything OK?' Mary asked, looking worried.

'Yes, yes—it was Mackey's fault.' Fruma paused for effect, grinning.

'I met Mackey today—I mean Reverend Mackey—at the beach, he invited me back for something hot at his place,' she said innocently, before realising the implication. Mary and Peter glanced at each other knowingly.

'You know what I mean! He was very accommodating—very kind.'

'A-ha.' Peter replied cynically, appearing to herd a floret of broccoli onto a fork. He gave up and stabbed it in the stem. Fruma felt unhappy about his somewhat non-committal reply. She expected them to say something pleasant about him.

'He was very kind. We had a good chat, and it seems we have a lot in common—we're both ex-teachers, and both intrigued about the island's history,' she elaborated, spooning out a couple more baby carrots, more out of nervousness than desire.

'I guess it's nice to meet someone new, dear,' was the best that Mary could offer before continuing,

'All I can say is—Fetlar is very mysterious, lots of skeletons in cupboards . . . . ' Peter tutted and looked at his pipe before placing it back in his pocket. Then, as if the act of eating suddenly became a serious ritual, they all finished the final leg of the meal while listening to the radio. A Scottish woman rattled on about Health Care. Fruma noticed she spoke in long vowels, staccato consonants, soft rolls and interrogative endings. She decided the woman's ambrosial accent could almost beat her first love: the melodious, singsong Irish accent, with its added H's to everything. Bones were checked for any remaining meat and then placed neatly on the side of the plate. A last minute decision about who would have the last roast potato flittered politely around the room; consequently, it sat there wasted. When the meal was over, Peter turned the radio down, so the woman was left mumbling away on the windowsill. His mood had lifted—as if the Scottish woman had soothed his troubled thoughts.

'Here—don't do what Mary did when she first came here . . . . ' he said, with a hint of mock mysteriousness. Mary giggled girlishly. Fruma leaned in to hear more, glad of the change of atmosphere.

'That's right! I asked one of the old women, she's no longer with us, bless her—I asked her if she could tell me about the history of the island, and this old lady—well! Her whole face changed from pleasant, you know, normal, to almost angry and she turned in the opposite direction—she literally turned around and faced the other way!' Mary explained animatedly. Peter guffawed into his pipe, which made him cough.

'What Mary didn't realise—' he started to say, then he lowered his voice to the level of the mumbling Scottish woman. 'What Mary didn't realise, is that history—when you ask about history—for Fetlarians this means gossip. So she thought Mary was asking for all the juicy island gossip!' Mary roared with laughter at this point, tears springing from her eyes. Fruma chuckled.

'I was mortified!' Mary admitted, dabbing her eyes.

'I can imagine,' Fruma agreed. Holding a serviette to her mouth, she let out a gentle belch.

'Makes you wonder, doesn't it? That's why I say—skeletons in the closet,' Mary confirmed, collecting up the plates. Fruma helped her take the dishes out to the kitchen. Mary leaned in close, almost conspiratorially, all the laughter made her appear momentarily drunk.

'There's a whole generation of people that never married on this island, it just never happened, and no-one knows why, which is odd . . . you'd imagine that most folk would try to hook up with one another —slim pickings—you know. They're as tight-lipped as I don't know what about it.' Fruma raised her eyebrows.

'I asked one of the old boys about it once, and got the same reaction: anger—well—not right away, he looked thoughtful first, but when I pushed the issue, you could see the anger was just under the surface, so

I just left it.' Mary busied herself with a huge, steaming bowl of rice pudding. Fruma was shocked at the size of it—she figured she could dive in and never reach the bottom. It wouldn't have looked out of place in a school canteen. Like all presented food, it made the guest feel they had to consume a fair portion of it, out of politeness. It made her feel queasy.

'I'm absolutely stuffed—' then seeing Mary's face drop, 'I'll make room for a little, but I won't be needing any breakfast in the morning,' she half-teased. Mary grinned sheepishly.

'What other plans have you made this week, then Fruma?' Peter shouted toward the kitchen. Fruma joined him at the table.

'I want to drift a bit, but I'm planning on visiting the Interpretive Centre tomorrow, Mackey mentioned it—looking forward to knowing more about the island.' He wavered, as if he wanted to be truthful but didn't want to put her off. Mary spooned out generous portions of rice pudding into bowls.

'Aye, it's not bad, it hasn't got anything of real value there, but there are lots of old photos and some artifacts from Brough Lodge, and Leagarth House.' Mary interrupted him, he put up his hand, 'I know, I know. Mary reckons it's the Laird Museum.'

'I don't—it's just that if they took out all the things they retrieved from the Lairds houses, they'd not be much left!' Looking sideways at Fruma he whispered,

'She's not wrong really. Anything that was any good went Edinburgh way—I guess they don't trust us with looking after it.'

'No, that's not it Peter, you know that—it's just that we haven't got a proper curator. It's very hard for someone to give up everything to come here for just five months of the year.'

'I-i, joost as you say,' he agreed, and lit his pipe

again. Fruma surprised herself by eating all of her pudding, then feeling like she needed her own space, she retired to her room for the night. An hour passed before Mary spoke.

'So, that Mackey is trying his wily ways with her then?' she said with a venomous sneer. Annoyed, she snatched up some knitting she'd been working on.

'Now then love, that's all in the past, I think Fruma's got her head screwed on, she seems level-headed enough. Let's say no more about it, eh?' he warned, attempting to bring to life the fragile embers in his pipe. She knitted in silence and decided she'd make some Cornish pasties for dinner the following day.

Malcum leaned forward to turn on the radio; this produced a nasty, hacking cough, as if an infection had taken on a physicality, and was trying to communicate. Annie Lennox's contralto voice rang out while a synthesizer held a long note—it was one of his favourite Eurythmic songs: 'Sweet Dreams'. Distracted, he caught sight of the unfortunate figure out the corner of his eye. He knew it was too big to be a normal sized person because he couldn't see the head of the figure. It was just a torso, legs and feet that shambled along in wet, tattered clothes, as if the person just walked out of the sea. He presumed it was a man because the figure wore men's trousers. His hands were in front of him, reaching out; not dissimilar to the old monster movies where the slow moving ghoul makes a laughable attempt at capturing a running, screaming individual. Turning the wheel as far as he could, he only just avoided him.

'Shit!'

He felt the post van tip sideways, then a bang; the front wheel had wedged tight into the bank, the engine still running. Annie allowed the chorus to take over. Malcum inched forward, hands shaking, grabbed at the radio knob, missed, grabbed again— then firmly turned the knob to the left before turning the engine off. Catching his breath, he looked in every direction; but he knew in his heart that the man wasn't real. Needing confirmation, he realised he'd have to get out of the van. Stepping into the foot-well, he lifted his body into the passenger seat. Opening the door with trepidation, it confirmed his suspicion; there wasn't a soul to be seen, not even in the distance.

So what the hell was that?

A solitary skylark started singing; its long, liquid

warble angelically hung in the air like a shiny bauble of melodrama. He looked back at the van—water was creeping into the tarmac from what Malcum assumed to be a crack in the radiator.

'Bloody hell! Just typical!'

He leant into the car and grabbed his mobile, at that moment William drove around the corner a little too fast, saw the post van and skidded to a stop.

'You OK, Malcum? You alright?' he shouted from the wound-down window; the concern in his voice almost sent Malcum into tears—he choked them back.

'There was a man—there was a big man,' he replied, obviously shaken.

'Come and sit in my car for a mo. I'll ring Ted—see if he's around to get you out,' William said soothingly, emerging from the car. Malcum decided to take his advice. He could see William's lips moving, but didn't hear what was said, his own mobile sat motionless on his lap. His teeth sought out a loose strip of skin next to his thumbnail. He bit it off and sat there chewing, replaying the scene and fretting about the damaged van. William finished his phone call, and happened to notice a flow of liquid he assumed was coming from Malcum's post van. The water was black, which he thought odd, considering that anti-freeze is normally tinged with fluorescent hues of green. He returned to the car, determined to get to the bottom of the incident.

'So, what's this about a big man then?' he asked, accusatorially. Malcum swallowed hard. 'Almost hit a massive bloke. Really big.' He laughed nervously, knowing how it sounded; if the roles had been reversed, he would have goaded William about it for weeks. Malcum twiddled with his mobile.

'A massive bloke?' Malcum was annoyed at hearing his words repeated back at him.

'You think I've really lost it,' he bleated resentfully.

'I didn't say that. Go on.'

'I was going along normal like—a man—a big man, suddenly appeared on the road. Weird he was, bloody weird—his clothes were tattered—you know—like a shipwrecked man. It was his size that got me, I'm talking *really* big, it wasn't normal.' Speaking it aloud seemed to give him some inner strength; as if it made it more real.

'I don't know what to say. Did you check outside?' William started to leave the car. Malcum stopped him.

'There's nowhere for him to go,' he said darkly, 'he just disappeared—if he was even there at all,' he paused, 'I've—um—I've not been well of late.'

'Well, that'll be it then Malcum, happens to all of us, nothing to be beating yourself up over.' Malcum frowned, wondering how often people saw abnormal sized, shipwrecked men on the side of the road. They sat in silence for a while.

'So, you've not been well then?' William enquired, to fill the tense silence.

'Dunno really, nondescript stuff, cough, feeling sick, headaches, generally feeling unwell. Probably just a Shetland cold. I've been trying to get my blood pressure sorted out too, absolute waste of time—no disrespect to the trouble and strife.'

'Oh, none taken. I don't trust modern medicine 100% either. It's alright with a definite diagnosis, but this other nondescript stuff—as you say . . . . ' Malcum was starting to feel his 'old self' returning.

'Did you get hold of Ted?'

'Yes, he's just coming back from the ferry, you're lucky because he wasn't due back until the later one—bit of a blessing for you,' William offered, smiling piously. Malcum didn't like 'Churchy' types and hoped he would keep his religious sentiments to himself.

'Look, I'm happy if you just leave me here—panics over now—I can just wait 'til Ted comes.'

'No reason why I can't wait with you. Oh, Malcum, I meant to ask you, do you normally put anti-freeze in the radiator?' Malcum turned sharply, irritated at such a question.

'Of course I do! Why?'

'Well, I—oh, never mind, the water coming from your radiator seemed a different colour—don't worry about it. Anyway, I'm curious, you said this guy was big, how big?'

'I'm never gonna hear the last of this am I?' he replied bleakly.

'Listen, I won't tell if you want to keep it quiet, there could be loads of reasons why you hit that ditch. My lips are sealed.' Malcum was relieved.

'Appreciate it mate. I reckon this guy was at least nine feet, without exaggerating, and he was big too, you know, heavy—unbelievable really—his clothes; they sort of looked like he'd been in a shipwreck, you know what I mean? Sort of ragged, the trousers were raggedly at the bottom, reminded me of Robinson Crusoe. He looked like he'd just walked out of the sea, didn't have much time to look because I had to swerve —oh look—here's Ted.' He was glad of the diversion. Ted had pulled up behind the post van and was preparing to drag it out.

'Look—cheers mate, I'd better get out there.'

'Drive carefully, and look after yourself too Malcum,' he said seriously. Malcum nodded, took a deep breath and walked towards the grinning Ted.

CHAPTER FOUR

Sue had gone out for the evening with visiting relatives, the twins were sleeping, and Holly was in her room, so Liam took the opportunity to question his father.

'Dad, has anyone ever gone metal detecting on Fetlar—you know—just take one out and see what they can find?' He tried to appear nonchalant.

'Not that I know of. I'm pretty sure you need permission from the landowners before you go off tearing up the land,' Trevor replied distractedly. They were watching the 2014 Fifa World Cup Final: Germany vs Argentina. Trevor hated the Germans, so whoever played against them was to be encouraged.

'Right, so you just have to find out who owns the land then?'

'As far as I know, mind you, I did hear that they frown on folk digging around as it might encourage the tourists. The last thing the Fetlarians want is a load of strangers turning up and taking an interest, especially at lambing time, or when the ewes are pregnant so they get spooked, it could cause them to miscarry their lambs.'

'OH COME ONNNN!' Trevor shouted at the TV. Liam felt a surge of excitement and pride over his discovery. He figured his Dad was right; they'd have to know who was digging, and where.

'But Dad, there must be tons of hidden treasure on Fetlar, can you imagine?' Trevor reached for another can of beer and sat back in his seat.

'Oh yeah, but to get the right people over to do the job would cost a fortune, it needs to be done properly, not just some amateur digging up the landscape with no clue at all. There's an art to it—like excavation, or an archaeological dig. No different at all in a place like Fetlar.' Then half-leaping out the chair,

'You've GOT to be KIDDING! Still no score! They'll have to go to extra time.' Trevor turned to Liam as if he were a gnat mildly bothering him.

'Why you so interested, anyway? You hated it last time we went, you did nothing but whine the whole time.'

'Yeah, only because we didn't find anything decent.' Liam sat forward, trying to get his dad to turn his head.

'But here Dad, can you imagine?' Trevor's eyes remained on the game, he swigged his beer and thought about it.

'Actually, it would be really great—look, if there's ever a right moment I'll speak to Jack or someone, just to see how the land lies. I don't know, maybe it's different for people who live here.' Liam left it at that. He was sure now that he'd have to keep his treasure a secret; at least for the time being. He sat back and enjoyed the football, regularly glancing at his watch. It wouldn't be long before he could fondle the cup again —he was becoming quite the night owl.

'Liam. LIAM. BED, you missed the best bits,' Trevor said, nudging his sleeping son. A quiver of expectation ran through Liam's core. He checked his watch—it was 11:00pm, he only had two hours to kill before he could safely bring out the cup.

'Sorry Dad. Tell me about it tomorrow,' he said, heading upstairs. Trevor rolled his eyes; he knew that explaining it would never be the same as experiencing it as it happened.

'The bloody Germans won anyway,' he said forlornly.

'Night, Dad.'

Trevor thought it strange that he had to wake Liam three times during the game. He figured it must be the unpolluted air, remembering the family's first week on Fetlar; no-one got up before 10am—even the twins.

Liam closed the bedroom door, slipped into his pyjamas, and grabbed his library book about Vikings, but found he couldn't rest. This feeling had grown exponentially over the last few days, but tonight, he felt it had reached a level that couldn't be ignored. An overwhelming pressure was coming from somewhere; as if *something* was getting at him. It was a persistent niggling, not dissimilar to what he felt when walking home after finding the cup. But now it felt as if it was inside him, like a brewing irritation.

He walked around the room, using his body as a kind of sensor. As he neared the wardrobe, the feeling increased. He opened the doors and yanked the hung clothes aside, he tried to force his mind to make sense —then it became clear to him; it was coming from the black wood. Removing it from its hiding place (inside an old sock, behind some old comics), he felt the room wobble. He felt light-headed and gripped the wardrobe door. The wood seemed to fill him with an energetic desire. The cut on his wrist started tickling, so he peeled away the wristband to see what was happening. The edges were pulled apart like a fissure; it had formed a deep groove, with an intense crimson centre. He resisted the urge to dig his nails in and scratch until it bled. Using the sleeve of his brushed cotton pyjamas, he gently rubbed the cut. With the tickling sensation being so exquisite, and the soft cotton not rough enough, he had to increase the pressure. Now he couldn't stop. He dug further in, using his nails through the cloth, frantically grinding the swollen, tender edges, deepening the wound. It was so pleasurable, he couldn't stop—until he reached something hard. In utter shock, he paused, thinking he'd hit a bone—but then he thought it should hurt more than it did. He looked down, fully expecting to see his arm a bloody mess, but the wound seemed to be in the same state as it was before he'd started scratching.

Confused, and overwhelmed with emotion, he ran to his bed. Retreating under the safety of his duvet, he wished he could go to his parents and tell them everything, knowing they'd help him (after scolding him first), but he could live with that. He seesawed between choices, but he couldn't do it; he couldn't give up the beautiful cup. He couldn't bear the thought of someone else gazing at her, holding her, *possessing* her. He turned on his side, realising he was still clutching the wood. He turned it over in his hands; it was highly polished, with a marble-like grain and light purple streaks running through the black surface. He wondered why the piece of wood was so important, he understood the coins and a bracelet, but this seemed to have no purpose. Yet in his heart he knew it had the *most* purpose; he just didn't know what it was. It was why he hadn't thrown it in the bin.

Feeling like his mind was a mixed up jigsaw puzzle, he wished he'd never taken the metal detector, until an unexpected feeling of joy spread through him; like pure white light . . . *Don't forget the cup! It's all worth it for her!* Placing the wood back in the old sock and back in its hiding place, he checked his watch: it was 3:30am. Shocked, he sat down on the bed, the last time he looked it was 11:00pm. He was losing time again. It was only three hours until he needed to be ready for school; he worked out that he could have an hour with the cup, sleep two hours and then catnap on the ferry. He opened the wardrobe and brought out an old games box, the contents long gone, now replaced by the wrapped treasure. He laid the treasure out systematically. First the twenty-six coins, then the flattened band, then the cup. Trembling, he carefully picked up the cup and held it aloft like he'd seen the priests do on the TV at Easter. He felt he'd never need anything else in his life; friends, girlfriends, or even his family, as long as he could gaze at her; as long as she was with him. His arms ached, so he placed the cup on the dresser, picked up two coins, and then added two more. He quivered with the thought that she was watching him. Playing out an imaginary bartering scene, he put the coins in a sock, and holding them out he whispered:

'Look my friend—I'll give you two silver coins for some bread, a fair bargain.' The coins were taken from the sock and offered to the imaginary person. The coins clinked in his hand. He liked the feel of them. Inspecting one of the coins closely, he fingered the cross at the centre, marvelling at how they could have been struck yesterday; the features were sharp, not smooth from wear.

He turned back to the cup. This was the third night he'd stayed up caressing and admiring her beautiful, golden body. He ran two fingers from the bowl down the slender neck, the way a lover would explore a willing partner. He'd never felt so alive, as if he now had a purpose in life. He wondered if this is what real love felt like, if it was, he'd never seen it exhibited by his parents. His friends didn't talk about their crushes or girlfriends with such rapture. Before, he'd been as good as dead—now he'd been reborn; reclaimed and reawakened by her sheer majesty. He decided it was more than love—it was . . . but he had no words for it. Then the word came to him: Real.

Philip rose from behind an acreage of desk. He was short but stocky, and looked to Fruma to be in his early sixties, she thought he had an air of 'army' about him.

'I've come to take a look around your lovely museum.'

'You're very welcome. The main room here illustrates the island history, and the back room—just through there—has some items recovered from archaeological digs, the geographical parts of the island and some relics from Brough Lodge. Just let me know if you need any help. Is it a flying visit or are you visiting relatives on the island?'

'No. No relatives, I'm only here for three weeks. I'll take a look round then.'

'No worries, if you have any questions just ask,' he advised, before returning to the desk. He typed slowly on a laptop, with alternating index fingers. She wandered around the various exhibits, but she was really looking for the picture of Heed. She didn't really know why it was important, but it was. Not all the photographs were named so she figured she'd have to ask; and that made it seem like bad taste—especially with the black water. She found a section on Jamesie Laurenson, there was a portrait of him when he was older. His shallow, but prominent forehead, large face, full eyebrows, long philtrum and small eyes made him look a force to be reckoned with, almost Neanderthal; or maybe the artist's rendition had exaggerated those features.

'He looks quite a character—this Jamesie Laurenson,' she said in a purposely raised voice. Taking the hint, he joined her.

'He was, and strong too—look.' Jamesie was dressed in the ubiquitous Shetland gear: a Shetland jumper, heavy cotton trousers, flat cap and wellingtons; the photo showed him holding an extremely long oar out at arm's length.

'He was an amazing storyteller too, we've got tapes here, but his accent is quite hard to understand—I can put one on if you want.'

'That would be great. Mackey mentioned there is a picture of the boy Heed in the museum? It seemed quite an interesting story—for the err . . . history of the island I mean . . . Mackey told me about it.' She knew she was gabbling. He nodded and walked over to a display towards the centre of the room. He pointed at a small 6 x 4 photo.

'Such a tragic story. This picture of him was taken about a year before he died—he's the one there, in the middle. I guess Mackey told you the story?'

'Yes, briefly . . . .'

She looked closely at the picture. Heed's face was difficult to see as the picture was taken at some distance away. He appeared to be standing with friends. One had orange hair, was as lanky and tall as Heed, and proudly holding what appeared to be a prize fish.

'This black water returning is not taken as a good omen—it's got everyone's nerves standing on end. All we can say is that it happened about the same time that this lad Heed fell ill, although we can't really tell if it was linked to him, but small islands like this can be very superstitious, as you can imagine.'

'Are there any photos of his father and mother here?'

'No, his mother still lives here, but Haby—no—I'm afraid not. He disappeared you know, in the 1960's . . .'

'Yes . . . I've been told.'

'In those days, they didn't have the inter-island ferries you came across on, they used these rowing boats,' he pointed at another photo nearby, 'they took all manner of things over the water in them.' The photo showed a sixareen; a Shetland rowing boat that could be crewed by six people. Two planks had been placed across the hull, and an old-fashioned car balanced precariously across the planks.

'Skittles, I see what you mean . . . . '

'Indeed, so getting off this island doesn't go unnoticed. No-one knew what happened to him. They figured perhaps he fell over a cliff, or maybe he committed suicide, who knows? Heed was only about four when it happened, poor lad. Da Anderson will tell you stories about that family, but you have to take his stories with a pinch of a salt; he's the main story teller of the island now, he'll be glad to talk to you—he'll talk to anyone about the history of the island. You know, somewhere around, we have a tape of Heed talking if you're interested, most folk here don't want to listen to it—it's a bit old now but I can put it on for you. At some point we'll digitise these old recordings. The main Shetland museum might have more info if you're down that way, it's worth having a look round.'

He fumbled around behind the desk, forgetting he'd promised to play her the Jamesie Laurenson recording. He produced a cardboard box with some tapes inside. He rummaged, mumbling while he searched. Fruma carried on her visit, staring into the faces of all the ancient islanders—their expressions reflecting the hard life they'd endured. Women with weathered faces wore knitted shawls around their shoulders, and scarves wrapped around their heads; but no trousers, only full length, heavy dresses. Their clothes were frayed and timeworn; even the children looked old. All the men wore a moustache or a beard, as was the fashion, and a hard wearing country jacket with a Shetland jumper underneath. A flat cap kept the head warm. She thought monochrome photos always made the past seem harsh—as though the lack of colour reflected the lack of joy in their lives. But the music of the Shetland Islands would indicate the opposite. Unlike some of the more mournful tunes of The Western Isles, most songs were written in major keys; joyful, inspiriting tunes played for the family, or at gatherings, where folk danced and celebrated their harsh existence. She was under no illusion that it would have been a tough and arduous life living on Fetlar all those years ago; having to fetch their own water and spending their lives in what was tantamount to a mud-floor hut. Gazing at the photo of a woman inside a croft house using a spinning wheel, she noticed the woman wore many layers of clothes.

'Here it is,' he announced wearily, and loaded the tape into the player. She chuckled inwardly at how antiquated and quaint it was to still use tapes. He paused before switching it on.

'I warn you—some folk find it quite disturbing. It's not long, but I'm not sure you'd not want it any longer than it is.' He pressed the button. It took her by surprise, the sound of a distraught boy ranting, at times interrupted by a woman she presumed to be his mother. Heed's voice changed countenance now and then, but what shocked her to the core was the number 237 that Heed mentioned in quick succession before falling into a wailing, shrieking voice. He switched it off after seeing the colour drain from her face.

'You OK?' he asked, concerned. Feeling incredibly disturbed, she tried to pull herself together.

'Yes—yes—it is quite scary hearing him,' she said, glad he'd switched it off, overwhelmed by the same number appearing again.

'I did warn you—but can you imagine how a simple folk would've taken it?' he mentioned in earnest.

'I can imagine they thought he was possessed!'

'True indeed, but things happening to bairns is always more upsetting isn't it?' He wondered why he'd even mentioned the tape, as he himself had forgotten how disturbing it was.

'Nobody likes to see or hear a child in pain. Has anything else strange happened on this island?' He was glad to oblige and change the mood.

'We had a documented murder a long time ago now, haven't got an exact date, I think it was recorded in the Yell Parish records. It's quite a mystery. Some local men had been fishing and had just landed their catch, this was on Lamb Hoga where they cut the peats, some folk had crofts there, families, amazing really considering the terrain, anyway they moored up the boat, and one man was nearing his home at Burgalstou, and he thought it was strange that there was no smoke coming from the house, and his children had not run to meet him. The house door was open, and the man found his wife and children dead. They'd all been killed and there was blood all over the place. He alerted the other Crofters who were making for home by shouting and waving his jacket. They came and saw what had happened. There were no police, but the minister was the justice of the peace and an investigation was held. They found a dry wooden clog at the foot of Selli Geos below the house. They concluded that pirates had come ashore and killed the mother and her children. It was mentioned that a strange vessel had been seen between Fetlar and Skerries—but it was too late to do anything. After that, the area was supposed to be haunted. Horses cleared out when the sun went down, and the croft fell into disuse. Eventually, the stones were taken from the house to build a dyke on Lamb Hoga—but it's quite the mystery.' He was glad she seemed to be recovering. He wondered why Heed's tape was even allowed in the museum; but considered that as long as it was, he'd play it to those who were curious.

'Fetlar seems to be an intriguing place. I may well pay a visit to the museum on the mainland on your recommendation. Have you been curator for long?'

'No, only about two years—moved here about ten years ago. I'd visited loads of times before I decided to settle here, I'm a bird watcher really, but it's hard to find folk willing to run the museum. I got involved by accident, now I'm running the place. It was supposed to be temporary, but you know how things are. Anyway, I found an old croft I liked, bought it, did it up and properly retired here.'

'So what do you make of Fetlar then?' she asked boldly. He squirmed a little and ran a hand across the back of his neck. He walked over to another photograph, deep in thought; as if he'd never seen it before. She followed him.

'Do you believe in—in strange forces?' he asked, still staring at the photo. She was taken aback at the question.

'I don't know. Can you elaborate?'

'The supernatural—what I mean is—do you think there is more to life than just this, what we can see?' He indicated with his hand towards the room. He appeared to be uncomfortable, out on a limb.

'I'm not just talking about the usual ghosts and the like—I mean a different governing force.' Knowing he wasn't making sense he changed tack. 'I'm not talking about the main trow folklore of the island, although that belief is fading now, only a few folk believe that they still operate here. Da talks about the trows living in the 'in-between'—like a different plane of existence.' He fidgeted some more before continuing.

'But I'm not talking about that, I mean something

'bigger, more Universal . . . . ' She was unnerved by his openness.

'I don't know, but I've not had any strange things happen to me until I came here.' Immediately, she regretted her words.

'Have you seen something?' he asked, excited.

'No—No. I haven't seen anything as such, just a feeling really.' Nodding, he seemed to deflate. But she felt he was warmer now; as if they shared a secret.

'Sometimes I feel the island is caught between different time zones.' He studied her for a reaction. She shrugged and tried not to wear her heart on her sleeve. She toyed with the idea of telling him about her vision, but then realised she hadn't spoken to Mackey yet; and she didn't want to make matters worse, knowing people like to gossip.

'But it seems a very active place—very raw—I mean, I'm not the only one who thinks there are places on the island that have a strange atmosphere. But if you talk to the old folk about the history of the island they don't remember much, just people—relatives mainly. It's like a dark cloud comes over them if you ask about the history of the place, the older Fetlarians I mean, not us incomers. I have to say, I was surprised when I came here that they didn't have that much info about the island before the Brough Lodge era, that's earlier than the 18th century. Still, that's Fetlar for you—it is what it is.' Then she felt him suddenly withdraw; as if a switch had been activated. But his mention of 'island history' confirmed Mary's earlier conversation. He seemed awkward, knowing he'd run off at the mouth; she knew he'd gone out on a limb.

'Fruma—good to meet you.'

'Same here,' he said before realising, 'Philip—good to meet you too, I mean . . . . ' The skin surrounding

his nose blushed a faint reddish purple revealing fragile spider veins that crept across his cheeks.

'Well, I'll take one more look around and then
leave you in peace.'

'You are welcome Fruma—it's quite a lot to take in
in one visit. I'll only charge you this one time, seeing
that you're here for three weeks,' he said, tapping his
nose conspiratorially. Noticing his veins had
retreated, she wondered if the nose tapping had sent
them rushing back into his cheeks. She took another
look at Heed's photo before leaving.

'Thanks again for your insight and stories.'

'No problem, or as the Fetlarians say, "never leet!"
which means—don't mention it!'

CHAPTER FIVE

Malcum examined the post for Stakkafletts, glad there was only a couple of letters and a parcel that needed to be delivered. He was totally preoccupied by his accident, and about what lie he should spin. The van had been fixed, but his ego was on high alert. Ted had told the whole island that he'd crashed the post van because he was drunk; Malcum thought he'd got off lightly, considering the truth. He only hoped that William would be discreet as promised—although he figured the nurse's husband must be used to keeping secrets. He knew better than anyone that it only took one person to mention an incident, and then, like Chinese Whispers, it would become so much more—he himself was skilled in this art. It wasn't really out of malicious intent, but people liked to know what was happening on their front doorstep, and they loved a good story. Stealth-like, he opened the gate of a house belonging to an elderly, sharp witted, sharp tongued Fetlarian couple. He knew it would be hard getting anything past them. He hoped they weren't at home, but the dogs heard his footsteps and reported back to Doreen. The curtains twitched, and quick as you like, she was on the doorstep, her husband Angus not far behind, shuffling along in his green carpet slippers.

'How's du? We heard!' Doreen said, a wry smile emerging.

'Aye, tell em, an tell aa da dogs i da toon. You came a cropper?' Angus declared gleefully before brushing roughly past Doreen. With newfound energy, he virtually sprinted down the path to see the damaged van. Malcum followed meekly behind, he still hadn't come up with a good enough excuse. Angus walked around the van, inspecting every scratch, then leaned over near the front and touched the paintwork.

'That'll be where you hit. Rabbit was it?' Malcum leapt at the suggestion.

'Yeah, that's right, a bloody rabbit. Bloody thing— caught me off guard!' he chuckled inwardly.

'We don't swerve for rabbits round here. You been on the—err . . . . ' Angus motioned with his hand that Malcum had been drinking.

'No. Nothing like that, this rabbit was a big bugger, huge—and before I knew it, I was in the ditch,' Malcum explained. It was a harmless lie; rabbits get under everyone's feet in Fetlar.

'Mm . . . lucky Ted was around. Still, you's in one piece and that's to be thankful for.' His inspection complete, Angus started back to the house. Malcum was opening the door of the post-van, when he realised he was still clutching Doreen's letters in his hand.

'Shit.'

He got out and carefully opened Doreen's gate. Paranoid, he rushed up the path and hurriedly shoved the letters through the letter-box, then rushed back down the path before they could come out and ask him more questions. Doreen and Angus watched him from behind the net curtains in the kitchen.

'He comes o da kind! All that drinking!' Angus said with gusto. Doreen grunted in agreement, and quickly picked up a pair of binoculars, focussing in on Malcum who was absent-mindedly looking at the damaged van.

'I think he's losing more hair,' she said. 'Time for a brew.'

Malcum had a parcel for Trevor at the top end house. He got in the van and reversed carefully, not wanting to make any more mistakes, or give anyone more reason to gossip. He rang the doorbell and Trevor answered; his dogs, anxious to get out, squeezed past his legs into the garden.

'Mace—get back here! Rufus!' Trevor shouted, ignoring Malcum. He called again, but the dogs were too busy sniffing at something at the bottom of the garden.

'Gotta sign for this one Trevor.' Trevor took his eyes off the dogs for a minute, then signed for the parcel before running to retrieve his recalcitrant hounds. Malcum was left on the doorstep holding the parcel. He watched him in amazement; and then realising he was still holding the parcel, he threw it onto a heap of shoes in the porch, tutting at Trevor's indifference.

'Dogs—they never listen!' Trevor shouted into the air, pulling them away by their collars, before noticing their discovery. It appeared to be two dead otters, both lying on their backs, side by side—seemingly in good condition.

'Malcum, what do you make of this?' he shouted up at the scowling Malcum, who hurried down to investigate, quickly forgetting his indignation.

'Not seen that before Trevor. They look fresh.' He was as pleased as punch; now they wouldn't have to discuss his accident, and he'd have some news for Da Anderson.

'Strange,' Trevor said, grabbing a twig and poking one. It twitched. They both leapt backwards.

'Blimey! It's still alive! Should we call someone?'

'I suppose you could call the RSPB warden, she'll know what to do,' Malcum offered. Trevor started back towards the house.

'It's not the only thing, a lot of dead things been

turning up—well—OK—one more thing, we found a dead seagull in the backyard two days ago. This one was really dead. It was the same as the otters though, it hadn't been touched. Just seems unusual. What do you think?' Malcum shrugged.

'It does seem odd, I suppose.' Then, as if the otters were old news, he turned to walk away.

'Well, I'll leave you with that then, must get on and finish me rounds.' Malcum was looking forward to a nice cup of tea and a gossip with Da and being out of the public eye.

'Err—OK—so I guess I'll ring the warden then. Is it 339?' Trevor enquired, surprised at Malcum's indifference.

'Aye, that's right—339.'

Malcum drove slowly to Da's, still spooked on the road. Every corner tested his courage, the anomalous shipwrecked figure having become a kind of tulpa. If he passed a person taking a walk, he would momentarily superimpose the shambling figure onto them, thereby causing himself great distress. This made him miserable and slightly withdrawn. Cautiously, he pulled into Da's drive, being overly wary of scratching the paintwork against the stone walls. Da was in the garden drinking tea; in fact, in nearly every island photo that included him, he would be shown holding a mug of tea—like some kind of mascot. He was now one of the few remaining elders of the island and made sure that everyone knew it. He was a wily, lithe fellow who kept his ear continually to the ground. Chief gossip and official stirrer, he seemed to have an uncanny knack of involving people in the latest scandal even if they were innocent. In fact, because of his meddling, no-one ever knew the truth of any story, so gradually the island became a miasma of anecdotes; the past mixed up with the present, confusing the incomers and delighting the natives who'd rather people didn't know the truth.

'How's du? You want a brew?' Not waiting for an answer, Da got up and head to the kitchen.

'You know it. I guess you heard? I'll never hear the last of it.' Malcum sat down heavily on the garden seat, and picked at an old spot scab on his head. The sun was so intense he wished he'd worn sunglasses. He raised a protective hand to his eyes and looked at the elevated view from Da's garden, right across the East side of the island; all the way to Funzie, and out to sea.

'He'll rise ida moarnin wi a wattery head, when da cock craas when he's gyaan ta bed,' Da shouted from the kitchen. Malcum looked up, sure it wasn't going to rain; there wasn't a cloud in the sky.

'I suppose you heard about me and the ditch?'

'Aye, I did.' Da shuffled out bearing two mugs of tea. He slopped some tea on the concrete and the sun lapped it up immediately.

'A rabbit?' he said sarcastically.

'You know me Da—I squish rabbit's heads for fun. I'm at . . . let me think . . . 407 now.'

'Food for da Bonxies,' Da said quietly, staring straight ahead at the view as if he'd never seen it before.

'No Da, this was serious. I saw a man—a really big man.' He looked at him expectantly.

'A big man? How big?' Da became animated at the news.

'He must've been at least nine feet tall. He was shuffling along like he'd been hurt. He wore clothes—

like shipwreck clothes—you know, all Robinson Crusoe style, tattered and torn, especially around the ankles. It all happened so quickly. He looked as big as he was tall. Heavy, very heavy, he was coming for me —I know it—he had that look in his eyes—his big, dark eyes!' Deep in thought, Da nibbled on a raggedy thumbnail.

'I hear dee. You saw a man. Folks have seen lots of things on this island. Not heard that one before though.' He turned around smiling mischievously. Malcum blushed.

'It's as true as the day is long Da. Never seen anything like it before either—and hope I dinne see it again! It's got me going all crazy, looking over my shoulder. I keep thinking I'm going to see him on every corner.'

'Where was this?'

'Aith way.'

Da nodded, returning to the view. Malcum knew he could trust Da with personal things. Da only gossiped about other people and the same for Malcum; it became an unwritten rule between them.

'Oh, and another thing, I was doing my rounds and Trevor found two dead otters in his garden—well the dogs did. He poked one and it wasn't dead, it just twitched. He called the Warden. He also said he'd found two dead seagulls not two days before in his garden.' Malcum was pleased to talk about something else, and two dead seagulls sounded better than one lone seagull that could've been caught by a cat or dog.

'Two dead otters? Two?'

'A-ha. Only they weren't dead—one twitched when Trevor poked it.' Da cocked an eyebrow at Malcum.

'And two gulls? *Two* gulls you say?' Malcum nodded enthusiastically.

'What kind?'

'Not sure, he just said they were seagulls.' Da gravely shook his head. They sat in silence, enjoying the unusually hot weather.

'Weather's on the change. There's a woman arrived, she's poking into the island's history,' Da mentioned, with a faraway look on his face.

'Oh, you mean that lady staying with Mary and Peter?'

'Aye.'

'I guess she's just curious.' Malcum didn't understand what Da's problem was. Da released more venom.

'It's bad enough with the newcomers nosing around into our history let alone tourists—present company accepted, of course.' Da flattered, patting his shirt pocket for something.

'You mean the black water?' Malcum offered, he enjoyed all the juicy gossip, but only if he wasn't the subject.

'Yes. No—I mean poking into Haby and Heed's business. No good can come of it. Something's on the change for sure, for sure, in more ways than one. I can feel it in the 'fluence.'

He reached into his waistcoat pocket and pulled out a pipe. It was a dimpled, wooden, squat pipe, designed to fit in a shirt pocket. To Malcum it looked like half a walnut. The stem could be turned around, so it looked like a small 'a'—for easy pocket storage. Malcum watched him fill it with rich, dark, vanilla tobacco that looked like shredded wood chips. It lit easily with a lighter. Da sucked the contents in, swilling them around his mouth before releasing. With no wind, the smoke hung in the air like the new gossip. Malcum sniffed deeply; he'd always liked the smell of Da's vanilla tobacco.

'How do you know she's poking around?' Malcum

asked, watching the grey-blue smoke cloud obscure part of the view.

'Philip. He was telling me that she was asking questions about them. What a piece o' wark! She doesn't even live here! Tellna me! And this black water again —we don't want the past brought up . . . . '

'Du can say 'im!' Malcum said, mimicking another of Da's phrases. Da ignored him.

'I saw some men, taking measurements at Tresta they were, when the black water came. Mainland men I think they were—more meddlers—we don't need the likes of them here, we can sort out our own problems,' Da said, in a low voice.

'Mainland men, how do you know?'

'I've no proof, but who else would be interested in our little island's ways?' he spat out.

'Anybody interested in geology, or archaeologists, historians.' Malcum reeled off, with a hint of sarcasm and amusement. Da made a noise of disgust. They sat in silence except for the puffing of Da's pipe and the call of a snipe.

'How's du today then Da?' Malcum asked, attempting to change the subject.

'Oh, nay so bad. Kinne complain. You feeling more yoursel'? Apart from the big man you thought you saw?' Malcum cringed, but decided to let it go.

'Well, it's sorta taken my mind off it all, couldn't say really. Christine took some bloods—let's hope they don't find anything nasty.'

'Mm . . . . ' Da murmured through his pipe.

'I'm not a lover of medicine. You do me right with my arthritis, don't have a lot of patience with these medical doctors, it's not like it used to be,' Malcum stated. Da nodded, saying,

'The old ways are always the best.' He held the pipe in his hand and tapped the bowl twice.

'That's it, you see me right don't you Da.' A small drop of water fell on Malcum' s nose. He looked up.

'Like I said, weathers on the change,' Da repeated. Malcum looked at Da with disbelief until another drop sploshed into his tea; then another.

'Owre weel—looks like that's it then,' Da confirmed, before disappearing indoors. 'Sees you then Malcum.' Malcum swallowed his tea in two large gulps, depositing the cup on top of the draining board in the kitchen, and ran for the post van. As soon as he closed the door, the heavens opened.

'How does he do that?' Malcum said, carefully reversing out of the drive.

As Fruma stood on deck and watched Fetlar recede from view, she was overcome by a strange sadness; as if the island were yearning for her, or sorry to see her go. Considering she'd island hopped for the last few days, this emotion took her by surprise.

'I'm coming back, don't worry,' she said quietly.

Nature seemed to respond by blowing cold air through the gaps in her jacket, so she buttoned it up. The Fetlar summer seemed to have evaporated, so her dream of sitting peacefully in the sun and 'finding herself' often ended in a brisk march in an attempt to keep warm. She used this as an excuse not to stay in one area for too long before retreating back to the guesthouse or visiting another island. But if she were truthful to herself, the remoteness of Fetlar scared her. It was like a mirror, reflecting the truth to all who looked—and the truth that she hadn't yet discovered was that she didn't know *how* to be alone. On top of all that, her mind seemed filled with alien ruminations and emotions which usually involved either her dream or vision, with a smattering of Haby and Heed thrown in.

On the other side of the deck, she espied an aged couple, identically dressed in the latest waterproofs, passing a pair of binoculars back and forth. To Fruma, they seemed to possess an invisible, binding tether. She figured they'd probably been married since they were children and communicated by telepathy. It started to spit with rain, so she retreated to the car.

Aging always caught her by surprise when she glanced into the rear view mirror; as if it were merely a trick of the light that she was old. She'd convinced herself that the liver spots on her temple were old stains from years of dying her hair, and the permanent frown wrinkles at the top of her nose and surrounding her lips would disappear once she'd found what she was looking for. In fact; the wrinkles were due to decades of disapproving of most people's lifestyles, and an underlying feeling of being disconnected from everything. At age sixty nine, she'd written off all ideas of a love in her life; she contemplated that older people only got together to share the price of a burial plot. Retirement didn't help, it simply forced her to do 'something' rather than sit at home and do nothing. All the while she'd been busy teaching at the school, there was always someone to come back to, there was always hope; there was always a troubled child that needed her. This became like an interminable escalator; more children were born and went through the school system, and she was there to catch the ones who managed to fall off.

In all her years at the orphanage, she had only one close friend: Ben, he was the same age as her—back then, they were almost inseparable. The most difficult time in the young Fruma's life, was when the orphanage placed her with foster parents, leaving Ben behind. She didn't understand why he couldn't come and live with her too. That was bad enough, but when she repeatedly asked if she could see him again, she was told he'd died in a car accident. Totally devastated, she felt responsible for his death, convinced it'd only happened because she'd abandoned him. All that remained of their friendship was one small photo of the two of them, taken in the orphanage garden one Sunday afternoon.

Although her foster parents were kind and encouraging, she never made any real connection with them. Her self-loathing and anger was so deep she hardened her heart, cutting herself off from any chance of happiness. As a teenager, she studied hard, and made it her life's ambition to become a teacher—that way she would never have to leave any children behind again.

It was decades later when she had another shock. Her only close friend (who was also a teacher, and a burgeoning romantic interest), was also killed in a car accident. This hit her hard, and all the old feelings arose; that she could have prevented it; that she was somehow responsible. Consequently, from then on, she never made any new friends, always keeping people at arm's length. She couldn't bear the thought of finding someone and losing them again. It was the reason she couldn't keep a pet, even though she loved animals.

The years flew by, and about a month before she was due to retire, she had a jarring realisation; at some point she would have to be alone for good—so she gradually lessened her connections with everyone at the school. She cancelled shared lunches and stopped turning up for school events. When the day arrived for her to retire, she didn't attend the party that the school had planned for her; instead, she sat in a coffee shop and stared at the childhood photo, telling herself it was time to stop being childish and grow up. She was about to tear up the photo when someone asked to sit opposite her; it was lunchtime and the coffee shop was short of seats. The photo was placed back into her wallet and never looked at it again.

The boat lurched to the left, jolting her out of her smouldering resentment and cynicism, and she reminded herself why she was making the trip to the Lerwick Museum—to see if she could find out more about Haby and Heed. The last time she'd felt such a thrill was when she was seven and had stolen raspberries from a neighbouring garden. Unfortunately, her stained lips were a giveaway, and she was forced to clean the orphanage hall floor every day for a week.

Disembarking at Gutcher, she drove the relatively

quiet road towards the Ulsta ferry terminal. She stopped for a sheep that had strayed onto the road, the top of its fleece had slipped sideways, so it looked like a badly fitting toupee. Two leggy, panicked lambs belatedly ran after their mother, bleating. She decided she liked Yell; particularly the peat moors. The peat digs reminded her of an oily chocolate cake that had great slices taken out of it. The slices were neatly stacked slabs of peat bricks that dried out in the sun, eventually be collected up and used to heat people's homes later in the year. Somehow, she found Yell less lonely. Not that Fetlar wasn't friendly, but there were less people, which made it seem emptier and more honest; as if it wore its heart on its sleeve. Settled onto the Ulsta ferry, she decided to migrate upstairs to the passenger lounge to stretch her legs, grab a hot drink and look at the view. As she half-juggled with scalding coffee in a flimsy, plastic cup, two women appeared beside her. One offered her a cup holder, and with some difficulty she placed the cup inside, smiling with relief; pleased to be thought of by a stranger.

'Thank-you.'

'Nay bother,' one of the woman replied, who appeared to be nursing one ear.

'You here for a long visit?' they asked in unison, appearing to be sisters—possibly twins. Both had identically styled hair. Like fine basket-ware, every strand was incorporated into a long, black interwoven plait. Their drab, woollen skirts kissed their ankles; and, as if to add a splash of colour, a floral blouse hugged each of their torsos.

'I'm staying on Fetlar for a few weeks,' Fruma replied, a little nervous at being approached and questioned so boldly. The women nodded as if to confirm their suspicion.

'Where do you bide?'

'I'm staying with Mary & Peter Smith—a lovely couple,' she wondered why she added the extra qualification. The two women nodded again.

'Haven't seen them for a while.'

'I think they're too busy running the guesthouse in summer,' she reasoned, realising she was running off at the mouth. The two women were making her feel unnerved; as if a human wall had blocked her path.

'Strange place Fetlar—odd goings on,' one of them remarked. The other looked glum.

'Black water, that's not a good sign, but still, you're visiting at the right time of year, all the islands are pretty in summer.'

'Where do you ladies bide—I mean live?' She figured she might as well find out more about them as they'd bothered to take such an interest in her. However, they weren't forthcoming with that information.

'We don't go to Fetlar. Most people don't stay on Fetlar long, only those who have their work there. Most folk come and go, they say it's because there's nothing to do there, but it's not that, it's the atmosphere—something not quite right—it's the Prophecy, it's all in the Prophecy,' one said, turning to the other who confirmed it by nodding enthusiastically. Fruma's pulse quickened at the word *prophecy*—no-one had mentioned this, not even Philip. One of the women continued.

'The island doesn't forget, it's like a photographic negative, it's imprinted in its mantle. Look to the place where it's divided.'

Fruma thought the comment odd, but then the two women seemed as quirky as Tweedle-dum and Tweedle-dee. Then, turning as one entity, they walked away.

'Thanks for the cup-holder!' Her thoughts drifted again to Heed's ramblings, and the number 237.

'The island doesn't forget'.

Taking a seat by the window, she watched a fog bank creep across the water, slowly erasing the view. Back on the car deck she tried to catch a glimpse of the two women, but there was no sign of them. She figured they'd returned to their car. It was a slow drive to Ler-wick, the fog only occasionally clearing on higher ground. To lift her spirits, she put the radio on and hummed along while contemplating what was said:

"Look to the place that's divided."

She was excited about the cryptic comment and news of a prophecy. With this new 'real' event, she felt she had something concrete to take to Mackey—then she could slip in her vision and dream as a side issue. Then she realised it would be better to tell Mackey everything that had happened from the beginning. But most importantly, meeting the two women made her feel she wasn't going mad after all; that the women were real people, not just some hazy spectre or vision. Ultimately, she was embarrassed by what had hap-pened to her; she considered real life worth discussing —not some crazy, night tossed notion. She comforted herself, that if it all went wrong, she could always leave the island when she wanted—no ties—no cries.

As she pulled into the museum car-park, the fog decided to lift, and the sun took a curtain call. She noticed it lifted everyone's spirit, people started to smile—the sun being some kind of northern narcotic. The stone steps to the revolving doors of the museum that led to an impressive foyer. The expanse of stone floor seemed to lower the temperature of the area, and the weight of the stone floor seemed to act like huge space boots, as if to stop the building floating away. If people spoke, their words echoed into the upper atmosphere of the building. Opposite the main entrance was a gift shop, completely open to the foyer where Shetland books, postcards, and other knick-k-nacks lined the walls. To the left, a photographic exhi-bition graced the corridor that led to the toilets. The entrance to the right led into the museum proper, and a flight of stairs promised a café, and the Shetland Archives. Two women were at the reception desk—they glanced up at Fruma with ready smiles.

'Do I have to make an appointment to visit the archives?'

'No, just go upstairs and it's to the right, someone will be there to assist you,' she said reassuringly. Fruma climbed the stairs to the mezzanine floor where a small seating area was provided outside the Archive room that overlooked the lower museum floor. She briefly leaned over, curious to see how it high it was; then looked up—entire boats were suspended from the three storey tall building.

The first thing that hit her as she entered the archives, was a massive table that commanded the middle of the room. Computer monitors lined the opposite wall. A wall of bookshelves boasted old tomes and reference works. The room exhibited the feel of a library, with a few folk either reading or wading through computer archives; there was an overtone of hushed excitement at the possibility of discovering a treasured, long-lost ancestor.

'I'll be with you in a moment,' an assistant announced. She nodded and took a seat. Not sure if she was allowed to browse the bookshelves, she simply held on to her cardigan. She overheard a conversation. A lady had come all the way from Australia, attempting to track down a relative from the 1960s. Before Fruma could learn more, another assistant arrived to deal with her.

'If you'd like to sign in first, it would be appreciated. In this visitor's book here.' Fruma dutifully filled out her name and where she was staying.

'Now, how can I help you?' She noted his Shetland accent was different, compared to the female receptionist downstairs.

'I'm interested in finding out more about Fetlar—in particular, about the black water . . . .'

'Fetlar?'

'Yes, Fetlar.'

'Black water?' The assistant raised an eyebrow.

'Yes, apparently it happened before in 1768, and again in the 1970's, the sea turned black along the coast . . . and again recently . . . a few days ago.'

'That can't have been local to Fetlar. I can take you through the—'

'That would be fine,' she interrupted, irritated with the assistant's repetition of her words.

'Oh—and one more thing. Is there any way of looking into the details of a Haby and Heed who lived on Fetlar, would you have any information about them?' The assistant looked long and hard at her.

'Well, I would need a surname,' he stated. She blushed.

'Oh, that's true, he didn't give me a surname—only they're very unusual names and not native to Shetland as far as I've been told,' she replied, squirming, realising she had not come prepared at all.

'Sorry, I really need a surname. But the black water we can look into.' The assistant moved to a computer terminal and expertly pulled up an archive.

'This is all we have, one account: "1768 Shetland. Sea disturbance. Marine eruption off Shetland." It seems the sea turned black and muddy, many fish died, but it doesn't say it happened in Fetlar,' he said in a somewhat disgruntled manner, as if she were wasting his time.

'Oh? I have it on good authority that the Minister of the time recorded an entry in the Parish records, so I'm pretty sure it was Fetlar,' she said, with an air of superiority. Her hackles rose, annoyed at his dismissive attitude. She also felt he was hostile toward Fetlar itself; she puzzled over her reaction, and the idea that an island needed defending.

'Well—I'm afraid that's all we have. When you find the surname of those people I'll be able to give you more details. Now is there anything else I can help you with?'

'No, that's just fine—thanks—I'll go take a walk around the museum.'

'Nay bother.'

She left the archives with the same feeling she remembered from Parent's Day at school. It didn't matter what she'd say about a child, some parents would find any excuse to be surly. Walking around the exhibits, her eyes darted around at place names, searching information plaques, desperate for one mention of Fetlar—but it never seemed to appear anywhere. She felt a kind of melancholia; as if Fetlar were a forgotten relative to mainland Shetland. With the Archive room finally emptied of visitors, the assistant picked up the phone.

'Hello. Is that Frater Niven? Hi, it's James from the Shetland Museum archives—yes—a-ha—you told me to ring you if someone came in asking about Haby and Heed—aye, that's right, and she enquired about the black water—yes—female—probably in her late sixties—her name—let me see—her name is Fruma Langthorne. Yes, I have an address too—OK—goodbye.' The assistant continued his furious tapping on the computer keyboard.

CHAPTER SIX

After the recent bleak, autumnal shift in weather, Fruma was glad to see Fetlar once again bathed in the gentle glow of the sun. Unfortunately, so were the insects, who used every opportunity to gang-up on all warm-blooded creatures. Luckily, by midday, a wind had arrived, and they were consigned to shelter once again in the depths of the grasses and sheltered spots. Fruma decided to take Mackey up on his promise of keeping an open house. When she arrived, he was on his way out to exercise the dogs and coerced her to go along; his bribe—a large flask of hot chocolate and some home-made muffins.

'Nice day, hope it lasts,' she said brightly.

'Never trust a *Joolie* sky, Shetland is known for having four seasons in one day.'

'I've noticed.'

'So—I'm looking forward to hearing about your travels,' he said, letting the dogs off their leads.

'Actually, it's all been a bit weird Mackey.' She searched his face. She didn't know why she trusted him, but she did, even after only one meeting.

'I'm listening.'

'You'll think I'm bonkers. These sorts of things don't happen to me Mackey,' she said darkly.

'Listen, I believe that a man rose from the dead, can you top that?' Tickled, she burst out laughing. He motioned her to a bench overlooking the beach, it was dotted with vestiges of yellow paint that made it look like it had a case of the shingles.

'Right, so I'll start at the beginning. The first day I was here, something happened, it was like I had a vision—just over there,' she pointed in the general direction.

'I was watching the sea and then the whole area changed atmosphere, it went all misty. I turned round, and I saw some coloured—some black men— they were wearing long robes, they walked slowly across the grass; that piece of land between the beach and Papil Water?' She pointed again.

'It's called The Links.'

'Thank-you. Oh, they were carrying books too. Anyway, I figured I must have drifted off to sleep, being tired from all the travelling. Then, the next night I had a dream—' she paused, expecting a humorous quip.

'Go on—I'm listening, it's very interesting to me. Please.'

'In the dream, I saw hands holding a golden chalice filled with a black tar-like liquid, I didn't see who was holding it, but the liquid was thick, and slowly spilled over into a black body of water.' She paused.

'A voice said to me—"Who is your master?" And then the number 237 was repeated over and over.' She spotted a flicker of recognition cross his face. She decided to keep back the part of the dream about the dog holding the wood as it involved Quincy, and she wasn't sure how he'd take it.

'And then, the next day, that black water appeared. Don't you think that's a strange coincidence?' He smiled as he poured hot chocolate into plastic cups. The dogs had crept back, bored with themselves.

'I don' t believe in coincidence Fruma,' he said calmly.

'Why not?'

'I believe that God has an overall plan for everyone but we don't see what he sees because he sees everything from a distance—even the future. It's the difference between seeing a hurricane from space and being at ground level experiencing it chaotically. That's what our lives are like—often we're coerced on a path, and we don't want to go, often because it's uncomfortable; we resist the way of change just because we don't understand, or can't understand because we can't see ahead. Your experience is part of His plan—you just don't have the foresight to see where it will lead,' he stated matter-of-factly. He offered her a muffin and broke one up for the dogs to share.

'But this has never happened to me before I came here,' she protested, not entirely happy with his reply.

'Yes, but the time is always right Fruma. I know you said you're not religious, but I believe that life is a bit like a game of chess—except you play against the ultimate player: God!' His face lit up at the thought.

'I think it was Stephen Hawking . . . he said that Einstein had been wrong . . . he was talking about black holes—oh what was it? Einstein said something like—*"God does not play dice,"* and Stephen Hawking remarked later saying: *"Not only does God play dice, but he throws them where they can't be seen."* I think that's a marvellous way of putting it!' he chuckled.

'So you think what happened to me had meaning then?'

'Absolutely—everything has meaning, we just haven't put all the pieces of the puzzle together yet.' Fruma noted the 'we'.

'What about "Who is your Master?" What do you make of that?' Mackey paused.

'That's quite interesting—who is your master—I think I'd like to hang fire on that. I get the impression it's not something we can answer right now, not with any accuracy. The answer will come in time, I'm sure.' Frustrated at not receiving an instant interpretation, she continued.

'But that's not all. I was visiting the Interpretive Centre, and Philip played me the tape of Heed while he was rambling, it was really quite eerie, but when Heed started chanting that number—237—I could've fainted!' Recalling the event, she gripped the plastic cup tightly.

'It's been a while since I heard that tape . . . so you dreamt about the same number too?' Mackey said, before remembering his formal role as Minister; political correctness overtook curiosity.

'Are you OK? Not too shaken up I hope?' He leaned forward, providing a placatory hand on her arm.

'No—but I was pretty shocked. Do you see what I mean though? In fact, it's more than a coincidence. How could I dream about that number when I've never even met the boy?' He pulled his mouth to one side. He had some ideas, but was unsure if she was ready for them.

'Look—don't worry. I'm more curious now than frightened or upset.' Smiling weakly, she allowed his hand to remain on her arm.

'Has anything ever happened before like this?'

'Never. Miss Ordinary. I don't believe in ghosts or anything, or at least I've never seen any to say they're real, and on average I don't remember my dreams.' He looked thoughtful again.

'I never asked you before—why are you *really* here, Fruma?' The question took her by surprise. Many answers flooded her mind, all of them sounded trite.

'To find something . . . for meaning—to find peace?'

'What do you mean by peace?'

'Maybe peace isn't the right word. I want to just be —I want to find out how to be happy, and to know what I want in life. My whole life I've been there for others—now I'm retired, I want to be there for me.'

She searched his eyes for some sort of recognition or approval, but he seemed removed, without emotion.

'That sounds incredibly selfish now I'm hearing it out loud.' He shook his head.

'Inner peace doesn't happen overnight. You have to learn how to listen Fruma. But maybe not in the *normal* way . . . . '

'I did try, and then these other things started coming up. It's unnerving, like there's no solid ground,' she whinged defensively. He squeezed her arm.

'Sorry,' she said in a small voice.

'No—no 'sorries' here. This is what I'm here for— remember?' She looked down, nodding.

'Then I found myself restless, sometimes with thoughts that seemed alien to me. I wonder if it's something to do with what's been going on here?'

'Could be. You mentioned you were an orphan the first time we met. Do you mind me asking—do you know anything about your birth parents or family?'

'No. Nothing. Someone might have mentioned a distant relative, but I was just a child. To be honest Mackey, I never looked—I didn't want to. If they didn't want to know me, then why should I bother with them?' she said indignantly.

'I understand, but what about close friends?'

'Oh, come and gone. I know some people, acquaintances, but no close friends now, I'm—err— I'm too busy at work for friends, and the children need me—it takes up all my time you see.' He looked at Fruma with sadness and concern, before his thoughts drifted.

'" . . . There is not a single thing as empty and needy as you, who embrace the Universe: you are the investigator without knowledge, the magistrate without jurisdiction, and all in all, a fool of the farce."

That's from Montaigne—actually it's about vanity, but I think it describes the ego too.' She went to protest but he was more forceful.

'You will never find yourself on your own you know. We can't. We can't get outside of ourselves, we can't observe without engaging the other side of us— our ego—and believe me—the ego is a powerful master, it decides . . . . '

'Oh, I've heard it all before about the ego!' she snapped back.

'The small voice inside that either thinks its superhuman or the most wretched thing on the earth —are you aware of it?' he returned forcefully.

'Not really, it's *me* that decides. I make all my own decisions.' He started laughing; it was a gentle, non-vindictive laugh; but she simmered with annoyance at being confronted.

'It *is* you Fruma—you and your ego are one—we can't see if our ego is fooling us without someone else, we make wrong decisions all the time because we don't notice that '*it's*' in charge. We're not mindful of our behaviour until someone else pops the bubble— that's why psychologists and analysts exist . . . . '

'So now I need therapy?' she said, with a murderous look. He smiled.

'*See*, that's your ego speaking—coming back with defence—why are you being so defensive?'

'Because you're trying to tell me that I can't do anything on my own—but I've always had to do things on my own!' she shouted, standing up, hands on hips.

'I didn't say that you can't do anything on your own, but if you're saying you don't need help, then why am I here? We all need help at some time in our lives Fruma,' he said gently. Defiant, she faced the sea; not wanting him to see her frustration.

'Now I understand,' he said in a low voice. 'Who is

your master, Fruma?' She turned around, and saw mirth in his eyes. Angry, she ignored him, and returned her gaze to the sea. She wanted to scream, tear down mountains; break things. It was Quincy that changed her mood. He walked over, sat on her foot, then leaned his head against her—almost romantically. Seeing him looking at her with such an expression, she erupted into laughter. She laughed so hard she thought she might pass out, then she made Mackey laugh trying to explain why she found it so amusing. The laughter eventually turned into heaving sobs and tears. He went to say something, but she held up her hand, and pulling a tissue from her pocket, she cried into it. Embarrassed, she turned back to face the sea, her shoulders wobbling. He gave her some space. After a while, her tears diminished.

'I don't know what I want—I think that's the problem,' she said in a small, sad voice. He smiled to himself.

'That's the most wisest thing you've said to me in the short time I've known you. Now things might change. Admitting that something's wrong is the first step. Shall we take a walk around Papil Water? The dogs are getting restless.' She held onto his arm as they walked in silence. Suddenly they heard the throaty calls of Greylag geese; there were three of them, just enough to allow them to fly in the classic V formation.

'Do you know why geese fly in formation?' he asked. She thought about it.

'Not really.'

'It helps them to conserve energy. It's all about wind resistance, the bird in front flies slightly higher than the one behind, reducing the wind resistance, then they swap round when the one at the front gets tired. You Fruma—you're always the front bird, there's never been anyone behind you to let you rest. When did you give up trusting?'

'I don't know—maybe I never did,' she replied glumly and squeezed his arm. They walked quietly for a few minutes.

'By the way, I went to the Shetland Archives, trying to find out more about Haby and Heed. Well, I have to say, I'm quite embarrassed about the whole thing really—I wasn't prepared at all. The assistant asked me for a surname, but of course you didn't tell me that, so the names Haby and Heed meant nothing to him. But I did find out that they only have one account of the black water but it's not attributed to Fetlar.'

'Interesting. The surname by the way is Finn. F.I.N.N.'

'FINN? OK, thanks. But we know, according to what you said, that the black water on Fetlar happened twice before don't we?' He nodded his head slowly. Fruma stopped.

'It's really odd—here's another thing. When I was speaking to the archive assistant, he seemed, I don't know—sort of offhanded, and I felt—I felt judged. I was annoyed that he wasn't ... oh, how can I put it? It was like I was the only one defending Fetlar, like Fetlar was sad it had been forgotten and no-one cared about it anymore.' He seemed thoughtful.

'To some extent it is forgotten. There's still folk living on the Shetland mainland who don't know where it is. I remember one lady who thought it was part of Unst. There's a sadness here too. I feel it.'

'Yes, but I've only been here for a few days—why would I care so much about it? This is what's puzzling me, it shouldn't mean anything to me—I'm only here on holiday.'

'But you're not only here on holiday are you? You're

looking for something else. What does time matter in all of this? Does it matter that it's so few days? It's how you feel Fruma, that's the important part. Something must be important here because you're dreaming about it. You don't dream about things if they're not relevant, or important to you. Maybe you've found something really special here—just for you—isn't that what you've been looking for?' She looked down.

'I must admit, it's all getting under my skin a little. I can't stop thinking about it—it's almost an obsession, and I don't have control over it.' He pointedly turned around and faced her, saying:

'There's nothing wrong with feeling something,' he paused, 'maybe it's the first time you've actually felt something, Fruma!' His comment hit the mark; she felt like she'd been hit with a cricket bat. She gulped back more overwhelming emotion.

'Maybe you're tuning into the island's energetic system, every place has one; ley lines, most churches are built on ley lines . . . you know, a long time ago, at every scattald boundary there was a church, so there were twelve chapels all in operation at one time on Fetlar.' He waffled on. 'This island has the capability to heal people, you know that Fruma? It's one of the reasons why I chose it. It's the serpentine stone in the island; it has special powers of . . . .'

Suddenly there was a splash. Quincy had launched himself into Papil Water. Mackey shouted, but the dog ignored him, swimming out to the centre. Then he seemed to change his mind, turned around and started swimming back. He was carrying something in his mouth. Mackey encouraged him, but as soon as he climbed out of the water, he started moaning at him.

'Bad Quincy! When I say come back, you damned well come back!' His rebuke seemed far away to Fruma, who felt as if she'd been shot. She sank to her knees. As Quincy stood there with a piece of driftwood in his mouth, she recalled her dream. Shocked, she leaned forward and gripped the grass, as if holding its earthy stems grounded her back to something that made sense. She didn't even object when Quincy started shaking himself right next to her. He dropped the piece of wood and then ran off towards Tresta beach. Mackey, not noticing her condition at first, started shouting after him; and then, as if sensing it, he turned around. She was turning the driftwood over in her hands, mumbling the number 237—over and over.

'Fruma—FRUMA!' But she didn't respond.

'Fruma, STOP.' He broke the spell by snatching the wood away, and knelt down next to her, worried. She looked up.

'What's happening?'

'You were chanting. That number. 237.'

'Was I?' She felt distant and disorientated, until she remembered.

'I should have told you, that was in my dream too! I saw a brown dog—it was your Quincy holding the wood. Why is all this happening to me?' She looked at him, helpless.

'I don't know, Fruma. I really don't.' He helped her to stand.

'Can you walk?' She nodded, but really was uncertain of anything.

'Just give me a minute.' He called Quincy; this time the dog decided to follow orders.

'There were some markings on that wood . . . I'm not sure, but I think it might be Hebrew,' she said quietly. Now it was his turn to look unnerved, he scanned the area.

'Let's go back shall we?' he said seriously. With the dogs safely on leads, they marched back to Mackey's.

A car passed them on the road, they both waved in unison as if nothing had happened. She stopped him.

'I didn't tell you before, but the very first time I saw you, I recognised Quincy straight away.' He said nothing, but looked dismayed. She'd hoped for some of his strength to buoy her up—now she felt as if she'd ruined everything..

'I couldn't say anything could I? I would've looked mad telling a stranger I'd seen his dog in a dream. But it was definitely Quincy holding the wood—I'm sorry I didn't tell you before.' He seemed irritated at first, but then seemed to soften.

'Sorry Fruma, I do realise what a shock it must have been for you, and feeling like you had to keep it all bottled-up too.' Then, as if he didn't want to be outside a moment more, he said, 'Let's get back inside and talk—I'm sure we could both do with a cuppa.'

Arriving back, she noticed that Mackey had brought back the piece of wood; she saw him put it in the greenhouse. He stared at it for a moment and then closed the door. Then he checked twice that the door was latched. Inside, she huddled herself into the sofa while he made the tea. She picked up a cushion with a soft, velvety cover and held it over her solar plexus. She noticed something was different about the room— Mackey had cleared up. He arrived with two large mugs of tea, handed one to her, and sat in the opposite armchair.

'Thanks Mackey. You OK? I thought you looked a bit rough there for a minute yourself.'

'I didn't have a very good feeling at Papil Water. I haven't felt that for a very long time.' He slurped at his tea that was too hot.

'I thought that too—the first time I walked around it, like the atmosphere changed, it was sinister, yet the beach seemed normal and peaceful.'

'Hmm,' he said before going quiet again.

'Did I really chant that number?' She didn't remember anything—just Mackey shouting at her.

'You did.'

'Just like Heed.' They both sat quietly, cradling their tea. A blackbird flew onto the window sill and looked in; seemingly sure of no threat it started preening itself. At that moment, she envied its uncomplicated existence. Irritated that Mackey seemed to be in his own world, she broke the silence.

'So where do I go from here? Is this going to happen everywhere I go—me falling into mystical swoons or chanting? I mean, do you have any clue what's going on?' she asked in earnest. He looked at her with compassion.

'I think you're picking up on past events, or catching glimpses. The spiritual veil down at Tresta might be thinner, and people like you are able to see through,' he suggested, knowing his explanation might not be received well.

'People like me?' He sighed.

'Look Fruma, I say people like you because this doesn't happen to just anyone . . . .'

'So now I'm just some weird—witch-like woman. Jesus! Just give me a crystal ball and I'm off, telling everyone's fortunes and predicting the future!'

'I didn't say that, did I?' he said, rolling his eyes. Frustrated, she stood up which frightened the blackbird, it flew away sounding an alarm call. This irritated her; but she was really irritated with herself. She stood at the window, wishing she could swear—it always made her feel better. Mackey joined her at the window. The sun played hide and seek as they watched the bird feeder being noisily attacked by a few bickering starlings. He chose his words carefully.

'All it takes is a small trigger event—a memory—

you've definitely never been here before?' She shook her head, his words made her feel even more alone. She began to wonder if he would be any help at all; at times he made her head spin with his crazy ideas.

'I have to say, I've not seen anything like this, it's very unusual . . . . ' She turned around half-angrily, but he put a calming hand on her shoulder.

'But that doesn't mean it's going to *keep* happening. It might only be confined to Tresta.' The doorbell rang. Mackey excused himself. She listened, it was a man at the door—she heard Mackey say that he had someone with him and another date was made. She felt a sudden rush of embarrassment at taking up so much of his time and decided she'd leave when he returned. She was like a horse at the starting post when he came back in; half pacing the floor.

'I'm going.'

'You haven't finished your tea,' he said, surprised.

'No—it's OK—I think I'd like to take some time to clear my head, I need some time to myself.' He looked truly sorrowful.

'I'm sorry I don't have any answers at the moment, and I'm sorry if I've offended you—it wasn't my intention, Fruma, it really wasn't,' he said sadly. Seeing his expression, she felt overwhelmed with regret.

'I know none of this is your fault, I'm sorry I behaved so impetuously. Look, I just need some time —just to clear my head—and decide if I want to stay; you can understand that can't you?' He appeared to brighten up.

'Of course I can. Will I see you another time? I understand, it's all a bit much, but you know I'm always here if you want to talk. Don't think you're alone with all this Fruma. You can even come round if you want a game of cards or a change of scenery, we don't have to talk about the island.' He stood back to let her go.

'Take care out there Fruma. Don't go without telling me, will you?'

'I won't. Thank-you. Thank-you for listening to me going on . . . and for being there for me.' There was an awkward moment when they both felt they should either hug or shake hands, and then he appeared to be lost in thought again. She put an end to it by walking away and saying:

'Penny for them!'

'Oh yes—sorry—take care Fruma!'

The good weather was still holding, so she decided to walk towards Aith. Walking helped release the tension, as if the cornucopia of the logical, natural world replaced the nagging feeling that she was somehow connected with the island's history. She reached the top of the hill near the entrance to the community hall and looked out towards Lamb Hoga; at that moment she seriously considered leaving; that at least everything was less complicated back in Gateshead. She also reminded herself it was boring. She visualised her empty two bedroom house, her messy front garden, and her neighbour's endless suggestions for planting shrubs that waited for her. At least here she felt she was interesting, even if it was all crazy. On Fetlar; for better or worse—things happened. She wasn't just another nameless face, and Mackey made it obvious he wanted to see her again. Feeling a surge of confidence, and with more than a dash of inquisitiveness, she made up her mind to stay. It was final. She couldn't leave without answers. She made up her mind to visit the Shetland Archives again, now she had the family name: Finn. She set off walking, remembering Mackey's words:

"That doesn't mean it's going to keep happening—

it might only be confined to Tresta."

'Skittles! I didn't tell Mackey about the two ladies on the ferry!' She felt as if the words didn't belong to her; as if saying them out loud meant they belonged to whatever was happening; that *it* owned her by proxy; that *it* was making her think and act. Her thoughts were disturbed by the sound of thunderous hooves—a flock of sheep fled an unknown threat. She looked in all directions, but saw nothing that could equate with their sudden flight. She was totally alone on the road. She continued walking, and castigated herself for not mentioning something as crucial as the two women, it was the only real evidence she had, apart from the wood. She also realised it meant it was more serious if it wasn't just confined to Tresta—then she spent the next fifteen minutes worrying herself stupid about early onset Alzheimers.

It was 2:30am, and already daylight; the Shetland simmer dim was either hated or loved by the incomers —as the sun would dip slightly below the horizon for only half an hour before rising again. Many installed thick blinds, so they weren't woken up at some ungodly hour. Even plants were known to be stressed at not having a chance to rest. But Liam didn't notice or care about what was going on outside—he only lived for his treasure. He was getting bolder, starting his adoration earlier, but that came with the risk of someone walking in. Maybe it was an unconscious desire to be caught, as the pressure would increase to unbearable levels until he removed the cup, and play-acted for the next few hours. He was becoming quite proficient at being a king, a trader or a potential thief. Although he didn't need any encouragement to spend hours stroking, fondling and caressing his cup, he would often lose hours; sometimes as soon as he entered his bedroom. At times he totally lost contact with reality. Sometimes he was more aware and worried about it; but not being able to share his thoughts with others made him feel very isolated.

Before finding the treasure, he used to be a vigilant teaser; it was how he and his sister communicated—now he was too tired and preoccupied to goad anyone, and his behaviour was not going unnoticed at home or at school.

'Liam! You're going to be late for school again!' Sue bellowed up the stairs. To Liam, her call was like a muffled voice from beyond—one minute he was holding the cup, the next, he was being called for school. He rolled over, feeling so tired he thought he had the flu, but with a raging hunger that pulled him to the breakfast table. He contemplated doing a 'sickie', it would give him time to catch up on some sleep; but today was sports day, and he normally enjoyed participating, being a fair runner. He hurriedly brushed his teeth, and went to change into his school clothes, but then realised he hadn't undressed from the previous night. He looked down at his shirt and trousers that looked as if they'd been walked over by a hundred sheep. He pulled a jumper over his shirt and hoped his mother wouldn't notice his trousers before heading downstairs.

'Come on Liam! What's the matter with you? You look terrible—what happened to your school trousers?' She looked him up and down. He shrugged.

'I think my trousers ended up in my bed somehow —anyway—it's Sports Day today; no-one will notice. I'll get changed at school,' he said reassuringly, shaking cornflakes into a bowl. He piled on teaspoon after teaspoon of sugar and filled the bowl so full he couldn't eat it without drinking some of the milk first. Liam's sister watched all this and turned round to fake smile at Sue.

'I wouldn't bother with *him*—I'm gonna win today, I just know it—I can *feel* it.' Holly said, beaming at Liam who didn't bother looking up. She frowned. It was usually easy to wind Liam up, but these days she noticed he seemed so preoccupied.

'Running? It's *so* easy. But Shotput—well—that takes *real* skill,' Holly boasted, but to no avail. Liam shovelled soggy cornflakes into his mouth like he hadn't eaten for days. Sue also thought it was odd that he wasn't rising to the bait. She'd got so used to the two of them arguing at mealtimes. Another puzzle was how her small framed daughter had the strength to throw a heavy Shotput and Discus, yet Holly had won every year at their old school—without fail. Sue began to wonder if she knew her children at all.

'Good luck today Holly, and you Liam—Liam? Are you running today?' Sluggishly, he looked up, he'd been daydreaming about showing off his gold cup in assembly, and everyone *oohing* and *ahhing*.

'What? Oh yes—running. I always run. Nothing new.' He returned to his slurping and crunching. Holly looked at Sue, rolling her eyes exaggeratedly and shaking her head like she'd seen her father do.

'Something up Liam? You seem so tired these days,' Sue asked. She had a brush in each hand and was simultaneously brushing each twin's hair, which made them both giggle and stare at each other. Bored, Holly left the table.

'I'm meeting Sarah at hers, see you later Mum— wish me luck!' she said, grabbing her jacket.

'Good luck darling!' Liam's eyelids were beginning to droop. Sue watched him and put a finger to her lips.

'Ssssh!' she indicated to the twins who crowded around the table to watch their older brother. Liam's eyelids closed and his head gradually tipped forward. Sue tiptoed over to the kitchen counter and picked up one of the twin's water bottles. Quietly, she pulled back the cap, crept to the table, took aim and squirted as hard as she could. The water shot out at speed, slamming into Liam's right eye. He jumped up and knocked over his bowl. The twins leapt up and down, laughing and clapping. She sniggered. Liam glared at her, wiping water from his face.

'Sorry—I couldn't resist! You were asleep!' she shouted above the twin's racket.

'Was not. I was resting my eyes. God, you're worse than Holly!'

'You can clear up the mess,' he said grumpily.

'I always do,' she retorted, with the confidence of a mother still indulging herself.

'Look Liam, you're not fit to run today, surely you must know that? Why are you always so tired these days? Do you need to see Christine?' she asked, while tugging a jumper over one of the twin's heads. Liam shrugged. He surreptitiously rubbed his cut through his wristband; it was getting worse not better. He contemplated showing it to his mother, but then realised he'd have to reveal that he didn't know how it had happened. He was glad the weather was cool enough so he could wear a jumper over the wristband.

'I don't know Mum, can't seem to sleep these days. Perhaps it's hay fever—I've heard that can make you feel drowsy.' He sniffed for effect. She snorted.

'You've never suffered before, besides, hay fever is something adults suffer from.' She wondered if she was right. 'I'll get some hay fever tablets when I go to the shop next OK?' He nodded and grabbed his school bag, slinging it over his shoulder.

'Bye Mum. See ya kids,' he waved to the twins, who quietly waved back. She sighed and thought about talking to Trevor. Liam slept on the ferry as it sailed for Unst. He dreamed of men building impressive structures. He appeared to be watching from a sling in the clouds, he was swinging to and fro, holding his gold cup, shouting commands from a high position. The men sweated under the hot sun and hated their King. He didn't care; he ruled over them all—he had the right. Then he dreamt he was only a prince who desired to be King. His sister was next in line—he had to kill his sister and claim the throne. He was woken up by falling on the floor. The ferry was doing a sideways roller due to rough seas, and he tipped right out of the side seat. His sister and her friend were over the other side of the room looking green—they didn't have the will, or desire to mock him.

CHAPTER SEVEN

Lerwick was experiencing some incredibly hot weather, even surpassing all previous summer records; whereas in the last two days, Fetlar lay under thick clouds and chilly temperatures. She was glad to get away from the gloomy island and visit the Shetland Archives again. As much as she was genuinely excited at the possibility of finding more information about Haby and Heed, it was still far easier for her to fall back into patterns of old behaviour; of burying herself in other people's lives rather than face her own. The archives were busy, and her heart sank when the same assistant she'd dealt with before asked her to sign in and take a seat. While she was waiting, her eyes fell upon a poster:

Lecture by visiting European Scholars:
Dr. R. Robinson & Dr. Luthier
The Papar - A Priestly People
September 17th, 6.30pm—8pm
In the Auditorium. Free Admission.

Seeing this gave her goose bumps. Not only because the word *Papar* was so close to the name *Papil*, but because of the associated picture. It showed men in long, white robes that had crosses on them. They were holding staffs and appeared to be in a procession. The men were similar to her vision men although they were Caucasian not black. She made a mental note of the name, intending to ask Mackey on her return. Another assistant entered the room.

'Are you being seen to?' he enquired.

'Not at the moment,' she said, relieved.

'So, how can I help you?' he said, balancing a tower of books in his arms.

'I'd like to enquire about a family name if possible.'

'Of course, step over to the desk, I'll need to use the computer.' While he offloaded his books, she was aware that the other assistant had glanced over at them.

'Now, what was the surname?'

'Finn. Haby Finn. H-A-B-Y. I was wondering when he came to the island—I mean Fetlar—maybe you could tell me where he originally came from?'

'Let me see, Finn . . . two n's?'

'Yes, two N's.'

'Haby—unusual name . . . . '

'Yes, it is.'

'Finn—yes—we have one record that a Haby Finn lived on Fetlar, only one record, and that was about his disappearance in 1965, it says here—' He turned the screen around for her to see.

'" . . . Haby Finn was said to have ventured out one night and never returned. Locals say that no boats were missing . . . " in those days there were no ro-ro ferries you know,' the assistant said, with a twinkle in his eye. Fruma nodded, warming to him more than the other assistant.

'" . . . He leaves behind a wife: Lily, and son, Heed. Police found no evidence of foul play."' He turned the screen back around.

'Yes, that's the same as I've been told. So there's no other information about his arrival on Fetlar or where he was from?'

'I'm afraid not, although the names are rather odd. Do you know where this name originates just out of interest?'

'No, I'm afraid I don't. All I know is that he was a Finn.' The assistant took off his glasses and rubbed his eyes.

'I think he may have been one of the last Finns on Shetland if he disappeared in 1965. I don't know if you know, but the legends say the Finns came from Norway in small canoe type boats and infiltrated many lands in the north. They were mistrusted because they were associated with dark magic and shape shifting. It was also said they were 'seal people'; possessing a skin or garment like the covering of a seal, enabling them to take to the water and cover vast distances no human could. Another extraordinary power the Finnfolk was said to have, was to transform at will into the shape of any bird or fish. I think Fetlar holds the record for Finn stories, the Finnigert Dyke on Fetlar was reported to have been built in one night by Finns.' The assistant tapped furiously on the keyboard.

'There are several folk tales from Fetlar about them.' He scrolled down the screen.

'There's one about a farmer of Kolbenstaft who only had a low turf wall to protect his crops from livestock. A Finn came to him in a dream and offered him kindness in return for the farmer's kindness he once received. In the morning, the farmer woke up and found a stone wall enclosing his name.' She interrupted him,

'Enclosing his name?' The assistant looked puzzled.

'Sorry, misread it, enclosing his *land*,' he continued, 'this was supposedly the Neolithic Finnigert Dyke —the stone wall that divides Fetlar almost in two; from North to South.' He typed on the keyboard.

'Yes, the name Finnigert looks like it might originally have come from Finna-garðr 'Enclosure of the Finns'—there's lots of references that can be looked up. So you see, this is just one story, but the Finns had much influence on the folklore of the Shetland Islands.' The assistant paused.

'Can I help you with anything else?'

'I think that's all, thanks. Oh wait—' she pointed to the poster, 'this looks interesting, this Papar talk, does it have anything to do with Papil Water on Fetlar? I mean—there is a Papil Water on Fetlar . . . . '

'Can you make the presentation?'

'I'm a tourist, I'm only here for a few weeks, but I guess there must be some connection?'

'Oh yes, there will be. The Papar were thought to be priestly clerics—there's the Papar Project online so you can read more about it. The 'Papar' name had turned up in many places: Scotland, Shetland, and even in other countries like Norway and Iceland, so a project was set up, with the aim of finding more information about these Celtic religious communities.'

'Interesting, I'll take a look at that when I get back.' The assistant started tapping on the keyboard again when the telephone rang.

'Do you mind if I . . . is that all for now?'

'Yes, thanks very much, it's been very useful. Thanks again.'

Fruma looked at the poster again; feeling as if someone had walked over her grave. She remembered what Mackey said about not believing in coincidences. As she was leaving the Archives, she realised she wouldn't have to wait to talk to Mackey—there must be a Shetland library; and most libraries have computers. She checked with the women at the front desk of the museum and was given directions.

Full of nervous energy, she settled in front of the computer terminal and typed in: 'The Papar Project'. Reading through, she noted the purpose of the project was to acquire a better understanding of everything to do with the Papar, and the various Papil locations, she also noted there were different ways of spelling the name: Papay, Papae, Pabbay, Payble. She clicked on the Shetland tab, there was a Fetlar reference; it mentioned Papil Water but nothing of any use to the mystery. She doubled back to the introduction page and scanned the contents, settling on the place-name evidence, then moved further down to the historical evidence, noting the Norwegian influence. Scanning the page, her eye settled on some startling evidence from the *Historia Norvegiae* (History of Norway).

" . . . *and the Papae have been named from their white robes, which they wore like priests; whence priests are all called papae in the Teutonic tongue. An island is still called, after them, Papey. But, as is observed from their habit and the writings of their books abandoned there, they were Africans, adhering to Judaism . . .* "

Fruma became filled with a whole range of emotions; from elation, wonder, incredulity—to a kind of dread at this *African* revelation. She kept re-reading the passage and wondered what Mackey would make of it, his words ringing in her ears:

"I think you're picking up on past events, catching glimpses."

Had she seen a vision of these Papar? Now she was beginning to believe what Mackey had already seen in her. She availed herself of the coffee machine. This new information, made her think; that sometimes life throws you a curve ball when you least expect it. Full of caffeine spiked courage, she decided to look up her old orphanage on the internet. On tenterhooks, she typed in:

Windy Nook Orphanage, Tyne and Wear.

There was no orphanage with that name. She tried another search.

Orphanage, Gateshead, Tyne and Wear.

The top listing was a 'Zion Orphanage'. Out of curiosity, she clicked on the link; it was a Jewish Orphanage in Israel. She balked at the 'Jewish' reference turning up again. Her thoughts also drifted to the Hebrew lettering on the wood—she wondered why she hadn't asked Mackey about it. She dug around some more and checked out a site:
Former Children's Homes—it listed two 'Cottage Home' sites in the area, but neither was called 'Windy Nook'. She checked other links, but it yielded the same result. She wondered if she'd remembered correctly, but was sure she could never forget such an aptly named place. All the girls complained about the draughts that came from the single glazed sash windows on the east side as it blew straight into the girls dorms. The garden, however, was quite the opposite; being set in a dip, looking up at the four storey house. Tall beech trees stood at the back, alongside deeply layered, clipped bushes—behind them dogwood, hawthorn, elder hedges, and other shrubbery. All the foliage made it a *windless* nook; a place that Fruma and her friend Ben would disappear into whenever allowed. She recalled that one of the beech trees had a natural hollow in its trunk and they

would hide items away from the keen eyes of the other children, and the orphanage 'Mother'. Fruma also remembered another beech tree she called 'George', because it had muscular, manly boughs. She leaned back against the computer chair, wanting to feel something behind her, holding her, supporting her; now even her past seemed thrown into question. Returning to a default mindset of self-preservation and self-hate, she blamed herself for dragging up memories, that she should never have come to the Shetland Islands in the first place, and that she was yet again getting involved in affairs that had nothing to do with her.

This sent her into a panic—questioning why she kept repeating the same mistakes. She entertained thoughts of returning home, but knew she'd only feel like a cuckoo in her own nest. She contemplated ringing Mackey just to hear his calming voice; but realised that meant she couldn't cope on her own, and they'd already had that conversation. Then she had another realisation; that maybe she'd have more luck with another browser, but the computer only had one installed.

Hunger now overtook her frustration, and she drove back to Commercial Street and settled in a busy café. The sound of bacon frying was soothing; like white noise, and in that calm moment Fruma realised she couldn't possibly go home without some kind of closure of the whole affair, no matter the cost. That Mackey was right—she couldn't *find herself* on her own. Emerging from the café, she noticed an air of excitement; a visiting cruise ship had chucked out its brood of tourists, the main shopping street was bustling with happy shoppers, all gabbling loudly in foreign tongues. As she neared Market Square, the sound of music wafted from tiny outdoor speakers attached to a wall. Raspy violins, throaty accordions and a flunky bass breathed a Shetland reel, making the tourists smile as they purchased Shetland knick-k-nacks. She looked at the quiescent behemoth of a cruise ship that waited for the shoppers in the harbour; it stood there like a patient mother, or a bully, overshadowing everything moored there. As a brief divertissement, and to avoid the crowds, she decided to take a closer look. She turned down a side street with uneven stone steps that were worn smooth, imagining them to be treacherous in the frost and snow. The steps led to the harbour road where the cruise ship sat like a monstrous, white, cardboard cut-out. The almost militaristic layers of decks gave her the idea of a floating prison, and she wondered what would happen if a person hated the six-week cruise after only three nights.

She bought a 99 flake from the corner shop before heading back to the car and finally back to Fetlar. It was upstairs on the Yell ferry, looking out of the window and drifting off, that she recalled the Hebrew letter *shin* on the wood, and how she'd remembered it was Hebrew. A Jewish boy who'd attended the school for one month, would forget himself and write his name in Hebrew; she would make him translate it underneath in English: Schneur. The 'Sch' part of his name, when spoken, made a soft sound like 'shh' this was how the letter shin was pronounced on this occasion. The letter she saw in the piece of wood was like the letter shin; but instead of looking like a three--pronged pitchfork with no handle—she realised it had an extra prong. She reminded herself to ask Mackey about the wood and hoped the new found *Papar* would provide another stepping stone in the Haby and Heed mystery.

Lucy liked going out on her own; it made her feel grown-up. She kicked a piece of driftwood, it landed in a deep heap of black, stinking seaweed. *Flonk.* She wanted to kick it again, but didn't want to sink up to her ankles in the smelly, black stuff. Turning to the sea, the wind picked up; feeling chilly, she thought about returning home. Scouring the beach, she went in search of something else to kick. Just over near the burn's outflow, there was something flat and yellow. Holding her arms out to balance herself, she carefully navigated the large, round stones; she liked the dull knocking noise they made when they toppled together. She then made her way across the short, stretch of beach with smaller, gravel sized stones.

She bent down to view the specimen—it was a piece of yellow plastic, once part of an old fish packing crate. She kicked it towards the sea, intending to send it back, wanting to see it float again—but it didn't budge. So she picked it up and threw it like a Frisbee. It sailed through the air and landed on the wet sand. She ran down and picked it up, determined to launch it back into the sea. As she bent down, a bird flew low overhead; the swish of wings and squawk made her jump. Startled, she looked up—the bird was now flapping away in the distance. Turning back, she grabbed the plastic and threw it as far as she could. It hit the water with the most unrewarding small *slap*, but at least she'd sent it back for another adventure. The sea accepted it, but then it came back in on the next wave.

Bored, she shrugged, and decided to head home. About ten yards away, she spotted something bright green that stood out among the gravel, small stones and tufts of grass on the foreshore ahead. It wasn't very often that she stumbled upon such a find, bringing back mainly pieces of green sea glass and the occasional milky agate. Making one last effort, she finished walking on the big stones, rushed over, and attempted to pick it up, but it was half submerged in the ground. Digging around it with her fingers and using a small stone, she eventually prised it out. It was an elongated piece of serpentine that had been flattened, squashed and smoothed into the shape of a cigar by the passage of time, and tectonic forces. She wiped off the sand and mud on the grass and sat down to play with it. She thought it looked like a long, green sausage. As she ran a finger down the full length of the stone, she felt the stone move. The serpentine morphed into a slender green snake. She watched; repulsed yet curious until it flicked out a tongue. As if suddenly realising what she was holding, she threw it into the grass, but the snake came after her. She wasn't quick enough getting to her feet, and the snake lunged forward, attaching itself to her wrist. She tried to pull it off, but it burrowed into her arm, pushing aside sinew, and muscle, tunnelling deeper. Panicking, she couldn't find enough air as she slapped at her arm. She felt the snake reach her shoulder before passing out and hitting the ground.

'Lucy's been a long time—maybe we should go check on her,' Tim said, drying up the last of the dinner plates.

'Mm? Isn't it great she can go off on her own and we know she's safe, no dodgy blokes hanging around, no-one trying to drag her into the bushes—and now that funny black water has gone . . . . ' Shelley laughed bawdily at something the TV presenter was saying as she sat on the sofa with her feet up. The TV audience laughed at another terrible joke. He hated daytime TV; it was like having the worst comedian in your front room. He'd hoped that moving to Fetlar would stop her sitting around all afternoon; TV would be replaced by fresh air, long walks and a reawakening of their relationship. He stared at the back of her head; *She's back to her old tricks, doing bugger all, just sitting on her fat arse.*

'Look, it's been two hours, that's at least 1/2 hour longer than usual,' he moaned, checking his watch.

'She'll be alright. She's probably found some nice shells and stones. Let her forget the time, this is a timeless place—those were your words, ' she said, not taking her eyes away from the TV.

'All the same, it won't hurt to take a look. OK? I mean, I know the black water's gone now, but you never know . . . . '

Shelley didn't answer. He was desperate to get away from the sound of the presenter's voice. Feeling anger rise up from years of her worthless promises, he grabbed his jacket, slipped Bertie on a lead and went off investigate. He noticed it was blowing up for rain from the south, but Houbie beach was just at the bottom of the road, so it wasn't a huge expedition for Lucy. Lamb Hoga loomed in the distance like some tenebrous sphinx; an area they had yet to explore. He realised he didn't need Shelley to go on long walks with him, he could go on his own; *leave her to get square eyes, perhaps she might realise she's missing something.* He knew that was unlikely. He reached the concrete shed and spotted Lucy's bright blue jacket on the ground. She was motionless, her legs splayed out awkwardly.

'LUCY!!' he screamed to the world and gently turned her over onto her back.

'Lucy love. Wake up—wake up love!' He felt her

cheeks, she was cold. He picked her up, holding her close to his body; she drowsily came to, her eyelids flickering.

'Cold Daddy,' she said quietly. He picked her up, looking around helplessly, and then he remembered the surgery was just up the road. Cradling her in his arms, he ran as fast as he could, his lungs protesting. Bertie couldn't believe his luck; with no-one hanging onto his lead he decided to investigate the beach on his own. Panting hard, Tim attempted to open the surgery gate, but with Lucy in his arms it was difficult.

'Hello? Help! Christine!' William's head shot out of the front door.

'Tim? Oh blimey, hang on, I'll get Christine.' Tim looked down at his daughter; who was quiescent but awake. Christine opened the gate, then unlocked the surgery door, rushing in, Tim close on her heels.

'Put her down here. Lucy love—can you hear me?' she said urgently.

'Yes,' Lucy replied, in a small voice.

'Are you hurt love?' Tim quipped in. Lucy looked down. Christine checked her head for obvious signs of injuries, all the while Lucy just passively watched.

'What happened?' Christine said kindly, knowing that when children were quiet, it was often serious. Lucy shook her head and looked down.

'At least she's responding. Lucy, I'm going to take a wee look at you love, OK?' Lucy looked despondently at her father.

'Can you sit up while we take off your coat?' Lucy nodded. Christine noted that she was still not keeping eye contact. She pulled up the bench so that the back was upright. Tim took off her coat and hugged her, kissing her on the top of her head.

'Let's just check her out, now then Tim, you just sit in that chair.' Christine did as good an inspection as she could and Lucy responded well. She was sure there was no immediate injury to the body. Lucy looked down at her wrist and frowned.

'Tim, let's have Lucy on your lap to warm her up now.' He gladly went to pick up his daughter, cradling her, while Lucy just looked forward.

'What happened to you? Did someone frighten you?' he asked plaintively. Lucy nodded. He looked at Christine; worry stricken.

'Shall I ring Shelley—let her know what's going on?' Christine offered. He nodded reluctantly.

'Lucy, it's alright now, Daddy's here. It'll be OK. Was it a man that frightened you?' Lucy shook her head. Christine came back in.

'Shelley's coming down now.'

'Prised herself away from the TV has she?' he quipped bitterly. Christine smiled weakly. He cradled Lucy, continually kissing her on the head. She noticed that Lucy shifted position, which meant she was probably warming up. Sure there were no obvious injuries, Christine offered her some chocolate—Lucy's eyes lit up.

'She's feeling better,' Christine said, smiling. Shelley rushed into the surgery.

'Oh Lucy love, what happened?' Shelley sat on a chair and Lucy was swapped from Tim to Shelley. Tim frowned; wishing she'd cared as much earlier.

'Lucy, can you tell us what happened?' Shelley asked. Lucy turned her head into Shelley's body.

'Shall we go to the hospital then?' Shelley announced dramatically, as much for the onlookers as for Lucy, hoping to persuade her to spill the beans. Lucy's eyes widened, and she shook her head.

'Shelley, err—not sure we can force these things, she'll talk when she's ready. How about I pop up later, see how's she's getting on? Best you go home now, get back to some sort of normality. Just keep a close eye on her, any changes let me know,' Christine advised.

'We will Christine, we will. *Both pairs of eyes*,' Tim retorted, glaring at Shelley. They all bundled into the car. Shelley fussed over Lucy which annoyed Tim even more. He drove back in silence, anger seeping from every pore. The heavens opened and released large hailstones. They bounced off of the windscreen and the metal shell of the car like tennis balls. The hail was so loud, even Lucy sat up in surprise on Shelley's lap. Tim's mood was dark and foul. He was glad it was too loud to speak to Shelley; because at that precise moment he felt like hitting her.

'I can't believe you said that to Lucy, about the hospital,' Tim said quietly. Lucy was watching her favourite Disney video and wrapped up in her quilt. Shelley shrugged.

'Sometimes they play at being the centre of attention—yeah, you're right—maybe it was a bit mean. Seems she wasn't playing up,' she whispered, half guiltily.

'Oh, no shit, Sherlock! You should've seen her, I thought we'd lost her, I really did, sprawled out there on the cold beach,' he complained.

'Bloody hell Tim! Don't you think I wished I was there too?'

'In fact, I don't! I'm sorry—if you'd had your way, you wouldn't have bothered about her at all. You've got a short memory Shelley. Remember I said that she'd been a long time? What did you do? Watch more bleedin' telly.' He tried to ignore his Father's words ringing in his ears:

"She'll never amount to anything; not while there's a hole in her arse."

'Later we'll sit down and talk about it, mm? Get to the bottom of it—of what happened, that's more important, mm?' He mumbled under his breath about having to do everything around the house, and walked into the living room, intent on seeing Lucy. He knelt down, noticing how vacant she seemed. Shelley started clearing up the kitchen, she was used to him being unhappy about something she was doing; her watching TV, her sitting down, her breathing in the wrong direction.

'How about your favourite for dinner tonight? Pizza? From the shop?' she shouted from the kitchen.

'How about it love? Make you feel a bit better?' he

asked, looking into Lucy's glassy eyes—he noticed her hands still felt cold. He attempted to warm them up by blowing on them and rubbing them gently.

'Ice-cream for afters?' Shelley volunteered. Tim slowly stood up and trotted out to the kitchen.

'Ice-cream? Seriously? She was frozen to death out there! Christ! You really are bleedin' clueless!' he hissed, looking at her with contempt. Shelley looked crestfallen at first, then angry.

'I'm not clueless—if you watched more quiz shows you'd know that ice-cream actually does the opposite to making you feel cold.' He looking dubiously at her.

'Honest! Look it up if you want! Anyway, she likes ice-cream. Let's get the pizza on and see if we can coax some info out of her,' she proposed. He muttered something unintelligible before heading back to his daughter. He sat next to her on the sofa; she scooted over and settled on his lap, sucking her thumb. He hadn't seen her do that since she was two years old.

It was Lucy's favourite pizza: ham and pineapple, and she ate it on the sofa under the quilt; being hungry she wolfed down great mouthfuls, chewing noisily. Tim didn't feel like eating, so Shelley consumed the rest. He knew nothing would keep Shelley from food. He watched her eat and realised how much they were growing apart, or maybe she was devolving. After pizza, Lucy was feeling better and kicked off the quilt, deciding to play with some toys on the sofa. She fiddled with an old doll, flipping the head backwards and forwards enjoying the feel of the silky hair hitting her in the face. Tim took the opportunity to ask her some leading questions.

'Was the tide out down the beach? Did you find anything?' she shrugged. 'I kicked some stuff,' Lucy said, still flicking the doll's hair back and forth.

'Sometimes you find things, don't you? Some nice

stones, did you find any?' she shook her head and frowned. Shelley joined in.

'Can you remember what you were doing before it happened?' He glared at Shelley. Lucy looked down before replying.

'Something yellow . . . ' she said, concentrating hard. ' . . . then a bird came by and went down like this.' She illustrated the swooping motion the bird made with her hands.

'Was that it? Was that what made you get scared?' he offered. She shook her head and stuck out her bottom lip.

'Did you fall over?' Shelley asked. Lucy shrugged her shoulders.

'Was it a man?' Tim waved a dismissive hand at Shelley, he didn't want her putting ideas into Lucy's head.

'No.' They both sighed in relief.

'Shall we play ten questions?' Tim was pleased to come up with a solution.

'Yeah Daddy, I like ten questions!' Ten questions was something they all played regularly; as twenty was usually too long for Lucy.

'OK, I'll go first. Was it a ball?' Lucy shook her head, smiling.

'Was it a seal?' she shook her head.

'Was it someone you know?' she firmly shook her head. They glanced at each other, relieved.

'Was it a boat?' Shelley asked. Lucy shook her head and sat up, knowing her parents would probably never get it.

'OK, we're at four. Was it a woman?' Tim asked. She shook her head.

'Was it an aeroplane?' Shelley asked, Lucy smiled and shook her head.

'Seven, mm . . . I wonder . . . was it a spaceship?' he

said, pretending to look scared.

'No Daddy! Not a spaceship!' She was laughing now. Tim and Shelley laughed too, pleased to see their little girl come back to life.

'Eight. What about a flying pizza?' Shelley asked. Lucy was giggling hard and shaking her head.

'Nine. How about—how about the witch from Wizard of Oz?' Lucy shook her head solemnly because that witch really scared her.

'Oh no! Last chance! Err—err—a—err,' he said, pretending to flounder, waving his hands in the air.

'It's a snake!' Lucy shouted. He looked at Shelley.

'A snake? Does Fetlar have snakes?'

'Doubt it—far too cold.'

'A snake with a funny face. It was a stone and then it was a snake, it went into my arm—here,' Lucy said seriously, pointing to her wrist.

'Let me see,' Shelley said, gently turning over her arm.

'Did Christine find anything on her?'

'Nope, she wasn't hurt anywhere.'

'Does it hurt where it went in?' Shelley asked. Lucy shrugged her shoulders and looked down.

'What colour was it?'

'Green. It was just sitting there. I wanted to stroke it.' Lucy was becoming more morose. She covered herself with the quilt.

'Was it doing anything?' he asked.

'No. It just sat there, and then it changed and stuck out its tongue—not talking about it anymore!' Lucy announced angrily, pressing her head into Tim's chest.

'We don't have to talk about it. Well done Lucy, I'm very proud of you,' he said kindly, stroking her hair. Shelley opened her eyes wide at Tim.

'How about we see what's on the old goggle box?'

Shelley offered. Lucy nodded, but looked glum. The doorbell rang; it was Christine. Shelley showed her to the kitchen. Tim kissed Lucy on the head and wrapped the quilt around her.

'Back in a mo love. Do you still want ice-cream later?' Lucy nodded, then stuck her thumb in her mouth and watched the cartoon.

'Cuppa?' Shelley enquired.

'Lovely. Milk no sugar. How's she doing?'

'Well, we got to the bottom of it using ten questions. A game she likes.'

'Good, good, it's better when you make these things fun. So, is she feeling better? What was it?' Shelley looked down embarrassed.

'Can you believe it? She said it was a green snake!' Tim explained. Christine looked surprised; then a delicate smile escaped her. Shelley noticed this.

'It got into her arm—apparently—through her wrist,' Shelley explained.

'But we know there were no wounds on her,' Tim chipped in, shrugging his shoulders.

'OK,' Christine said slowly. She thought about brain disturbances.

'Anything like this happened before, ever?'

'Nope. Never. She's been quite a well child, really. Just the usual childhood stuff,' Tim offered brightly.

'What do you think?' Shelley asked hopefully.

'Well, I'm only the nurse; it might be worth her seeing the Doc tomorrow. Can I just have a quick chat?' Tim and Shelley nodded. Christine stuck her head round the door, she noticed Lucy was sucking her thumb.

'Does she normally suck her thumb?'

'No, not since she was . . . no, just today,' he remarked, looking worried.

'Hello Lucy, I can smell pizza, is it your favourite?'

Christine asked, standing to the side of the TV. Lucy nodded shyly.

'So, you feeling better? No more nasties?' She shook her head, grabbed hold of her doll and started playing with it, occasionally looking up to see Christine was watching. Satisfied that Lucy was looking better, Christine returned to the kitchen.

'OK, she's either just had a turn—not unheard of in children—or she's not seen something correctly, could be an eye problem. Has she ever fainted before?'

'No, nothing like that. She's quite a sensible girl really, that's why we let her out on her own,' Shelley explained. Tim wondered what *sensible* meant, considering that Lucy was eight years old; she wasn't his Mother-in-Law.

'Look, it won't hurt to see the Doc. Luckily, she's in tomorrow. Just to be sure. Now keep an eye on her tonight, she may well have a nightmare, so be prepared.' Christine got up to leave.

'Call me, if anything changes at all. Anything. I'll see you all tomorrow morning for the last appointment at 9.15 unless something else crops up in the meantime. Don't hesitate to ring, no matter how insignificant it seems.'

'OK, thanks for coming round Christine. Sorry about all this. A snake eh?' Shelley said, attempting to laugh it off.

'Don't worry, children sometimes see the world differently that's all. Bye for now.' Shelley closed the door. Then Tim did something he didn't normally do; he grabbed hold of Shelley giving her a huge bear hug. Shelley was taken aback—she'd forgotten how good it felt.

'It'll be alright Shelley, won't it?' he whispered, scared. She was shocked at his reaction, and not sure how to respond, as he was normally not one to collapse in a crisis.

'Tim, I'll be honest, I really don't know, but if we stick together we can get through anything, we're stronger together than apart—aren't we?' Tim pulled back from her and searched her face.

'Sure we are. Scary snake, eh? She must have been seeing things, praps she's not been eating enough and just fainted from lack of energy . . . . '

'We could speculate 'til the cows come home. Let's see what the doc says.' Shelley suggested. Tim sighed. This time they both sat on the sofa watching TV, with Lucy firmly sandwiched between them. They'd forgotten all about Bertie, who was having the time of his life exploring the island on his own.

CHAPTER EIGHT

Fruma observed the approaching rain clouds, it had done nothing but drizzle for the last two days. There were only a few exceptions; some small episodes of refulgent light. It was at those times that the island burst into colourful washing lines, like spring flowers responding to a nurturing sun. She looked to the distant coast where a boat appeared to be pinned to the sea bed. From the window it looked tiny, but up close it was probably quite a size, maybe even a tubby trawler or a research vessel. She could see a faint outline of another island, and wondered if someone on that island was looking out and thinking the same thought, or looking at Fetlar, and imagining life there. The people on that distant island couldn't see the black water arrive, being too far away; but to the people on Fetlar, close up, the black water had been shocking. Mackey's idea of God seeing things differently to humans had played on her mind. She posited that this was how everyone lived—that we see people from a distance, always on the horizon; it's a rare thing to 'really know' them—up close—so we can witness life's effect on them. Unless we spend long periods of time with someone, our knowledge of them stems only from personal judgement.

Two days ago, a sudden gale had churned up the sea, muddying the once distinct line between turquoise and inky black water. Now the sea just looked murky, like dark, stewed tea. She had heard of no great calamity in the community; no-one had died from the latest 'black water incident'. She wondered if Heed dying at the same time as the black water arrived was simply a coincidence, especially consider-ing the islander's level of superstition back then. She looked again at the front of the envelope she'd received that morning.

To: Ms Langthorne
'Da Ty Rigg'
Fetlar

She'd read it and re-read it; as if this repetition would springboard a clue as to the sender. She won-dered how anyone knew her surname and where she was staying. The cream coloured envelope was made of linen and opened easily as the gum had not adhered properly. She pulled out the note, noticing the extra thick paper that appeared to be handmade and hand cut. Apprehensively, she unfolded it—one line of writ-ing graced the page.

"Da stane at lies no i your gaet, braks no your taes."

Not being able to understand all the 'Shetlandeese' she racked her brains for who could've sent it on the island, having only spoken to Philip at the Interpretive Centre, Mackey, Mary and Peter. She thought about the two women on the ferry, but she'd not given them her name. Having not seen Mackey for a couple of days, and seeing the weather was threatening, she decided to pay him a visit, hoping he could decipher the message. With the clouds about to dump water, she was glad it was only a short walk to his house. He was in the greenhouse when she arrived, so she knocked on the window. He beckoned her in, but she stood at the entrance rather than brush past the packed foliage.

'Fruma, good to see you, how are you?' Mackey asked, dead-heading some rather fragile flowers.

'Good, good to see you too. I received this, this morning,' Fruma said, holding out the envelope. His eyes widened.

'What's this then?' he asked warily, preparing himself for another Fruma outburst.

'It's written in the Shetland dialect. I was hoping you'd be able to decipher it.'

'I'll certainly try—but before we go indoors, I want to share something with you.' He shuffled a few pots around to make room.

'It's really quite beautiful Fruma—I think you'll appreciate it.' Hearing that, she squeezed into what space was left in the greenhouse; the smell of tomato plants overloaded all olfactory organs. He pointed proudly at his protégé. It was a cactus, with one striking yellow flower at the centre. The spindly body sprouted long, spiky, black hairs, reminding Fruma of her own sporadic chin hair she occasionally had to pluck out. The flower's yellow petals were as delicate as fine feathers, with a flaming orange-red centre. The stamens looked like miniature, yellow washing up gloves. He beamed at Fruma.

'My Goat's Horn cactus is flowering; it hasn't flowered for seven years. You know, in its lifetime, it only ever gave me one flower—you couldn't have come at a better time to see it. Isn't it wonderful?' She looked at it closely, marvelling at the size of the flower compared to the body of the cactus.

'Reminds me of one those joke flowers that squirt water,' she teased.

'I know what you mean; you'd think the flower would topple that silly little body. It is such a delight to me Fruma. Have a sniff too, it's a wonderful scent.' She cautiously leaned in, inhaling the aroma. It filled her with images of desiccated, distant lands, full turbans and colourful bazaars.

'Mm . . . what a superb fragrance,' she leaned in again.

'Come inside for a cuppa, I was hoping you'd come back soon, considering the way it was left last time.' He put the watering can back in its place, ushered her out and shut and latched the greenhouse door. Noticing the wood had been removed from the greenhouse she made a note to herself to ask him more about it.

'The wind has a wily way of opening doors here— come on, come inside.' He showed her to the front room, and this time, she felt bold enough to approach the bookshelves while he prepared the tea. She scanned the titles: a lot of Psychology/Psychotherapy books, guides, maps, and old, well-thumbed Shetland books. Her eyes scanned higher, bibles and a tall, leather-bound work with strange names in several volumes. He shouted to her.

'Usual?'

'Yes, please.'

'When did you receive this letter?' He set a tray down precariously on a pouffe; then thinking better of it, he handed her a mug and placed the biscuits down on the chair opposite.

'Only this morning.' She pulled the letter from her cardigan pocket and handed it to him, watching him finger the envelope before pulling out the contents. He rubbed the paper between his fingers.

'Very thick,' he remarked. Carefully, he withdrew the letter and opened it, frowning. Fruma was unsure of what to take from his expression.

'Do you understand it?'

'Basically it says: da stane—the stone—at lies no i

your gaet—that lies not at your gate—braks no your taes—doesn't break your toes.' She looked shocked and instinctively tightened her cardigan around her.

'Toes? What about my toes? Is someone trying to threaten me? Who would do that? I don't even know anyone here, who do you think sent it?' she squeaked. Mackey looked at her and pulled his lips to one side. Fruma noticed that he did this when he wasn't sure. He smiled quickly.

'It's not really threatening—it's—well, it could be thought of as a friendly warning. It means: Don't stick your nose into other people's business . . . . '

'Don't stick my nose in? Hardly friendly. I must've really upset someone on this island.'

'I honestly don't know what to think . . . . '

'How does anyone know my surname?'

'I don't even know your surname—good point.' He then glanced at the address on the envelope. She stood up and paced the room, her mind whirring.

'It must be about me looking into the Haby and Heed thing. I can't think it could be anything else can you?'

'No, but why is that a problem you looking into it? It's not a secret—Haby's disappearance is on public record.' He returned the message to the envelope and handed it back, she noticed he looked drawn and tired.

'Do you think I should leave or something?' she suggested, sitting back down on the sofa.

'No, I don't! You're not breaking any laws . . . . '

'But what about island laws?' she intimated. He gave a dismissive snort.

'I never intended for any of this to happen—you know this,' she said gloomily.

'Of course. Look, maybe it's because of this black water—people are just getting unnerved.' She made a face.

'So they blame me?' She looked away. 'As if I haven't had enough of this weirdness myself—I meant to tell you the last time I saw you, but it slipped my mind—on the way down to the museum, I met two strange women on the ferry, they gave me a cup holder and quizzed me about where I was going and staying. I reckon they must've been sisters because they looked the same—same black hair, plaited in the same way. I thought, surely they must be sisters—they dressed very old fashioned too.'

'Were they from Yell by any chance?' he suggested, grinning. He rubbed his hands up and down his thighs as if he couldn't contain himself. She hadn't seen him do this before; it unnerved her.

'They didn't say—why—do you know them?' She was cautiously hopeful.

'I don't personally, but some folks would on these islands. From your description I'd say you met the Tait sisters!' He sat back, still grinning.

'Ohhh, the Tait Sisters! Of course! Why didn't you say so?' He rubbed the bridge of his nose.

'I can see you're going to be trouble today. The Tait sisters lived . . . . '

'Lived?' she interrupted in a squeaky voice. This made him guffaw.

'I'm afraid so. They *lived* on Yell in the 1960's, they were a notorious pair. One was caught for stealing and the other frequently got herself into trouble playing around with married men. They were hardly ever apart. They both died in a car crash in the late Sixties, no-one quite knows why, but people think that alcohol might have played its part.' Shocked, she grabbed her tea.

'So what you're saying then—they're ghosts?'

'Yes, they're ghosts all right, haven't heard anyone

talk about them for a long time—well—you know—I heard that they appeared to people in the past.'

'But why did they appear to me? I'm not a native Shetlander or anything?' She put her cup down and picked it up again; twice.

'It's not common for folk to see them, but maybe we shouldn't be so surprised, we've talked about this before . . . how long have you been here now?' She sat forward to face him.

'Almost two weeks.' She waited for him to return with something, but all he did was nod and look thoughtful, which aggravated her. She went to the window and watched the sycamores sway. It hadn't rained yet but it soon would. The leaves turned, showing their pale undersides; like one might lift a palm to check for rain.

'Remember what we talked about—the path is never straight forward for a seeker like you.' She felt overwhelmed at being called a seeker, and for this new information. Feeling tears forming, she attempted to sniff them back. The overwhelming need to let rip and ball her eyes out had been held back by sheer willpower—she could no longer hold back. He was immediately at her side with tissues. She turned around and instinctively leaned into his shoulder. He allowed the storm to pass, gently patting her on her back.

'T-he-e lett-er—it rea-l-ly up-set me.' She took staccato breaths. 'Bu-t then wi-th th—ose wom-en . . . . '

'There—that's good—that's what you need; let it all out. Most people spend years building a hard carapace around them—coming to this island where you're confronted with yourself, maybe for the first time in your life, can trigger all sorts of emotions—it's quiet here, there's room to allow things to surface. It can happen any time you know Fruma,' he waffled. She nodded into his shoulder and snivelled.

'I think-k—k emotions can get you into- into tro-o-uble,' she stammered, a fresh round of crying imminent. An appliance in the kitchen clicked. Hail clattered against the window, throwing the room into partial darkness, muffling the sound of her sobbing.

'Now you're reflecting the weather too,' he said warmly. She laughed and dried her eyes, emerging from his shoulder; at that point, the hail paused too.

'I'm sorry to burden you—with all my stupid troubles . . . . ' He raised a palm in the air.

'No apology necessary.' Then the hail fell at double speed accompanied by a clap of thunder. They both listened, enjoying the momentary diversion. She felt calmer, the tears were drying up, but she felt emotionally drained. She spoke up over the noise, the hail providing a screen so her words felt less exposed.

'Those two sisters said something strange to me though. They said, 'look to the part that's divided'—or something like that—no—'the *place* that's divided', and they mentioned a prophecy—that it's all in the prophecy—and something about a negative imprint and the island remembering.'

'Interesting, there are a couple of prophecies about this island . . . but one is old and doesn't make much sense. The other one seems to have come true in part.' He grabbed a worn folder tied with elastic bands from a shelf. He pulled out some papers. The hail stopped, and the room became brighter. They both sat down on the sofa.

'The weather does seem to be mimicking you, ' he said seriously.

'Don't! I'm trying to calm things down,' she replied shyly, blowing her nose.

'This is the modern prophecy,' he prodded the paper, 'it says—"there will be a mansion on da Ripples", this seems to foretell Leagarth House being built—the big house down at Houbie?' Fruma nodded.

'"Soldiers on da Vord Hill," apparently there was a watch stationed on Vord Hill during the war, "and a harbour in da Dullins." This was thought to mean that Papil Water would no longer be separate from the sea, so ships or boats could harbour there. And lastly, "Nothing but the shepherd and his dog". There's been much speculation about this last one, some folks think that the island will depopulate; leaving, as it says, nothing but the shepherd and his dog. The other prophecy is called 'The AdderStane'. Now this is more of a mystery.' He let her read.

The AdderStane Prophecy

From the North, a taste forbidden
The shells of youth abandoned here
Lay sleeping in, a dreamless sky
Limbs fortell an ancient why
The tirrick calls, the land is still
Wanderer's hand a heavy load
The AdderStane, this sleeping rock
Walks the road redemption shows

Whirl in stars in winter stirs
As summer sun fast fades
The queen of heaven riding high
Cosmos turns, AdderStane replies
The menacing north is put to right
Dybbuk fool to one is turned
To set them free, she must calm
Unfailing end to free the shore

'Very enigmatic. Not sure I can get my head around that. I think I'd be inclined to believe the Tait

Sisters were talking about the other prophecy because they mention the place divided, and you said something about Papil Water no longer being divided from the sea.'

'That would be looking at it *rationally*—yes—and maybe you're right . . . . '

'The other one—this AdderStane—makes no sense to me at all—but then, why would it? Why would they be referring to that one? Especially as those sisters told me to look to the place that's divided—and it doesn't seem to mention anything about being divided.' He returned the papers to the folder.

'That's what I mean, no-one can really decipher it. All I can think of that they could be referring to, is the Finnigert Dyke. A wall was built hundreds of years ago that was said split the island in two, almost exactly in two.'

'One of the assistants told me about this, that the Finns might have built it and they were often mistrusted. Why would they want me to look there I wonder?' Then suddenly remembering,

'But Haby was a Finn too . . . . '

'That's right. There were more Finns here at one time, way back in past centuries, the graveyard here had some old graves, but since they extended it and moved some of the old stones, their graves seem to have disappeared; maybe I should've photographed them when I had the chance,' he said to himself.

'The assistant reckoned that Haby could have been one of the last Finns here on Shetland.' Mackey looked thoughtful but said nothing; all that moved were his eyeballs.

'So this Haby, what did he do for a living then?'

'He was a fisherman, worked away most of the time, so folks tell me.'

'And Lily—she was a Finn—I mean; is she a Finn

too?'

'No, she married Haby, he was the Finn; she took his name by marriage. She's a recluse now, did I tell you?' She felt him drifting again, then realising she had much more news to tell him, she brightened up.

'There's more Mackey, do you have time?' This seemed to break the spell.

'Tea?'

The sun had come out and bathed the room in a welcome stream of sunlight. Fruma slipped the envelope into her pocket and decided it was probably something she'd never get to the bottom of. Mackey came back with a pack of chocolate biscuits and steaming mugs. He motioned her to help herself.

'Something to help the tea go down.'

'Thanks. Anyway—I went to the archives to find out more about Haby and Heed—but nothing more is known, anyway, I saw a poster on the wall about a talk that's being held at the museum—but the thing is, the picture showed what I saw, similar to my vision—men in robes—they weren't exactly as I saw, they were shown as white men for a start, but it got me thinking, about Papil Water . . . . ' She stared at him intently.

'What do you know about the Papar?' She announced it with a certain amount of glee, hoping it might be news he didn't already know.

'The Papar? As far as I know, they were Celtic priests. Christians. Papar means Pope, there's lots of places on Shetland with that name, Papil Water, for example . . . . ' She interrupted him.

'Did you know they were African Jews.' He was taken aback.

'What makes you think that?'

'It said so online, some reference in the Papar Project—I went to the library and used the computer there. I thought that was really interesting, considering my vision of those men—and me finding the Hebrew lettering on the wood—no coincidences eh?' He leapt to his feet.

'Let's take another look. It's been years since I looked at this. Pull up a chair.' He went over to his large desk and switched on his computer. The screen leapt to life, the backdrop featured an aerial photo of Tresta beach.

'The internet is pretty good here; we're on that Shetland Broadband Scheme—here we go—The Papar Project.' She pushed her chair nearer so their arms were touching. He smelt of Cussons soap and old wardrobes.

'No, not there—further down,' she advised.

'Says—Island of Priests, err—da—da—da—this raises another significant question for our understanding of the fate of Christianity in the locality; why did the Vikings give the 'Papar' name to these places if the priestly communities were immediately dispersed? Interesting.' He read on, squinting at the screen, scanning the pages. She tried to lean in, but was almost on top of him, so she leaned back.

'There's a Shetland section here—oh and Fetlar—oh wait—here—there were very few early documentary references to Fetlar—I mean—so many of the traces are now gone—we know about the ancient Haliara Kirk up on the hill overlooking Houbie—let me go back a minute.' She was getting exasperated and now didn't care about leaning heavily against him.

'Fruma—look at this from the history of Norway— just looking at the historical evidence . . . says—blah blah—inhabited by Picts—wait, this is interesting—

" . . . *and the Papae have been named from their white robes, which they wore like priests—but, as is observed from their habit and the writings of their books abandoned there, they were Africans, adhering to Judaism . . .* "'

He turned to Fruma with the look of someone who'd just found gold. She looked smug.

'I know—that's what I found.'

'Africans adhering to Judaism? I didn't know that.'

'But you knew about the Papar Project before I brought it to you—you're telling me you didn't know they were African Jews?' He swooned back in his seat.

'I honestly have never read that before, I promise you Fruma, I've never seen it before—well I never— they were African Jews!' She balked, convinced he was teasing her.

'Oh come on!!' Irritated, he looked at her, serious for a moment.

'Fruma, we haven't known each other very long, but I'm not playing around, I didn't see it until today—I didn't know they were African Jews.' She backed off.

'Sometimes we're not meant to see things, it's like you're blind until you need to see it—until it's the right time—you know what I mean?' he said, moving the chair closer to the table.

'I have a friend, he's really anti-religious, you know the type?' she shrugged,

'I suppose so—sort of—'

'He became a Catholic overnight; it was an overnight conversion.' He watched a frown wrinkle her temple.

'It happens. Anyway, he'd been a Catholic for a few years and watched the film 'Alive' for the second time —remember the film? The one where the plane crashes in the Andes, and they have to resort to cannibalism?' She looked thoughtful, he continued.

'Well, the odd thing was, he'd seen the film before, but had never noticed that they were Catholics, and that they said the Rosary throughout the whole film—yet it's odd because that's what the film's about—remember?' She racked her brains.

'It was about faith wasn't it?'

'That's right! Because my friend had converted—changed his life which now included rosaries and prayer—it enabled him to see something that didn't register in his mind before, it was a mind-set change—his intentions had altered. Anyway, that's obviously what happened to me. Until you came along, I was blissfully unaware. I wasn't looking for it—so I didn't see it—it wasn't what I focussed on—but now we're looking, it does . . . does that make sense?' He leaned back against the chair.

'Maybe that's true for me too; if I hadn't had that vision I wouldn't have had the reason . . . ' he finished her sentence.

' . . . to pick up on its importance. Exactly!' He silently clapped his hands together.

'I did some digging too—your name is Jewish, did you know that?' She slightly wavered, wondering how much more she could take.

'It comes from the word 'Frum'—to keep kosher—to keep the Jewish Law. It's quite an unusual Jewish name too.'

'No—really? Back then I didn't really care—I wasn't interested in my past or my name, it didn't hold anything for me,' she paused, 'but I did check out my old orphanage—' she smiled weakly, ' . . . which didn't exist.' He stroked his upper lip; something he did when he was thinking.

'But they only had one search engine on the computer at the library, so maybe it wasn't representative.'

'What was it called?'

'Windy Nook.' He typed it in. 'You're right, no orphanage.' He checked another browser that showed the same.

'There's a Windy Nook History Society.' They both scanned the pages as he scrolled down.

'No mention of it.' He scanned faster.

'Oh—stop—education—praps it's under that.' He read it and shook his head.

'Are you sure it's . . . . ' She placed a hand on his shoulder.

'Don't. Of course I'm sure it was called that.' He swung round.

'But they're pretty good at keeping records about these places . . . . '

'I checked out all the other orphanages in the area —there were two in Gateshead—but no mention of mine.' He turned back to the screen and shrugged. He typed in some other information, scanned the pages. Deflated, she decided to sit back down on the sofa.

'So what does that mean?'

'It doesn't mean anything—perhaps they pulled it down—look—it does seem unusual—' She sprang into the air like a flea that had spotted lunch.

'Unusual—weird—strange—odd—no explanation— she must be mad—she's a nuisance—a busy-body— this bloody letter says so!' He stood up to placate her.

'No—no—I'm so sick of this. All I wanted to do was come to a remote island and bloody well have a nice time, listen to the bloody birds and—and—now it's like my life has got huge holes in it—nothing's making sense—now I'm seeing frigging ghosts—' She retrieved the envelope from her pocket and threw it like a Frisbee. It landed on the chess board, knocking over the top heavy King. She put her hand to her face.

'Sorry—I'm sorry—hope I haven't broken anything.'

He stood there looking sad.

'Even *that* is symbolic,' he pointed out wryly.

'Listen Fruma, I think you're meant to be here, maybe you've always been here—somehow.' She sat down looking miserable.

'That doesn't help,' she whined.

'Look—I don't know why this is all coming up, but perhaps it's time to stop denying it's happening,' he said gently. She went to object, but he held up a hand.

'No. Let's stop and think shall we. You're being shown something aren't you? Maybe we have to get to the bottom of it—I mean—there's no way you can stop it happening can you?' She opened her mouth again, but he shot straight back.

'Just because we don't have the wisdom in the matter, doesn't mean that we should treat is as a trick of the mind—or merely a—a folly.' He knelt down next to her and placed one hand on the arm rest.

'You are special Fruma. People don't send notes to strangers who stay for a holiday. It's something about you. You seem to be the catalyst. Something is going on—not just to you, but to other people on the island too.'

'Other people . . . . '

'Yes. People are starting to report hearing strange whisperings and voices. A young girl passed out on the beach—I won't mention names, but either way, it's affecting others. Now you see why people might be getting unnerved?' It comforted her that she wasn't the only one, and she brightened up a little.

'I didn't mention it to you before because I didn't want to worry you. In fact, everything that's happened to you has been a blessing—it's like your channelling clues—those sisters mentioning the Prophecy for example . . . I think it's all good Fruma, even though it may not feel that way.' He made her look into his eyes.

'OK?' he said warmly. She nodded, then looked down.

'Please stay Fruma—I know that leaving has crossed your mind on more than one occasion. Let's get to the bottom of this together, shall we? Try not to think of it as a burden, but a curious and intriguing puzzle.'

'Easy for you to say, ' she said, half smiling. He looked down and ran his fingers through his curly hair. Then he gave her such a look of warmth and friendliness that she knew at that moment she'd fallen for him. She blushed at her own thoughts.

'Oh—do you mind if I take that letter? I might show it to Da, see if he has any ideas who sent it,' he said, standing up.

'Of course—sorry about your chess set.' He waved away the idea. She stood up to face him.

'See, that's better—you're already looking brighter, let's work together eh? We don't know what God has in store for us—I know you don't . . . . ' It was her turn to raise a hand in objection.

'I'm beginning to believe that this is something more than the ordinary—I can't go so far as to say I'm now a Believer, but I'm sorry I've been so childish about it all. I haven't acted very rationally . . . . '

'I'm not surprised you were anxious, and I'm not judging you, *and* you're not alone in all of this.' She nodded and fiddled with the toggle on her cardigan.

'Stay for some dinner tonight—nothing special— pasta and sauce? Let's ban all talk of the island just for the evening?' She beamed.

'I'd like that.'

CHAPTER NINE

The jackdaw lowered its bill, raised its wings slightly, and with a sudden burst of energy thrust itself forward against the window of Sue and Trevor's house. Its mate responded with a guttural cry, the sound appearing to come from a deep, ancestral bone.

Kaaaarr!

A milky, semi-translucent eyelid slid over the eye of the first jackdaw. It pecked twice on the window. Sue was in the kitchen writing an email when she heard it. The first smash against the window made her jump. The half cry, half cluck reminded her of the primitive sound of the Velociraptor in Jurassic Park. Mace decided the creatures weren't welcome and barked his disapproval. She roused herself from the chair to investigate. A second smash hit the window. She stepped back, unsure if they'd break the glass, then head out the back door to confront them. She had trouble stopping the dogs from escaping; they barked indignantly from behind the closed door.

Kaaaarr!

The other bird joined in. They both hopped onto the grass and raised their wings threateningly. With trepidation, she fenced with them; advance and retreat. Each time she edged a little closer until eventually they flew off. She inspected the glass; luckily it wasn't broken. It looked like a three-year-old had traced dirty fingers all over the window where they'd pecked at the putty. She went into the kitchen and filled a bucket with hot, soapy water, and set about cleaning the windows. She spotted Shelley walking across the car park.

'Morning Shelley!'

'Hi Sue, how are you?' Shelley walked over, glad of the chance to chat.

'Not too bad, and you?'

'OK, I guess. I'm just taking Bertie to the Links— thought the walk might be good for us both.' An islander had spotted Bertie roaming the grounds of Leagarth House, and returned him to the family the same evening that Lucy had had her fright. Sue ignored Shelley's remark, preoccupied with the birds.

'I just had to shoo away jackdaws, two of them, smashing themselves against the window and making that eerie sound—really creepy— 'specially close up. They made a right mess of the windows,' Sue complained, pulling up her sleeves.

'Are you sure they were jackdaws, not crows?' Shelley then realised her remark wasn't appropriate.

'Strange behaviour, I wonder why they're doing that?' Unnerved, Sue pulled out a burgundy scrunchie and tied up her hair. She just wanted to relate the story; not speculate.

'Any more dead animals turn up?' Shelley asked, trying to elicit more of a response. She pulled back an impatient Bertie on his lead, glad it wasn't just Lucy that had experienced weird things.

'No, thank goodness.' Sue moved on quickly. 'So how's Lucy getting on?'

'Still withdrawn at times. We've tried all sorts of things, taking her over to Yell Leisure Centre for some swimming . . . she forgets for a while, but then something comes over her and she goes back into herself. I don't know what to do. Thank goodness for Bertie, she totally dotes on him now—probably more than me or Tim. If she doesn't improve . . . then I'll have to think about . . . . ' She didn't want to utter the word 'leaving'.

'I don't *want* to, but what choice do I have?' Shelley said defensively, more to convince herself than Sue.

'It's difficult if she's ill—'

'She's not ill—'

'But that fainting fit, did you ever find out any more about that?'

'What do you mean?' Shelley asked, guardedly.

'What did the doctor say in the end?'

'She was very good with Lucy, she thinks it's a shock that Lucy will get over in time. We have another follow-up appointment next week; hopefully she'll feel better, though she seemed to think that Lucy's snake thing could have been any number of normal child-hood things. She did mention . . . ' she struggled with her words, ' . . . making a referral.' Sue sighed com-passionately.

'At least it's being looked into. It must be really worrying for you both.' Shelley screwed up her face as she attempted to push back tears that were just under the surface.

'I guess you heard the latest? At the school?' Shelley offered reluctantly.

'Sort of . . . . '

'Lucy had an incident at school.' Sue made an 'Ohhh' noise. She had heard about it, but wanted to hear it first-hand.

'She complained of feeling ill, but I didn't want to keep her home unless it was *really* necessary, you know what I mean?'

'Of course.'

'I did say to Heidi that she could ring me and I'd

come and collect Lucy if she was still not feeling well—
but Wednesday is her favourite day—anyway, apparently she looked very strange, and then walked out
into the middle of the classroom and starting chanting. Now see what you make of this—"there's nothing
quite as dead, as a dead, dead, deader"—that's what
she kept saying. What the hell does that mean?'
Seeing Sue's concerned face, Shelley's face crumpled,
she fanned her face with her hand. Sue looked around
to see if they were alone.

'Come inside . . . . ' Sue offered. Shelley reached in
her pocket for a tissue and shook her head.

'No. Bertie needs his walk. Me and Tim—we had a
terrible argument. Tim reckons I should've let her stay
home. He thinks I'm being insensitive. I'm not—it's
just that . . . it's hard being here on my own, not
knowing what to do. You can't just get up and go
somewhere to make things better—like the Playgroup
or wander around a shopping centre. It's so difficult.'
Shelley attempted to pull herself together. Sue gave
her a sympathetic look.

'I miss my friends, my parents too—it's not the
same talking to them on the phone. Then I tried to get
Tim to agree with having a holiday but he's too busy
with his work—I know he's only just started, but
surely family comes first—I mean if one of yours was
—you wouldn't . . . . '

'Oh Shelley, it must be so difficult for you both.'

'He blames me for it—the first time—all because I
wanted her to have a bit of freedom you know? It's
been lovely seeing her go off exploring on her own—I
mean—where could she do that where we've come
from? Oh, I don't know—thanks for listening Sue. I
just don't know what's going to happen next.' She
blew her nose, smiling awkwardly.

'Can you and Lucy get some time away?'

'I could. I could stay with Mum and Dad, but that makes me feel like I've lost the challenge. I wasn't too sure about coming here in the first place, but Tim was really keen—he kept on about the remoteness, and I thought it would be a new start for us all, and Lucy could grow up somewhere safe.' She sniffed.

'Liam had an invisible friend when he was four, but he grew out of it, maybe it is just a passing phase,' Sue offered hopefully.

'We've argued more on this island than ever before —I really can say—since our whole marriage. Maybe it's because we both worked down south, so we had less time to get on each other's nerves.' There was a small pause, so Bertie took the opportunity to whine and pull on the lead.

'I have to go.' Sue nodded, but didn't want to be the first to move away, knowing there was more to come. A haunted look came over Shelley, she spoke in a low voice.

'She keeps on saying there's a hole in her. It scares me that she won't accept it when I tell her there isn't any hole. I even got her to stand in front of the mirror and showed her. Christine has tried to tell her too, but she won't believe it.'

'God, that's awful—it's a strange thing to see isn't it, snakes, especially when we know there's none on the island. Hopefully it will pass—she's eight isn't she?' Shelley nodded.

'Fantasy and reality can get blurred. She just needs time, each child is different. Liam still believes in fairies and goblins and things, but Holly, she didn't have an ounce of make-believe in her body, that's how she came into this world—a born cynic. Used to crease me and Trevor up at how spot on she was about the world.' Shelley cut in,

'Well, guess I better get on and take old Bertie out.

Look—thanks Sue. Sorry I got all . . . . ' Sue waved away her comment. Bertie tugged on the lead. Shelley went to walk away, but she turned around instead.

'Oh—I meant to ask you—how's the Carer job going?' Shelley asked, attempting to get back to normal.

'Fine. I might even take on another client soon: Mrs Henderson. I'm going to pop in on her tomorrow to see what she needs.'

'Lucky you—bit of extra cash coming in, how many folks do you look after now?'

'Just the three.'

'Kids OK? And Trevor?'

'No problems there as far as I know.' Shelley went to walk away.

'You know where I am—if you want to talk,' Sue offered seriously. Shelley gave a hint of a smile, still embarrassed at being upset.

'Thanks—I'll see you then.' She loaded Bertie into the car and head off to Tresta. Sue carried on cleaning the windows and wondered why the two of them had never gotten together regularly, considering they were virtually neighbours. She felt guilty lying to Shelley. The twins and Holly were fine, but she was worried about Liam's odd behaviour, and decided it was time for Trevor to have a word with him.

As if things couldn't get much worse, a fog arrived on Fetlar. It was as if Nature had saved up the worst type of fog and emptied it out over the island; the dense, lingering mist seemingly filled every available gap and orifice. Five days passed, and it still hadn't lifted. Some islanders feared their livestock would be lost, and the children's safety was on the mind of most parents. It wouldn't be the first time that someone had been lost on the island due to inclement weather; it's too easy to get turned around and walk over a cliff edge. If it were possible, the fog seemed even denser at the ferry terminal. Car headlights could hardly penetrate it, making progress slow. The disembarked cars were virtually brought to a standstill before crawling across the island like a colourful caravan of snails. Reports from the two neighbouring islands were that they had clear weather; blue skies even, and this was the same forecast for most of Shetland.

The fog amplified the general negativity and darkness and made Malcum's job take twice as long. He was convinced that if he saw the shipwrecked man again, he'd not escape; he'd be dragged off into the mist and become another missing person like Haby. He wondered if it had been foggy on the day Haby went missing, or maybe Da's suggestion that the trows took him was more accurate. Nearly every islander stopped him for news, but he had no answers for them, and they'd slink back into the safety of their homes, to emerge only when necessary. Da opened his front door like everyone else did—with trepidation. When he saw it was Malcum, he breathed a sigh of relief.

'Oh—it's just you.' Malcum nodded, he was in no mood for being teased.

'Very odd this fog. Feels like something's going to emerge from it—na, dat in traath!' Da said testily. This scared Malcum, so he ignored him.

'How's folk taking it?' Da asked.

'Not good Da. It's just adding to the fear—building it. Some folks are even thinking about keeping their children home. I've only been to six houses, but it's like a broken record. As if I know anything about it? As if I can stop it? I just saw some kids on the road . . . is it safe for them to play out?' Da shook his head, shrugged, and looked down. Da felt the fog reflected the Islanders mood, and now he had the nagging feeling that someone else was going to get hurt; just like Lucy and Heed. Malcum shivered on the doorstep. The arrival of the fog had lowered the temperature. Usually in the summer, Fetlar maxed out at fifteen degrees Celsius. Then the autumnal shift reduced it to nine degrees, but the addition of the fog made it feel more like seven degrees, and with the two weeks of odd happenings, it felt not only physically colder; but the kind of cold that seeped into a person's thoughts.

'I don't know Doctor, I guess it got worse since the fog, but it was pretty bad about a week before it, I just can't catch a full night's sleep, it's so draining. I know I don't work as such, but I still have the housework to keep up with . . . I fell asleep when I was hoovering yesterday morning—so I thought I should come and see you—I didn't want to bother you, really.' The Doctor nodded seriously and scribbled something on her pad.

'Take these half an hour before going to bed, hopefully they should do the trick, OK?' The nervous patient nodded and stood up to leave before turning to Christine and saying,

'Busy morning again Christine?' Christine murmured something in a noncommittal tone, pretending to be looking for a lost prescription.

'Goodbye then!' the Doctor said, attempting to be cheery and upbeat.

Christine finally closed the door on another busy morning surgery. The doctor raised her eyebrows at Christine and hurriedly typed the patient info into the computer. Christine fussed around and put the prescriptions away. Five minutes passed in silence. The doctor, finishing, sat back in the seat.

'I see what you mean.' Christine plonked herself down on the spare seat, relieved to hear a professional off-island opinion.

'I can honestly say I've never seen anything like it, with that number of people complaining and with no real cause, never, not in twenty years, and what with the phone-calls to the surgery, I just couldn't fit everyone in,' the Doctor said, shocked. In a hurry to catch the ferry, she stuffed items into her surgery bag, not wanting to get stranded on the island. Christine nodded, looking miserable.

'I don't know what to say to them anymore. Nearly everyone has turned up at the surgery in the last two weeks. It's the same story, bad dreams, hearing whispering voices, and then young Lucy . . . who's not improving,' Christine replied miserably, almost to herself.

'I know,' the doctor agreed, then wondered if the water supply needed checking as she packed the last of the equipment away.

'Doesn't matter what time of day, everyone's scared if they'd but admit it, that black water started it all— and now this fog!' Christine moaned.

'Yes, I heard about that black water—funny business. That happened once before didn't it?' she enquired, while hurrying out the door. Christine followed her into the foggy car-park, shivering in short sleeves in the cold mist.

'Sometime in the 1970's. Then a boy apparently died of old age. Not sure how true that is . . . but I don't want that sort of thing happening when I'm here on my own.' The doctor went quiet, then she faced forward, staring vacantly into the fog. Puzzled, Christine peered through the windscreen. The doctor turned the ignition key, still staring ahead. Christine went round to the passenger door and bent down. The doctor wound down the window, still facing forward and said:

'It will reveal the truth within itself.' Christine, unnerved and confused by the comment, didn't know what to say. Something in her was afraid to follow up. The doctor, seemingly coming around from her comment said:

'Look, I must go, give me a ring in the week if anything ramps up, and hang in there, you're doing all you can be expected to do. Must dash!'

Before the car had gone ten yards, it slipped into the fog as if it had never existed. Christine rushed back into the relative safety of the surgery, feeling like she was the last sane person in the world holding the island together. She'd even visited Mackey at William's suggestion, but she was so nervous, she ended up saying everything wrong. When Mackey asked her what he should call her; Chris, Christine or even Nursey—she ended up saying:

'You can just call me Christ if you want.' Much mirth was had at her expense, about her lack of beard and long robes. William had never understood why she was tense around Vicars; neither did she, but she didn't like hypocrisy, and figured that ordinary folk could do the same good works without having to attend a Church. They did however agree that a Community Meeting would be a good idea, to give everyone a chance to air their views; a problem shared . . . either way, she decided that whatever was playing games on this island, it was not going to play them with her, and she was not going to give in to it. Then she reprimanded herself for making it seem more than it was—that maybe it was some kind of mass hysteria brought on by gossiping and winding each other up. She was comforted that nothing had happened to herself—or William, which in one way made her feel guilty, and another, truly relieved.

Mackey backed into Da's parking space at the top of the road. As he walked down the rough track to the house, he could just about make out the path in the fog. He remembered what a fine view it used to be, being so high on the hill—but the fog had stolen all reasons to have impressive views, or windows. One of Da's old sheepdogs sidled up to Mackey making him jump; it laid itself low in a submissive gesture. Mackey made a fuss of it before continuing. The rough dirt track lead to a gravel driveway, and finally to Da's croft house, where Da snooped at him through the curtains before coming to the door. As it opened, Mackey caught the smell of linseed that wafted from the recently oiled oak door. Taciturn, Da stepped aside for Mackey, holding his cap protectively to his chest.

'I-i Mackey, how's du?' Da enquired cautiously. Not waiting for an answer, he went out to the kitchen to put the kettle on. Mackey wiped his feet; he knew the way to Da's front room.

'Tea?'

'Is the Pope Catholic?' Da roared with laughter. Mackey was beginning to feel like a teapot with the amount of tea he'd consumed recently.

'I'll sit myself down shall I?' Mackey said loudly. He inspected Da's bookshelf; nothing had changed since he last visited. In no particular order, tatty gardening books rubbed shoulders with a few Shetland novels, and stacks of ancient 'Shetland Times'. Mackey figured that Da didn't need a lot of books because he carried all his stories around in his head. Some small tools and forgotten, dusty trinkets were crammed onto the bottom shelf. Like many Shetlanders croft houses, every corner and nook are taken advantage of, stacked with boxes containing items once useful (and might be useful in the future). He chose a seat away from the window; the non-existent view was beginning to offend him as much as someone picking their nose in company. He noticed a substantial sized spinning wheel in the corner and a bag of different coloured wool next to it. He deduced it was Da's mother's wheel as he'd seen many pictures of her working in this room.

Da arrived with an elaborately decorated bronze tray, filled with bronze tea-making accoutrements. The teapot was bulbous bodied, inset with oval, black jet stone; the engraving modest; mainly braiding, simple flowers and swirls. A long, tapering neck led to an onion domed lid with a daisy atop, encased in leaves. The handle was large, like that of a zinc watering can. The bronze cups were heavily engraved around the same inset stone, with a brushed metal interior. Wrapped Cantucchini slices sat amongst differing sized lumps of amber rock sugar in a plain bronze bowl; a pair of dainty matching tongs alongside. The small milk jug was slender with no handle.

'That's quite a setup you have there,' Mackey remarked; he'd forgotten how much Da liked to put on a show. Da methodically poured and added components as if they were precious gems.

'The ritual of tea making is important, and I like it done properly, especially if I receive guests,' Da said, smiling sweetly. 'So, what brings you here this fine summer morning?' he said sarcastically. Mackey let out a tinkle of nervous laughter.

'I need to pick your brains about something,' he said cautiously, withdrawing the envelope from his jacket. Da eyed the envelope and said nothing.

'Milk?'

'A smidgen.'

'There's a lady, a tourist, staying with Mary & Peter, she received a letter recently—was wondering what you make of it.' He passed the envelope to Da, watching him closely. Da put on some reading glasses. The mantelpiece clock chimed twice.

'No-one knew she was coming here, so that makes it stranger still,' he added.

'I'm sure you know what it means,' Da said, and gave the letter back to him, 'it means don't stick your nose in where things don't concern you, and I happen to agree!' he spat out. Mackey noted, but ignored Da's splenetic mood.

'Maybe you can explain to me what you think she's done wrong to receive such an unfriendly letter.'

'Sa naethin, bit saa wid—investigating something that has nothing to do with her.'

'This is all public information Da . . . . '

'It's just that it's happened before, she seems to be at the heart of it, poking around in our affairs, then that black water again,' he paused, 'asking questions that most folk wish was left behind, like about Heed. I know because Philip told me, listening to old tapes, private island stuff.' Da turned and faced the viewless window. A breeze blew through the open back door; as if attempting to blow Da's hotheadedness away.

'So why are Heed's tape and photo in the Interpretative Centre then? So people can hear about the history, surely?' Mackey asked, bemused.

'Historical accident. That tape shouldn't be in there,' Da cringed.

'The truth is—I don't know anything about this letter. I mean, who knew she was here as you say? It's all very odd, and she's not making it any better for hersel', now we have that Lucy girl all upset, and they're newcomers, we don't need to go upsetting them.'

'I understand. But we also encourage visitors to the island too. I wonder if I should visit Lily?' Da slapped the table.

'Lily? She's nothing but a sad old lady living weth her ghosts, she's no for ös ta caa oot a kailyard.' Mackey racked his brains but shook his head.

'Enlighten me Da, that last saying . . . . '

'I mean—she's a poor thing, useless really, she's had it, there's nothing left, she can barely look after hersel'! She lost what was most dear to her—two things—it broke her heart it did—you leave her alone —we don't need her getting all upset too. Don't you start poking around again,' Da whined.

'I haven't seen her for ages; at least two years now —' Mackey mused.

'And it's best left that way. We don't want more things stirred up. Aye—nothing more to say on the matter.' He thumped the armchair.

'So another island mystery, eh Da?' Mackey said, trying to lighten the mood. Not wanting to leave it there, he continued.

'Listen Da, Fruma—Miss Langthorne is different, I'll say this because I know you can keep a secret,' he paused, wondering whether he should repeat Fruma's news, 'she's seen the Tait Sisters.' Da looked surprised.

'Really? Where?'

'On the Yell ferry, they spoke to her, gave her a message even,' Mackey replied, glad to diffuse Da's anger and gain his interest.

'Dösta! Dösta! They've not been seen for many a year!' Da exclaimed, half excited, he rubbed his palms together.

'They gave her a cryptic message about looking to the place where it's divided. That's very cryptic, yes? And they mentioned the Prophecy.' Mackey searched Da's face for recognition. Da paused and looked out of the window.

'Mm ... that is a strange message. I'll have to think about that one. Could mean many things and those Sisters were known to be untrustworthy,' he said, with a small amount of contempt.

'What did they say about the Prophecy?'

'They said that it was all in the Prophecy, and that the island remembered everything.'

'That'll be the island's old serpentine bones; it has a way of making the past known . . . . '

'I know. You realise Da, we're probably the only ones on the island that believe that. That's why I came to you with this letter.' Da waved a hand dismissively.

'I don't know anything about that.'

'Yes, but that's not all that's happened to her. No— best not to tell you much more without her permission, but I'm just saying that something else may be going on here—she has been quite upset about it all!'

'Well, I'm not surprised, talking about the island out of turn—this community is falling apart and you bring in a stranger—into—into our inner circle!' Da declared, unable to contain himself.

'Inner Circle? Oh come on!' Mackey said, guffawing. 'You mean—you, Malcum and Ted? We don't have an inner circle on this island, most of us just get on with our own thing and come together for community get-togethers. This isn't the eighteenth century—I mean—we even have Broadband now, or is that all witchcraft to you Da?' Da made a noise of disgust and sipped his tea.

'I'm going to say something now Da Anderson and you will listen well. Fruma is the nicest lady Fetlar has ever had the pleasure of opening her doors to. She genuinely cares about the island and would be horrified—yes—horrified to think that you think she had anything to do with these strange events, I think she would genuinely be in tears! She was shaken up enough about the strange letter that she received, she even mentioned about going home if she wasn't welcome.'

'Now, let's not be too hasty, I did'ne say she wasn't welcome, I'm joost saying it's odd that it's all happened since she arrived, as you once said—there are no coincidences . . . . '

'Oh, now you remember what I said, how convenient, but yes, you're right, there are no coincidences, but you've taken it all to the dark side Da Anderson, and with no proof whatsoever! An innocent woman's life—a retired teacher who'd always wanted to visit Shetland . . . . ' Da looked down submissively, scowling.

'No—' Da tried to defend himself.

'Now Da, I won't put up with much more of your witch-hunt on Fruma, you're the only person who's got a bee in his bonnet about her, and it's not warranted!' Mackey spluttered, acidly fuming, his white curls waving wildly about his head. Da knew when to sit quietly. Mackey gulped his tea and tried to calm down. It started raining, setting a gloomy atmosphere.

'Raining,' Da announced. They sat in silence, listening to it pound on the window.

'Wonder if that's the end of the fog,' Mackey said, thinking aloud.

'It did this before—then it goes straight back to fog. Fog and rain; then more of the same.' Da put his cap back on.

'Look, all I'm saying is—if it's *that* upsetting for her, I mean, she is only a visitor, it's not like she has family here,' Da whispered, so as not to inflame Mackey's wrath. Mackey rubbed his temple and looked at the floor.

'I know Da, but I think something is opening up in her, as if she's found something about herself, and to me that's important and something I wish to support —you know—as a Minister,' Mackey stated passionately. Da made a face and returned his gaze to the window. He didn't trust Ministers.

'I know you understand these things Da, that's why I'm bringing it to you, I didn't have to—you know that —what with my role in the community . . . . ' Mackey hoped to flatter him.

'Aye, I ken—and I'm not insensitive to people's feelings, it's joost . . . . ' Da leaned forward, 'we can't afford to lose more people. These new incomers—well —they're not as strong as the ones we had ten years ago, don't know what it is, but, they seem less— err —'

'Spiritual?' Mackey offered.

'Well, that's one way of puttin' it. Look—you and me, we know there are other forces at work on this island, but these new folk, they don't believe the same, you know what I mean? Take Malcum for instance, he knows that odd things happen here, he's even experienced some himsel', but he stays around, it doesn't make him want to leave, it doesn't even enter his mind —but these New-Uns—they need to be more open-minded, more in touch with the island and its ways, this takes time—you know this,' Da proffered kindly, as if he were Mackey's father offering advice.

'I do, I do. It's like a whole different language and they're struggling to become familiar,' Mackey started to feel a token of affinity return between them.

'That's it! You got it! They need time, but if we have more of these odd things happening, they may not wait, they'll fly the nest back to safety and familiarity, it's so easy to do these days—just up and leave, rather than stick around and learn.' Mackey nodded, knowing there was some truth in his words. Da refilled their cups.

'So, this is where we are—I mean—Fruma, and what is happening to her. I don't know—maybe you could talk to her, answer her questions—I don't know.' Mackey raised his hands in the air, not wanting to push Da in any direction.

'We'll see, we'll see—let's see how things go, eh Mackey?' Da replied cautiously, not really wanting to get involved. Mackey took the hint.

'Those Tait sisters did mention the Prophecy, and I hadn't told her anything about that beforehand—'

'If you're talking about the AdderStane Prophecy, I think it would take better men than us to try to understand what that's referring to, but it's interesting.' Da had spent years trying to fathom what the AdderStane Prophecy was all about. Normally he wouldn't talk to an incomer like Mackey, who'd already acted as though he owned the spiritual keys to Fetlar; but with the recent events coming up, he thought it was time to see what Mackey knew. He took off his cap and scratched his head.

'I've been thinking about this AdderStane prophecy, what do you think it means? I know you read a good many books, religious books too—and—well—I thought you might have some ideas,' Da said, looking at Mackey sideways. Mackey sighed and wiped a hand over his face.

'I have to confess, I really don't know anything much about it, I thought the term AdderStane came from an adder stone—you know—rocks with naturally occurring holes that go right through them. I've seen old drawings of snakes going through holes in the rock —maybe that's where the idea comes from? Anyway, I know it's considered lucky and often used like an amulet to ward off disease or negativity. I know the Druids held them in high esteem, but we don't have a Druid tradition here. Maybe it's a reference to witch-craft? Or maybe linked in with the bedrock stone here; serpentine has so much folklore attached to it—it's said it's supposed to help you discover past life experi-ences—if you're into that kind of thing—'

'Yes, the serpentine has been known to help in the old ways—but Druids? No—No—Druids here on Fet-lar. They wear pointy hats don't they?' He looked thoughtful, 'No—that's not them . . . . ' He attempted to change the subject.

'This Queen of Heaven reference, what do you make of that?'

'Well, to me it might indicate Mary,' Mackey added a qualifier, 'the mother of Jesus . . . Christianity maybe?' Da indignantly puffed out some air.

'What about *the menacing north is put to right*?'

'Maybe it's something to do with the clearances? All those people displaced with nowhere to go . . . I never liked the north part of the island particularly—'

'Aye, I agree. I avoid it. No reason to go there,' Da said, fiddling with his cap, he then remembered he had something to show Mackey.

'Oh, I almost forgot, I was looking through some old photos and I found these.' He handed them to Mackey, who looked at him, puzzled.

'I took those in the 1970's . . . . '

'And?'

'They're photos of the Hjaltadans stone circle.'

'I can see that . . . . ' Da looked exasperated.

'It's the markings—I hadn't noticed them before. I don't know why, but it seemed important to show them to you,' Da said half-irritated, hoping Mackey wouldn't make a fool of him. Mackey looked closely at the photos. He turned one around a couple of times.

'Hang on—this looks like a Hebrew letter!' Mackey exclaimed. Da leaned forward.

'Hebrew? I thought it might be ancient rune markings.'

'Suppose it could be, but it looks quite plain to me. That symbol there—that's what's called a four-pronged shin.' Da screwed up his face.

'Hebrew? On Fetlar?'

'Seems so. Might be something to do with the Papar,' Mackey said thoughtfully. Da looked at him, puzzled.

'Long story. Can I keep hold of these, for now, to do more research?' Mackey asked. Da waved them away.

'Keep 'em. I can visit the stones any time I like, don't need pictures of them—as I say—not quite sure why it seemed important to give them to you; maybe it's just another mystery, and I know you like mysteries as much as I do.'

'Yes—almost as much as you like gossip,' Mackey replied teasingly. Da played with the sugar tongs.

'How do you think this will all end then?' Da asked sadly.

'I haven't a clue. I've been praying about it. It does

seem like something has disturbed the natural order of things. The AdderStane Prophecy was written heaven knows how long ago—maybe it was only applicable at the time it was written.'

'This dybbuk thing in the prophecy, what do make of that?'

'Dybbuk, yes, there are many differing stories. It's said that a dybbuk is a malicious spirit, it enters the body of a person who's committed a sin, it can be got rid of, but only by certain people—I mean—we're talking Jewish origin here—in Judaism there would be people, perhaps considered more holy than others to do it. I was surprised to see it when I first read the prophecy, but just recently it makes a lot more sense, considering that we may have had Papar on the island.' Da shifted in his seat.

'Papa Stour—those Papar come from there, that's what I was told,' Da mentioned casually.

'Apparently not. The Papar came from all over Europe, in fact, according to the Paper Project—you know about that?' Da shook his head.

'Well, according to Norwegian history, the Papar were African Jews that had Hebrew books, and kept the Jewish Law.' Da winced.

'Africans? On Shetland?' Da said, Mackey couldn't help himself.

'That's right Da—blicks—darkies—jet black they would've been, with faces like coal . . . . ' Mackey guffawed at Da's screwed up face. Then Da leaned forward so enticingly that Mackey also sat forward, so as to catch every word.

'Here—here—changing the subject—they say that Lily kept someone in her house in the past, she was very protective of it and that it wasn't—how can I put it? HUMAN—maybe that's this dybbuk thing.' Mackey looked at Da and burst out laughing, but Da didn't see the funny side of it.

'No—no—seriously—stramp apon a snail and shö'll stick oot her hoarns—how would we know? As you say, we are not a close community anymore, we don't know the comings and goings of everyone like we used to. I tell thee, *someone* is weaving a spell, maybe I have got the wrong woman; maybe it is Lily after all. Less a less, I never thought of that,' Da said, combing back his hair at this new revelation. Mackey groaned.

'Will you stop with your fortune telling!? She's been through enough—those are your words Da!' Da looked sheepish and started putting the cups on the tray.

'You're right—of course. I'm joost worried. Worried how it will all end.' Mackey stood up and sighed.

'Aren't we all?' Mackey decided he was in a strong position to ask Da a question he'd never had answered by a local.

'Da, I'm wondering, perhaps it would help if you told me what you thought about Haby? Everyone has commented on Heed, but nobody speaks of Haby.' Da looked like Golem who'd just found the ring—the thought of having the upper hand was almost too much for Da and he almost took delight in refusing him. But these days, not many came to him for stories, and everyone (apart from Malcum) mistrusted his sources. He gleefully pointed to the sofa and Mackey took the hint. Da rubbed his hands together.

'He was a funny fellow, he wasn't from Fetlar, as you know—or anywhere on the Shetland Islands, he came and briefly stayed in one of the run down croft houses before meeting Lily. I remember the first time I was introduced to him; you know me, what with being psychic . . . . ' Mackey stifled a guffaw and almost choked.

'Sorry, dry throat, please go on, it's fascinating.'

'So, the first time I met him, what I noticed were

his eyes, big, deep pools they were—he was handsome too, I could see why Lily fell for him. He was what you'd call 'half-cast'. He spoke pidgin English, told us he was from Norway; that he'd travelled on a fishing boat and then hitched a ride to Fetlar. We confirmed this with someone reliable on Yell. As I was saying, it was his eyes that got me, I felt like I was being drawn in, I didn't like to look at 'em. He was accepted into the community the same as anyone was, it was different in those days, new blood was a real novelty and no-one could stop talking about him for months. Then he got his hooks into Lily, and she was a fine catch for any man in those days. Have you seen pictures of her when she was younger?'

'No, can't say I have.'

'Hit's no for da kyunnen's göd ta be owre cosh wi whitrits,' then he saw Mackey frown, 'it means innocent people shouldn't mix with shady people. This is exactly what happened when these two came together. You could see Lily, slowly over time, started diminishing, like her life-force was sucked away. You'd be hard pushed to not call her a real beauty—outside and in. Long, fair hair, gorgeous green eyes, and the most beautiful singing voice any of us had known on these islands. When she sang, the birds didn't dare open their beaks for fear of being upstaged.' Mackey inwardly rolled his eyes.

'He sucked out all her life-force. After a while he became a little secretive, then he became even more secretive. Even the lads on the boats said this. He liked his own company, but not just that—dark—something awful dark about him; almost sinister, I would even go so far to say he wasn't totally trusted by the community. Even when he went missing, the Community almost breathed a sigh of relief to be honest—not so for Heed—not so.' Mackey nodded and felt sorry for the island's misfortune.

'People were awful suspicious in those days, though Mackey. At one time here, everyone believed in evil spirits, njuggles, trows and even witches. There are so many tales of men who wouldn't go fishing if they crossed the path of a suspected witch—you know . . . . ' Da lowered his voice.

'There was a time when there was a whole different language used on the sea—the fishermen were not allowed to talk about things of the land for fearing bad luck, so they invented their own words, even for everyday things of the land, it was OK to name the things associated with the sea, but things of the land had to be called something different on the sea; even their wives, do you understand? Can you imagine?' Mackey pretended to look shocked, he'd heard this story before, but let him continue.

'Aye. You didne want to spook your catch. So the horse was called da russi and the cow; a boorik.' Da chuckled to himself.

'And the cat—well—the old cat had several sea names, depending on the district; da foodin, meaning a light-footed animal, da voaler, due to their wailing, da spjaaler, meaning a player, and da skaavin, this was the most common, it means the shaver!' Da imitated a cat washing itself. This tickled Mackey no end.

'This all came from Norwegian waters this Norn language,' Da explained, enjoying Mackey's amusement.

'Aye, that Haby he was up to something. Some say he used spells to bewitch people, and that's how he got our Lily, but I could see why they'd say that. He was a Finn you know.' Mackey nodded, hoping Da would tell him something he didn't know.

'A long time ago a walrus was killed on this island, it was said they thought it was a shape-shifting Finn.

Anyway, trouble was, in the end, everyone grew afraid of him, and wouldn't cross him. Someone reported strange men on the island and he was seen arguing with them, but I don't know how true that was. Many avoided him, but poor Lily couldn't. Luckily for her, he was at sea most of the year. But the strangest thing none of us could fathom—was how much she mourned him when he was gone. We were all puzzled and convinced that he'd put a spell on her.' Da paused and stared at the white fog as if hypnotised.

'I was certain that the trow folk took Haby. It's the only explanation. Perhaps he's somewhere out there, in their world—it could exist alongside ours—but we can't see him, like a magic spell, a veil—and Heed— maybe he saw it too, and it drove him mad—I mean, he died of old age you know!' Mackey shook his head compassionately and realised there was nothing more to be known from Da, that he was just stuck in those memories, like the fog. Da got up to look out of the window, he gripped the wooden windowsill.

'Did you drive here?' he asked, solemnly.

'Yes, I know it's not far, but I didn't fancy walking. It's not often I'll admit that the island frightens me.'

'That's very wise. Very wise.' He seemed distant.

'Dey'll hear o da pairtin at never heard da meetin— guess that's the way of things.'

'Meaning?' Da continued to stare into the blank canvas of fog.

'Folk are more interested in the bad news than the good, like gossip. Sometimes I stand here for hours just looking into the fog—sometimes I see things . . . . ' Mackey decided it was a good time to leave. Looking at Da, he saw a sad old man longing for the way things were; he realised there was a lot of sadness and regret on the island.

'I'll go now Da, thanks for the tea and the stories.'

But Da didn't hear, so left him to his memories.

CHAPTER TEN

Fetlar (1965)

'So it's my faul' I 'ave to work away?' Haby shouted at Lily. She glared, angry at being confronted, normally he didn't question what she did when he went to sea for months on end, but she knew he was right—which made it worse. He felt his hand involuntarily form into a fist, all his negative energy directed into a single point.

'You . . . . ' He struggled with his words, 'You make a fuul of me Lily. Everyone know abou' you and Thomas—not me!' he growled, pulling sharply on his trouser braces, a habit that normally relieved tension for him—but not today. She moved forward to comfort him.

'Ikke rør meg!' he exclaimed, pulling away. 'So I'm turn a blin' eye? An' Heed?' he complained, turning his back on her, he placed both hands firmly on the mantelpiece in an attempt to control his rage.

'Leave our son out of it!' she objected. He spat into the open fire, the fire spat back at him.

'Heed knows nothing about it . . . what? You think I'd bring him here? The family home, stays the family home,' she retorted, unable to say her lover's name. He paced the room a few times before kicking over a wooden chair; she'd never seen him so enraged.

'Is that suppose to make me theel better? Tha—tha my wife play with other man, but she not brung him home?' With his mouth pulled into an ugly sneer, he took a step towards her, his fist raised. Instead, he swore and turned away from her.

'Føkk!' He wanted to express himself in English, but no words emerged. His anger and ego willed him forward to a conclusion. She stepped backwards, not recognising his face. The anger brought an ugliness with it. He wasn't a typical looking blonde haired, blue eyed Norwegian—she had been attracted to his foreign, dark sensuality; he carried an air of mystery with him. However, it turned out he was quite the opposite in the bedroom: he was virginal and recessive, and she had to be patient with him. Things only improved marginally in that area, but it didn't matter at the beginning of their relationship, because he was so different to other men.

But this was the first time she'd seen him this aggressive before. A part of her was sexually aroused by this display of forcefulness; that it might have been different in the bedroom if he'd been a bit more fiery; then she might not have taken a lover at all. She knew that underneath, he was really a benign soul; slightly troubled by life, even when he didn't need to be—but at times he became dark and guarded and far too secretive; a real Jekyll and Hyde character.

Haby, like an unguarded pressure cooker, was almost at blowing point. He paced the room looking for things to smash, mumbling in Norwegian. He wasn't used to feeling this level of anger; it had to be discharged, it had to go somewhere.

'I am getting air before—before—I . . . . '

A terrible regret hit her; she suddenly wanted to hold him, reassure him, tell him it was all a mistake, a stupid night of passion—several stupid nights of passion. She wanted to do something to fix what she'd broken, but it was too late—she knew that—she'd betrayed him in the worst way possible. She leaned against the mantelpiece, sobbing with true remorse—

she couldn't bear the thought of hurting him; only remembering him as the gentle, sweet Haby she first met. She remembered the day he asked her on a date ten years ago; his English was poor, and the Shetland accent only confused him further; but he'd obviously worked hard on a speech. He seemed so full of life and wonder in those days—so different from the local men who were often surly in nature. It was only later that he started withdrawing and acting strangely at times. She sat down in the armchair, her sins tipping the scales of self-loathing. She wondered what would happen to her family now.

It was a bitterly cold winter; one of those winters that even the salt from the sea couldn't penetrate. Everything was in a state of frigid torpor; the well water, vegetation, the animals . . . part of him wanted desperately to forgive her; that it was just an unguarded moment; something he himself could fall foul of. He'd seen many men forsake their wives on strange shores—even for other men. The other half of him wanted revenge, and at that moment it was the winning emotion. He flew out of the front door, leaving it open. She rushed outside, calling his name, but he was gone. As he marched towards Tresta, a bottomless anger overwhelmed him, so powerful that it wouldn't allow him the luxury of tears. He envisaged everyone laughing—laughing at his ignorance, while she copulated with gay abandon, her face turning serious the more intense the pleasure became, moaning his name—Thomas—that fiend whom he'd treated as a friend from day one. He kicked a large stone across the path. So many questions went through his head: Why didn't anyone tell him? Was it because he was a stranger? That he was different? He figured they must have known what was going on; nothing goes unnoticed on an island of only a hundred people. He punched the freezing air; it was useless—how could he ever trust her again? How could he look anyone in the eye or talk to anyone without feeling betrayed?

At Tresta, the sea appeared sludgy at the shoreline, the waves acting as if drunk, overcome by the sub--zero temperature. He hurried to the one place that he understood and loved; as a person would to a comforting mother: Papil Water. His sanctuary, and its surrounding indurate peat, were all transformed into one huge, dark brown block of ice. He admired it for a while before tentatively approaching the edge; he put a foot out in front of him and pressed down. No sound, no movement of the ice. Not even a crack. Gradually he crept forward, his arms out to his side; the ice appeared solid. Now he was a quarter of the way out. He hoped his concentrated efforts might subjugate all thoughts of Lily, but they only made them stronger. Every step fuelled more murderous hate, voracious anger and bottomless resentment—every step he imagined a terrible image of hurting her in some fashion. Every cell, every atom became infused with negativity.

He continued, one step after another while Tresta held its breath; he was now standing in the middle of Papil Water. The tears that could have saved him remained inside, trapped by hate, locked and barred from erupting; instead, a stream of consciousness flowed from him as he raised his hands to Heaven and spoke in Hebrew, which translates as:

'Powers of the kingdom be under my feet and in my hand. 237 Glory and eternity take me 237, direct me in the paths of victory. 237 I command, in the name of 237, the Splendour, Intelligence and Wisdom, 237 Crown me. Spirits of the water lead me to truth 237! In the name of 237, open to me 237 open to

me 237 open to me 237 open, open 237 open 237 open 237 237 237 237 237237237237237237237237.'

Uttering this racing invocation raised such a rapturous force within him that the ground trembled. He heard a crack, like a gunshot. He stopped chanting, his body filled with an overwhelming energy, every cell of his body vibrating. He was hardly able to contain it. Visibly shaking, he looked down—sure he saw a shadow of movement; he peered into the striated gloom. A glow appeared, a tiny ray of light widening, as it lit the brown ice from underneath. Something enormous was surfacing, he knew it was monstrous, but he didn't care. He desired it, ached for it, he wanted it, he'd never felt such power—at last—he'd conjured it! The radiance grew stronger until Papil Water was no longer murky, but illuminated with white light. He shot his arms into the air and waited to be taken, crying out with the effort, he shouted one last prayer.

'Open to me, my sister, for the opening is within you. My children shall enter only through you. If you do not open your opening—I am closed; and I can't be found, so open to me—open to me. Open the gates of righteousness. I will go in, and I will praise HaShem. This is the gate of HaShem. To find and cleave to Him.'

Then, as soon as it had come, the light slowly diminished, retreating back to where it came. He screamed at the sky, and shouted, now the tears came, weakening him. The area darkened down even further. He heard a crack in the ice, another smaller one; then another. He let out a mournful cry, he had an image of Heed, of Lily smiling, and then, only regret

—a terrible, intense, heart wrenching regret. He moved his foot and noticed water on the surface, now it was a rising, steady flow. Crying out, he wasn't sure whether to attempt to walk away. He made one tentative step, gradually pushing his weight forward, and then his boot slipped through into the piercing, icy water, his body followed. He swallowed needles of ice, his body agonised with pain. He flailed around, but could make no headway, and soon he gulped no more air, his body spasmed as his lungs filled with the shocking, frore water in aching gulps of death. One more gulp and he was still. His body, now limp, lay floating—then something tugged at his boot. Another tug. Then he was pulled under, into the abyssal depths. The water became ice crystals, expanding, creaking until Papil Water became one and closed its entrance.

Heed, was in the bedroom, he'd overheard his parents shouting, which was unusual, and then the sound of the front door slamming. Then it went quiet. He slowly opened his bedroom door and peered out before venturing shyly into the hall. Poking his head around the living room door, he saw his mother sitting in the chair. Feeling her extreme sadness, he ran to her and hid his head in her dress, afraid of her copious tears. Lily made no attempt to hide her feelings, she stroked his hair, saying:

'So, lamb. So, so!'

Heed didn't understand what was happening when the policeman arrived and asked his mother questions, but he did remember her anguish, and he remembered the haunted look of the other islanders.

Fetlar (1975)

Ten years on, Heed had a vague remembrance of his Father's hair being black and that he was tall. Photos don't do people justice; they don't speak of his father's coat that exuded a gamut of aromas throughout the year, or the occasional Norwegian song that erupted from him, or his calloused hands that expertly fixed fishing nets. Lily no longer displayed family photos, never talked of Haby, and because there were no regular family memories to share, Haby drifted away from them both. Ten years on, and Haby's body had never turned up; most of the islanders presumed he'd been washed out to sea. Nevertheless; Heed grew up happy, he enjoyed the simple island pleasures: caving in the summer, and helping out the folks at lambing time. But Heed's particular penchant was fishing at Papil Water. Unlike his Father, who was a natural with anything to do with water; Heed struggled to catch anything of a decent size—but his enthusiasm more than made up for it. He planned to fix up his Father's old boat when he was a couple of years older and earning a wage.

It was one of those rare days in spring, when the island is teased with a promise of summer by a single, poignant, hot day, that Heed decided to head down to Tresta to catch the whopper of a trout that had eluded him the previous week. It would be a lovely surprise for his mother (a nice fish supper), and he could practice some new techniques he'd read about. He ambled along the beach and looked out to sea. The tide had retreated, leaving flatfooted gull prints and the squiggly casts of the elusive lugworm. For a change of view, he decided to sit with his back towards the camouflage coloured flanks of Lamb Hoga. Other than a noisy bunch of Oystercatchers that flew overhead, he was alone. He thought it odd that nobody ever fished from the Papil Water—he only ever remembered his father bringing home fresh trout. It seemed most locals preferred sea fishing, or maybe it was just a tradition that had never been broken. He set up, casting out as normal, hoping to lure out the 'big boy' with some new flies he'd made that week. Da had loaned Heed his big landing net, and he felt ready to haul out the tarrying monster. After half an hour of trying and getting tiddlers (which he put back), he cast out the furthest distance ever, pulling back the line—jerking it—making it wiggle like a fish in distress.

Suddenly the line went taut. He pulled again, but it seemed the hook had caught on something. It wasn't behaving like a bite, so he pulled a little harder. The hook was definitely snagged. He cursed and tried pulling the rod from every different angle, eventually, he felt the line give way and then go taut again, and then it was free—this time, he was able to reel it back in. But something was on the end. The line was almost reeled in, so he flicked the rod to the side so it wouldn't snag on anything, and out came a mass of line, weed and a dark object. He cleared the hook and went to pick up what looked like a piece of wood; he hesitated—the atmosphere had changed—he felt it as a wobble. He picked up the drenched wood and turned it over in his hands. It was obviously part of something larger. It had lettering which he couldn't fathom; he then felt a strange sensation, as if everything sped up, and vibrated, all instincts told him to drop the wood but he couldn't. He kept turning it over and over, faster and faster, he couldn't make it stop;

his tongue uttered alien words that scared him, he needed to stop; to breathe, as if the black water, like air, flowed freely into his lungs. He struggled, gasping for breath, clutching the physical air as if it had hands around his throat. Then, as suddenly as all the craziness had arrived, it ceased. He looked down at the wood; the number 237 appeared to be roughly engraved on it. Experiencing sharp chest pains, he fell backwards, before finally passing out. When he came around, the sun had almost set, and he experienced strong pangs of hunger; of a kind that almost made him lose his mind. Rising to his feet, and feeling somewhat unsteady, he gathered up his fishing gear; including the piece of wood, and head home. Every step seemed to produce a deep ache, so he walked slowly, which only prolonged his misery. Stumbling into the doorway, Lily caught him heavily in the hallway as he crumpled to the floor, knocking the wind out of her. He pleaded for food and water like a shipwrecked man.

'O my gorit! Göd be aboot wis!' she exclaimed, hurrying to the kitchen to get some bread and a glass of milk; and there in the hallway, he ate like he'd never seen sustenance before, gulping voraciously—which scared her. He drank the milk in such huge gulps that she refilled the glass four times before he slowed down.

'There, there Lamb,' she whispered, stroking his hair. He made a terrible noise through his nose because he was ramming food in so fast; it appeared to her that he'd skipped the 'chewing' stage. When he'd finished, he said nothing, he was panting heavily, his chest heaving. He attempted to stand up. She assisted him, but it was difficult because he was much taller than her. They both staggered into his bedroom where he fell onto the bed. She lifted his legs to swing him onto the mattress and put a pillow under his head. She stayed by his side all night; he woke frequently, sweating, speaking in a strange tongue she didn't recognise, before falling back into a nightmare filled slumber.

Ted woke with a start, gasping for breath. At first he wasn't sure where he was. What a dark dream, he thought. Throwing on some clothes, he ran downstairs, grabbing a fresh bannock from the table. He ignored his mother shouting, and head out the door, sprinting to Heed's house. They'd both planned to go to the mainland in a few days, and Ted wanted to tie up some loose ends. Ted had grown up with Heed, they were good friends, so it was with reluctance that Lily let him in; Ted being as precious to her as Heed. She didn't want him to be unduly upset by Heed's supposed illness.

'Why can't I see him?' Ted asked.

'He's not at all well, Ted,' Lily said. He noticed she looked tired. Seeing Ted's bright, hopeful face, she gave in.

'Just poke your head around the door then—doctor said he's coming sometime today, but Ted—he's not himsel',' she whispered. He bundled into the porch. He was as tall and lanky as Heed, except for his bright, ginger hair. Heed used to say he could light up the room with his hair. He opened Heed's bedroom door just a crack.

'Heed,' he whispered, 'Heed, whaas up?' Heed lifted his head slightly, turning towards Ted, a look of sheer horror on his face, before turning away and letting go a stream of alien words. Scared, he quickly closed the door. Lily was standing in the hall, continually fingering the bright beads around her neck; they were beads that Haby had made many years ago.

'I know, lad. Come in, have a cup of tea—make you feel better.' He nodded, shock whitening his normally ruddy complexion. She fussed around him and then sat down.

'He came back from fishing down at Papil, Oh, Ted, he just collapsed in my arms, and then asked for food —ate it like he was starving, he's been in bed since yesterday,' she confided, hanging onto her mug for comfort.

'He looks . . . he doesn't look himself—and those strange words,' he said, wide-eyed, looking to her for answers.

'I don't know what to make of it. At times he keeps saying 237, over and over. Something awful has happened, dat in feth!' They sipped their tea in silence.

'I had a terrible dark dream, everything was dark, black water, and I was suffocating, never ken such a dream!' he explained, glad of the hot tea.

'Boys a boys!' He took off his cap and put it back on again. This was Ted's way of relieving stress. She leaned forward and squeezed his knee.

'Shame you didne go fishing with him'. He nodded. She noticed how muscular Ted's arms were becoming from working in the fields; his hands dwarfed the mug of tea. She concluded that time was running away from her, or she was living at a different pace from everyone else. She remembered when they were boys and would sit in her kitchen; they'd eat whatever happened to be going spare, the two of them could have been brothers they were so alike in character.

'I have some work with Tommy—out at Aith—some rogue yow,' he paused, 'you'll let me know how he is then Ma,' he said sadly. He'd always called Lily 'Ma'

ever since she could remember. He rose from the seat, towering over her, she saw him to the door.

'A freend i da wye is better as a penny i da purse Ted.' He nodded, appearing crestfallen, and walked with his usual long strides down the path.

The conversation about the recent good weather took a backstage to the event that happened the same day Heed took ill. It was all the islanders could talk about. A group of fishermen had taken to the sea for a spot of fishing, two boats and six men. Suddenly one of the men cried out,

'Waatir! Waatir!' The sea had turned inky black all along the coastline; there was nothing they could do but row into it. They looked in all directions—the water was so black the fishermen couldn't tell which fish they'd caught until they'd hauled them in the boat. Returning with just a few fish in their buckets, they desperately rowed to shore, relieved to see the landing pier ahead. The men couldn't get out of the boat quick enough. Close to the beach, in the shallows, floating like massive prehistoric creatures was seven-foot conger eels. They counted eleven—all dead—and various other dead fish, the like that had never before been seen in these waters. The men were scared to put their feet into the blackness and rushed through the shallows to get to land as soon as physically possible; some of them shouting, and some screaming as their feet touched the eerie water. One islander not particularly afraid, was Thomas Brown. A fierce-looking giant of a man; he hauled in the seven-foot monsters by hand—every one of them—and laid them out along the shore. The whole island turned up to poke around and comment. The children were pulled away from the black water which remained in the bays for eight days.

Then the islanders found out about Heed.

The children of Fetlar were the lifeblood of the island. Without them, the Fetlarian's felt the future of the island was doomed. So when something happened to a bairn; the locals went into a blue funk. People continually dropped in on Lily to offer various remedies, and to gawk at the boy's strange state. Even the local Minister tried to exorcise him, but was unsuccessful; in fact, it only made him worse. Lily sent the protesting Minister away; she couldn't bear to see Heed suffer more pain. Now it seemed that he had a new symptom; he was aging—fast. Day after day she sat by his bed watching him grow old, his skin becoming wrinkled just like her grandfather's. Then his hair started thinning and losing colour. It took two weeks for Heed to die, puzzling the doctors who tried many treatments.

For Lily, losing her only son in such an inexplicable way, sent her into a tailspin of depression. He continued to babble in a strange tongue and never returned to a state of sanity; in the end he didn't even recognise his mother. The medical establishment took Heed away, but he died in transit to the hospital which made it all the worse for Lily who didn't want him moved. It was an awful day for her. She knew something inside Heed cried out for people to just leave him be, she knew in her heart he wouldn't have wanted to die among strangers. Some Islanders blamed Lily, saying it was some kind of retribution for her previous adulterous actions; others blamed the trows. For weeks, just like the black water of 1768, a flurry of superstitious activities arose, where no chore was carried out without first appeasing the trows. Even simple things like putting the washing out had a ritual assigned to it. Everyone returned to the Church, delighting the Minister who took great pleasure in frequently relating the story of the woman taking adultery. Either way, superstition was raised to the giddy heights among the Islanders, and only the passing of time lessened their un-Christian, superstitious practices. Heed's death unnerved everyone, and as the island's story teller Da repeated often:

'Der a hantel ta wite whin onything misförs.'

Which means: When something goes wrong, there's plenty of blame attributed.

CHAPTER ELEVEN

'Mm . . . this mutton is de-licious,' Trevor announced, sucking the juices from his fingers and licking the rim of the plate.

'Dad! That's disgusting!' Holly protested, grinning. The two twins copied their father's actions.

'Don't encourage them Trevor,' Sue whispered seriously, as she ladled more gravy over her vegetables. Liam ate in silence which didn't go unnoticed. He chased a carrot around the plate before staring at it; as if it were about to come alive. Holly looked at her mother as if to say, *he's weird,* Sue made a face at her and shook her head discouragingly.

'Love? You enjoying the mutton?' Sue asked Liam. He didn't answer. Sue looked over at Trevor.

'Your mother is asking you if you enjoy the mutton Liam—but then I know you're not as keen as us, are you?' Trevor interjected, trying to let him off the hook. Liam suddenly realised he was being spoken to.

'Tis glorious meat, succulent, juicy and worthy of praise!' he proclaimed, prodding the air with his fork for effect; then fell back to chasing a carrot.

'Weirdo,' Holly sneered. Sue poked her.

'Is this some sort of play you're working on, or something to do with a history lesson?' Sue asked, hoping he would say yes and she could stop worrying. Liam became anxious; he didn't mean to say it. He was becoming confused more often these days.

'Oh, something like that. Vikings, I'm interested in

them,' he said truthfully. Sue lightened up.

'The school must have some books on the subject, have you checked?' Trevor asked, pinching a spare Brussels sprout from one of the twin's plates.

'Yes, I brought a couple home.' In fact; he'd taken out every book the library had on Vikings.

'Is everything OK at school? No trouble? No bullying or anything? You still friends with Simon?' Sue enquired. Liam nodded an affirmative to all the questions.

'It's all fine, Mum.'

'Are you sure? You seem to be more tired these days,' she observed sadly.

'Yeah, Mum, remember when Liam's face fell in the plate? So funny!' Holly prompted, laughing with glee. Sue shushed her.

'You will tell us, won't you—if you've got any problems? It's not good to hide things,' she searched his face. Liam sat upright upon her mentioning the word 'hide'.

'But I haven't got any treasu—TREASON! That's what it is, against the King!' he shouted, making the twins jump, jabbing his fork upwards again for effect. Holly giggled. He blushed, realising he'd almost given himself away.

'Sorry, just practicing, some play we're doing—well —not a play, just some skit thing . . . . ' He hoped they'd lose interest.

'I thought it was rather convincing,' Trevor said, smiling, 'Got any more?' Liam puffed himself up, his speech already memorised.

'I say to Thee, do not seek to deceive the King, his reach is far, he knows you have the treasure, why do you persist in this treachery. YOU—' he leaned forward with his fork aimed towards his sister, 'will pay for your disobedience and learn the meaning of

PAIN!' And with that, he lunged forward across the table. Holly yelped and leapt backwards, almost toppling her chair. Sue gasped in astonishment. The twins stopped eating. The dogs barked just in case something interesting was going down. With the whole table paused, Liam silently shrank back into his seat.

'Pretty good. I can't wait to see this production,' Trevor said to Sue, who looked at him with a look that said: *we don't know our son anymore*. The dogs fussed around the table thinking this was a cue for a walk—Liam leapt at the chance to take them out and get away from all the probing. He smiled weakly and rushed to the kitchen, grabbing their leads, the excited dogs whining, barking and jumping.

'Just gonna take the dogs out!' he shouted. The door slammed.

'Wha—?' Trevor said, looking puzzled. Sue shook her head and wondered why kids' lives seem to be so much more complicated these days, convinced she had a much simpler upbringing. She wasn't falling for Liam's act; patience was required. Maybe a chat with Christine was the way to go. Trevor suddenly went pale.

'The fog!' He ran to the door, but Liam was gone.

'I forgot about that!' Sue said, panicking. Trevor rushed out the door. Liam was walking in the general direction of Houbie Beach, but visibility was so reduced that he could just about make out the tarmac after each step, and the dogs were pulling him this way and that. He wasn't lost; he knew he was on the road that ran down to the surgery. It was then the dogs stopped pulling and went quiet. He paused; hearing something running fast towards him. Not thinking rationally, he let fear rule his heart and turned around.

'RUNNNN!' he shouted at the dogs, hoping he or the dogs wouldn't run into a ditch. He could hear it catching up, it's breathing laboured, it sounded big and heavy. He reached the Stakkafletts car-park—Trevor was shouting his name near the top of the road.

'I'M HERE—RUNNNNNN!' Liam screamed, panicking Trevor, who caught him, hanging onto his arm, he ran with him, they all crashed into the porch at once. Trevor shut the door, and then checked every window, just in case, but the same white view was reflected back.

'Shit!' Liam said, bending over double. Sue came out, alarmed

'What's going on?' she asked.

'Running. Liam told me to run. Blimey kid, you sure got my hackles up!' Trevor wheezed, getting his breath back, he released the panting dogs.

'Something—something running towards me fast. I could hear its breathing,' Liam explained, out of breath.

'Who would be running in this fog?' Holly probed.

'Right—THAT'S IT!! I'm not taking any more chances, you're grounded—you're all grounded until this fog lifts. All this bloody peculiar stuff going on, look at Lucy, she's a mere shadow of a girl. I'm not letting that happen to any of you—I'm just not Trevor!' Sue shouted hysterically, almost in tears.

'It's OK, I agree, it's not safe, not worth the risk, I'll ring the school tomorrow, we'll sort it out then, OK?' Trevor acknowledged her fear, rounded up his family members and ushered them into the front room. Liam looked meekly at Holly, who folded her arms and glared suspiciously at him.

'The Simpsons is on—come on—we're all going to watch it together—as a family—and forget all this spooky stuff or we'll all be having nightmares at this rate.'

'Being home with Liam is enough to give me nightmares,' Holly piped up, sniggering. Liam shot her a severe warning glance, and for once she backed off, scared of something else that's crossed his face. Sue, Trevor and the two twins crowded the small two-seater sofa while Holly sat in the single armchair. Liam sank into the big bean bag feeling gloomy and frightened. Sue looked around at her brood and considered for once if she'd made the right choice in coming to Fetlar. Liam's fear didn't last long; soon he was thinking about the coins clinking in his hands and fondling the cup.

'Mum, I'm just gonna clean up my room, after all, if we're gonna be stuck at home, I'd better make a bit more room for my—for my—acting—you know, in the play? Need some room to act out the lines, yunno, like an actor?' Trevor, Sue and Holly looked at him like he was an alien, then saying nothing, returned to the TV. Liam took that as a 'yes' and scooted off quickly upstairs. Trevor looked at Sue, who shrugged. He leaned in.

'Since when did he ask permission to go upstairs? Have you heard about this play from Mrs Dunbar?' Sue shook her head and looked worried; then mouthed,

'Later.'

Liam went to his bedroom and jammed the door. He had another of those weird pressure headaches again; it made him foggy headed, and affected his thinking, so he lay down on the bed, and kept the cup under the

duvet just in case someone walked in. He'd developed an acute sense of hearing, preferring not to play music in case he missed someone walking around. In fact, he hadn't listened to his favourite bands in ages. He put some coins on his belly and fondled them under the covers. They felt cool until they got heated by his body, so he'd have to bring them out to get cold again before placing them back on his belly. Then he held the cup above his head, imagining he was doing a sacred ritual; he mouthed rubbish speech in a low whisper. He turned the lion towards him, fingered the outline and found himself humming a tune he'd never heard before. He was also careful not to fall asleep with it in his hands in case someone walked in, so every five minutes he would hide it, check if he was feeling sleepy, and then bring it out again if he wasn't. He checked his watch, it was 7.45pm. This obsessional behaviour was tiring in itself, and occasionally he found himself dropping off, and would wake in a complete panic, the coins scattering onto the bed. He brought out a coin and studied it; he flipped it over and over.

'Four coins and no more, you strike a hard bargain Deader!' He didn't know where he'd got the idea of the Deader name, but he thought it sounded like a good name for a Dungeons and Dragons character. He pulled three more coins out from under the sheets.

'Four, I said FOUR!' He rubbed the coins together, enjoying the rasping sound.

'I cannot justify giving you more, you haven't finished your last mission. Last mission? Well, if you remember rightly, I asked you to frighten the girl, not to harm her, we need her alive and unsullied!' He spoke confidently, but not too loudly. Then he realised he'd told his family that he was doing some acting, so he relaxed a little. He held the cup to his mouth and rubbed it against his lips, it felt nice doing that. Sometimes, when he knew his family were occupied, he'd drop coins into the goblet; he liked the sound they made; a bright sound, like a metallic sun falling. At 9.45pm, he fell asleep looking at his watch, the cup lay on its side on his chest. He woke with a start, knocking the goblet to the floor, it rolled under the bed. Sitting bolt upright, he listened like a keen zebra. He heard the TV still on downstairs, no other movements, so he got up and retrieved the cup.

Somehow, two coins that had slipped down into his underpants; he felt them moving around—jingling, just under his balls. He reached in and fumbled inside, moving the coins so they met and pressed against the bottom of his balls. His penis shot up in response. He massaged it, leaving the coins there. Suddenly, all in a rush, he ejaculated. He was shocked at how quickly it happened, but extremely aroused. Normally, it took him ages to reach a climax—being nervous about people walking into his bedroom. He slipped out of his underpants and used them to wipe away the sticky mess from his groin—then he shoved the underpants under his mattress. Picking up the coins, he rubbed them on his sleeve—he planned to wash the underwear, and dry it in the wardrobe. This became his new nightly ritual, with even more reason to retreat to the privacy of his bedroom.

Sue pulled down the blind and sat on the bed.

'What's going on, what happened out there?' she asked. Feeling cold, she grabbed her nightgown and put it round her shoulders.

'I don't know, but there was something out there— then when Liam shouted, I didn't think twice,' Trevor said, squeezing a pimple. He could see her in the mirror; she looked small, like she'd lost weight. He joined her on the bed.

'We can't let them go out in that—mist—fog. Surely at some point the—the police, or someone's going to have to get us off the island,' she said, and looked at Trevor, fearful.

'I don't know what to think. I guess it's only been a few days—it's hardly an emergency yet. You seem like you've got the weight of the world hanging round your neck.'

'Yes, but with the kids in danger . . . . '

'I'm pretty sure this fog will lift. And I think Liam is getting so good at acting, he's too believable; I think anyone would've run at his command, it's infectious.' He came up behind her, folded his legs under him and started kissing her neck. Unconvinced, she pulled away.

'Don't, not now. Weirdness aside, I'm really getting worried about him.' He kissed her shoulder blade and traced his hands down her spine, he knew she liked that. She shivered.

'You cold?' He ran a palm up and down her back to warm her up.

'A bit, I think I'm just worried, I can't concentrate on things like that,' she said truthfully, turning around, 'not until we've talked.' She brushed his hairy chest downwards as if to brush off imaginary crumbs.

'Let's get to bed, we can snuggle and talk.' They quickly undressed and hopped under the quilt. She nestled into his shoulder. He grabbed her hand, laying it on his chest, placing his hand on top of hers.

'What do you think's going on with him?'

'Not sure. He does seem more tired—praps he's just getting used to this lovely, clean mountain air!' he suggested, inhaling deeply.

'Mountain? What mountain?' she laughed involuntarily.

'Well, it's sort of high up, on the map,' he paused, knowing how stupid it sounded, 'The Shetland Islands are just one big mountain range really,' she laughed explosively.

'Idiot!'

She punched him playfully. He was pleased; at least they could still joke considering the circumstances. He wouldn't tell Sue, but he'd felt more than a feeling outside, he'd heard something running, something other than Liam. He made up his mind to talk to Ronald in the morning.

'You wouldn't have me any other way, surely?'

'Seriously though—don't you think he's acting strange? I wonder what he does in that bedroom.'

'Teenage boys in their bedrooms? Surely I don't need to spell it out for you?' He felt up under the covers. She slapped him gently.

'I'm being serious, I've got a bad feeling, something's not right about him, I mean, fancy falling asleep during dinner and breakfast? It might have been funny at the time, but when you add it all up, it isn't really Trevor, maybe he's ill, maybe we should speak to Christine about it?'

'I don't know, that's a bit drastic isn't it? You know teenage boys go through all sorts of—yunno—puberty stuff, it's probably just that, maybe he's had a bit of romance at school that went wrong, and he's over-thinking it, licking his wounds. It's not a crime to be private is it?'

'No, but you know Liam, he's not *normally* so secretive and that acting lark was a bit over the top, don't you think?'

'I thought it was pretty convincing, maybe he's just getting into acting, just trying things out, look, I don't want to pry too much, but I could talk to him, casually if you like, how's that?' She lifted her torso, turning on her side to look at him, then paused, wondering whether to say it.

'Do you think he might be . . . gay?' Trevor turned with just a momentary hint of horror in his eyes, before 'societal protocol' took over.

'What makes you think that? That's a bit of a jump isn't it?'

'But it might make him anxious; he might have these—these feelings, but doesn't know what to do with them . . . I couldn't bear to think of him feeling alone.' He considered her words.

'No—I really don't think he's gay, and we can't ask him, that would make things worse. If he is gay, he's gonna have to come to that conclusion on his own.' He squeezed her hand. 'And even if he is, he's still our boy. Doesn't change anything.' Somewhat unconvinced, she backed down. They lay there quietly contemplating what they would do if he was; knowing whether they liked it or not—it would change their lives.

'Anyway, that's all I'm asking, for you to talk to him, I might just have a chat with Christine, it won't hurt, I mean, especially after Lucy had that outburst at school. Shelley is really worried, she's trying to get a proper holiday, but what with Tim just starting that new job, he doesn't want to ask for leave.' He played with her hair and she nestled back down into his shoulder.

'Yeah, I know, he told me, he said life's really stressful at the mo, he knows he should take some leave, but I mean—I would too—but I'd worry about my job. I mean—there are so few jobs here as it is, he was lucky to get one, especially with no experience,' she said.

'Must be awful, can't imagine really, upping sticks and coming to a remote island, then with Lucy being unwell—at least with Liam, he's still eating—more or less—' she said, before realising that lately Liam just picked at everything.

'Look, he was never keen on lamb, let alone mutton, what do you expect? You've been having it for dinner quite a bit yunno,' he reminded her, flopping his hand down on top of her hand.

'I mean, we had it three times last week—you could cook him something else . . . . '

'I want him to get used to it, it's good food, better meat than we'd get down south,' she said, playing with his nipple.

'Don't change the subject!' He pushed her off.

'I'm not—look—I thought we all enjoyed it here, I'd hate to think that Liam has changed his mind and isn't telling us, I'd hate to think he was sitting in his room mourning for the old life.'

'Old life? You mean the Gray's son who wouldn't leave him alone and his continued difference of opinion with his form tutor? Not sure he'd be pining for that.' He tickled her stomach. She wriggled away.

'Noooo—I mean just other stuff, like his online adventure game he liked to play, they used to really get into it—'

'Yeah—until his character got killed off and we couldn't speak to him for a week! It wasn't healthy him sitting in that room all night—' he said, catching himself. Sue looked at him, worried.

'I know what you're saying, in the early summer he was out at every opportunity, exploring, he made friends at school, he seemed happy.'

'That's right. He seemed happy, now he looks tired and a bit vacant sometimes, I guess that's what I mean, you can't reach him, like he's on another planet. And then that outburst at Holly, he really scared her, jabbing with that fork!' She spoke in a quieter voice, as if Liam could overhear, 'I didn't recognise him—it scared me, let alone her.'

'As I said, maybe he's just getting really good at acting. Look, I *will* have a word, promise, I am still watching him . . . how can I not? He's still my boy.' She twined her legs in his.

'That's all I wanted to hear, that you're watching. I can't always do that when everyone's at home, what with the cooking and the twins, and now everyone's stuck at home. Have a chat—I'll be happy then—and maybe—' She grazed his pubic hair with the back of her hand,

'Maybe I'll be able to relax now, you know?' she said, in the sexiest voice possible. He gently cupped her breast.

'Oh yes—I know.' He pushed her back and rolled on top of her. His hand groped for the bedside light to switch it off. Pushing him off, she leaned over and turned the light back on.

'And another thing—do you know why he's wearing that dirty old tennis sweatband around his wrist all the time?' He groaned.

CHAPTER TWELVE

Mary cleared away the plates, and then stood at the kitchen sink, praying the fog might clear.

'Would be nice to get out there and do some gardening, I've got some plants to go in,' she grumbled. Peter tutted and turned over a copy of the Shetland Times.

'Odd weather—bright sunshine on Yell and Unst. Folk are not happy, not happy at all. Da reckons something's happening, don't know what, but he's been going on about it.' Mary said, spooning trifle into bowls. Fruma didn't say much, feeling somehow responsible for everything. She hadn't told either of them about what she'd experienced—her mind kept replaying the burning scene from the 'Wicker Man'.

'It's been bright sunshine too everywhere else—this fog does make things difficult—like going for walks,' Fruma replied, tucking into the creamy pudding.

'It's not just difficult, it's downright disruptive! The children have been kept from going to school you know—everyone is really worried, never had the like— and folk have been telling me they feel like something's coming, you know how it is, things get amplified especially in a small community like this,' Mary said wearily, before serving herself. Fruma noticed that Peter seemed more quiet than normal.

'Well, I'm off to Mackey's—I'll see you good people later,' Fruma announced, taking the bowl to the kitchen.

'You don't have to do that! You're a paying guest!'

Mary shouted at Fruma. Peter frowned in Mary's direction. Shocked, Fruma stuck her head around the door.

'Sorry—creature of habit. It's your fault Mary, for making me feel so much at home!' Fruma said, defusing the situation. Mary calmed down, realising she'd gone over the top.

'Glad you feel at home here, what with all that's going on, other folk would've left by now,' she said solemnly. Peter stood up to look out of the window that once housed a view of Tresta Bay. He sat back down again and lit his pipe.

'You religious Fruma?' he enquired, catching her by surprise; she blushed involuntarily.

'Me? No—I mean—me and Mackey we're just interested in similar things—history—you know—things like that,' she mumbled, Mary offered Peter another huge spoonful of trifle. He shook his head.

'So, see you later then,' Fruma said cheerily.

'Have a good evening, mind yourself in this fog!' Peter shouted. Mary continued clearing away dishes.

'This fog is driving everyone round the bend—me included!' Mary offered. He didn't respond. She carried the plates to the kitchen and looked out the window, feeling slightly claustrophobic. She felt cheated having such a gloomy summer; especially when winter reigned for at least eight months of the year.

Fruma walked along to Mackey's for a change, although she wished she hadn't, it seemed the fog was even thicker and denser than before, as if you had to cut your way through something more than just water vapour. A car passed her on the road, it slowed down; she could just about make out a wave from the occupant. Letting herself in, she hung up her coat in the porch.

'Only me!' she shouted and paused. She heard

something drop on the floor with a thud, it sounded like a book.

'C-come in!' he shouted back weakly. She poked her head around the living room door, he was pushing his hair back, his shirt was undone by two buttonholes; she noticed his white hairy chest and his strong, long legs in his Craghoppers. She felt a twinge of lust, but pushed it to the back of her mind.

'Sorry, did I wake you?' She flonked down on the chair opposite him. He attempted to do up his shirt, but got the buttons mixed up; she resisted the urge to button them up for him.

'This house is becoming awfully familiar.' She realised she'd never noticed the colour of the sofa before; deep maroon with chestnut swirls. She stretched her legs out in front of her and felt for the first time that Fetlar was her real home; as if her house in Gateshead was for another Fruma—a pre-Fetlar Fruma.

'Had you been knocking long? Sorry, I must have dozed off, it's been a long day it seems,' he said, rising to adjust himself.

'Long day? On Fetlar? Can't imagine it—' she teased. Mackey looked at her and smiled.

'I do have long days you know,' he grinned, 'once or twice a year. Tea?'

'Yes, no rush, I've just had dinner. You had dinner yet?' Mackey nodded. He sat back down, obviously tired. She was bursting to tell him her news, but waited.

'Problems in paradise?' she asked, getting comfortable, adjusting cushions.

'Well, sort of, and I'm having these very vivid dreams, not altogether very pleasant really, nothing I could put my finger on, just waking up—like a half nightmare—but couldn't tell you what about. I've also been speaking with folk on the island, they've been drifting in for the last two days now, worried about the weather, each with their own problems, hearing voices, seeing things—properly spooked they are, and I'm not much use, I mean, what can I tell them? What can I do?' he said, somewhat forlornly. She frowned.

'That's not the Mackey I know—intrepid, cope with anything minister I've come to know and love!' She realised she'd spoken a truth and blushed. He brightened up.

'Thanks. I needed that. That's made me feel better already. Fancy something a little stronger? I've got some rhubarb wine that Doreen made—it's very fruity.' This made her laugh. He joined in, breaking the depressive atmosphere. He went to the kitchen doing a comical Charlie Chaplin walk, which made her laugh again. She followed him out.

'Where's the dogs? Lost in the fog?' Mackey came up behind her and made her jump.

'Asleep upstairs. Worn out, they've been running like maniacs this afternoon, seemed quite agitated about something, anyway, they're asleep now.' He handed her a glass of pink wine.

'Lovely colour,' she noted. He sighed and took a huge swig; he stared at her in a somewhat sad, absent-minded manner.

'You've always been here, Fruma—' he whispered.

'Eh?'

'I said, want some more wine?'

'No you didn't—you said to me—"you've always been here, Fruma."'

'Pretty sure I didn't . . . why would I say that?' They both paused, trying to work it out.

'And why would I want more wine—you just poured it!' Puzzled, he drank the wine down in two large gulps. She frowned.

'It's been a bit like that today—things not making sense,' he said, wiggling his empty glass, she shook her head.

'I haven't had this yet. And perhaps you'd better slow down a bit . . . . '

'Oh come now, I think I can have one more . . . . '

'Mackey! You being a man of God an' all!'

'Nonsense! They're always mentioning wine in the Bible,' he said mischievously. 'Being a man of God doesn't mean I can't have a tipple every now and then,' he changed to a fake high voice, 'anyway, it's sort of an occasion.'

'What occasion?'

'I've been doing some investigating—get this—about the Ebionites, from the term 'ebionem' meaning poor—a Jewish Christian movement around the early centuries of Christianity. They believed in Jesus as a Messiah, but not as God—they also kept the Jewish law and customs, very interesting, not much is really known about them. They were known for their excessive ritual bathing—it made me think of Papil Water and your robed men—perhaps they were Ebionites.' He paused for effect.

'I also stumbled across someone called Frumentius.' She blinked.

'Frumentius? But that's so similar to . . . . '

'Your name? I know!! Well—you could've knocked me down with a feather too when I found out that this Frumentius character founded the Ethiopian Church. Apparently he was consecrated as Bishop under the title of Abba Salama, he was known as the Apostle of Ethiopia. I wondered . . . Frumentius is also taken to mean 'upright' which is similar to your name; keeping Frum, or kosher! Fascinating, absolutely fascinating! Who'd have thought it, we didn't know each other a few weeks ago and now we seem to be involved in a

proper Shetland Island mystery about some—some—
Christian Jews!' He said excitedly, before realising
that the term 'Christian Jew' wouldn't please either
the Jews or the Christians. Fruma felt suck-
er-punched. The strong wine didn't help.

'Does this mean I'm a Jew, then?' she asked, per-
plexed. He caught her change of mood.

'It doesn't mean you're anything, just because you
have a Jewish name, I mean, Rebecca is a Jewish
name and many women have that name, they're not
necessarily Jewish—or Miriam or Mary for example.'
But his comment made her feel sad. The strangest
feeling came over her; she realised that she desired an
identity; that she would've liked the chance to belong
to something, or somebody—especially as she'd never
married.

'Rebecca or Sarah is not the same as Fruma though
is it? I mean, how often do you hear that name? Come
on,' she said cynically. Realising she was right, he gave
her a weak smile. The dogs woke up and came patter-
ing down the wooden stairs, they both made a fuss of
them.

'Looking into what names mean, what does Haby's
name mean?'

'It means to hide . . . it's Jewish.'

'Another Jewish name?' She balked at the coincidence. Feeling shocked, she was glad of the wine,
emptying her glass with one swallow, she held it out
for more. Mackey obliged.

'That's true. I guess I didn't think anything of it
because I've always known his name was Jewish.' He
paused. 'No. No. Oh my word!! Why didn't I think of
this before?' he shouted, making Quincy bark.

'I've no idea,' she replied, sarcastically.

'Oh, sorry, I'm so used to discovering things on my
own. Haby's name. Haby—'

'Repeating it doesn't help.'

'It's a shortened version of Habbakuk!'

'Never!' she replied, grinning.

'No, I'm serious.' He shot over to the bookcase and grabbed a large tome and started flicking through it.

'It's this Old Testament story.' He read quietly for a minute. 'Just reminding myself—that's right—Habbakuk, well, he was a minor prophet. This was after King Saul, David and Solomon, quite an important time really. The country was split in two; Israel in the north and Judah in the south,' Mackey saw Fruma's face and assumed she was getting bored, so he shortened the story.

'Basically, Habbakuk complained to God about the people's wickedness and God replied, telling him he would destroy them, so Habbakuk prophesied to the people that God would destroy them—and he was right. God told Habbakuk that he would do it, but Habbakuk didn't understand why God would use such wicked people to punish his own chosen people, it's really a story of having faith—that God can use any instrument He wishes to accomplish his plans; even using so-called 'evil' people to achieve it, we just have to trust that He knows what to do.'

'I see,' she said, then thinking aloud, 'look to the place that's divided.' She looked at him. He didn't understand at first. She urged him to understand with her eyes.

'You mentioned the country was split in two—divided—in Habbakuk? So the Tait sisters—maybe in a veiled way they meant Haby was divided . . . . '

'You mean—oh, I see what you're getting at. Maybe. Maybe.'

'It's a bit of a long shot though,' she stated dubiously.

'No, not at all—I like where you're going, or maybe

what I said before—about the Finnigert Dyke—it divides Fetlar almost exactly in two doesn't it.'

'Maybe that is it—after all, Haby was a Finn, and if the Finns built the Finnigert Dyke then . . . . ' Mackey went quiet again.

'Fascinating.'

'I think we've worked out one clue then. It could be talking about Haby or the Finnigert Dyke.'

'I want to go back to these Papar and see what happened to them,' she said. Returning to the computer screen, he opened the Papar Project web page. After searching for a while he found the right section.

'It says here, "In the days of Harold Fairhair, King of Norway, certain pirates, of the family of the most vigorous prince Ronald, set out with a great fleet, and crossed the Solundic sea; and stripped these races of their ancient settlements, destroyed them wholly, and subdued the islands to themselves." So it looks like they were killed off then.' He scanned the page again.

'No wonder I felt sad—maybe the same thing happened here? I mean, it's called Papil Water for a reason, isn't it?'

'Absolutely. Like Skutes Water, the main place where our water supply comes from; a skute is a small boat, maybe they used to fish there at some point,' he said, reaching for an old, cold tea on his desk, finishing it off.

'Maybe the Papar were killed there—at Papil Water,' she said absent-mindedly. He clicked on another page. She noticed an image and stopped him.

'What's that?'

'The Papil Stone—haven't I showed it to you before?'

'No. I think I would've remembered.'

'It was discovered at a place called Papil, at Burra, on the Shetland Mainland . . . . '

'Hang on—there's a lion in the middle—'

'And maybe those little men at the top of the stone are the Papar—they've got little croziers,' he looked closely, 'and little bags or satchels.'

'No, wait—that lion—that's what I saw on the chalice in my dream, you know?'

'Really?'

'Absolutely, I remember, the chalice was very ornate, and the lion had its tongue hanging out. Skittles! This is quite something, isn't it?' He suddenly shot out of his chair, then sat back down.

'OHHHHHH—THE LION—why didn't I think of that before?' He groaned, rubbing his face hard with his hands.

'Brawn no brains?'

'No, I mean—*the lion*—I wonder if it means the Lion of Judah!' he shouted excitedly.

'So, explain.'

'The lion is the symbol for the Jewish people, the line of Judah . . . . ' He started tapping on the keyboard.

'I thought the Star of David was the symbol they used.'

'Yes, well, that came about around the 12th century; the Zionists started using it around 1897—it says here: "The Lion of the tribe of Judah. The lion was the ancient symbol of the tribe of Judah. Jacob described his son as *a lion's whelp*" —that's in Genesis 49:9—it says—"the standard of Judah in the Israeli encampment is said to have been a *lion*. It was the symbol of strength, courage, and sovereignty"—yes, and Ezekiel's vision of the chariot, it had the face of an ox, a *lion*, eagle and a human. WOW! This is so exciting!' He started typing again. A picture of a flag appeared on the screen. She looked closer at the green, red and yellow flag with a lion in the centre.

'Yup—well—this is also starting to tie up, ' he observed.

'The Ethiopian flag! Ha! Well, that is most interesting!' she stated, taken aback.

'Put the Papil Stone next to the flag . . . that's it—look, they're almost identical.' This new information sobered him up.

'They're in the same pose—and—' He quickly typed.

'Yes, I'm thinking about those Ethiopian Jews again—but that's not the flag they use now . . . ' He furiously typed on the keyboard again. A flag with the same colours and a blue five-pointed star within a blue circle graced the centre.

'A five pointed star . . . interesting. The blue circle is supposed to represent peace—hang on—it says here that the Ethiopian flag with the lion on was linked to the Ethiopian Church in the 1800's! Well—call me a master sleuth if you like!' He sat back proudly in the chair.'

'It's all coming together—especially if the Papar were Ethiopian Jews . . . now do you believe that it's important you being here?' She shrugged.

'Now we just have to work out why you were shown this cup.'

'And what this 237 means.'

'That I can help you with. It means 'the place of death.' He looked sheepish, realising he hadn't told her. With this piece of news, Fruma felt as if their friendship were somehow hollow.

'Actually, when I say death, it doesn't have to be literal, it's a place of No-thing and of Some-thing . . . in fact, it's much more complicated than that.'

'How long have you known this and not told me?'

'You see, I didn't want to scare you off—you've got to admit—it doesn't sound very good does it? Besides you didn't ask again,' he tailed off. She didn't know whether to feel insulted or let down that he'd kept the information from her. She suddenly mistrusted him—now she thought it made sense of Mary and Peter's ignominious comment concerning him.

'Is this all some game to you Mackey?' He groaned.

'Absolutely not! Look, it's been a long day for me and I'm not thinking straight. I didn't mean to upset you.'

'So, you think I'm that fragile that I wouldn't understand what the 237 meant?' She crossed her arms indignantly.

'You were struggling with what was happening at the time, and you've got to understand that nothing has happened like this to me before either. I'm grasping at straws and trying to keep a community together at the same time. These recent events have got everyone standing on the knife edge of panic. I wasn't exaggerating when I said that people are really feeling scared. This fog has only added more confusion. Can you not forgive me one small slip, especially when we've come this far together? I said I'm here for you Fruma, can you be here for me too? Can you not trust me?' She felt all her anger dissipate, realising for the first time she'd had only been thinking of herself. She felt ashamed that she was so self-centred—that here was a total stranger, willing to spend time listening to her problems without ever complaining.

'I don't know what to say. Sorry isn't enough, but all the same—I'm sorry Mackey—I really am. I'm just a mixed up old woman who's spent most of her life living in my own world.' He looked at her with compassion.

'Actually, I think you've been incredibly brave hanging around. People who have no siblings often find themselves in your position—of not feeling like they fit; and being an orphan—that can't help either.

Don't be too hard on yourself. I had to take things as they came up—as they happened to you, and with a certain amount of caution . . . . '

'I know. I understand now. How did you find out about the 237?'

'I've known for quite a while. I discussed this with Lily a few years ago when I first came to the parish. She told me about Heed. But when you found that wood, I didn't know what to do. It cemented the idea that you are important in all this. You see, I think that wood might have been used by Haby.' He paused to see if she was OK. She was staring out the window at the white view.

'Skittles, how do you know it was used by Haby?'

'I was thinking about the Hebrew lettering. Lily told me he was playing around with spells—when I saw the wood I realised it might be Kabbalistic spells —but that's all I know, really. The Hebrew letters combined have great power. It was a zayin, on the piece of wood that Heed found on the day he was taken ill—she showed me a photo of it. Zayin is the seventh letter of the Hebrew alphabet, also equal to the number seven. It has many meanings, the seven days of Creation, it could also be thought of as a weapon, like a spear, a cutting implement, it indicates the struggles in life, or the last day of Creation which is the rest day for Jews—The Shabbat—the time of peace. The Jews have a meaning for everything, and the Hebrew letters equal numbers in the Tanach—you might know it as the Old Testament.' He stopped, 'You might not want to hear this—sorry—don't want to bore you.'

'No—go on, I'm an ignoramus when it comes to religion.'

'Well—the Hebrew Scriptures contain a code, it's called the Bible Code, future events are said to be embedded or encoded in the Scriptures, like the 911 event; it was actually encoded in the Bible. It's fascinating. I spend a lot of time studying the Hebrew Bible and other Jewish works, I mean . . . . ' He got up and grabbed a Bible from a nearby shelf. She interrupted him.

'But I thought you were a Christian?' he sighed heavily.

'Of course I am. Look—this part . . . . '
He flicked through the biggest part of the Bible, 'this is the Old Testament and this . . . ' he flicked through the remaining pages, 'is the New Testament. I mean—not understanding something of the so-called 'Old Testament' would be crazy, don't you think?' He waved the book in the air as proof of the weight of his argument.

'I never thought of it that way,' she said thoughtfully.

'Anyway, nobody *reads* the Bible, it reads you, or reveals you. Some say that by reading it you become part of it—that it lives and breathes, and you make your own commentary as you read. Anyway, I'm going off subject. Haby would have used a combination of letters and words to reach his goal. I don't know whether he achieved it, or what he was looking for. It's said, in the past, that Jewish Kabbalists made a Golem.'

'Golem—reminds me of The Lord of the Rings— some sort of creature?'

'Yes, a clay creature made without a soul, made from magically assembling Hebrew letters.'

'Haby didn't make one of those did he?'

'Not as far as I know . . . . ' Then he remembered Da's comment when he last visited him, about something not human at Lily's.

'So Haby's the cause of all this trouble on the island, it goes way back . . . but it's older than Haby—

you said the black water started in the 1700's.'

'That's right, but it doesn't explain what happened recently.' She turned to him saying,

'So what did you think when I first told you of my dream and vision?'

'Well, the 237 sparked my main interest—but you've brought so much more—the Jewish Papar—it just spring-boarded me into looking deeper.'

'So what do we do now?'

'I'm going to speak to someone who might be able to help us. Can't guarantee anything—but I'll try.'

'You mean Lily?' she said, quick thinking. He nodded.

'Just out of interest, I didn't see a saying, I don't know what a saying looks like; I saw the letter shin on the wood, but not an ordinary shin, this one had four prongs, not three.' He started laughing.

'What?'

'You saw a four-pronged shin on the wood? But there were very faint markings on the wood—I checked . . . . ' Without waiting for a reply, he picked up the photos that Da had saved for him. He showed her the one with the Hebrew letter.

'Yes, that's it. You see, it's got four prongs, not three.' He made a swooning noise and looked at her with renewed admiration.

'You going to tell me?'

'Da gave me these, I went to ask him about your letter, oh, you might want it back.' He handed it to her. 'He didn't know anything about the letter you received by the way—but these photos, Da thought I might want them. He seemed a bit embarrassed, like he didn't know why he wanted me to have them. They're from the Hjaltadan Stone Circle . . . and *the stone circle is at the boundary of the Finnigert Dyke!*' Fruma leaned over to relieve the tension in her stomach.

'The place that's divided . . . . '

'It just gets better, doesn't it?' she said quietly. He rushed to the kitchen.

'More wine? The night is young . . . . '

'You'll have to drive me home—' He waved away the suggestion.

'I'll get you home, don't worry, it's only two seconds away.'

'Now, you have to tell me the significance of this—' Mackey finished off her sentence, ' . . . four pronged shin. Yes, of course.' With glasses filled, he began.

'I'm going to shorten the story. This is a very special letter. It's only found on something called tefillin— basically, the Jews use items to help them when praying or reciting the Psalms. This letter is on the box that is placed on their temple. Hang on.' He went over to the computer and almost missed the chair.

'Whoopsy. Here. Look.' She carefully made her way over and leaned heavily against him; the wine giving her courage.

'See? See what I mean? The box around his head, see the four-pronged shin?' She studied it carefully, a small, black box was placed above the temple and set in the centre, midway, between the eyes.

'I can see it.' He turned around, and they almost knocked heads. She wished it had been more than that, she was feeling squiffy and was open to a romantic engagement. But it wasn't on his mind, so they both returned to the sofa.

'It's a very special letter. You know about The Ten Commandments? Course you do. Well, these commandments were not written by Moshe, I mean Moses; they were *given* to Moses already carved, on a kind of sapphire stone. The letters were hovering within the stone, even the letter that had holes in them, the hole inside the letters just hovered. Anyway, this four-pronged shin only ever appeared on the first set of stone tablets. When the people made the golden calf, despairing that Moses wouldn't return from the mountain, Moses broke the first set—he smashed them for the peoples' great sin of not believing. When he smashed the stone tablets, all the Hebrew letters flew back to God. So the next set of stone tablets he had to write or carve himself, but it was missing part of what the first set had—which I think was the oral law—' he frowned, 'I can't be sure of that.'

'So there were *two* sets of the Ten Commandments?'

'That's right. Anyway, here's the lovely bit about it. If you write the letter shin in black ink and then focus on the white space in-between the letter there will be four columns. These are the four lines that form the four-pronged shin. They are the wake, the reflected light of the Luchos. Sorry, the Luchos is the Hebrew word for the stone tablets. It's like the four-pronged shin is the negative imprint of the three-pronged shin —it's called 'white fire that surrounds black fire'. The black fire being the revealed part of the Tanach—the Old Testament, and the white fire is the unrevealed secrets of the—of God, who is limitless. The four columns also represent the special four letter name of God. That is why this four-pronged shin is so special to the Jews. Now it only appears on their tefillim—for teshuva—when asking for repentance for their loss of faith, because they lost the first set of the ten commandments. But why it's on the Hjaltadan Stones—I don't know.'

It all went over her head, but she enjoyed his enthusiasm. While he tapped furiously on the screen, she felt her eyelids drooping. Half an hour passed when he finally spoke.

'I found something really interesting here Fruma.

It's from a Yogic source—it talks about the letter shin being like a tooth—in particular, it mentions a 'serpents fang'. It says—a tooth is used to break down food, so the serpent fang 'represents the power which kills the false personality, and its sense of 'seperateness'—this is fascinating stuff! It goes on to say—the shin represents the limitless extension to the mode of consciousness—this is common to most people. Apparently, it implies a kind of *conscious immortality*!!' Grinning, he turned around to find her asleep. He sighed, poured himself another wine and continued reading about the two different shins, that they corresponded to the ascending and descending force of the Serpent power—meaning human consciousness. He chuckled to himself, thinking about the serpentine stone that ran right through the centre of Fetlar, and remembered something about the Kundalini: the 'coiled up' energy located at the base of the spine —a Yogic idea. People are taught different ways to release and awaken this energy for purposes of spiritual enlightenment. His thoughts returned again to the Serpentine Stone.

'Maybe that's what the Tait Sisters were talking about! The serpentine stone that divides the island in two—it goes right through Vord Hill and the Hjaltadans!' Speaking aloud woke Fruma. He knelt down beside her.

'Fruma, you're not going to believe it—but I've found something else . . . . '

CHAPTER THIRTEEN

Frater Niven walked with purpose towards the meeting held at No. 237, St. Julian's Lodge. Before Frater Niven knocked on the door, Frater Alick had opened it, and saying nothing, he held out his hand; their handshake stating their deeper purpose. They retired to a small side room. Frater Niven accepted an orange juice and a slice of cake and then unloaded his briefcase of the relevant material for their meeting.

'The Lion must meet the Eagle,' Frater Niven announced, handing Frater Alick a bland, pastel blue, A4 wallet. Frater Alick placed one hand on top; he psychically scanned the contents through his fingers.

'Bensalem is shrouded in darkness. I will set up the meeting for this week. As far as I know, the lion was still on the island two days ago.'

'Look for the Queen of Heaven,' Frater Niven stated authoritatively. In silence, the two men ate and drank. Someone moved around in another room, a chair leg scraped the floor. Frater Niven rose from his seat and extended his hand, Frater Alick took it saying;

'It will bear evidence of its own Truth within itself.' Frater Niven turned and left the building, exiting via the narrow side street; into the Scottish world of men and secrets.

Mackey tried to find the parking spot next to Lily's house and only managed after two attempts; the fog made everybody feel they were learner drivers again. He wasn't sure if Lily would talk to him, but perhaps news of Fruma might heal old wounds. He noticed she had trimmed the hedges which made it easier to negotiate his way to the front door. He peered through the porch window, nothing had changed; Heed's coat still hung on the hook, as if he still lived there. Not wanting to presume entry, he knocked loudly on the inner door and then retreated to the front door. He knew to wait, as she often painted, and didn't like to come to the door straight away. But today was different, she opened the door immediately. He was taken aback. What he expected to see was an older woman with mid-length, unkempt grey hair that could never decide whether to be up in a ponytail or down. Instead, she had a smart bob haircut that made her look as if she'd finally entered the 21st Century. She still dressed casually; old slacks and a Shetland jumper, but then everybody dressed down until they needed to dress up. Her beautiful green eyes hadn't changed, he could've stood there gazing into them forever.

'I-i Mackey. Come in for a brew.' He was surprised at her change of attitude as they'd previously parted on bad terms. He habitually smoothed back his mass of curls that immediately disobeyed him, flopping back to either side of his head.

'You look well, the new haircut suits you,' he said.

'It was getting on my nerves. And besides, it was time.' Her small frame slipped through the half-open door into the kitchen, and he sat down on what looked like a new two-seater sofa and wondered how he would start the conversation. He decided it was best to be straight with her, at least he would have tried to help Fruma. She returned with mugs and sat down opposite him.

'I like what you did with the place, you must be feeling better?'

'Not really, although someone persuaded me that a small makeover might lift the spirits; it has a little.' He made sure he set his mug down on the coaster.

'My aunt passed last year, and I inherited the family home, on Yell, remember Aunt Marie?'

'Just about. Does that mean you're leaving us? Look, I know it—' she waved away his comment.

'I'm only *thinking* about moving on Mackey, it may not be possible. There's nothing left here for me, but sadness, and I'm determined not to die a lonely, unhappy old widow that no-one likes.' He scoffed.

'You must admit, to an extent, you cut yourself off—'

'The islanders have their own ideas about me—look, let's not fight. We're both too old and the island is too unhappy to bear us fighting, anyway, I think I know why you're here,' she said, without a hint of mystery.

'I'm here on behalf of a visitor.'

'Yes, they said she was here.'

'They?'

'I had a visit.' He frowned, then remembered Fruma's letter.

'So someone else knew about her staying here—did you send the letter, or them? Whoever they are—' he said warily.

'What letter?'

'Fruma—the lady I've come about, received a letter, more or less telling her to keep her nose out of the island's business.'

'You're jesting . . . . ' She lightly chuckled.

'No, I'm not, and she didn't find it very funny at the

time, she thought her life was in danger,' he said melodramatically.

'I want to show you something, hang on.' She left the room and returned with an envelope which she thrust into his hands. Puzzled, he opened it, noticing the envelope was made with the same thick paper. He read it, looking astonished.

'This is the same letter that Fruma received—exact same—word for word. I don't—'

'Haby received this same letter a year before he went missing.'

'What the heck is going on? Who are these people and why didn't you tell me about all this before?' he whined, nervous that he was no longer the one in command.

'I couldn't tell you everything—I wanted to—but I was told—told you were just someone there for me, at the time . . . . '

'So, all that time I spent with you was a lie?' he said incredulously. She stood up, wringing her hands.

'No, but there is so much you don't know Mackey. Look, I was grateful for your kindness, but I have to say, you did impose yourself far more than I encouraged, you must know that. And I was vulnerable at that time.' He carefully placed his hands on his knees and sighed.

'I'm the minister for the island, I provide spiritual help for many people here—'

'Yes, but I'm not a Christian and you knew that—I should never have allowed you to drag me into that church. If it wasn't for Da—' She swished back one side of her hair; obviously irritated, before continuing.

'I wasn't myself, back then—I was weak. Look, let's leave all that in the past now, I've moved on, and hopefully you have too. Either way, your visitor is very important. None of us can ignore what is happening on the island, and neither can my two contacts.'

'Well then, it appears that we're totally in your hands,' he replied, looking miserable. 'I haven't even told you what happened to her.'

'You don't need to—I will speak with her directly.' He looked as if all his toys had been taken away. She saw his dismay.

'If she wants you to come along, then that will be fine,' she said warmly.

'If I hadn't been there, I think she would've gone home long ago—so I hope you give me some credit.'

'Still after reward, eh Mackey? Nothing changes,' she said sarcastically.

'No—no—I helped Fruma because she was lost—is lost.'

'Of course you did,' she said precociously.

'Hang on—I've had just about enough of . . . .'
He went to stand up. She leaned over and pushed him back by the shoulder.

'I'm winding you up—don't get all hot-headed about it,' she said, commandingly. He made a noise of disapproval, but gave in. Satisfied, she sat down again.

'I know I made a mistake with you Lily, and I wasn't going to make the same mistake with Fruma—anyway—I'm learning too, and I—I don't feel the same way about her as I did you.' She smiled knowingly. He quickly changed the subject.

'I found some more of the wood. Quincy went into Papil Water and fished it out, dumped it on poor Fruma's lap. Then that awful 237 chanting began—she really does seem connected.'

'The same thing happened to her?'

'I'm afraid so, it was very disturbing, now I understand how you must've felt—with Heed.' She nodded sadly.

'Rather you two finding it than some other poor

soul. '

'I think we should burn it—'

'No! We must be careful what we do with it—it could have consequences—for her. She is linked now, she's part of the solution Mackey.' They briefly sat in silence.

'So these people you talk to, who are they?'

'Mainland men. They've been watching Fetlar for a very long time.'

'How do you know you can trust them?' he said, with lacerating cynicism.

'They've told me things that have come true. I believe them and so will your visitor.

'Fruma—her name's Fruma . . . . '

'But we won't know anything *for certain* unless she bears the sign.' He frowned, hating not being in the loop. Feeling a twinge of stress backache, he shifted in his seat, and put a cushion behind his back.

'Christine—the nurse came to me, worried about how everyone was feeling. She wanted to call an island meeting. Do you think your people can sort this out before then?'

'I don't know—depends on whether you can convince her to come here and take her clothes off.' She paused. 'If you haven't already that is. ' He sucked in air sharply, then scowled at her being so blatant.

'Since when have you become all prissy? It's true. There's no telling where it will be on her body, she said, unhooking her legs from underneath her. She stood up and took one step towards Mackey; smiling, powerful—in command.

'The Queen of Heaven riding high . . . . ' He stood up to face her.

'That's from The AdderStane Prophecy! '

'Now you're beginning to understand,' she said smugly. 'Your lady will bear a birthmark.'

'And how long have you known this?' He couldn't help but be indignant. Lily stood her ground.

'That matters not Reverend.'

'So I have to convince her to come here? What if she doesn't want to come?'

'If she wants answers and you want this island to become peaceful again, then you'd better convince her.' She crossed her arms. 'After all—you're good at convincing.' He implored for mercy with his eyes.

'Something has been uncovered that shouldn't have been, it's been removed from its place of rest. It was what Haby was looking for but didn't succeed. He was too dark and negative, and it consumed him in the end. I know it. I felt it. I tried to ignore it, but the darkness almost consumed me too. Heed paid the ultimate price. Bring her here Mackey, and soon, before this place tears itself apart,' she commanded.

Fruma had booked the boat trip to Noss over a week ago, impressed with the advertising blurb boasting of 20,000 Gannets, 25,000 Guillemots, 2,000 Kittiwakes, all among the staggering backdrop of 181metre cliffs. She'd invited Mackey at the last minute, but apparently something important had come up, so he declined. Over the phone, she'd toyed with asking him if he was going to visit Lily, but found herself silenced —dumb. She pondered this, wondering if it was because she didn't want be discussed by them, that unconsciously, she resented Mackey talking about her experiences; that she wanted to talk privately to Lily, woman to woman. She also worried that if the two of them met without her, the mystery might reach an early conclusion, and she'd be sent packing— 'Thanks Fruma, you were very helpful—we know what's going on now, so your presence is no longer required.'

She castigated herself for thinking everything had to be about her; that it was more likely to be about the Parish Church—maybe it was an emergency meeting about the lack of parishioners. Maybe the Scottish Church had decided to offer free, stunning locations to lay your spent body if you attend Church twenty years before your death. There would be a wee card that could be stamped by the Minister upon leaving the Church Service on a Sunday. She ticked herself off for uttering such a blasphemy; but she missed his company. She was beginning to feel the relationship was more than just friendly; he also contributed to the glances, innuendos and subconscious touching. She did notice that he seemed distant when she asked him to Noss. She was glad when he'd suggested they meet up in two days time, after the Hamefarin celebration had ended.

The few scattered clouds and light breeze made it a comfortable temperature, just perfect for spending a few hours on a boat trip, and although the spectacular guano stained cliffs heaving with noisy, feathered bodies kept her occupied, she still found her mind wandering back to the puzzling mystery. The boat moved off, and very soon pulled into a cave where an athletic assistant showed the visiting party underwater video footage, in the clearest water she'd ever seen. This only made her mind wander to what could be lurking in the depths of Papil Water. She mentally slapped herself; was it not possible for her to leave Fetlar behind for a few hours?

It had been a good, but tiring day, and she'd decided to go back on the later ferry. It was an amazingly tranquil crossing over the Yell Sound. She went upstairs and slipped out to a balcony which gave her a virtually unobstructed view ahead. She couldn't help but think of the film 'Titanic'—in her fantasy, she replaced Kate Winslet at the front of the ship with outstretched arms, Mackey behind her, about to kiss her . . . she indulged in this whimsical notion for the entire ten minute journey. Disembarking the Yell ferry, hers and virtually every other car raced across Yell, making her realise for the first time why it was called the 'Yell Run'. She arrived only just in time to board the Fetlar ferry.

Halfway across the Bluemull Sound, they hit the fog bank. It appeared as a light fog at first, then as the ferry powered through, it gradually became denser and colder, with the feeling that something resided within, something tangible, almost as if the fog consumed the island. She hadn't noticed how menacing it felt before. Nobody stayed up on deck, there wasn't any point—there was nothing to see. She likened it to eternally walking through blank pages or an empty artist's canvas; then was amazed at how imaginative and insightful she'd become since the recent events.

She wondered if Mackey was right; perhaps she was feeling something for the first time.

She retreated downstairs to the relative warmth of the passenger lounge and thought about her day. At the Fetlar ferry terminal, all the cars crawled through the fog, she was the last in the line. Suddenly, there was a loud bang on the side of the car—she stopped abruptly. A face appeared in the window. She yelped. It was a teenage boy, and he was indicating for her to wind the window down. She did, but only a crack.

'Sorry, got caught in the fog, I missed my ride. Can you get me back to the council estate—to Stakkafletts?' It took her a moment to digest the information before she waved the youth in.

'Thanks. That would be a long walk home.'

'No problem—you live here?' she asked, calming down.

'Yes, we're at No.2. I'm Liam.' She acknowledged him with a slight turn and nod of the head.

'Tricky driving in this fog eh?'

'It is. How long have you lived here then? I take it you weren't born on Fetlar?'

'No. We've only been here a few months.' He paused before saying enigmatically,

'Bensalem is in trouble.' Puzzled, she turned around to ask him to explain himself, and then slammed on the brakes. *There was no-one else in the car.* She checked the empty back seat. Panicking, she fumbled with the radio while keeping one eye on the road. She drove on with some inane music channel blaring out pop music. She was close to screaming. Driving as fast as the fog would allow, she tried to fill her mind with images of birds and high cliffs—anything. Returning to Mary's, she ran into the house. Mary and Peter were in the living room and heard her rush in.

'You OK?' Mary enquired, before realising some-thing was terribly wrong. Fruma shrugged, there was little point in telling them what had happened.

'Looks like you could do with a cuppa.' Fruma nod-ded. She concentrated on the sound of the TV; an interview, people speaking. Mary went off to organise the tea. She was just beginning to calm down when Peter turned to her and said:

'Did he frighten you?' She was so stunned she couldn't reply. Unmoved, he sat in his seat, puffing away on his pipe. He half turned to her.

'How was Noss?' Then, seeing her shocked and white faced said:

'You alright?' She gulped, nodded, tried to answer, struggling with feeling shocked out of her body.

'What did you just say?'

'I said—how was Noss? Been a while since we've been there, I guess it hasn't changed much, loads of birds there still?' Peter queried before returning to the TV.

'Yes—lots of birds—no, can't imagine it has changed, maybe a few more birds . . . . ' Mary came back with a tray of mugs and some cake.

'Enjoy yourself? Everything OK?' Mary asked again, busying herself with cups. Fruma remembered her trip, glad to bring a more rational reality to the sur-face.

'Yes, it was err . . . really lovely, especially showing us the underwater video, fascinating, spectacular scenery too,' she said, feeling like she was on the verge of breakdown.

'We went on that trip when it first started, he did it on his own then—he's got an assistant now hasn't he?' Mary asked. Fruma nodded.

'An enthusiastic American, she was amazing, a veri-table fountain of knowledge.' She struggled with wanting to blurt out what had happened—but that meant she would have to tell the whole story, so she kept quiet.

'Thanks for the tea and cake, I really needed that.'

'You're welcome. It's a long journey back.' Mary looked at her differently. Fruma ate and drank in silence while a woman rattled on, advertising a soap powder which inevitably led into a 'washing' song. The inane singing and dancing didn't help Fruma's mental state. She kept picturing the teenage boy looking in at her from outside the car; this creeped her out more than anything had so far.

'Right, I'm off to bed. See you in the morning, then.'

'Sleep tight, Fruma, don't let the bedbugs bite!' Peter called out. Normally, on any other occasion, she would've teased him about having bedbugs in a B+B, but she just wanted to go to her room and shut the door. Going straight to the window, she closed the curtains, not wanting to see any more of Fetlar's white parchment. For a while, Mary and Peter watched TV in silence. Then Mary spoke.

'Did you see her face? I wasn't her was it?' Mary offered. Peter turned around, a shadow of fear in his eyes.

'Certainly wasn't the same person . . . don't know who it was though.'

'That's right, it wasn't her—don't say anything— there are far too many strange things going on. We need to calm things down.' Mary said forcefully.

Fruma was in her car heading towards Mary's. She couldn't work out what had just happened, she was sure she'd already driven through that evening, but this time no teenage boy knocked on the window. She arrived at Mary's and rushed indoors, then stopped, realising this had happened before. And why was she rushing?

'You OK? How was Noss?' Mary enquired. With an overwhelming feeling of déjà vu, and feeling a little nauseous, she uttered a small 'Yes'. Mary realised something was wrong.

'Looks like you could do with a cuppa,' Mary said firmly. She nodded, searching Mary's face for some kind of recognition that this had just happened only ten minutes ago. The TV audience was laughing at a silly, slapstick routine. Peter chuckled into his pipe. She was confused; remembering that the last time this happened Peter said something incongruous. *Last time?* Turning around Peter asked:

'How was Noss? Been a while since we've been there, I guess it hasn't changed much, loads of birds there still?' Peter said, smiling brightly.

'I—I—yes—I guess so—I—don't feel too well—sorry —I might just go to bed Peter. Tell Mary I'm sorry—I know she just made the tea and everything . . . . ' She rushed from the room. Peter called out.

'Sleep tight, Fruma, don't . . . ' Fruma finished his sentence, ' . . . let the bedbugs bite!' Frowning, he experienced the same feeling of déjà vu. Fruma paused, then continued to her room Shrugging it off, he returned to the TV. Mary came back in with a tray of teas and cake.

'Fruma's not feeling well, she just rushed upstairs— you know—I couldn't help but feel it was because of something I said . . . all I asked her was—were there still lots of birds at Noss?' Mary shrugged.

'I hope she's not picked up some virus from them birds,' she muttered, pouring the tea, 'That's all we need; illness on top of this bloody, miserable fog!'

CHAPTER FOURTEEN

'Liam is just not himself, he's constantly distracted, sullen, and even the other students are noticing it, especially his close friends. He only comes to life in drama class, but he always plays the same character, it's like a stuck record,' Liam's teacher complained. Sue tutted into the earpiece.

'You mean like he's hamming it up?'

'Exactly! It's quite sweet really, and no-one expects miracles, but I think he actually believes he is the character, very odd and disconcerting, and he often doesn't come out of character, so his form tutor mentioned.'

'We have been meaning to have a word with him, but I guess we didn't get round to it, but now you've rung we'll take this opportunity while he's home to get to the bottom of it. He's been falling asleep during meal times.'

'Yes, apparently that's been noticed here from time to time—as if he's animated and alive one minute, then knocked out the next.' They both paused.

'I have considered talking to the Nurse here, but she's pretty overloaded, you've probably heard that it's a bit strange on this island at the moment, maybe it's affected him some way.'

'Maybe, is anyone doing anything about it?'

'What can anyone do about the weather and bizarre incidents?'

'Look, Liam's a lovely and talented boy, would be a

shame for him to fall behind, I'll wait to hear from you, and if there's anything we can do to help . . . . '

'Speak to him Trevor, today, after dinner,' Sue whispered sternly after Liam disappeared upstairs. Liam had been noticeably quiet again, making the usual excuses, most of time, the same ones. Sue missed hearing him wax lyrical about his walks around the island, the birds he'd seen, or a tale he'd been told. Trevor girded his loins to confront him, but now his head-teacher had rung, he couldn't deny it any longer—something more serious was going on. He went to Liam's room and listened at the door. There was no music playing, and even though he wasn't keen on Liam's music, he would've given anything to hear a thumping bass line right now. He listened a while longer. He could hear low voices, they didn't sound like Liam. Alarmed, he knocked on the door.

'Liam. Liam, OK to come in?' Silence. Trevor tried the door, it seemed to be jammed. He pushed harder, the door gave way and Liam was staring at him from the bed.

'Door was jammed . . . . ' Liam made a play of switching TV on. Trevor sniffed at the air.

'Jesus, what's that smell? I'd crack a window if I were you!'

'What's up, Dad? I'm busy—my favourite program-me's coming on.'

'Favourite programme—my arse! You haven't had TV on for three weeks,' he groaned inwardly at his own ineptitude; thinking Liam might now clam up. Liam turned off the TV and sat up higher against the headboard.

'Come off it—something's going on. Mrs Drydon—your headteacher just rang us—and let's face it, even she thinks you've been acting a bit over the top—look, are you in some sort of trouble? Is it drugs or girl trouble?' Liam shrugged.

'Drugs?' Liam shook his head.

'If it's girls—then I know a thing or two about that!' Trevor offered, inviting himself to sit on the bed. Liam shot up in the air.

'You sat on my leg!' he shouted hysterically, fearing the cup was almost going to be discovered. Trevor stood up.

'I was nowhere near your leg! Look, Liam, this is madness!' Liam made a play of straightening his quilt, at the same time slipping the cup up higher.

'I'm sorry. I'm just having a tough time at the mo—I've got—err—problems.' He looked down. Trevor breathed a sigh of relief.

'I thought so. Do you want to talk about them?' Liam shrugged, knowing he couldn't possibly reveal what was going on.

'Let's just say I can't get her out of my mind! It's driving me crazy!' This time there was no need for acting. Trevor nodded sagely. He remembered an obsession he once had with one of his teachers; it lasted three years until his parents moved from the area.

'Is it some girl at school? Is she teasing you?' Trevor suggested, glad to be talking some sense at last. Liam shrugged.

'Well, yes, there is one in particular—but it's all of them. I can't stop thinking about them. I want them all, at every moment of every day, beautiful, golden, shiny—' he said animatedly.

'Shiny?'

'Oh, you know, they are so bright, glowing with beauty, I can't stop myself sometimes,' he said, realising he was going overboard again.

'Most boys have a crush on just one—or two,' Trevor said, before remembering that he once fancied three girls at the same time.

'I like something about every one of them, there's the one with beautiful eyes, one with lovely hair . . . . ' Liam started to make a round shape with his hands.

'Oh boobs? Well, who doesn't like them?' Trevor said seriously. 'I have to say I'm slightly relieved, I thought you were going to say you were gay or something!'

Liam laughed, in some ways he wished he was, at least it would make sense.

'Look, what can I do to help? Your school work is obviously suffering, and your friends are saying you're acting out of character—how about talking to the nurse, maybe she's got something to calm you down for a while.' Trevor added before lowering his voice.

'I have got some soft porn mags if you err . . . need to . . . . ' Trevor paused, Liam looked horrified.

'Dad! You're suggesting . . . OH GROSS OUT!' Trevor was not at all phased.

'Sometimes, at your age, things get heated very quickly, and you can get frustrated, even depressed if you don't find some way of . . . err . . . relief. Now look, I know what it was like, luckily for me, when I was your age, a very obliging neighbour would come round every now and then, she was older than me but—'

'Too much info!' Liam pretended to cover his ears, then realised that if he didn't show any interest, his Dad might involve Christine. He pretended to be thinking about it; and then dramatically threw his hands in the air.

'I guess I could try it just once, maybe it will help.'

'Good. Good idea, you'll feel better, and 'praps you'll meet a nice girl at school when all this funny island business is over eh?'

'Maybe, yeah.' Liam twiddled with the TV remote.

'Look, I'll just nip next door, I've got a few I've finished with you can have, and if you want some new ones, just ask—don't be shy.' Liam nodded. Trevor tussled his hair, then disappeared next door. Liam wondered how anyone knew when they'd finished with a porn mag. He quickly shoved the cup in his bedside drawer. He was glad he could blame his problems on puberty; although he knew that most of the time he was out of control. At some point, he'd have to admit he had a seriously weird problem, but not yet, he still wasn't ready to let her go. Trevor returned with three magazines.

'They're good ones—clean—as I said son—just let me know. Well, I'm glad to have had the chance to talk. Now back off a bit with the drama, and things will be fine, OK?' Liam nodded.

'Thanks Dad, these are bound to help.' Trevor smiled, relieved it wasn't anything odd he had to deal with, as all teenage boys go through some trouble.

'Oh, and another thing, Mum wants to know why you keep wearing that dirty, old wristband? I don't care what you wear, but she was curious.' Liam fingered the wristband, thinking of a good story.

'It's the fashion at the mo Dad, but it does need a wash sometime, I'll put in the basket. OK?' An idea came to Trevor.

'No problem—oh—and I'm thinking of getting the table tennis out, putting it up in the front room, not much room in there I know, but fancy a game?' Liam nodded, knowing his Dad would soon get bored, and would have to go to work at some point, so he'd be left alone again. Trevor closed the door and head back downstairs. Sue was in the kitchen peeling potatoes, the twins and Holly were playing a board game. He crept in so the kids couldn't see him.

'Men's troubles. No problem, I took care of it,' he whispered proudly to Sue. She turned around, beaming.

'That's all it was?' she whispered, surprised.

'All?' he exclaimed in fake shock. 'Lucky I don't say the same thing about your PMT!' Sue frowned.

'It's like dogs that can smell a female dog in heat and can't get to them—drives them crazy, it's not nothing!' She motioned him to whisper.

'I guess he can't stay a boy much longer can he? Thanks love.' She kissed him on the cheek, relieved it was all over.

'Girlfriend?'

'Several it seems!' Trevor beamed proudly.

'Several? My word! Takes after his father!' Feeling a sense of accomplishment, he grabbed her by the waist and sneaked a hand under her apron. Laughing, he ran out into the living room to the children playing snake and ladders.

'Now then—who's cheating—Holly?'

Liam pulled back the wristband, the cut had remained an angry, red wound for longer than he thought was normal. The edges of the cut had slightly hardened, leaving a tender pink centre that occasionally oozed smelly pus. Not being able to stand the smell, he quickly covered it up again, hoping it wouldn't get any worse, but realising it had probably been left too long. Two days ago, he'd washed the wristband, but it needed a fresh bandage every day, and although he did sneak out some bandages from the first aid kit in the kitchen, they soon soiled. He took the soiled ones to school, depositing them in the school bin rather than at home. He still had no memory of how he'd procured his wound, but intended to show Christine his injury when the fog lifted. It was a wake-up call for him, knowing the school had rung to complain, and he wondered if it was ever going to be possible to break the cycle, to wean himself from his obsession. He even contemplated throwing the cup into the sea, but then would sweat all over at the thought. He considered burying it, just for one night—to have a break. He realised his biggest mistake was digging it up at all. Every time he went through this torture, he'd always say to himself:

'Tomorrow. I'll do it tomorrow.'

But then he'd go through the same thought process the next day. For Liam, daytime slowed to an unbearable, agonising crawl, and he constantly checked his watch or the school clock, willing time to go faster. Arriving home, he ate his dinner merely as a perfunctory courtesy, while attempting to care and be part of the family. But it was all contrived and factitious, because his mind would inevitably drift upstairs to his secret hoard in the wardrobe; his paramour; the only thing that mattered to him in the whole, wide world.

In the community hall, the atmosphere was one of excitement, but with overtones of gloom that occasionally broke out like a solemn solo every now and then. Most of the islanders had been grounded for nine days and were feeling downright cranky. They tried to forget their white oppressor that gave no sign of letting-up. If there were a ritual, or a prayer that could be offered to appease the weather god, then the inhabitants of Fetlar would have been on their knees, pleading for release.

But a Hamefarin (Home Coming) has always been always a joyous occasion, one to lift the spirits, and it couldn't have come at a better time. Angus and Doreen's two daughters had arrived home for a short stay; one now lived in Australia, the other in Canada. They exhausted themselves, flitting around the room, swapping old and new memories and meeting newcomers. The band assembled on the stage to tune up. This was the cue to push the tables and chairs to the side to allow room for the dancing. Many Incomers had learned to dance reels and jigs over the darker months, and much hilarity was afoot when one of them made a mistake or forgot the moves.

Apart from that, dancing is a very serious business on Fetlar, as it is throughout all of Shetland, and synchronisation is important when twenty or thirty people take to the dance floor. And so the Islanders were transformed into powerful dancing shamans, summoning their own magical totems to push back the foggy melancholia. Some danced to forget, some forgot to dance, choosing instead to down many glasses of forgetting, whilst gazing hypnotically at the young lasses.

There was one family missing. Tim and Shelley had decided that the fog was the icing on the cake, and Lucy had drifted into a deeper state of depression, so they made the difficult decision to leave Fetlar for good. This made Da more paranoid, and a little more hysterical, and like an infection, caused a corporate gloom to spread over the island. Sue, Trevor and their children were looking forward to the their first Hame-farin celebration. They'd embraced all the ways of the Fetlarians, the remote living bringing a joy they could-n't find in a busy town, or in a full filo-a-fax. Tonight they were weary, but grateful to have an excuse to leave the house. The twins were playing in a side room, and Liam sat on the side of the dance floor dreaming about his mistress. Every now and then, someone would attempt to talk to him, but he wasn't listening; soon it would be over and he could return to his golden lover, the one that made his heart leap more than any girl (he imagined) ever could.

His sister had joined a group of girls from a neigh-bouring island, they were talking and watching the adults swish around the dance floor. The music sped up indicating the end of the dance was near, and the accordion played the closing notes, hanging long on the final chord. The audience clapped, and the pant-ing dancers swapped partners or readied themselves for another round. The young and old brought together in a timeless waltz of life. It was a welcome diversion—the whispering voices of the night silenced by the merry making, and the black water confined to the dark, distant past.

For folks who wanted a break from the music, the Community Room at the back of the hall was open. Da, Malcum and Ted, took the opportunity to discuss the island events.

'Nice to see folks enjoying themselves, what with all this . . . upset,' Da said, arranging the balls in the rack on the pool table. Malcum was tired of hearing about it all, but desperate not to miss any news.

'The birds were quiet a couple of days before the fog, but now it's worse—it's like they're waiting for something else to happen,' Da said sadly, his breaking shot downing two balls. Neither Malcum nor Ted encouraged him.

'We'll get no more tourists to the island if it carries on like this, they'll be no extra money to be had, then what will Barbara and Lawrence do then? Sell up shop I guess, then what will we do?' he bleated.

'It isn't the fog that scared the tourists away, Barbara said they had complaints before then—people hearing things. That's what scared a load of tourists away,' Malcum replied, hoping this was new information he could spread.

'Probably just otters scratching around . . . ' Ted advised, ' . . . or whales—it could be whales singing, they can sound unearthly sometimes.' He watched Da pocket another ball. He tutted loudly.

'Either way, the tourists left—and that's not good for business,' Malcum replied, with an air of resentment. Malcum was annoyed that no-one accepted what he said at face value without having an opinion—or several. Ted shook his head at Da pocketing yet another ball, and at being reminded of the unnatural happenings. With no further reaction from anyone, Malcum continued.

'Apparently, it fair shook 'em up it did, Barbara said the tourists felt threatened, felt like something big was going to come into the tent.' Malcum scared himself with his description. 'There was one other person in a nearby tent, he heard it too, you know what it's like; in the middle of nowhere in the dead of night. ' Malcum said gloomily.

'Did someone explain to these people that it's probably just otters or maybe even a sheep loose,' Ted said dismissively.

'Yes, but they said they'd camped all over Europe, in places where horses, sheep—where all sorts of animals would come round in the night, it wasn't any of that, it was a feeling, a menacing, a foreboding, they were clearly suffering from lack of sleep and were very troubled. There was nothing she could say to make them stay Ted,' Malcum added. He'd further embellished the story. The couple was upset, but they hadn't camped all over Europe.

'Course there was nothing they could do! How do we—any of us stop what's happening here, we're all acting like it's normal when it bloody well isn't!' Da shouted, Ted missed his shot and glared at Da.

'I tell thee, when da wirm muvs, it's time ta flit, we can't ignore what's going on under our own eyes,' Da said loudly.

'Da's right,' Malcum said quietly, remembering his own apparition.

'And that woman is still here poking around, aye, nothing good can come of it—dat in feth!'

'What woman?' Ted asked guardedly.

'A woman, a tourist that turned up the same time as the black water came—*exactly* the same time,' Malcum elucidated for Da.

'Da mair you steer inta dirt da waar da stink gets!' Ted said, knowing that Da never did anything but get everyone else worked up. Da's eyes narrowed, he spun around to face Ted.

'I'm joost saying, we should stop acting like everything's normal round here, we need to keep our wits about us . . . for everyone's sake.'

'Live in fear you mean? Walk around looking over our shoulder, stop living, stop enjoying life because the bogeyman might get us,' Ted shouted angrily. But in truth, the returning black water had unnerved Ted no end.

'I'm ginne say it because no-one else will . . . . ' Da kept his voice low, even though there was no-one else in the room. 'It's something to do with that Adder-Stane prophecy! I'm telling you! I've had time to think aboot it!' Da whispered.

'That old fairy tale—OH COME ON! You don't even know what it means!' Ted shouted, snorting in disgust, while over-chalking his cue.

'It's not a damned fairy tale—it's true—my old Da told me from his old Da—dat in feth!' Da said, knowing that to an extent Ted was right.

'Your old Da?' Ted said, smiling. He looked at Malcum, who looked away.

'We all know he was a storyteller like you—this is 2014, not the—the medieval times, there's no creepy ghosts, or hill-folk . . . or trows even.' Da pulled a face.

'There might be witches, they used to hang 'em, we've still got the gallows to prove it,' Malcum piped up. Da waved away his suggestion; then thought better of it.

'Maybe she's a witch, that might explain things,' Da said thoughtfully.

'Supernatural rubbish! It's all in these people's minds, that's what! You're all delusional and just making things worse!' Ted scoffed angrily.

'Rubbish? With so many people affected? Look at that young family we've just lost! How do we stop more from leaving? No. No. I won't listen to that! I'm joost saying—there's no smoke without fire. Something's caused this te happen, we kinne deny that it's happening, all these things—together—all at once—we've never had this before, not on this scale, not even in Heed's time. Look—I'm *joost* saying that's all—and tha's the facts!' Da confirmed and thumped his pool cue on the floor. They all fell silent for the next few minutes; the only sound the crack of balls being hit. A loud cheering came from the main hall and a lone violin rang out.

'You know, I haven't forgotten Heed—that was the damned strangest thing. I'll never forget that—he was never the same again. None of you saw him at his worst,' Ted reflected, looking solemnly into half a glass of beer.

'I haven't forgotten Heed either, but we kinne close our eyes to what's happening now. Der mony a change in a simmer dim, far less a winter's nicht, who knows what we'll ken next? This all happened when that woman arrived—I tell dee—it's no coincidence—she's been snooping around.'

'Snooping around?' Ted shot back. Da sighed exaggeratedly.

'That's what I've been *trying to say*—she's been looking into Heed's history. Mackey came to me. Sounds like she's getting proper involved, an' she's no family here . . . . '

'Look—I know I haven't been here very long, but this woman visitor seems very nice, she waved at me in the post van, I don't know her, but I just can't see her being involved with anything, yunno, shady,' Malcum remarked, before shrinking back into his chair.

'Well Malcum, when you've been here as long as us, you'll know—you'll know, you don't drag up the past for no good reason!' Da snapped.

'Now Da, a closs mooth maks a wise head, maybe we shouldn't start slinging arrows.' Ted advised.

'Dey dat live langest will see ferdest! Du can say 'im!' Da shouted. He banged the pool table.

'I tell dee—she arrived and the black water came, then,' he lowered his voice, 'then she started asking questions, listening to island tapes. Heed's tape . . . . '
Ted moved closer to catch his words.

'Now why would she want to do that?' Ted asked

protectively. He recalled Heed's distorted face when he was ranting, it wasn't something he wanted to hear or see again. It was bad enough that he often dreamt of Heed's horrible wailing.

'Why indeed? Unless she's not what she seems. ' Da drew them both in by beckoning them over. 'And someone's written her a letter to that effect. Mackey showed it to me. Someone else was warning her to keep her nose out of our affairs.' Malcum and Ted looked surprised. Da now had them in his pocket.

'That's right—she did—I delivered it to her. I'd forgotten about that!' Malcum looked at Ted, who'd lost all colour in his face. 'Who do you reckon sent it?' Malcum whispered. Da smiled, knowing they had no choice but to believe him.

'Don't know. Someone who cares as much as we do about the island, we have to stick together.' Malcum looked at Ted, to gauge his reaction.

'That's not all. I saw her car parked at Lily's this evening. Guess she took her moment when no-one was around to hassle a frail, old woman.' Da reported. Ted frowned and reached for his whisky, downing it in two gulps. Lily had once been a part of Ted's life when Heed was alive. As the years went by, they both found themselves drifting away from each other, neither wishing to relive the past, but Ted would still defend Lily as if she were his own mother.

'We might have to take . . . . ' Da paused, pulling his two listeners even nearer, 'we might have to take action, nothing too drastic, just enough to warn her off—then all this business will stop and we—the island —can get back to normal. I tell dee, this fog will go if she goes, I ken, I really do.' They were interrupted by Ronald, the Community Council Chairman who entered the room saying:

'Now then people—a hen in Skaw is a gös at Moola.'

Da and Ted scowled, returning to the game. Malcum went to the bar to order more drinks. Ted and Da looked knowingly at each other.

Bored, and fed up with the same music droning on, Liam slunk into the men's toilets. He sat in the only cubicle, listening to the cacophony, and extracted a gold coin from his trouser pocket. He caressed it, turned it, held it up to the light, marvelling at how old it was. He heard the main toilet door fly open and footsteps. Someone prepared themselves to ease their burden at the urinal. He heard the fumbling of cloth and a rip-roaring fart that lasted at least five seconds, and whoever it was burped too. Giggling, Liam clamped a hand over his mouth. He'd heard his Dad fart before, and of course, his friends; but never a stranger. He imagined it to be Malcum or Ted. The sound of flowing urine bored him, so he turned the coin, tracing the cross in the centre. Whoever was out there started singing, it was a dirty rhyme and he worked out it was Ted; he could tell from the way he spoke; as if from the front of the mouth; he was a real Fetlarian, born on the island. Then he heard Ted speaking as if someone else was there with him.

'Leave off–leave off–you shall not enter—you shall not emerge. It is neither yours nor your share. Return—Return . . . . ' Liam strained to hear more.

'The sea is swelling; its waves are calling. I am held in the holiness of the King.' Ted paused before saying in a different man's voice:

'But who is your Master?' Then he zipped up and walked out. Liam's pulse quickened, he thought they were strange words for Ted—they were more likely to be something he would come up with when acting out. Feeling spooked, he decided to leave too. The door flew open, and Trevor waddled into the toilet,

'Li-am? You—you inna?' Trevor, who'd had a skinful, laughed bawdily and burped. Liam tentatively opened the cubicle door.

'Eh—see—you haven't bought any—of those—those maggs-sazines with you—eh? Have yer?' he slurred.

'Course I haven't! Where would I put it? You'd see it—it'd be too big.' Liam pointed at his small trouser pockets. Trevor tutted, lowered his head and slowly raised an arm as if it were leaden, and pointed to the main door. He attempted to slap Liam's head as he went by, but missed. Liam returned to the hall and watched his mother enjoying herself, dancing formally with William. They were deep in conversation. Trevor sauntered back and almost knocked over his beer glass.

'Oops—sorily.' Liam walked over to him.

'Dad, I'm going home—I'm bored,' he said fake yawning and stretching. Trevor looked at him, then looked past him.

'Enjuying yurselk then?' he said, before raising his glass and loudly cheering on Angus and Doreen who took to the dance-floor. Trevor's beer swished around in the glass like stormy waves.

'DAAAAD! I said, I'm going home. I'm SO tired.' Liam made sure he made eye contact this time; he pulled Trevor's arm to make him look at him.

'Whaaas? Whass you wanna go hame for?? Oh— dos what you want—yous old enuff.' Liam ran to find Malcum. Realising Liam had gone, Trevor shouted:

'Careful, bees careful . . . . ' Then he forgot what he was talking about, peered into his glass, looked up, and cheered again for no reason at all. Liam tapped Malcum on the shoulder, Malcum jumped. He'd been thinking about what Da said.

'Whas that? Oh, it's you Liam, you wanting to go home? Had enough have you?' Liam nodded and swigged some coca-cola out of a bottle. Malcum had drawn the short straw when it came to taking people home who didn't have a car. Since the fog arrived, no-one walked anywhere on the island. Malcum had parked the minibus right next to the entrance, so they didn't have to fight the fog.

'You must be feeling a bit hemmed in,' Malcum asked, starting the engine. Liam didn't answer him.

'I say—you feeling a bit trapped at home since this fog? I know you used to like walking around the island.' Malcum put all the lights on and could just about make out the gravel track.

'I'm OK, I've got some things to do at home,' was the best Liam could muster, he didn't dare say any more because he couldn't be sure his tongue, or the pressure in his head would interfere, so the half mile journey home was made in silence. Malcum was pre-occupied with trying to see everything. Sometimes he even wished he'd see this man again just to prove that he wasn't seeing things, but then would supersti-tiously scatter the thoughts, as if thinking about the man would bring him back. Liam was preoccupied with what he would do when he got home. He planned to bring her downstairs and show her to the living room, even to the dogs.

Malcum dropped him off, and Liam ran inside, not wanting to spend a moment longer in the clawing fog. He stopped when he heard a howl and then castigated himself for thinking it was anything more than the Ronald's dog missing his owner. He immediately rushed upstairs and grabbed the cup; that way he would alleviate the horrible, nagging pressure. He jumped from the top of the stairs to the landing, ignoring the leaping dogs that were anxious to see him, and went to the kitchen and poured himself a glass of milk. He rushed back into the front room, held the cup high in the air, then placed it on the table and pretended to do a ritual over the gold cup and coins, before downing the milk. The dogs looked expectantly at him.

'This,' he said to his canine audience, 'is my Mistress. Isn't she the most beautiful, gorgeous, wonderful thing in the whole world?' He grabbed a coin and started skipping around the front room, knowing she was watching. It felt so good to have her out in the open, not hidden away in his room, always in fear of being discovered, hiding his love under the duvet. He rushed over and grabbed the cup, thrusting it into the air like a figure skater would throw a partner onto his shoulder, and spun around. The gold caught the overhead light and dazzled him like a disco ball; he accelerated before collapsing on the sofa, exhausted and dizzy with infatuation. The dogs tried to join him, but he pushed them off. He kissed the gold cup. He stroked it. He fondled and traced the lion. The coins he let slip through his fingers onto the floor, at one point he imagined he was the one who gave Judas the coins that would betray Jesus.

'Take these, your payment!' he said, pulling off the sofa cover and wrapping it around his body like a robe. Liam always remembered that particular story from the one time he'd attended a Religious lesson at school. It was a powerful part of the Jesus story, betraying a friend for riches. He understood the attraction, the pull of something over another. He would even consider selling his family rather than giving up the cup. He danced and canoodled for another half hour before an overwhelming tiredness engulfed him. He went upstairs, sacredly wrapped the cup and coins, laying them safely back into hiding, and sauntered downstairs to watch cartoons—a dog either side of him. Expecting his family to return at any moment, he fell asleep and dreamed of men marching and hammering wood. He didn't even wake when the Jackdaws returned in the early dawn—their beaks crashing and sliding down the glass, while the two dogs barked and backed away into the kitchen.

CHAPTER FIFTEEN

Fruma re-read the letter. She even sniffed it. Was it possible, it smelt of the sea? Looking at it, feeling it, holding it, all helped her to believe that it was real. A part of her was grateful for the physical proof she carried around in her jacket pocket. The pressure to visit Lily had increased, and at times she had to stop herself driving to Lily's house, petulantly demanding answers. Although she trusted that Mackey would talk to Lily, it was a matter of when. She re-read the letter again, pacing the room, brooding indignantly; some things that happen *do* concern her. They concerned her the moment she'd heard Heed repeating the same number from her dream. They concerned her when she'd held the wood and uttered the same number. If her curiosity were monitored on an ECG graph, it'd be one, big, never-ending spike.

She decided to take a chance that Lily wouldn't be going to the Hamefarin, and slipped away before Mary and Peter could ask any questions. She wondered if it was too audacious to park right outside Lily's house, but then parking in the Stakkafletts car-park as if she were a resident on important social business, could also be considered brazen. She took a chance that people would be more interested in having a night out than caring if Lily might be ambushed by a nosy tourist. The thick fog still draped itself over Fetlar, but for once, she was glad of a smoke screen. She hesitated at the porch, then, before she could stop herself, she walked in and knocked three times. No answer.

Weighing up her imprudence with loss of courage, she turned to go—Lily hesitantly opened the door. Seeing Fruma, she swung the door wide open, saying nothing.

'I'm—I mean—I've come about . . . . '

'I know who you are Fruma.'

'Mackey?'

'Yes. He visited a couple of days ago. Please come in.' Filled with nervous excitement, Fruma imagined this was how people felt before their fortune was read; the possibility of revelation, brought about by information a stranger shouldn't possess. At the same time, an arrogant part of her considered that her presence might bring succour to an old woman; weighed down, burdened with the past, until she saw Lily face to face. To Fruma, Lily appeared to be confident, charismatic and spoke with only a light touch of a Shetland accent.

'I'm making tea—would you like some?'

'Absolutely, I wasn't expecting anything . . . how much did Mackey tell you?'

'A little, but I didn't let him explain the whole story. I wanted to hear it from you. It is important you tell me everything.' Lily showed her to the sofa and went to the kitchen. Fruma was surprised and extremely relieved at Lily's attitude, considering someone had told her she was a recluse. Lily came back bearing two, plain mugs.

'I presumed you wanted milk, but I haven't put sugar in. Did you want sugar?'

'I can drink it without, it's good of you to see me— considering—everything.'

'Why don't you start at the beginning? Don't miss anything out,' Lily ventured. Fruma nodded, then felt the letter in her pocket to make sure she wasn't dreaming.

'OK. The first day I arrived, I had a kind of vision at Tresta, I saw these men; they had dark skin and wore light robes. It was winter because the frost was over everything. They were carrying books too. I thought I must be tired, all that travelling, that's why it happened. Then that same night, I dreamt of thick, black tar falling from a golden chalice. I figured that because of the black water—' Lily put up her hand.

'Let's not analyse what it means—just the bare facts for now.' Fruma had a sharp recollection of being a child, questioned as to why she'd stolen the raspberries from the neighbour's garden. The orphanage 'Mother' had the same manner as Lily; the coolness in the voice, a patient wall who *might* yield given the right circumstances. Fruma continued.

'So, I saw a brown dog holding a piece of wood, and then a voice said to me, Who is your Master? That's odd, isn't it? And the same 237 that Heed—your son repeated over and over . . . . ' Lily nodded stoically. Fruma noticed that 'Mother' look from Lily again. She recalled her surprise as a child when 'Mother' had slapped her hard in the face for some misdemeanour; remembering the sting of the ring on her lip; a pearl of blood on her tooth.

'Then the next day the black water came. You can imagine how shocked I was. Then to meet Mackey— and his dog was exactly the same brown dog, I mean *exactly*, uncanny, everything about him. I didn't tell Mackey at the time—how do you tell someone that?' Lily interrupted.

'Let's move on.' Fruma tried to put aside the rising indignation at being cut off yet again.

'After that, I visited the Interpretive Centre—I heard the tape of Heed.' She stopped, embarrassed at talking about Heed as if she knew him.

'It was the number 237—the same as my dream you

see.' She moved on quickly.

'Then there was the letter. Mackey told me some-one was asking me to mind my own business, but then no-one knew I was here.' Lily indicated with her head for Fruma to continue. Fruma frowned, feeling under pressure, not sure she'd got the chronology of her story correct.

'Then I met—Mackey calls them the Tait Sisters. They told me to look to the place that's divided, they seemed to know—they knew that the island was in trouble, they said something about the Prophecy.' Fruma paused before Lily could cut in again. Lily picked up her tea, Fruma copied her. They both drank a few gulps.

'Please continue.'

'OK. I'm just trying to think, I can't quite believe I'm here, it seems like aeons since I first arrived and what happened that first day. Well, I guess that leads on to Quincy finding the piece of wood at Papil Water. Seeing him standing there with it in his mouth, I was quite—you know—I felt quite sick—he dropped it at my feet, and then all I remembered was Mackey shouting at me. He said I was repeating—chanting that number and turning the wood around in my hands.' Fruma noticed a shadow of recognition on Lily's face. Lily had puckered her lips, pushing them to one side.

'Is this too painful?' Fruma asked.

'No, it's important, you must tell me.' Feeling happier that Lily was showing *some* emotion she continued.

'Mackey told me about the Finnigert Dyke, and a little about—about,' she waved a hand in the air, 'about Haby—what he did for a living. Oh hang on—I got the letter after that—oh no that's right. Where was I?'

'He told you about Haby.'

'Yes, and then later, I went back to the archives to find out more about—' Fruma paused, trying to gauge Lily's reaction to her intrusion, ' . . . your family.' She looked away.

'I couldn't stop thinking about it. They didn't tell me any more than I had found out, but I did see a poster about the Papar, and that started me and Mackey looking. It really spiralled from there—then Mackey found some history about someone called Frumentius—the founder of the Ethiopian Church— such a similar name.' She brightened up at the coincidence of it all. 'I mean—you couldn't make this up could you?' She insisted. Lily gave her a wry smile.

'That led on to the Papar project, and made us think that I saw these Papar in my vision. It seemed to make sense. Oh yes, and the lion, the lion on the chalice I saw in my dream—that same lion was on the Papil Stone and on the old Ethiopian flag. It turns out these Papar were African Jews! It all sounds so incredible when I'm saying it! Is there any more? Let me think, de—de—de—err—well—there is something recent that happened, Mackey doesn't know this—I was coming back from Noss, I arrived at Fetlar, and I picked up a boy hitching a lift from the ferry terminal. He said something odd, 'Bensall—no— Bensal . . . . '

'Bensalem?'

'That's right.' She smiled coquettishly.

'It's a very old name for this island,' Lily stated.

'Well, then the boy disappeared! Just disappeared. Honestly, I didn't know what to think! And as if that wasn't enough torture, I got back to Mary's, and it all went wrong there too. I thought Peter said something, but he didn't, and then it all happened again, like déjà vu, with no boy the next time—I'm very confused— maybe I didn't . . . . ' Lily shook her head, interrupting again.

'It will be confusing; don't try to make sense of it just now. There will be strange echoes. The boy, do you remember?'

'Liam. I didn't forget that. Liam.' Lily nodded. Fruma remembered another important point.

'And the marking—there was a Hebrew letter on the wood too.' Lily nodded.

'Mackey has given me the wood.' They both paused.

'And that made me think about—no, I would digress—I don't think there's anything else that's happened, at least that's the end of the weird things.'

'Thank-you. I can imagine you have lots of questions, but there is one thing I need to do—to see—before we move forward.' Lily braced herself, knowing this could be the final tipping point—that Fruma might object, but she had to take the risk.

'I need to check something on you,' she moved forward in her seat, as a placatory gesture, 'I know that sounds odd, but please, I need you to trust me.' Fruma's eyes blinked fast, unsure.

'We could wait until Mackey is here if you prefer.'

'Certainly not. I have to say, if it means getting some answers then . . . there must be a reason for everything that's happened,' she said, bracing herself. Lily asked Fruma directly and slowly:

'Do you have—somewhere on your body—a birthmark? It will be quite a considerable size . . . . ' Lily was taken aback at Fruma who immediately started disrobing. Fruma was glad Mackey wasn't there, or she might have been too shy. She pulled the blouse out of her trousers and unbuttoned her the last three buttons on her blouse. She stood side on, lifting the blouse to the bottom of her bra, and pointed to the birthmark. Lily leaned in to get a closer look. Just below Fruma's armpit on her right side, it was clearly marked, like a dot to dot. A wonky 'W' made of five, dark brown circles sitting on an overall lighter brown patch. The outline of the birthmark, the fine edge itself, was wine red in colour. Lily gasped and touched it, making Fruma jump, which in turn made Lily jump. Fruma swung around, protectively clasping her hands to her breasts.

'Sorry,' Lily said, realising Fruma's vulnerability. She stepped back, beaming, then realising that that was inappropriate too, she stopped smiling. To give Fruma some space, she rushed over to a table on the far side of the room and picked up a piece of a paper. Fruma buttoned herself up, eyeing Lily's movements cautiously; like a cat who watches when its Master brings the vacuum cleaner into the same room. Lily showed her the paper which was obviously a photocopy of an original, older document; it showed the exact copy of her birthmark.

'That's it! That's my birthmark!' Fruma squeaked. Lily chuckled at Fruma's childlike manner.

'Yes, your birthmark.'

'I used to call it my 'wubble-u' when I was a child,' Fruma said in a quiet voice. They both gazed at the image.

'The outline of your birthmark Fruma—does it remind you of anything?' Lily asked, with a hint of humour. Fruma looked closer. She turned the paper to the right, but still couldn't work it out. Lily turned it back to the original position.

'The outline is the island Fruma. The outline is Fetlar.' Fruma was trying to ignore the remark as she tucked herself back in, then Lily yanked her out to the kitchen, to a map on the wall. She raised the photocopy up to the map. Fruma put her hands to her mouth and gasped.

'Skittles! It's been there all along. It's exactly the

same shape, outline—even with Lamb Hoga sticking out!' She paused before saying, 'All my life, I've been wearing Fetlar!' Lily couldn't help but chuckle, it had been a long time since she'd felt how good it was to laugh.

'That's not all. Come on, sit down for a minute,' Lily said, almost reverently, leading her back to the front room. Fruma didn't know what to think, her heart was playing pick-up sticks with her stomach.

'You OK with this?' Lily asked. Fruma nodded; overwhelmed but excited at getting some answers— unsure of where it would lead.

'The five brown marks on your birthmark, those five marks make up the constellation Cassiopeia,' Lily said gently. Walking over to her bookcase, she picked up an oversized, coffee table book. Fruma craned her neck to see the title. Lily opened it at a marked page; the constellation Cassiopeia, its characteristic wonky 'W' shape stared back; she held up the photocopy, marvelling at the similarity. Fruma gasped again, this time laughing openly with wonder.

'But what does it all mean?' she implored her, convinced now that Lily had all the answers, and that Mackey was only a minor player in the proceedings.

'Does Mackey know about this?' Lily shook her head. 'He knows some of it—the rest, he may have worked out for himself.' Lily breathed in hard, and then let out the air in a slow, steady stream.

'Fruma, knowing this and seeing it is really quite . . . OK, there's no other way of saying this—this means you are unique—not just unique—you are someone *very* special—sorry to put this on you, but you are,' Lily said, placing her hands on top of Fruma's hands. Fruma didn't know whether to laugh or cry.

'You deserve to know everything Fruma, but I can

assure you, it's going to change your life from now on
—you won't be able to go back to what you were.'
Fruma swung from fearful one minute—then
astounded and shocked the next.

'Will I be in any danger?' she asked guardedly,
'Only the letter said—'

'No, not on account of the letter. You don't need to
worry about the letter—I only know this much—you
are safe here, and I know Mackey is very fond of you,
so you are also safe at his house. I'm going to tell you
what I'm allowed to tell you—what I've been given
permission to tell you, now you have confirmed that—
now I'm really certain *you are who we thought you
were*,' Lily asserted.

'It sounds so important and dramatic—how can
anything be *that* dramatic about me?' Lily sat back,
the realisation that all of her time spent with Haby
had pointed to this moment, everything she'd been
through with Heed, all her efforts to keep the things
hidden—to keep Haby's actions secret.

'Did Mackey ever mention the AdderStane
Prophecy?'

'I read it, but we came to no real conclusion.'

'The AdderStane Prophecy speaks of what was, and
of what will come to pass—including you.' Fruma
shook her head and sank back on the sofa. She
pointed to herself, a question mark in her raised eyebrows; she had tears in her eyes.

'I'll start at the beginning, but it's a lot to take in.
You see, something incredibly important has been
removed from its resting place. I thought I'd never see

this come to pass in my lifetime, I was assured by others, there was a great possibility that it would. Something has been hidden here for many centuries.' Lily paused and looked flustered, no longer the 'Mother' character that Fruma originally experienced.

'I'm not quite sure where to start—your turning up out of the blue caught me out, I was expecting to have time, and have it all laid out properly. OK. I could tell you a story first of how this *something*—this *item* came to be on Fetlar. Centuries ago, the Papar landed in secret here, their cargo consisted of many artefacts. The native people, the Picts, were eventually converted to whatever the Papar believed, and allowed the Papar to bury the sacred item along with precious treasure—for safe keeping—what with the island being so remote. The Picts swore to keep the secret safe. Later, the Romans arrived here, they were also searching for the item, having heard a rumour that it was hidden on the Shetland Islands, it's why they fought the Picts and overcame them, but they were unsuccessful at finding it, or any information about it. We still have remnants of their arrival and settlement at Snabrough, on the West side. Actually, we only know it's a Roman fort because there's evidence of a fortified well—the Picts wouldn't have bothered to fortify their wells—anyway—I'm digressing—the Romans eventually left empty-handed.'

'The men that came here and buried the treasure, do you think they're the ones I saw in my vision? The Papar?'

'Quite possibly, you do seem to be led by other forces.'

'How do your people know about this?'

'I'll come to that later. Or they'll tell you themselves. I am just trying to think how I can put this simply, I'm now going to tell you the story about the sacred item that was buried here by the Papar. The Jews . . . you might remember from history: 'The First Temple'—does that ring a bell?' Fruma looked uncertain, amazed to hear the Jews mentioned again, considering all that she and Mackey had discovered.

'The First Temple? Where God would have a dwelling place on earth, where his spirit resided, the Ark of the Covenant? Does that ring a bell too?'

'I've heard of it—briefly—somewhere along the way I'm sure.'

'Well, the First Temple was not allowed to be built using tools made of iron, because iron was used in war, which would defile the temple; so something else very special was sought to cut stone for the temple, but first it had to be located.'

'The First Temple—what time in history are we talking about here?'

'Err—about 800 BC I think, at the time King Solomon ruled. The stones had to be cut using a very special tool, a unique tool that had been made *during the six days of Creation.*' Fruma shook her head slowly in wonder.

'You mean, like the original Bible story everyone knows, about God creating the world?' Lily nodded.

'This was the same item the Romans were hoping to find here, this was a creature called the Shamir.'

'The Shamir . . . .' Fruma repeated dreamily.

'Yes—now—the Shamir was about the size of a barleycorn, a tiny worm, but a powerful worm that could cut any stone, by just its gaze, and there was no stone that could resist it. Unfortunately, King Solomon didn't have possession of it. This is how the story goes; only the Archdemon Ashmedai knew of its whereabouts.' Lily paused to see if Fruma was still interested; Fruma indicated she was by nodding furiously.

'So the story goes that they had to trick this demon

to give it to them. This demon—when he visited the Earth—went from house to house, listening to the Jew's debates and was also known to drink from a particular mountain well. On top of the well, this demon placed a large rock. Now before he took a drink, he would examine this rock before he opened it, presumably to see if anyone had tampered with it.

Knowing this, King Solomon gave his chief man a chain, engraved with the divine name of God, a bundle of wool and a skin of wine, and sent him off on his deception in the hope of securing the Shamir. The chief man drilled a hole in the rock covering the well, drained off the water, then stuffed the hole with the bundle of wool and then filled the well with wine. Later, Ashmedai removed the stone, not realising it was wine until he drew it out, but it put him in a quandary, knowing that wine was the temptation of men, he went back and forth in his mind about what to do, but being so terribly thirsty he drank it anyway and fell deeply asleep. King Solomon's man then chained Ashmedai around the neck with the divine name of God. When Ashmedai awoke and realised he was chained up, the King's man said to him;

'The name of the Lord is upon thee.'

Thereby sealing the demon to his fate, the demon was now under the control of man. King Solomon said he would set the demon free if he told him where to find the Shamir. The demon told him of the moor-hen that kept the Shamir safe; the Shamir was given to the moor-hen for safe-keeping by the Angel of the Sea. To attain the Shamir, a trick was played on the moor-hen. King Solomon sent a servant to the nest of the moor hen, who laid a piece of clear glass over it. When the moor-hen came back to the nest and found it couldn't feed its young because of the glass barrier, it flew away and fetched the Shamir from the secret place, hoping to use it to cut a hole in the glass to save its young. At that point, the King's man shouted, terrifying the moor-hen, making it drop the Shamir and fly away. By this means, King Solomon's man lifted the glass with the Shamir on it—not being able to touch it himself—and returned to King Solomon. The poor moor hen, distressed at losing so precious an item, and having broken its oath to the Angel of the Sea, committed suicide. Have you seen the Papil Stone Fruma?' Fruma nodded.

'Remember the strange bird-men at the bottom?' Lily went to a pale blue A4 folder and pulled out another piece of paper with a picture of the Papil Stone on it.

'The bird-men at the bottom with the long beaks . . . see? This depicts them holding the Shamir in their beaks. In the carving they are shown as bird-men, a kind of amalgamation of Solomon's men and the moor-hen possessing the Shamir. See there, the Shamir is given a man's face on the carving, as if the Shamir had thoughts of its own, which of course it didn't—it was God's instrument.' Fruma seemed to radiate joy with every new revelation; her face ached from continually smiling.

'So, were we right then? The men shown at the top of the stone—they're Papar?' Fruma asked.

'Well, that's the next part of the story.' Fruma was now totally under Lily's storytelling spell.

'Where did I get to? Oh yes—the Papar arrived on Fetlar's shore—these Papar were in possession of the Shamir many centuries after the First Temple fell. The Shamir first belonged to King Solomon, as I said, and his eventual wife, Queen Sheba, then gave it to their son, Menelik the First, who eventually became emperor of Ethiopia . . . . ' Fruma gasped at the Ethiopian reference. ' . . . through the centuries it finally ended up with these—these African or Ethiopian Jews who practiced Christianity, but kept the Jewish Law.' Lily said, leading her to the conclusion.

'The Papar!' Fruma said quietly, 'We were right!'

'Yes—now—as I said, the Papar buried the Shamir along with the treasure—it's here—somewhere on Fetlar. My sources fear that its burial place has been disturbed—or worse still, someone has found the Shamir. Just imagine Fruma—something that was made at the beginning of time, at the six days of Creation, was buried here, on a small remote island in the middle of the north sea!' Lily said, prideful tears welling up at the idea, and being able to share the story with the right person.

'What's even more amazing, is that I bear a birthmark of Fetlar!' Fruma paused. 'But what if someone —*unscrupulous* has found the Shamir?' she said delicately. Lily stroked her neck before answering with a serious expression.

'*Then God help us all.*'

They sat quietly. Fruma was trying to take it all in. She hadn't learned what this still meant for her; was she a Prophet? Some sort of Seer? But she didn't feel comfortable asking; as if this final piece of news would be the end of the mystery. She waited for Lily's cue; receiving nothing she changed the subject.

'They must be having a good time—at the Hamefarin—Mackey asked me to go with him, but I didn't feel comfortable.' Lily ignored Fruma's comment, appearing to be deep in thought.

'Living with Haby was like living with two different men. He was loving and attentive and yet the other side was unyielding, demanding, and sometimes cruel,' she paused, 'I took on a lover Fruma.' Lily said with tears in her eyes. Fruma wasn't sure whether to comfort her, so she did what she was used to doing with the children; she opened a space, and allowed Lily to fill it.

'Haby had felt drawn here, by the power of the Shamir—I was later to find out—it pulled him here. The good side of him wanted a fresh start, and he took advantage of the good fortune that came his way. He was clever with his hands and made little scenes with anything he could find; grass, shells, vegetables . . . .' She chuckled.

'He was very kind. I wasn't used to men paying attention, not the way he did. He seemed to reach into my soul. I was only twenty three and it was a wild time, trying to teach him better English, this was the time when we ourselves were almost forbidden by our own teachers to speak our own dialect. Unbelievable really! Now we're trying to get back our language—our heritage. Anyway, he would help me with chores, and help other people in the community. We were married within a year, and everything seemed so bright for the future. Then he started having bad dreams. The dreams would stay with him all day. He went off on his own for long walks, he was often seen at Papil Water, standing on the edge; yet at the same time, he was home here with me. Two places at once? This started a rumour, his surname being used against him. I never questioned it at first, until I fell pregnant, and then something changed in me, I became fearful— this was a new feeling for me—I had nothing to fear on this island—then I realised I was becoming fearful of him! Of having him and losing him. It was irrational, I know. He went to sea for his work, and I only saw him maybe once every four months. Every time he seemed to come back with a darker soul. I found him one night swaying to and fro; he was holding his temple and speaking gibberish. At least I thought it was gibberish. Those were the bad sides of him. Sometimes he'd come back from sea as I first met him, full of warmth for me, and for his boy—for Heed. He was a good father. Heed hardly ever saw that blackness in him. I don't know why I betrayed him, I think I was weak, I felt alone, and Thomas . . . . ' She turned to Fruma; almost in a pleading manner,

'You see, Thomas was always here. He fished locally, and was lucky enough to have an inheritance from a distant relative. He was living in the community, unlike Haby. The next thing I knew we were seeing more of each other, and then . . . but I never brought him here—not to the family home—that would've been wrong, for Heed too. Heed never knew about us, I was discreet. But most of the island knew— how could they not? You can't hide true feelings for another. I knew Haby was getting mixed up in something that was beyond his ability, he even half admitted that he was trying to find something, but he wouldn't tell me what. Then I was approached by some Mainland Men—they called themselves The Fraters. They warned me that Haby was in too deep, what he was doing was dangerous, they told me very little details at first, but that it affected the island, what he was doing. They asked me if I knew what he was doing, they told me about his past and where he was from. Haby had told me—told everyone he was from Norway, but it wasn't true. He was born in England and was taken to Norway as a child by foster parents. They showed me his birth certificate. They told me things only I could know about him. I felt cheated at first—that he didn't tell me the truth, I suppose he had a right to some secrets. I found him once at Papil Water, passed out on the bank. Next to him were pieces of wood with strange markings on them—well— you found a piece Fruma. He was doing spells down there, I was sure of it. I tackled him about it and he was relieved to be able to share. He told me that something ancient had been buried here, that someone had told him in a dream, that every so often he would receive instructions; he wrote them all down. He said there was a big reward for the person who discovered the treasure; that a group of religious people were looking for it.' She wiped tears from her eyes.

'He said he only wanted the reward so we could have something nice as a family. I told him we didn't need anything else. Then he came back from work after a long six months; he'd found out about me and Thomas. He was crazy, I'd never seen him so distraught. He took off. And that was the last time I ever saw him. I knew nothing about his past, I only ever knew one thing. It was after I'd found him looking at a picture. He hid it when he saw me coming, but I confronted him when he was in a better mood. He told me that he remembered one person when he was a child and that she had gone—she'd died.' Lily got up and went to a drawer. She handed Fruma a small photograph of two children, it was summer, and they looked happy in a garden.

Suddenly Fruma screamed and held out the photo to Lily. Lily wasn't sure what she meant by it. Fruma made a snorting sound and pulled at her short hair. She tried to speak, but it made no sense. Then she started shaking and fell back in the chair. She kept holding out the photo to Lily—imploring her. Lily was beside herself, not knowing what to do. Then the tears fell, then Fruma started wailing and howling. Lily was so frightened, and panicked, she rushed from the sideboard to the kitchen; back and forth, not knowing what to do, memories of Heed's ranting too clear in her mind, until gradually, Fruma quietened down. Lily rushed a box of tissues over to her, but she was still not making any sense. Twenty minutes later, thoroughly spent, Fruma laid the photo gently on the side of the chair, and wiped her face and dripping nose. She reached into her pocket and pulled out her wallet. Smiling, laughing and with a few more tears, she extracted a small photograph and handed it to Lily. Lily gasped, her mouth hung open like a drawbridge. Saying nothing, she kept looking at it—and then looking at Fruma; from one to the other.

'This—this is you?' Lily asked, still astonished at seeing an identical photo. Fruma nodded, still grinning and weeping.

'I was told he died in a car crash. We were in the same orphanage together; Windy Nook. But his name wasn't Haby though, it was Ben.'

'That's right! That's apparently what his birth certificate said, the Fraters told me . . . Ben.'

'A foster home had been found for me, and about a week later I was given the news that he'd died. Maybe they thought I would get on with my life if I stopped thinking about him—I mean—we were inseparable . . . my goodness Lily, my goodness!' Lily picked up the two identical photos, marvelling at them. She reached out for Fruma's hand—which Fruma gladly took. Then Lily rushed over, and the two women wept fresh tears in each other's arms. After they were emptied of all emotion, Lily got up and poured two large glasses of port. She handed one to Fruma who downed it in one gulp. The warm, silky glow slid to her stomach, calming her. She nodded her thanks to Lily.

'Haby was told the same thing; that you'd died in an accident Fruma. He was so sad about it. He told me all your memories, of the garden where you spent time together, and your special friendship. But the one thing he never did was tell me your name—it was like he couldn't voice it, it was too upsetting or him.'

Hearing this, Fruma cried a few more tears.

'But what I can't get over is how you are tied to Fetlar, with your birthmark. Did he ever get a chance to see your birthmark at any time?' Fruma shook her head.

'Not that I'm aware of . . . but it was different in those days, you must know yourself, we were far more modest. I don't see how he could've seen it.' Lily picked up the photos again and laughed with wonder.

'I don't suppose you have any pictures of him do you Lily?' Fruma asked plaintively. Lily looked down, embarrassed.

'I'm sorry Fruma, it was all too painful—I burnt them all one night. I was in a low place, it was just before Mackey came to the Parish. But I do have some photos of Heed—can I show you those?' Fruma started crying again, this time because she finally had some answers, more than she could ever have imagined, or hoped for. She wondered what Mackey would say about it all.

'I've thought of nothing but him and Haby for the last three weeks, oh Lily—that would be lovely.' Lily touched Fruma's arm with such tenderness, that Fruma started crying again. While Lily was getting the pictures, Fruma put her palms together and thanked God. It was the first time she'd done such a thing since she'd heard about her best friend having the accident all those years ago. Fruma was so touched at seeing Heed's photos, wearing a permanent smile on her face.

'He's so much like Haby was when he was younger,' Fruma reflected. Lily sat on the sofa next to her, realising this changed everything for them. However, this was the end of what she knew; she herself had been given no more information, either about Haby or what would happen next for Fruma. Lily went to make more tea, and Fruma felt for the first time in her life that everything made sense—even if she didn't know any more about what the birthmark would mean—she had some kind of closure, yet a new beginning. She imagined Mackey's face, being told the story—and she thought he deserved to know. Lily came in with sandwiches and tea. Fruma tucked in immediately. Lily thought she could see Haby in Fruma, the same dark eyes, the nose was long, and went down and then up at the end, like a ski jump; Lily used to tease Haby about that. She pushed it out of her mind, knowing that the mind plays mean tricks sometimes; it makes you see what you want to see.

'Fruma, I have no more to tell you—I don't know what's next. I'll make a phone-call to the Fraters, they'll probably want to come here to meet you. I'm so glad you came Fruma—I hope you are too—now I can't wait to know the rest. It's been decades, having it in the back of my mind that you might appear one day. It's just wonderful, and perhaps now the island will know peace again, we've had our fair share of upsets!' Fruma wiped her mouth with a napkin, nodding.

'Absolutely. Skittles, those sandwiches taste good—didn't realise how hungry I was,' she said, her mouth full. Lily laughed out loud. The two of them shared more memories of Haby until early the next morning, and then Fruma decided it was time to go back to Mary and Peter's. Lily agreed to let Fruma know once she'd contacted the Fraters.

It was 3am, and the Hamefarin was still in full swing. Da and Ted had left early and waited at a lay-by just around the corner from Mary and Peter's house. Da's decision to confront Fruma had sobered him up, but Ted was still half-cut, and simply along for the ride.

'I just want to scare her a little, enough to stop her, make her think, I just want the island back to normal,' Da said, pretending to look at birds through binoculars. Ted was unsure, no one had been more affected by the black water than himself, but the drink was dulling his senses. They'd been sitting there for three quarters of an hour when Fruma finally appeared. Da started the engine, buoyed up with adrenaline, he rambled instructions to Ted.

'Look, it's best if I do all the talking, I'm just going to come up behind her and get her to pull over, flash my lights,' he said, bristling with nerves. He'd never threatened anyone before; especially a woman. Fruma was on her way back to Mary and Peter's, the fog still thick, so progress was slow. Da saw her and pulled out, came up behind her fast, beeped his horn twice, flashing his lights. Fruma slowed down and stopped in a middle of the road. Da looked at Ted.

'Come on then lad, let's deliver the message.' Ted was falling asleep, but followed Da anyway. Fruma stayed in her car, but wound the window down. Da rushed to her window before she could get out, panting with adrenaline, he mumbled his words.

'Here—you've got to stop poking around in other people's affairs, you're just a visitor—you're nothing to do with Fetlar—you're upsetting the balance, the delicate balance.' Surprised, she turned off her engine to hear him better.

'What? Who the hell are you?'

'Da. Da Anderson.' Then he kicked himself for telling her; for a split second he knew what he was doing was wrong, but he couldn't back down now.

'And I'm obviously not the only one who thinks that you're the cause of this latest upset to the island.' Then Ted moved in to speak.

'Aye, I'm—was—Heed's best friend. You's have no idea what it's like—when—when . . . . ' Da pushed him back. Fruma could smell whiskey on their breath.

'Let me speak laddy. Now we think it's best if you just pack up and go home, there's nothing for you here!' She went to protest. Annoyed at her refusal to listen, Da wrenched her door open, she tried to hold it back, but Ted moved in to hold the door too, half annoyed that Da had stopped him having his say.

'Please, I'm not here to cause any trouble, but things have been happening to me, you must under-stand . . . . ' Da leaned in, invading her personal space.

'I understand, oh I understand alright,' he could feel spiteful anger welling up.

'You visited Lily when you thought no one would see you didn't you? At the Hamefarin—I saw your car —bothering an old lady who's had enough trouble—' Ted interrupted Da,

'She's had enough upset—' Da turned round and made a face at Ted.

'But she doesn't *know*,' Ted protested, pointing at Fruma, 'she wasn't here when it happened to Heed!' Da waved him away, so Ted angrily kicked a piece of stone across the road.

'You see how much you've upset people with all your digging around? So, are you going home? Are you going to leave us all alone?' She made her mouth into a thin line.

'I'd like you to close my door—then we can talk.' With a sudden burst of pent up energy and frustra-tion, Da reached forward and yanked her arm, attempting to pull her out of the car. She made a strange noise; a kind of low growl. Ted decided he could be silenced no longer, pushed Da to one side, and grabbed her arm, she struggled to move over into the passenger side of the car but didn't have time. Ted was far stronger, he tugged at her, she screamed, kicking out with her legs. She came out of the car, half gripping the door—Da pulled her arm away while placating her with soothing words. Ted however, was angry.

'You caused this te happen . . . . ' Ted said, his face was red, she realised it wasn't going to help if she struggled.

'I'm sorry. I never meant to upset anyone. I found some wood at Papil Water and it was awful—that number 237—over and over—I didn't want any of this —but Lily told me . . . . '

'She didn't tell you anything, you *forced* yourself on her—you're a witch! You force yourself on everyone— you need to shut up—or—or we'll shut you up!' Ted spat his words at her. Da moved forward.

'Now Ted—hadd dee tongue! She knows now how much damage she's done, now leave her be—that's enough—let her go.' But Ted wouldn't be placated. He grabbed her by her upper arms and started shaking her; she was shouting, and Da tried to pull Ted off. Using the back of his hand, Ted slapped her across the face. She fell backwards against the car, her lip was cut, but she wasn't afraid. It was as if a strange peace fell on her. She raised a finger to her lip and then turned her finger around and showed the blood to Ted. Both men were glued to the spot. She took a step towards them, still holding up her bloodied finger. They took a step back, fearful.

'Lily told me, and showed me something that connects me to this island, and to Haby. It's written in the AdderStane prophecy. And—and you'd better listen carefully—because—because—I grew up with Haby, and I have the photo to prove it!' she said sternly. Ted protested.

'You canna draa a strae afore my nose an tell me it was a docken!' Ted shouted, he was shaking, but Da laid a hand on his chest and said to him gently.

'Der mony a guid man fann haalin up a docken . . . .'

Shocked, Ted realised the truth of Da's words, realised he was wrong. Tears started running down his face—and then surprisingly, for both Da and Fruma; he simply ran away like a scared child. Da called after him, but he'd disappeared—as if the fog had swallowed him whole. She now took command.

'Now listen Da Anderson, I have work to do here, if you want your island back you'd better back off.' She had to think quickly, yet a power moved within her, giving her a strength she'd never felt before.

'You'd better stop thinking I'm your enemy—I'm not—I never was—I was as much in the dark as you. But now I know—I have the birthmark—Lily confirmed it—it's—it's in the Prophecy. If you stand in my way the island will fail, and it will *fall*,' she moved forward, remembering what Mackey had said, 'until all that remains . . . is the shepherd and his dog.' Da gasped and dropped his head. She knew she was mixing up the two prophecies, but hoped it would be enough to make him back off.

'I had no idea, none of us could know—you have to excuse Ted, it was so hard for him to see Heed slip away; Heed didn't recognise him towards the end— that was hard on a teenage boy. He got in with a bad crowd for a while until he met his wife and settled down.' Even though she knew they had no right to attack her, she had more compassion for Ted.

'No—I blame you! Why didn't you just come and

speak to me? None of this needed to happen! But now I must go and get some sleep, Mackey's expecting me tomorrow—I mean, today,' she lied, yet she realised that was exactly where she wanted to be; somewhere safe. Knowing that he and Ted would be in trouble, Da continually rubbed the back of his neck and apologised profusely. She raised a hand.

'Look—I'll tell no one if you leave me alone—and let me—let me . . . look—I never wanted any of this, I didn't come here for this, but now I'm here and I won't leave until it's all over.' She checked her lip again, it had stopped bleeding, she licked it with her tongue, remembering the taste of the salty iron as a child.

'I'm very sorry, Miss—very sorry indeed—forgive me—it got out of hand—I should've come alone . . . .' She cut in.

'No Da—you shouldn't have come at all!! Now go home! Go home and wait—and be silent!' He backed away, half-bowing, then rushed to his car that was still running and backed up to his original starting position, almost coming off the road at one point. He turned the car around and drove off as fast as he could in the opposite direction.

Suddenly deflated, she staggered backwards, turned around, and leaned against the car door. She checked her lip again, but it wasn't bleeding. Shaking, she got into the car and looked at her lip in the rear view mirror. There was a small line of a cut, and her cheek was red. She reached into the passenger compartment and grabbed the baby wipes. Pulling out two, she placed them on her face, glad of their cooling effect. She figured it was best to get back to Mackey's, just in case the Universe had other ideas about what would happen to her. She banged on the door, but didn't wait before rushing into the sitting room. Mackey was flat out on the sofa, drooling and snoring;

obviously out for the count after a heavy night of drinking. As she stood there looking at him, she realised she couldn't remember what her own front room looked like. Fetlar felt like her home; it was her home. She sat down opposite him, his presence made her feel safe; and having time to be still, she contemplated what had happened at Lily's. Then, realising that her car was parked outside, and not wanting to cause Mackey any trouble with people gossiping, she decided it was best if she went back to Mary's to get some sleep. She drove back and fell into bed, fully dressed and emotionally exhausted.

CHAPTER SIXTEEN

Everyone in the house felt hemmed in. Sue did her best to keep the children entertained, but with Trevor at work, she kept less of an eye on Liam. The twins continually misbehaved, which annoyed the house pets as much as the humans, so Sue punished them. They cried real tears and then extended crocodile tears, grizzling into cushions and corners. Sue was at her wits end.

'We could play Snakes and Ladders again?' Holly calmly suggested as she leaned against the door frame. Sue looked at her beautiful fifteen-year-old daughter; clear-skinned, a little on the skinny side, but the long, heavy curls that extended down her back somehow seemed to swell her proportions. Sue wondered about Holly's future; in particular, romance. She realised she hadn't thought about that part of the children growing up—and living on a remote island would not make dating easy.

'That might keep them quiet for at least an hour . . . failing that—we could drug 'em,' Holly said, with a flicker of a sophisticated smile. Sue laughed.

'Don't tempt me, now, I'll get the board, you round up the boys.' Holly took the stairs two at a time. She paused at Liam's room and put an ear to his door. Hearing several voices she was curious and thought about rushing into his bedroom to see what he'd been keeping so secret for the last few weeks. She knocked on his door.

'Liam? Liam? Want to play snakes and ladders with

us?' Silence, then:

'No—go away!' But this only increased her curiosity.

'What you doing in there? Inventing a cure for cancer?' she said, pleased with her witty comment.

'I'm busy—I just want some time on my own!'

'Ok, baby brother!' But she was narked. Calling him *baby* would normally have brought forth a flurry of insults; teasing was part of their sibling rivalry and she missed their daily banter—somehow the house seemed colder without it. This further reinforced the idea that she should break in and disrupt whatever he was doing. Next door, the twins had succeeded in pulling out all the filling from a cushion. It looked as if the sky had been dragged in, with little soft clouds scattered around the room. Exasperated, she grabbed each twin by the arm, they both protested.

'Come on you little mischief meddlers!' she said and then laughed at how stupid it sounded.

'Snakes and ladders?'

'Yay!' The twins cried in unison and ran downstairs.

'Don't run!' Holly shouted, then realised that she wanted to stretch her legs too, and joined them.

'SWEETS!' The two twins yelled.

'No sweets, you *bairns* have had enough already.' Sue decided she preferred the Scottish word for children.

'They've taken the padding out the cushion upstairs—definitely don't need any more sweets,' Holly advised. Sue groaned.

'Come on, BEFORE THE SNAKES GET YOU!!!'

The game finished and the twins naturally drifted into playing with Lego. Sue took the opportunity to peel some potatoes for a mutton stew, and Holly crept upstairs. She cupped a hand to Liam's door, but couldn't hear anything. Her curiosity changed gear into overdrive, she stood up straight, wondering how she'd carry out the break-in. She figured she could put her arm against it and suddenly push forward, or she could use her right hip and leg to get a lower, heavier force in motion; but before she'd made a decision, and as if her body didn't belong to her—she'd kicked in the door. It flew open to reveal Liam struggling to hold a huge golden goblet in one hand, the other hand down his underpants. She didn't scream, she just took a huge intake of breath and covered her eyes with her hands.

'You LITTLE . . . . ' He rushed forward and grabbed her by the arm, dragging her into his bedroom—then he threw her onto his bed.

'Get OFF—what are you DOING!!' she shouted. Downstairs, the radio played one of Sue's favourite songs: 'You Really Got Me'. She turned up the volume and sang along badly, swaying as she peeled the vegetables. Upstairs, Liam covered Holly's mouth with his hand.

'WHAT ARE YOU DOING IN MY CASTLE BITCH?' He straddled her, pinning her down. She tried to speak from behind his hand, but noticed a terrible smell coming from his wristband; it made her gag.

'You've been spying on me haven't you? You just want my treasure, don't you . . . WELL YOU'RE NOT GOING TO STEAL IT FROM ME, DO YOU HEAR?' She continually nodded, shocked at seeing her younger brother so different and scary. He leaned over; his face near her face.

' . . . And, you're not going to say anything to Mum and Dad, are you, Holly, ARE YOU?' he said firmly. Her eyes grew wide, she was having trouble breathing. Something changed in Liam's expression; he softened for a minute, and then looked down at her pert, small breasts. Her eyes grew wider; she started protesting, desperate to escape his grip and the putrid odour.

'I could touch you—I could,' he said suggestively, his penis rising. She felt it against her, and protested, attempting to shake her head from side to side. She tried to move, but he seemed unnaturally strong for a thirteen-year-old. He had both her arms pinned with one hand and another across her mouth; the rest of his weight was on her groin and belly. Holly, being very slim, bordering on skinny, didn't have a chance. He stared at her breasts, and lowered his face, opening his mouth as if to bite her nipple, her whole body writhed in protest, he talked in a low voice.

'If you say one word about what you saw, I will—I will—KILL YOU—do you understand? It doesn't matter how long it takes, I'm very patient, it could happen at any time, Mum and Dad aren't always around, you could be in the shower, or out for a walk somewhere, no-one will protect you—then I'll get you—so—do you understand? If I take my hand away, you won't scream, you won't do anything and I'll let you go—you do believe I will do it, don't you Holly?' She nodded fervently, and wondered if she'd ever see her Mother again.

'It's quite simple sister—you don't say ANYTHING about this to ANYONE, and you will stay alive—simple —we have a deal yes?' She nodded again. Just when she thought she was going to be released, he bent over, his lips grazed her nipple through her t-shirt.

'I could just lick it, or even bite it like a cherry . . . tasty.' Her eyes rolled. She renewed her wriggling.

'But I won't UNLESS you swear to me not to tell anyone—GOT IT?' Her whole body nodded in agreement. Very slowly, he lifted his hand away. She half gasped for air through his fingers, her face wet with saliva. Putting his fingers to his lips, he licked them, smiling.

'Shh . . . remember, not a word!' She nodded, agreeing to anything to get away. He slowly eased away from her body; seeing her chance, she pushed him off and attempted to stand up, but she felt dizzy and sick. He just sat there smiling.

'You—you—YOU'RE FUCKING INSANE!' she shouted and staggered to her bedroom, slammed the door, and leaned against it; glad to have something between her and Liam. With nothing to bar the door, she put a flimsy, wooden chair against it. She looked down at her breasts, and rushed over to the wardrobe, yanked out a jumper and attempted to put it on. She panted heavily with anxiety, and couldn't lift her arms because she felt too weak. She started crying and fell to her knees, the jumper half over her head; she sobbed into the woollen pile. She renewed her struggle; but in the end she just pulled it off and threw it on the floor.

Oh my god, what the hell IS Liam? He's a monster —OH MY GOD! OH MY GOD!!

Her mind raced; she desperately wanted to phone her best friend, but didn't dare to. She picked up her mobile phone and put it down three times before finding the strength to pull the jumper properly over her head. She strained the delicate mohair weave; tugging on it, stretching it; she wished it could cover her whole body. Then she leapt into bed, curled up into a foetus position and sucked her thumb. Emotionally spent, she eventually fell asleep.

Liam searched for his trousers. In his panic, he kept putting two legs into one hole.

What have I done? To my own sister? But she deserved it, I mean, I wouldn't dream of kicking in her door, no, she deserved everything that happened!

Then he realised she may not keep her word.

I'll deny it—any of it—I'll say she was dreaming or something, act like butter wouldn't melt.

He went over to the window; the white wall of fog stared back at him—he knew it witnessed everything. It became his accuser, his judge. He closed the curtains, knowing that something tangible lurked in the fog. He sat on the bed and switched the TV on, then switched it off. Then the feelings came, nothing much at first—just a few gulps and tears. Then he threw himself into his pillow and really let rip.

What's happening to me? I don't understand why I did that.

He pictured his sister's face as she tried to catch her breath. He hated his sister at times, but he would've killed someone else for doing what he did to her. He beat the pillow against the mattress; over and over until he exhausted himself and needed a drink. Then a realisation came to him:

Where's the cup?

He scrabbled around; it had got knocked under the bed. He retrieved it and held it at arm's length—he hated it and loved it. He knew he was different because of it; that something else made him do things. He tried not to think about the black wood that was always there—inside his head. Carefully, he wrapped the cup in an old t-shirt, and then in a fit of pique and disgust, he threw it as hard as could into the wardrobe. In complete panic, he retrieved it and checked it for damage; he apologised and caressed it. He needed a walk to clear his head. He needed to be free. He couldn't stand the same four walls.

Holly was right—I am insane. It's the treasure—I should tell Dad—no—tell Mum, she'd be kinder—SHE WOULDN'T BE KINDER IF SHE KNEW WHAT I JUST DID TO HOLLY!

He lay back on the bed and listened for angry foot-steps, but none came, so he presumed that she'd kept her promise. He wondered if it was safe to go down-stairs and get a drink; he knew he'd have to emerge at some point. The terrible trap was, that even after all this upset, he knew the cup would calm him down, but he couldn't risk exposing it.

He went to the bedroom door and listened. He heard the radio blasting out in the kitchen. He strained to hear music coming from Holly's room; he'd had given anything to hear some terrible boy band playing, and her tuneless singing, but there was no sound coming from her room. He wondered if she was crying or phoning her friends.

I wouldn't blame her really, I couldn't hurt Holly, not for the world, the treasure made me feel that way —they'll put me in a mental home—like that one on the Mainland—I'll be drugged and drooling all day.

He hated himself and hated the island; he hated what he'd become. He closed the bedroom door behind him, and tiptoed along the landing, he stopped outside her door and listened, but it was completely silent; no crying, no urgent whispering. He almost thought of knocking, but decided it was too soon. He sneaked downstairs. The dogs didn't greet him; they just looked at him from their dog beds. He decided to ignore them, but was then suddenly overcome by a vision of Holly choking under his hand—it gave him a pain in the chest, so he pushed it out of his mind. Uncharacteristically, he went into the living room and started playing with the twin's Lego set. Surprised to be joined by their big brother, the twins showed Liam what they'd made. Sue had just finished preparing the evening meal.

'Now that's a sight you don't see very often!' Sue said, she leaned against the door, drying her hands. Liam looked up and gave her the sweetest smile possible.

'Hello Mum, good to see you.' He then made a fuss over one of the twin's Lego towers they'd built. Sue was puzzled, and more than a little unnerved by his reaction.

'Drink love?'

'Thanks Mum.' He smiled sweetly again. Sue noticed he'd been crying. She handed him a full glass of orange juice; he grabbed it and started gulping it down like he hadn't had drunk for weeks. Two lines of juice ran down his face and dripped onto the Lego. The twins watched this, and then looked at their mother who didn't do, or say anything. Almost finished, he gasped for air, his sister's face in his mind, her eyes wide, trying to speak; he pushed the image away again and fought back fresh tears. He wiped his mouth with the back of his hand and wished he could do the same with the image. Sue took the glass from him.

'Another?'

'No thanks—that was perfect. You know? Like when you've been running and someone gives you a drink and it's the best thing you've tasted—like—like mirage nectar . . . . ' Sue contemplated saying something, but decided against it, glad that Trevor would be home soon and would notice that something was up.

Upstairs, Holly contemplated leaving her room, but couldn't rouse herself from the bed. She knew there was no way she could keep what had happened from her mother, it was too upsetting; she knew her mother would sense it. To avoid any confrontation, she decided to say she wasn't feeling well, that way she could avoid dinner. Yet she desperately wanted to tell someone that Liam had really scared her; he'd threatened her the way a brother shouldn't. She put the quilt over her head.

I'll have nightmares—every night I'll see his horrible, smiling face.

She sobbed again, and wished she could tell her parents, she visualised her Mum holding her, and her Dad shouting at Liam, telling him he was wrong, and then Liam would be locked up somewhere far away. Yet at the same time, she loved her brother.

Maybe I shouldn't have burst into his room like that anyway—what did I think would happen? But what the hell was he holding in the air? And in his underpants?? He was freakishly strong too . . . .

Trevor arrived home, greeted by the dogs, twins, Sue, and even Liam, which he thought was downright strange. Trevor looked at Sue, who made a face like: *Don't ask!* He washed his hands and sat down, glad to be home. Sue handed him a beer, he cracked it, eyeing Liam with suspicion.

'Alright kiddo? Good day?' Liam nodded enthusiastically, his body belying what he was really feeling, as he bounced up and down on the sofa, playing with the twins. Trevor watched him, glad to see him out of his bedroom.

'Liam was playing with the twins and their Lego today, weren't you Liam?' He nodded, smiling in the same sickly sweet manner, which caused alarm bells in Trevor. Sue shot him a glance that said: *See, told you he was acting weird!* Liam pulled one of the twins onto his lap and started tickling him, the twin wriggled from Liam's grip and ran out into the kitchen to Sue.

'Everything alright Liam?' Trevor enquired. Liam nodded as he bounced up and down on the sofa.

'Why you doing that?' Trevor asked. Liam stopped, white faced.

'What—I haven't done anything!' Liam protested.

'I didn't say you'd done anything—look what is going on with you? I thought we'd talked about your behaviour . . . . ' Liam didn't answer, he got up and sat down at the dinner table. Shaking his head, Trevor organised the twins, then said to Liam,

'We'll talk after the meal if you want, if something has happened.' Liam swallowed hard, knowing he'd have to find a way to distract him.

'Where's Holly? She's usually the first one down,' Trevor asked. Sue shrugged. Liam was still acting strange, playing around with the twins, pretending the fork was a toy, making silly noises. Sue opened her eyes wide at Trevor; Trevor just closed his eyes and shook his head. Sue shouted up the stairs at Holly and thought she heard a faint reply. Thinking that meant she was coming down, she returned to the table, and passed round the dishes.

'Mutton stew. Lovely . . . . ' Liam said, as Sue spooned out two large portions. She looked at Trevor.

'You finish here, I'll go check on Holly.' This statement sent Liam into a semi-panic. He had to think fast, he knew he couldn't sit opposite his sister, so he pretended to have a pain in his stomach; although the tension he was feeling was real. He hammed up the pain, causing Trevor real concern.

'You alright?' Liam suddenly bent over double, fell to his knees and then to the floor. Trevor shouted up to Sue, who had her head in Holly's bedroom.

'Sue, SUE—it's Liam, he's collapsed!!' Sue rushed from Holly's room. Trevor was on his knees, not knowing what to do, while Liam was writhing on the floor. He decided to ring the nurse while Sue stroked Liam's head.

'The nurse is coming Liam.' She turned to Trevor saying, 'I thought he was acting a bit strange.' Then back to Liam, 'Don't worry, love, Christine will be here soon.' Liam got up slowly, but fell back down. He knew he'd gone overboard, the last thing he wanted was the nurse arriving.

'Feel a bit funny, that's all, what's all this fuss?'

'But your sister said she wasn't well either, so maybe we're looking at a stomach bug—hope it's not food poisoning!' Sue said to Trevor, who was only half listening. Liam, hearing this, pretended to make a remarkable recovery. He sat up slowly and seemed brighter, Trevor groaned,

'I just called the bloody Nurse!' Liam sat on the floor holding his stomach, he waved at everyone watching.

'False alarm! Feeling a little better now, I don't

want your delicious food to go to waste.' He attempted to get to his feet, but Sue stopped him.

'You stay there until the nurse—until Christine comes. How embarrassing, what with all the calls she's been having recently as well.' Liam nodded, pleased to have diverted all the attention away from Holly, yet knowing his piece of playacting would be his undoing. A part of him was glad of it, yet the pressure in his head would make him fight; he knew that.

Christine rushed inside to see Liam sitting on the sofa; Trevor sat next to him, looking embarrassed.

'Liam—how you doing?' Christine asked, pleased she didn't have to call the air ambulance in this fog. Liam looked forlorn.

'He's been acting strange Christine, for a couple of weeks,' Sue said. Trevor shot her a warning glance. Holly came downstairs after she heard all the commotion. She walked into the living room, feeling safer with her parents around. Liam spotted her. He shot up from his seat, not able to hold it in any longer.

'IT WASN'T MY FAULT! IT WASN'T MY FAULT HOLLY—PLEASSSSSE!' Holly shrank back. Trevor looked from his son to his daughter.

'HOLLY! What's going on?' Sue shouted. Holly turned and ran back upstairs. She sobbed loudly, in between saying it wasn't her fault either. The two twins, who'd watched the drama from the dinner table started crying too. This opened the floodgates for Liam, with tears flowing; he rocked to and fro, saliva dripping from his mouth. Trevor and Sue looked on, aghast. Sue grabbed the twins and coaxed them upstairs.

'I'm sorry, I'm sorry!' Liam grizzled. Christine bent down next to him.

'Sorry about what Liam? What's happened?' Christine asked kindly. Liam knew it was now or never.

'It's the treasure, IT'S DRIVING ME MAD!' he screamed and dissolved into more floods of tears. Christine took charge.

'Now take your time Liam, can you tell us what happened?' He rocked to and fro, then looked briefly at Trevor.

'I—I took your metal detector—I KNOW I SHOULDN'T!' Liam said, getting more agitated.

'It's OK Liam, I don't care about the metal detector —it's OK—it really is—just tell us what happened so we can get to the bottom of this, you'll feel better for telling lad!' he said in a soft tone. Liam snorted and sniffed back tears; mucus running down his face. Trevor grabbed a tissue from his pocket, he handed it to Liam who ignored him. A globule of snot fell and completely enclosed one of his shirt buttons; like a fly caught in amber.

'Come on Liam, let it out now—you can tell us . . . . ' Christine urged.

'I took your metal detector and I—I dug up some treasure!' Trevor looked at Christine who seemed bemused.

'OK—so you found some treasure—why is that so bad?' Liam turned to Trevor.

'When we were watching football, I asked you—and —and—you said it would be wrong to do that—AND I DID THAT WITHOUT PERMISSION DAD!' Trevor sat back shocked.

'Look, we can talk about what you're supposed to do another time, but why are you so upset?' Liam continued rocking to and fro, and then looked at Christine.

'It's embarrassing,' he said quietly, looking down.

'It's OK Liam; I've seen it all before. I've seen your Dad's bottom when he needed that tetanus injection.' Trevor looked doubly embarrassed and laughed.

'That's right; I wouldn't wish that on anyone!'

'THIS ISN'T THE SAME!' Liam shouted, hating the fact he had to spell it out for them—*why didn't they understand?* Christine decided to give him some space; she stood up and sat on the opposite chair. Christine mouthed to Trevor: *Do you want me to go?* Trevor shook his head fiercely.

'What happened with this treasure Liam, did it come alive?' Trevor joked. Liam shot him an angry glance, coupled with a monstrous undertone of hate. Shocked, Trevor looked to Christine, who looked concerned. Then Liam looked soft again and in distress.

'I can't stop thinking about it Dad. Every minute of every day—I just can't stop touching it.' Trevor leaned in closer and put his hand around his son's shoulders.

'We are still talking about the same thing are we?' Trevor teased, partly out of fear of what was happening. Liam stood up, throwing off Trevor's arm.

'NO YOU IDIOT! WE'RE NOT TALKING ABOUT THE SAME THING! A FUCKING PORNO MAG IS NOT GOING TO CURE THIS!' Liam started pacing. Trevor's eyes widened, and considering the circumstances, he decided to let Liam off for swearing.

'I CAN'T STOP THINKING ABOUT IT! WHAT DON'T YOU GET? I CAN'T EAT, SLEEP OR THINK— IT'S SO BLOODY STUPID!' He become more agitated, he started punching the arm of the sofa, so Trevor tried to stop him, then the dogs started barking. Christine intervened.

'Calm down—calm down Liam, or I'll have to call the doctor!' Christine said loudly, she hoped it would scare him, but it only made him worse.

'DON'T CARE! GET WHOEVER YOU WANT! GET THE KING OF ENGLAND . . . AND YOU CAN TELL HIM FROM ME HE'S NOT GETTING MY FUCKING TREASURE, IT'S *MY* TREASURE, HE'S A BORN LIAR! LEAVING ME WAS THE BEST THING HE DID, AND THAT BITCH UPSTAIRS, SHE CAN DIE, SHE CAN DIE FOR HER—HER . . . . ' Liam collapsed onto the floor. Christine shot over to him and checked if he was breathing.

'Liam? Liam, can you hear me love?' she said firmly. Liam groaned something.

'I'm just going to make a phone-call Trevor—don't leave him. Can I use your phone?'

'Can you use my phone? Course you can use the bloody phone, it's there!' Trevor snapped; his mood indurate. She called the doctor. Trevor leant down next to Liam.

'Liam, Liam, don't worry now—help's coming . . . . ' Christine returned.

'Because of this fog it makes everything difficult, the doctor has suggested we get Liam over to Yell, it's the quickest, and then from there she can call an air ambulance if need be.'

'That'll take 20 mins!' Trevor retorted angrily.

'I know—I know—but the air ambulance can't land in these conditions here, look, maybe Liam is just exhausted, but I can't risk it—I'm not a doctor. I'll ring the ferry crew now.' Sue came downstairs after hearing the shouting; she stood back at first then rushed forward.

'Liam! Oh Liam!' She fell to her knees next to him.

'Give him some room, love, Christine's just getting a ferry together to get him to Yell, nothing will land with this fog!' Sue wiped tears from her eyes. She whispered to Trevor.

'He attacked Holly—he threatened her, she's really

upset, I'm going to have to go back up, can you deal with this?' Trevor looked stunned.

'He attacked Holly? Is she alright?' he said in a low, frightened voice. Sue nodded.

'She just needs her Mum. OK?'

'What's going on Sue?' Trevor asked, in a small, sad voice, with the demeanour of a frightened child. It was hard for her to see him reduced to such a pathetic creature; she hugged him so hard he couldn't breathe. Christine came back with news.

'We're to get him to the ferry now, I'm going to get a stretcher for him, I'll need your help Trevor in a minute.' Trevor nodded, it snapped him out of his shock. Sue squeezed Trevor's hand, not wanting to release her grip.

'See you later love,' she whispered, 'ring me, won't you?'

'Of course, as soon as I know.' Christine and Trevor lifted Liam onto the stretcher, then disappeared into the thick fog. Holly was watching from the window; she saw faint figures before they disappeared. She felt numb. Sue ran back upstairs to the twins who were sitting in their bedroom looking sad.

'You boys, it's going to be alright. Liam's sick, that's all, he's going to the doctor to get well OK?' She hugged them both and switched on their favourite video and shut the door before running to Holly.

'Oh MUM!' Holly moaned, before breaking down into tears again. Sue held her tightly.

'You're safe now, you're safe now, there's something wrong with Liam so he's going to see the doctor, it'll all work out OK love.'

'I feel bad now I know he's ill . . . I SHOULD'VE TOLD YOU, BUT HE THREATENED TO KILL ME IF I DID!!' Holly shouted hysterically before breaking down again.

'I know—I know—you did the best you could Holly, you did the best you could!' Sue rocked her to and fro in her arms.

'You want a drink of something? How about a nice, sweet hot chocolate? The twins are going to need me too, and their big sister. Shall we all go downstairs so I can settle them down, and then we can chat some more?' Holly nodded solemnly. Sue went into the twin's room, they were both watching their video, but started crying when Sue came in and held out their arms; she pulled them both to her.

'It's OK boys, it's OK, would you like a milkshake? Chocolate milkshake?' Both boys nodded, blinking back enormous tears. They all went downstairs, Holly sat on the sofa with a twin either side and put on the TV, she flicked through the channels until she got to a nature programme.

'Yay, penguins!' Holly shouted as cheerily as she could. Sue came in with drinks for the twins; the brightly coloured straws floating at an odd angle. Sue settled them down and beckoned Holly into the kitchen. Holly looked back to see; they were holding the straws with their little fingers, and sucking contentedly, watching the penguins waddling around. Holly was grateful for the hot chocolate and sniffed its steam, inhaling deeply.

'It's half my fault really Mum, I crashed into his room, it was a really stupid thing to do—it really was!'

'No blame Holly, I just want you to feel safe, that's all.'

'I do now. I do.' She sipped the hot chocolate.

'When I burst in he was holding what looked like a big, golden cup and he had his hands . . . ' she paused and looked embarrassed. ' . . . his other hand was down his underpants Mum.' Sue nodded sagely, sighing.

'Then he went berserk, he grabbed me and threw me down on the bed, he was strong too Mum, really strong, I couldn't get away, I did try, I did!' Holly revealed, getting all upset again.

'I know you did, there's no blame here,' Sue said quietly. Holly nodded, sniffing.

'I know—but it was so *unlike* him. And his arm stunk something awful, I had to stop myself from throwing up, I think the smell was coming from that wristband he's been wearing.' Sue nodded, looking down.

'I don't know why he's wearing that—'

' . . . and he said—well—he said *he'd do things to me*, he touched my nipple. It was awful Mum, so awful —he was like a—a—like a dirty old man!!' Sue grabbed her chair and sat next to her, she rubbed Holly's back.

'He had his hand over my mouth, I couldn't breathe!' Holly recalled, growing breathless again with the memory

'I know love, I know, it must've been so frightening, you're safe now, safe now . . . . '

'I thought—I thought I'd never see you again!!' Holly whined, as she choked the tears back. Sue leant forward to look at her.

'He can't hurt you now, I know that doesn't change anything, but—he's going to get better, I'm sure of it, it may not be here, he may have to go to the hospital or something like that, but you won't be in any more danger, I promise you that, I really do—OK?' Holly nodded and clung to her hot chocolate, she gazed at Sue with the knowing trust that exists between a mother and daughter.

'I just want to check the twins OK?' Holly nodded; glad she could talk about it. Sue came back; she looked thoughtful.

'I'm going to see if I can find this gold cup you saw

—you OK here?' Holly nodded. Sue ran upstairs and cautiously entered Liam's bedroom. She picked up his quilt and searched his bed, but found nothing. She saw something shiny; a gold coin on the floor, she picked it up, briefly looked at it, then slipped it into her pocket. She pulled out his bedside drawers, but found nothing. She turned to the wardrobe and found the goblet, roughly wrapped in a dirty t-shirt. She sat on the bed and unwrapped it, gasping at how ornate it was, and heavy. Unsure what to do, she considered calling the Community Council Chairman. She went back downstairs with the cup.

'Is this it?' Sue questioned Holly, who gasped, partly out of fear.

'I guess so, I mean, how many of these could he have?' Sue shrugged.

'I found it in the wardrobe; maybe I should go and check everything else; that alright with you?' Holly nodded.

'I'm feeling a bit better now Mum, thanks.' Sue kissed Holly long on the forehead and disappeared upstairs. After searching deeper into his belongings in the wardrobe, she discovered the gold arm band, some coins inside his football boots, and more coins in an old margarine tub. She felt a sense of despair and dread come upon her and tried to dismiss it. Sue took them downstairs.

'Wow! That's a lot of coins! I wonder where he found all this?' Holly exclaimed. She picked up a coin and studied it.

'I've no idea, but can you imagine how excited he'd have been to find it? I mean, Liam can't even keep Christmas presents a secret!' Sue quipped. Holly picked up the armband and put it against her skin.

'NO! Don't do that!' Sue shouted. Holly stopped, fearful.

'Mum! You scared me!!'

'Sorry Holly. I don't have a very good feeling about any of this, I'm going to talk to Ronald, stay here, don't touch anything.'

'Mum, don't be too long, just in case there's a phone call.' Sue disappeared across the street to Ronald's house. Holly took out her mobile phone and snapped a picture of all the treasure; then took another to be sure. Sue returned with an excited Ronald in tow.

'Bairns, bairns!' Ronald said excitedly, he immediately picked up the cup, he turned it around in admiration.

'That's amazing! I wonder—where did he find it?'

'We don't know—we didn't get that far before they carted him off,' Sue reported, glad to be able to share it with an official person. Ronald was utterly gold struck. He picked up a coin and muttered to himself.

'What shall we do with it all?' Sue asked. The twins walked into the kitchen, Holly quickly redirected them back into the living room.

'I don't know, I guess I might speak to Mackey, he might know. But WOW! Spectacular! And you say your Liam was sitting on all this? Oh—how is he by the way?' Ronald enquired as an afterthought, without taking his eyes from the cup.

'I don't know yet.' It dawned on Sue that she didn't know; she slumped down into a kitchen chair. Ronald noticed and snapped out of his fugue.

'The ferry boys will get him there quick as they can, they've done this before; getting folk to the doctor—don't you worry now. Do you mind if I take all this to Mackey? I'll keep you informed about it?'

'Sure, get it out of here, at least it won't be here when Liam comes back—I guess it'll go to the Museum?' Sue was glad to be rid of it.

'Something as valuable as this? Noooo. It'll probably end up in Edinburgh. It's an amazing find, and Liam will be attributed—as—as finding it.' Sue looked around the kitchen, found a small box and put the items in.

'Do what needs to be done Ronald—you're the Chairman. Liam won't be in any sort of trouble will he?' Ronald shook his head.

'No—well, I mean—you're not supposed to just go digging around—but let's just say we'll put it down to experience this time,' he replied confidently. He had already decided to keep the treasure for the night before showing it to Mackey the following day.

'So, I'll be off now, leave you to think of your boy— night all!' Then suddenly remembering himself, he turned and said,

'You'll let me know how he is when you know?'

'As soon as we know.' Ronald disappeared into the fog, having every intention to keep several coins. Even from a distance, the black box weaved its ancient cantrip, manipulating all innocent souls, and those who had the misfortune of misjudging its power. On the way home, he found himself humming a tune he didn't know.

CHAPTER SEVENTEEN

It had only been a day since they'd met; but Fruma was impatient to see Lily again. Mackey had rung and asked her to come round, he sounded curt, so Fruma knew to get round to his house as soon as possible. She arrived and rushed in buoyantly. Mackey was at his computer; mouse in one hand, mug of tea in another. He didn't offer her a cup of tea, this made her feel uneasy.

'Have I got some news for you!' she said, trying to break the tension. He looked at her silently, eventually replying.

'If you want to make enemies of people round here, you're sure making a—doing a good job of it! You can't just knock on people's doors you don't know . . . . ' He stopped, realising he was shouting.

'You planned this, didn't you, is that why you didn't go to the Hamefarin with me? You were planning to go to Lily's?'

'Skittles! Is that what you think? I'm not that under-handed! It was a spur of the moment thing.'

'But she wanted me to talk to you first,' he lied, 'then I was supposed to bring you to her—then I could always act as a go-between—between the two of you—in case of awkwardness, arguments, and suchlike—' She looked down, realising that she'd sidestepped Mackey; usurped his position.

'Mia Culpa. Mia Culpa. Will you forgive me? It just so happens that we got on just fine—I admit it—it was a risk going to see her—but boy—have I got some news for you!' She raised an involuntary finger to her lip. He spotted it.

'What happened to your lip?'

'Da and Ted. They were waiting for me—guess I had it coming.' He rose up from his seat in righteous indignation; his face red. She shushed him.

'It doesn't matter, in the scheme of things . . . .' He started protesting again.

'LISTEN—listen. I've got some news for you. ' He looked at her solemnly for a moment and then, realising he might get some answers to the mystery; bounded off to the kitchen to make tea.

'I haven't had breakfast yet, do you want the full Mackey doorstop with all the trimmings?' She thought about it, having only picked at a piece of toast at Mary's.

'I could eat a whole Shetland pony,' she shouted back. She curled her legs under her and debated whether to tell Mackey about what Da and Ted did. Maybe the cut was a small price to pay for the upset that everyone had been feeling, and she had over-stepped the mark by visiting Lily. He called her into the kitchen. They silently ate great slabs of bread filled with Lincolnshire sausage, double fried egg and bacon. She ate like she'd never seen food. He eyed her cautiously, he felt the air had shifted, that she was somehow different. He struggled with annoyance too —he had wanted to be there when she met Lily. He wanted to be the instigator. He wanted to be the lead. But his annoyance didn't last long, because he had his own exciting news to share, in the form of a visit from Ronald.

'Why does food taste so damned good at times, when you least expect it to?' she said, then, seeing his peeved expression, she reigned herself back in.

'You know, you can come to Lily's—you're in this up

to your neck too,' she said, mouth half-full, grinning. Hearing this, he brightened up.

'I've got some news—but you first—can't wait to hear yours,' he said, genuinely grateful that she'd included him. She told him what had happened; becoming emotional when revealing that Haby was her friend at the orphanage. He became emotional too, even though he liked to be in charge, he cared for Fruma and shared in her news as if he'd been right beside her at Lily's. He was amazed, hearing about the Papar burying the treasure, and about the Shamir. She felt his warmth return and was grateful for it, she couldn't bear going through all this if she fell out with him. He had become a stabilising force. She realised that she loved him; and probably had loved him ever since their first meeting.

'My goodness Fruma, so what does it all mean? I just can't get my head around you being—with the birthmark . . . and the Shamir being here, on our small island.'

'Nor can I. Nor can I. It was bad enough finding out about Haby. Can you get the piece of paper with the AdderStane Prophecy on it; I'd like to read it again.' He obliged. This time, she read it aloud.

'From the north, a taste forbidden
The shells of youth abandoned here.
Lay sleeping in, a dreamless sky
Limbs fortell an ancient why.
The tirrick calls, the land is still
Wanderer's hand a heavy load
The AdderStane, this sleeping rock
Walks the road redemption shows

Whirl in stars, in winter stirs
As summer sun fast fades.

The queen of Heaven riding high
Cosmos turns, AdderStane replies.
The menacing north is put to right
Dybbuk fool to one is turned
To set them free, she must calm
Unfailing end to free the shore'

She marvelled at the Queen of Heaven reference. Instinctively, she touched her birthmark through her clothing.

'What's a tirrick?'

'The Shetland name for the Arctic Tern, there are many birds that arrive for summer, but the tirrick is— I don't know—somehow special. It hangs around the coastline, its swooping and diving is delightful. I liken them to swallows and swifts. The Queen of Heaven riding high eh? I bet that was a shock!' He chuckled with delight, visualising Lily's personal inspection of Fruma.

'You have no idea. At one time Mackey, I considered seeking help to get this birthmark removed, I mean it's not small, and if I was going to be with a man, he might have found it repulsive,' she explained shyly.

'I don't know about that—I mean—if a man loves a woman . . . . ' He blushed slightly. She noticed and inwardly hugged herself. She knew that he felt something for her.

'I don't suppose I? No—that would be asking too much . . . . ' She smiled coyly, knowing what he desired. She stood up and slowly removed her sweater. His blush deepened. Discreetly, she pulled up her blouse and went over to him, standing to one side, so he could see. He put on his reading glasses. His eyes first settled on her pretty, white bra before he mentally slapped himself. He studied the birthmark carefully. She wished he'd touch it, touch her, hold her —and more.

'Cassiopeia, there it is,' he said, with wonder, 'and the outline of Fetlar is so clear—fascinating—absolutely fascinating!' She stepped back, smiling. After her run in with Da, she'd spent the next day being quiet, alone in her room, convalescing, recovering from the shock of the news, and of being attacked. She dwelt on all that had happened, standing in front of the mirror gazing at her birthmark. She felt great sorrow too, for Da and Ted; because of their fear, they had to gang up on a woman—that Ted was still mourning the loss of a friend; *that* she could at least understand. And Da, she knew deep down he was telling the truth, that he never meant it to go that far.

'I have some news for you too,' he said proudly.

'Of course! I'm sorry—please, I'd love to hear it, although I'm chocka-block with revelation, I'll do my best.' He left a dramatic pause before speaking.

'The Community Council Chairman visited me yesterday, it seems that a boy called Liam.' Fruma stopped him, she reached forward and placed her hand on his hand.

'Liam?' He nodded, and was about to continue,

'That's the boy I picked up at the ferry terminal two days ago—I'd been to Noss—oh course, I haven't told you, well—I hadn't seen you. I was coming back from Noss and this boy Liam wanted a lift back to his house, the council estate—'

'Stakkafletts.'

'That's right. So, of course, I couldn't leave him there. Anyway, we were talking about how long he'd been on the island, and then he said something peculiar—that *Bensalem* was in trouble, and then he disappeared. Seriously Mackey, he just disappeared. Gone. I tell you, then it went all weirdly deja vu at Mary's, and Peter said, 'Did he scare you?' She tailed off, realising she'd interrupted him. He was nodding while listening.

'Lily said that Bensalem was an old name for Fetlar.' He shook his head in wonder.

'You have been so lead down this path Fruma—nothing surprises me now. Maybe he was reaching out to you, maybe he was in trouble, maybe you could've helped him like you helped the other children.' This must have hit something in her because she shot him an accusing glance.

'How could I? He disappeared! He was there one minute, gone the next! It was all a bit too weird for me, I'm afraid. I just bottled it up. I'm sorry—please continue, and I'll try not to interrupt.'

'I was going to say, Liam had dug up some treasure.' She interrupted again.

'Liam dug up some treasure?' She stopped, embarrassed.

'Yes—Liam dug up some treasure Fruma,' Mackey said pedantically. She made a face and looked down.

'I wonder if . . . .' Mackey looked at her, exasperated.

'From the north, a taste forbidden—do you think the prophecy is talking about Liam digging up the treasure? The *shells of youth* abandoned here—and the 'wanderer'—I wonder if that's Haby?'

'You could be right, or the shells of youth could mean yourself—you know—you leave your past behind? Shells of youth? Something like that?' Mackey said, his thoughts whirling.

'Anyway—let me just finish. *Then*—then he was taken off to hospital. It's unclear *why* he's in hospital —Ronald didn't say, anyway, he brought round the treasure for me to look at . . . not quite sure why, oh, maybe it's because I'm the Minister, the coins had crosses on them you see. Anyway, he's taken them back at the moment. But I took a photo—here—look.' He leant backwards in his chair to a cabinet behind him, picked up his iPad, and turned on the screen. He handed it to her—she almost dropped it in shock. Speechless, she put her hands to her face.

'What? What? What is it?' he said, alarmed, she put up her hand, stopping him, she paused as if in recollection and returned to the iPad.

'Well, I am shocked—but I guess I shouldn't be surprised. That's the cup from my dream,' she replied. He half hopped in his seat, all of a flutter.

'The reason I remember it, is because of the lion. So what Lily was telling me was right about the treasure, that it had been found—so that means Liam might have the Shamir—if it's the same treasure that is . . . and not some other treasure.' He sat back in his seat, chuckling and slapping his thigh.

'My good God! What an amazing coming together of—of—things!' he blurted out.

'Where is the treasure now? Does Lily know about it?' she asked, concerned.

'Ronald still has it, it's safe enough for now, but there was nothing else that small in the cup—if you say the Shamir is small. It could've been lost, or maybe it's still in Liam's bedroom. Do you think I should go and find it, go round to Liam's house? I mean—they know who I am, and I don't expect Lily's contacts want Ronald to know what's going on.' She shrugged, but was worried.

'I don't know, I don't even know what's next for me, now we have all this information. All I know is I have the mark. But the Shamir must be found before it's too late. I remember asking Lily what would happen if it falls into the wrong hands, she said, *"God help us all."'* Mackey chewed his thumbnail.

'Maybe it is time to give her a call, especially now the treasure has turned up, you're right; or it might be too late.'

Mackey and Fruma were standing in Lily's front room. It looked to Fruma as if Lily and Mackey were practising their synchronised pacing. All were nervous, knowing the final pieces of the puzzle would mean either saving Fetlar or failing. Fruma couldn't even contemplate how, or in what form her life would continue. Surely she couldn't go back to Gateshead as if nothing had happened and continue with her previous life? What did she expect? Maybe she had arrived on Fetlar just to set the wheels in motion, not *be* the wheels; these thoughts continually plagued her. Mackey combed his hair with his hands. He strained to see the visitor through the fog as he walked along the garden path; all he could see was a pair of shiny, black shoes. Anxiously, he wiped his hands on his sweater.

'Come in, come in,' Lily gushed, leading the visitor to the living room. Frater Alick nodded to each of them in turn before setting his eyes on Fruma. She detected a slight smile. Feeling nervous, Lily switched a side lamp on, plumped up a cushion, and then showed him to an armchair. Alick said nothing and sat perfectly upright, like a trained ballerina, with both legs clamped together. He was of medium height, and weight, his hair showed no sign of aging, was dark brown, greased, and parted in the middle. Mackey noticed his suit fit him perfectly; like a nut in a nutshell.

'Can I get you anything?'

'No, I'm fine, thank-you.' He pulled out the pale blue folder from his briefcase. Mackey noticed how perfectly neat his fingernails were; the white of the nail was an exact strip as if it had been cut against a ruler.

'Fruma knows everything I told you?' he asked. Lily nodded, she was clasping and unclasping her hands.

'Please, don't be nervous, any of you. We're all here because we want to see peace restored to Fetlar, and we, my other colleagues and I, want an important item returned to its resting place. But firstly to you Fruma. It's time for you to know the whole truth.' She took a deep breath and smiled awkwardly at Mackey and Lily.

'You spent the first part of your life in our orphanage, along with your brother, Ben.' Fruma took a sharp intake of breath, she stood up. Mackey immediately put an arm around her shoulders.

'Yes, that's right, she needs you Mackey. I'm sorry my dear, that we couldn't tell you. You were twins.' This time, Lily gasped out loud, tears falling naturally for her husband.

'That means we're related Fruma,' Lily announced. Fruma just stared, open mouthed. Mackey interrupted with a thought.

'Look to the place that's divided—Fruma—do you think the Tait sisters meant you and your brother being divided?' Fruma turned to Mackey, eyes wide; she could hardly bear the news.

'Why wasn't I told he was my brother, why did you make me think he was just—a friend,' Fruma said, accusatorily.

'We had our reasons—you were both important—but Haby—Ben—he was a darker soul. He couldn't find out about you, what you are—what you bear on your body, so we thought it best if we told you both different stories.'

'It was cruel of you, saying he'd died—I presume you planned that,' Fruma said angrily. Alick nodded.

'And as you know, we told him the same story.' It was Lily's turn to be angry.

'You caused him so much pain, both of them a lot of pain—was it really necessary?'

'You'll have to trust me that it was.' Alick said with such command, no more was said in that regard. Fruma sat back down, Mackey stayed by her side. She was glad of his support.

'What about our real parents? Why did Haby go to Norway?'

'We gave Haby to a couple from the Order, we thought it was best, he was far away from England— from temptation. We could only hope that he would eventually settle down, maybe marry, and forget about his past. But he was a difficult child, and restless. As soon as he could leave home legally he did. He drifted from one place to another.' Fruma interrupted.

'*Wanderers hand a heavy load . . . .* ' Alick bowed at Fruma, who looked delighted at uncovering some of the Prophecy.

'You understand. Good. But we kept an eye on him. Eventually he found the place he was looking for; Fetlar, but luckily nothing else; and he tried to use you to help him Lily—that ended badly, but perhaps it was for the best. We didn't want to get rid of him—but it was getting close at one point to being the only solution.' Lily looked full of remorse; as if the past had come back and sat on her shoulders.

'So you know what happened to Haby then,' Fruma asked. Lily looked heartbroken.

'He was swallowed up by his own darkness, greed and negativity my dear. 237—Papil Water enclosed him, it enclosed him in His Name.' Fruma had a sudden flashback, to hearing those words before—then she recalled the assistant's words at the Shetland Archives, when he misread from the computer screen: 'enclosed in his name' She chuckled in wonder. Everyone turned to face her. She apologised.

'So he's on the bottom of Papil Water?' Lily asked, she could feel no more sad than she already was. Alick made a face.

'Not exactly—it's very complicated—let's just say, he's not in this world anymore, and leave it at that.' He changed the subject.

'He was given the name Ben by your mother, but as soon as he could, he changed his name to Haby. It means 'to hide'. You might have already worked out how important names are for a person Fruma.' She looked at Mackey and nodded.

'He hoped he could hide his actions, be less obvious, but he had such a restless spirit, and he was easy manipulated by other powerful forces.'

'What about Heed?' Lily asked in a small voice. Alick looked at her with such a great compassion that Fruma walked over to Lily and held her hand.

'You chose an unfortunate name for him Lily—or was it Haby's choice?' Lily nodded.

'Haby—he said it was a special name—to him.' Alick shook his head.

'If you take out an E from Heed's name, you get the Jewish name: Hed—which means *echo*. I think Haby was hoping to use Heed if he didn't succeed in finding the treasure. Heed's own innocent goodness stopped the force, but unfortunately it turned in on him.' Lily shook her head sadly. Fruma put an arm around her and said comforting words.

'Your parents were good people Fruma.' Alick lifted a piece of paper from the blue folder and handed it to her. She read it aloud.

Seventeenth of September 1944

My Dearest Fruma

If you are reading this letter, then I am no longer in this world and you are with important people who will tell you that you are special; the last of a remaining line of people. I, your real mother, have kept this secret and my mother before me. One day Fruma, you may be called upon to help, entrusted with that which must pass in secret. If you doubt this letter, then I can tell you that you were given a piece of jewellery, a necklace, on your 12th birthday that bears this symbol. I'm sorry I cannot be with you, but know that you are eternally loved by me and your father. Your adopted parents will hold the secret and keep you safe. Finally, to prove the authenticity of this letter, I leave you with a small blessing you may remember from your dear adopted parents:

In the dark places—light—walk in truth and beauty.

Your ever loving Mother.

'My goodness,' Fruma said quietly. Mackey put his arm around her. She smiled weakly at him, glad to feel him holding her—stopping her from falling; her mind darting from one idea to another.

'I do remember that saying, my adopted parents would say this to me every night. And to think—I never really gave them a chance. I never let them in. Phew, it's a lot to take in, it really is, but why were we both in an orphanage?'

'It was the best we could do—there were so few of

us. The orphanage knew all about it. It was they who carefully watched over the two of you—until they realised you had to be separated. They saw Haby— Ben's temperament change, they saw his darkness Fruma, but you only saw the good in him.' Fruma looked back at the letter and then pulled from her trouser pocket a small bunch of keys. She separated the pendant; it always reminded her of an intestinal labyrinth, with its concentric circles. She handed it to Mackey to look at.

'I was originally given this pendant on a necklace, as the letter says, on my twelfth birthday. I stopped wearing it when I was about sixteen, people kept asking me what it meant and I didn't know, so I put it away. It was about twenty years ago that I discovered it again and attached it to my key-ring. I hadn't even thought about it for decades, I guess it was just always there. Now I know how precious this is, I might wear it again. Does it say in there what it represents?' Mackey piped up.

'It doesn't need to, I know what it means.' Fruma suddenly burst forth a recollection, from the first time she met Mackey.

'Of course! You have this symbol on your garden gate! Why didn't I see it? Why didn't I make the connection at the time?' Looking at her he smiled and chuckled at the example.

'At the right time—only when we're meant to recognise it, eh Fruma? Actually, it was there on the gate before I arrived, so I don't know who put that there. The symbol is the sevenfold labyrinth of life—it's a lovely pendant, obviously handmade. It's the symbol of growth and development of man, it's an ancient symbol, it also depicts the seven energy centres of the body. There's a riddle on how to get out of the labyrinth, but maybe that's for another time. It is a very special pendant Fruma—very special.' He handed it back to Fruma who smiled weakly, she felt as though part of her was slipping away, she felt almost drowsy, faint, but tried to pull herself together.

'So my real parents, what happened to them?' Alick pulled out another document.

'They were living in Poland during the Second World War and were captured whilst trying to escape to one of The Order's safe houses. Your father was taken to a concentration camp where he perished. Your mother was in another camp and found out she was pregnant with you. One of the doctors was taken from among the Jewish prisoners to work for the Nazi's—she was to ascertain if any of the Jewish women were pregnant, and if they were, they were to be immediately killed. This doctor decided instead to carry out abortions to *save* the women's lives, but it was towards the end of the War that she had second thoughts, and saved your mother from an abortion in the hope that you would be born, and the Jewish race would survive and continue—apparently it was highly risky for her to do this. A week later, the camp was liberated, and your mother was freed. The Order found her and took her back, but she was in a terrible malnourished condition and due to complications, she died in labour. As I said, there were—are so few of us, that we put we you with friends in the Orphanage, knowing you'd be safe there . . . we hoped that one day you would be drawn to Fetlar, and we had contacts that alerted us.'

'You sent me that letter?'

'We didn't. We sent one to Haby, to try to warn him off.' It was Lily's turn to speak.

'Haby received one, years ago. Mackey told me about your letter—the wording on his was exactly the same as yours.' Fruma handed Alick the envelope.

'These are echoes—simply echoes—there are other forces at work Fruma.' Alick said solemnly. 'Shall we continue?' Fruma nodded, occasionally looking down and fiddling with her pendant.

'Can I just ask one question, does this mean I'm Jewish?'

'Yes. You are—were—both Jewish. Your mother was a very enlightened woman, she requested you be named Fruma before she died, it's your grandmother's name. She also perished in one of the camps.' Fruma turned to Mackey, they both exchanged knowing looks.

'Yes, and more Fruma,' Alick said gently, 'you are the last of a line of people.'

'Sounds like something out of the Da Vinci Code!!' Fruma said, joking, then seeing Alick's expression, she looked aghast.

'Seriously? Last of a line of people?' she repeated.

'You, my dear Fruma, are the last of the line of the Papar, and the *only* one left who can safely rebury the Shamir.' With this news, she stood up and went to the window. Mackey went to join her, she held his hand tightly. She was feeling decidedly odd, and Alick's words seemed distant.

'Jesus Mackey!' she whispered.

'I know—I know!' he hissed back.

'Haby also wanted the Shamir Fruma, he knew through magic that it was here, and tried to raise it. Heed found part of what Haby used for casting his spells into Papil Water—the piece of wood—but when Liam finally dug up the treasure, it released all the negativity that Haby had created that resided in Papil Water, that's why the island is again under a negative energy, especially at Tresta. Liam digging up the treasure caused the black water to happen. It's like a kind of underwater shock—the bowels of the earth objecting to the wrong person capturing the Shamir.'

'It is frowned upon to dig for treasure here—is that why Fetlar doesn't look into many of its sites?' Mackey asked him.

'Yes, we block anything that comes up—that way there's no chance of stumbling on it.'

'But what about that black water happening in 1768? Did that mean that someone had found the treasure again?' Mackey asked.

'Like I said, there are other forces at work. We weren't the only ones looking for the Shamir.' Fruma looked into the swirling fog; finding out she was somebody totally different; a Jew and a Papar, utterly overwhelmed her. She stared out of the window and sighed.

'So what now? Now I'm not who I thought I was.'

'You need to find the Shamir, as Lily told you, and to bury it again. No-one else on this earth can do it. It has to be buried in the earth, it's too powerful to be in the hands of man. The cup that housed it is also special and we must retrieve that from your Chairman Mackey. If need be—we will take care of that. Look, I'm sorry to lay this burden on you Fruma, but there's a lot at stake.'

'Did Liam tell anyone where he found it?' Alick asked. No-one knew.

'What about the shin—the four-pronged shin?' Fruma said to Mackey.

'OF COURSE! On the stone at the Hjaltadans. Da brought me some old photos.' Alick smiled and nodded.

'All the players are in place.' Alick said in a distant voice. He turned to Fruma.

'The Shamir cut the first set of tablets—the Ten Commandments. It has been in existence—it has always been in the mind of God. But God works with humanity, he gives us choices, and inevitably, we usually make the wrong ones.' Fruma and Mackey gasped at the enormity of his words.

'The AdderStane Prophecy, can you tell us more? Haby is the wanderer, as you confirmed,' Fruma enquired. Alick nodded.

'There are three depths to the Prophecy: I can only tell you information on the simple level, that it's ultimately talking about you and your brother.'

'What about the dybbuk fool?' Mackey asked.

'That is yet to come Reverend.' A silence fell over them all. Fruma fingered her seven-fold labyrinth and wondered about her mother; what she looked like. Mackey's mind was on retrieving the Shamir.

'I could visit Liam's parents, they at least know who I am. I could ask to search Liam's room?' Silence. Alick appeared to be thinking. Mackey continued.

'If you could tell me what it looks like . . . . '

'Thank-you Mackey. You'll feel it first, if it's there at all, but remember, you will not be able to pick it up—you must allow Fruma to do that.'

Mackey took the car on Frater Alick's instructions, even though Lily's house was a stone's throw from the Stakkafletts estate. He wondered how on earth he could persuade Sue and Trevor to let him rummage around in their son's bedroom, and what if Liam had chucked the Shamir away, not knowing what it was? It could have been discarded, now sitting at the place where he found the treasure, or maybe the wind blew it away; this could all be a waste of time—and then what? He pulled up outside the row of houses, but couldn't remember which house it was; his head was buzzing with so much information. He took a moment to calm down, then he remembered—it could be one of two houses. Choosing one, he walked up to the back door and rapped loudly. A white faced Sue opened it, surprised to see him; immediately thinking the worst.

'Sue, it's the Minister, I need to talk to you briefly. May I come in?'

'Is it about Liam? Is he alright?' she said anxiously. Mackey kicked himself for forgetting that Liam had been taken to hospital.

'Sorry, I should have mentioned that—no, it's not about Liam's health, don't worry,' Mackey explained, Sue visibly calmed down. Holly was standing in the hallway.

'Hello Minister,' she said shyly. Mackey acknowledged her with a nod. Sue offered him a chair in the kitchen.

'Don't want the twins to get wind of something up, we'll chat here, do you mind?' Sue explained.

'How is Liam by the way?' Mackey enquired, his ministerial formalities taking over.

'Christine and Trevor took him over to Yell in the ambulance—it was so awful seeing him like that. Still, I'm just glad he's in the right place, I hope we hear some news about him soon,' Sue replied, glancing at Holly. Holly made a thin line of a smile.

'Sue, you're going to think it odd what I'm going to ask of you . . . . '

'Odd? Looks like odd is our middle name at the moment!' she said, resignedly.

'I understand. I know this fog and weird events are pushing folk to their limits, but I've had a visit from some—some religious people who've been looking into what's been happening on the island, they know about the treasure your son found, and they say that something crucial is missing—what I mean is—we need to find this other item if we want this fog to lift and to stop more weird events happening. I have an idea what the item could be—would you give me permission to check your son's room for it?'

'If it can help the island and Liam, then you go ahead. Maybe this treasure being dug up is the cause of the whole thing that's happened here? I certainly know it affected Liam—so please, find the item, and here's hoping that your religious people can help us!' Sue crossed her arms defensively. She felt guilty for not being assertive enough with Liam in the first place, knowing he hadn't been right for a couple of weeks. He gave a huge sigh of relief.

'You've no idea how grateful I am Sue, so very grateful,' he said, anxious to get on with the search.

'I'll take you to his room.' They climbed the stairs, Mackey braced himself for anything. She opened Liam's door, it looked like a normal boy's room, untidy and a little cheesy smelling. She noticed and opened the window.

'I'm going to leave you to get on with it Minister.'

'Mackey, please—call me Mackey, everyone else does.' She nodded and left, then returned briefly.

'I found some other items in the wardrobe—so don't be afraid to take a good look around. Good luck,' she said, feeling a flash of sadness at seeing a stranger in Liam's room. It made her think of a TV drama where the police search the room for clues after some poor soul had been murdered.

He carefully removed every item from the wardrobe and laid them out on the bed, checking pockets and shoes before placing everything back. No luck. He removed everything from the chest of drawers, he found one of the gold coins wrapped in a pair of underpants; he slipped it into his pocket. He checked under the bed, the mattress and the chest of drawers. Nothing. He picked up the metal bin, and felt a wave of energy, it made him dizzy. He sat on the bed attempting to push the feeling back. Remembering Frater Alick's words, he gasped in relief; the Shamir must be in the bin. At the time, Liam didn't have a clue about what resided inside the black wood, and had become so frustrated with the Shamir's power, that at one point, before his breakdown, he threw it in the bin. This was merely a metaphoric desire; of wanting rid of it.

He extracted the carrier bag, and tipped the contents on the floor, a few crisps and sweet packets stared back at him, he even checked the crisp bags—nothing. He posited the thought that this item could be anywhere. Feeling defeated and tired, he went to put the carrier bag back when he noticed some debris at the bottom of the metal bin; some old, stuck on boiled sweets, but peering closer he saw a small black piece of wood, about the size of a matchbox. His heart leapt. Overcome with emotion and relief, he reached for it, then felt a wave of sadness hit him. He almost burst into tears. This was the power of the Shamir. He reached in to pick up the box, this time, his fingers touched thin air. The box had disappeared! He peered into the gloom, it had changed position. He reached in again—his fingers flailed around in the thin air. He peered in, the box had moved again. So this time, he tipped it onto the floor, wondering why he hadn't done that in the beginning. Confident of capturing it this time, Mackey used all his energy to concentrate—he reached over, and this time, he saw it clearly, but the box seemed to momentarily vanish until he removed his fingers. Mackey was bursting with annoyance that he couldn't pick it up—he almost had it in his possession. The power of the Shamir increased the desire in Mackey, the same way it did for Liam—only in Mackey's case, he wasn't as innocent as Liam. The Shamir brought out Mackey's underlying desire to be the lynchpin of the island, to rule and lead men. Mackey swore, annoyed he'd have to bring Fruma to retrieve it. He went downstairs to talk to Sue.

'The item I need is upstairs on the floor, however, I cannot remove it, I'm going to bring someone who can, is that alright? Please don't attempt to remove it yourself,' Mackey said, knowing it was asking a lot from her, allowing more strange people into her son's bedroom.

'That's fine. No-one will enter the room until you have what you need.' She was glad that she might be rid of a potential threat to her family. Mackey thanked her and rushed back to Lily's.

'I found it Fruma! It disappeared every time I tried to pick it up. Can you—can you come and get it?' Mackey shouted, in-between gasping for air. Alick stood up.

'I told you, Fruma is the only one can handle it.' He moved closer to Mackey, who almost shrank into the floor. Alick narrowed his eyes.

'It saw you Mackey, it saw your deepest desires.' A shadow crossed Mackey's face. He whispered in Mackey's ear.

'You are a fool for trying to bypass Fruma—you are the *dybbuk fool*.' Shocked, Mackey stepped backwards. Alick grabbed him by the arm of his jumper and pulled him roughly back towards him, he continued whispering.

'You see now—its power. Resist it Mackey. Now you know, you must resist it. This is the nearest you have ever been to God's power on earth; through his Creation. If you truly care for this island, take Fruma to it

—now—and let her retrieve it.' Ashamed and guilty, Mackey's head nodded so hard in agreement, that Alick thought it might drop off.

'Fruma, it's down to you.' Alick leaned over with a low bow. Fruma didn't know what to make of the gesture, so she half-bowed, half-curtsied back.

'We'd better get going—Sue's waiting for us,' Mackey pointed out. It was the longest car journey Fruma felt she'd ever made; as if time itself was stretching. The fog appeared to be thicker, with searching fingers that threatened even the interior of the car. Mackey didn't say a word to her throughout the whole journey; he was so fixed on the goal and resisting his own temptations. They both felt it, a strange, sapping of strength. He seemed to drive slower and slower, the fog so thick there was no telling where the road started or ended. Fruma stared into the white wall of silence that now filled the car, feeling herself drift away.

THE ADDERSTANE – PART TWO

CHAPTER EIGHTEEN

$2-3-7$. Did she hear right? There was a noise in the distance; a police siren. Police? On Fetlar? Lying still, she realised that she was no longer heading towards Sue's house in the hope of securing the Shamir. She heard passing teenagers talking and giggling. Disorientated, she didn't dare open her eyes, too afraid of what she might find.

'Laura? Laura? Can you hear me?' Laura opened her eyes to a familiar face; it was Dr. Janis Kowalski, her therapist, who was looking at her expectantly.

'Sit up slowly, take your time now.' Laura's breathing became laboured and panicky.

'Did you say 237? Where am I? It doesn't sound like Fetlar but . . . . '

'I was counting down for you to come back. Just take things slowly, I told you this could happen, take your time.'

'Did something go wrong? I don't understand—'

'I know, it might take some time to adjust and assimilate the information—we talked about this.' Laura sat up, shocked and confused.

'But I was Fruma and there was a minister called Mackey, we were on a remote island. Oh my God—it—it felt so real!' Laura's therapist smiled.

'I know; and that was only a short session . . . . '

'I found out who I really was—the last of the Papar —it felt like I'd been there for weeks.'

'The feeling will subside. Just sit quietly.' Ignoring her, Laura looked down at herself; she was wearing a smart, white blouse, a black, knee-length skirt and black Suedette platform heels. It felt alien not wearing Fruma's walking shoes and casual trousers. She went to chew her fingernails, but they were painted and highly manicured. She stood up a little unsteadily, smoothed down her blouse and went to the window. She wanted a Fetlar landscape to stare back at her; even the fog would've been acceptable. She instinctively put a hand on the place where she had the birthmark, then frowned, knowing that here, she had no such mark on her body.

'Can you tell me what happened?' Janis asked. Laura leaned on the windowsill.

'I was a retired teacher. I wasn't happy at first, but I had a special birthmark, I had a purpose—the Prophecy was about me.' She felt hollow and alone knowing she'd never see Mackey again. An ache in her chest, overwhelmed her, then the tears flowed. Janis offered her some tissues. She knew that no amount of tears would bring any of it back.

'Come on now, sit back down, this is quite normal, feeling disorientation.' Janis pressed the intercom button. 'Mrs. Temple, can you bring through a cup of tea for Miss Harrison—look, I know it's upsetting— let's go through it together,' Janis said kindly. Laura took a tissue and dabbed at her eyes. Pulling the tissue away, she noticed black marks from her mascara. She knew Fruma wouldn't wear such junk on her face. Mackey's smile popped into her mind; the way he wanted to protect her and cared for her. She didn't have that here.

'I think I need to go—go home,' she announced, realising that her home was so different from Fruma's home in Gateshead; and neither were a patch on Fetlar. Her therapist frowned.

'I don't think that's a good idea, let's take our time —we need to go through the material while it's fresh in your mind. You've had a shock—a cup of tea will help.'

'Sorry Janis, but I think I'd like to gather—sort myself out at home, I'm feeling much better now— maybe it's best to have familiar surroundings to work this out—sorry.' She looked at the coat rack, and grabbed her black, silk jacket from the stand, holding it at arm's length; as if it belonged to another woman.

'I really think you should come back and discuss this, are you going to be OK going home on your own? I could call you a taxi?' Laura wasn't interested. The secretary looked up from the desk as she strode from the office. The harsh sunlight, like a spotlight, hurt her eyes as she ungracefully tottered down the side street. For a moment, the sun hid compassionately behind a building, giving her time to think. She paused and contemplated returning to Janis. She felt a pressure building in her chest and before she could stop it, she erupted into more tears. A picture of Quincy filled her mind and a realisation that he was not here in this life.

In this life? Yes, Quincy and Mackey are not here in this life, they belonged to Fetlar. I'd never be able to have a pet here, I'm not dirty enough, and I don't like dogs in towns, and anyway, I wouldn't want to be one of those people that let their dog crap where people walk.

This flooded in as a small consolation. A small sob escaped her.

This is ridiculous! But it was real—every moment

with Mackey, and Lily, and the Shetland Archives, the Tait Sisters . . . .

She realised she'd even be happy seeing Da's face right now. The island suffocated her, filled her, it pressed into her pores, it bound her to its landscape and people; as if packed into a concert hall waiting interminably for the conductor. She checked her handbag for car keys. Walking as fast as her shoes would allow, she emerged onto the busy high street. Eastbourne; a familiar scene, the buildings and concrete made it feel barren and parched. Across the road, she recognised her car—she rushed over, unlocked it and fell gratefully into the driver seat. She turned the ignition and went into 'automatic' drive mode. Her house wasn't far, about half a mile away. She pulled up and ran indoors, feeling a little less exposed to the world. Everything seemed familiar yet empty; as if it lacked soul.

She walked into the living room and sat on the sofa. A picture hung over the fireplace: Edouard Manet's 'Olympia'—the nonchalant truth of unabashed nakedness. Somehow this seemed foreign to her; the pale, naked body of a woman lounging on the bed, almost a construct, plain and sexless, with a matter-of-fact expression on the woman's face. The artful way the hand was placed to cover the pubic region made Fruma laugh; as if that were the only offensive area of the picture. A Negro woman presented colourful flowers to Olympia; her black skin juxtaposed against the alabaster limbs of Olympia. She liked the black against white—or was it something she wanted to be; naked, matter of fact, truthful, and open; to live in a different skin, to be someone else. The picture seemed redundant now she'd lived Fruma's life. It wasn't what was important anymore. She imagined, in a self deprecating way, that it was only ever an attempt to be artsy-fartsy, but in reality, buying the picture was the first time she had reached out to 'something else' rather than the going along with the usual banality of life. She'd read an article about fine art, and how everyone sees an aspect of themselves in a famous painting. She'd also watched an interview on TV; one of her favourite actresses recommended therapy, so she decided to see a visit a therapist. It was then that she became two creatures. One who remained shallow, vain, and banal—the other dawdled in memories, and began to explore her dreams. A year into her therapy, Janis suggested that they try life regression therapy. She wasn't sure at first, but they hoped it would get to the bottom of something that was revealed during a session: her sudden aversion to sharp objects, like scissors and knives. She never believed that she would have such a complete memory, along with the feelings associated with living another person's life. A part of her wanted to accept, yet she struggled with the other doubting half that couldn't accept anything as inexplicable as this.

She moved an arm to see if she could. It moved, and she despised its obeisance.

You are not called Fruma, you know this. Yes— who are you? You are not someone called Fruma; it's a stupid name, anyway. Time to forget all this rubbish and carry on with your life—you are Laura Harrison!

'SHUT UP! SHUT UPPPPPPP!' She felt the movement of air in her throat, she heard the sound but laughed at it—pianissimo to crescendo—it scared her, because it didn't sound like her voice—she wanted it to stop, all of it. She panted and moaned, her thoughts like labour pains.

Look on the bright side—you're not an old woman like Fruma, you're not sixty-nine—you're forty-five— Yes! HA! I've got twenty four years on Fruma!

With this egoistic revelation, she felt a little better. Now she thought the picture didn't seem too bad . . . .

It's precocious nonsense. I want the scruffy bookshelves and Christian slogans—I need Mackey. Stop doing this to yourself! Look in the mirror. The mirror doesn't lie. I'm scared. I don't want to be alone. I'm alone here.

She felt the dull ache of missing something; and then realised she'd never missed anything before. Flashes of Fetlar. The island was a beautiful, golden cup, its magic spilled over the roofs of her house; it filled her to bursting. She felt something was dying, she was dying or wanted to die; had she already died? She checked for a pulse but couldn't find one, she panicked—then realised she didn't know how to take a pulse. She thought about her friends.

'Friends. Pssh!' She had work friends and saw her ex from time to time, and the occasional old friends from school—but she knew they weren't real friends, not after the close friendship she had with Mackey.

How can I long for a non-existent, aging Reverend in his seventies?

Yet she did long for him, for something to make sense, he would have made sense, would have reassured her; and she needed reassuring. She walked over to the window. It was warm, it felt good—she remembered how cold it was on Fetlar, even in summer. She put her hand out to confirm it. Summer was indeed outside these windows, a proper summer, real summer; a summer that brands the skin. She thought about going to the Arndale Centre for a cup of her favourite coffee, hoping it would ground her back to reality. She looked at her watch: 2.35pm.

What day is it? Forget it—just forget all about it— forget all about this stupid regression therapy—all it does it make you upset. Concentrate on the coffee.

She grabbed her handbag; she was aware that Fruma would never have bothered with such an accessory. Her shoes felt wrong, so she rushed upstairs and opened a cupboard that was full of shoes. She missed the comfort of Fruma's walking boots.

Which ones? The red pumps? No—not with a skirt like this. Stop it. You must stop thinking about.

She selected a pair of smart, white, low-heeled, leather slip-ons. Not wanting to see any more of her empty home, she grabbed her keys and walked out into the street. The heat hit her momentarily like someone had blasted her with a hot hairdryer. Throwing the bag on her shoulder, she walked to her car. It was all coming back to her now; this life.

Oh, there's Mrs Gerter—wave—don't be all weird— you do know someone, you do belong somewhere.

Throwing the handbag into the car, she turned the ignition key.

What about speaking to Janis? It wouldn't hurt to

try.

She speed-dialled her, but all she heard was an answer message—she thought it unusual because the secretary always answers the call during the day. Ignoring it, she decided to phone a friend from work; but then thought better of it. Maybe she wasn't quite ready for that.

Take things slowly, that's the best way—Janis was right.

She lifted a hand to her cheek, feeling her smooth, youthful skin, so different to Fruma's downy, aging face and wrinkles. This at least gave her some comfort. She played with her long, brown hair, then looked into the rear-view mirror at the unexceptional looking woman who stared back. She recognised her face, but not without colour on her lips. Reaching into her handbag, she rummaged around for a lipstick, and expertly ran it over her lips; it looked gaudy. Grabbing a moist wipe she furiously rubbed it off.

Go! For God's sake, GO or you never will! MOVE!

Pressing a little too firmly on the accelerator made the car lurch forward, almost hitting another parked car.
'DAMN IT'!
She reversed and carefully swung out into the road, passing familiar streets, the church on the corner, the side street that led to the main road. She cautiously merged into the traffic, but was hesitant at the number of cars on the road, it was shocking after the empty Shetland roads. She put on the radio on, Annie Lennox's voice cried out in stereo. She sang along with gusto, but it felt all wrong. She couldn't stop the tears.

Struggling to turn the radio off while making a hard right turn, she didn't see the mother with a pram. Her foot came down hard on the brake, stalling the car. The owner of the pram looked at her accusatorially. The car behind bibbed its horn long and hard, shocking her into apologies.

'Sorry! Sorry!' she pleaded in every direction. The person in the car behind was angry and threw his hands into the air to indicate that she was a monumental pain in the arse. Unhappy at being judged so harshly, she sped off at breakneck speed. Arriving at the car-park, she snatched a parking ticket. The barrier rose, and all she could think about was Mackey in his Shetland jumper, Tresta Beach, and throwing balls for Quincy. If a heart could be broken, hers was in a zillion pieces. She let go of her anguish as she wound her way around the car-park looking for a space. For a moment she remembered the seven-fold labyrinth as she drove around in circles, crying like a toddler, hitting the wheel in frustration.

She felt everything was tight, there was no room, and far too much concrete and throngs of people; and it seemed to be getting hotter by the minute. Spotting someone leaving she waved her thanks and pulled in. She sat there for a minute, now desperate for her regular coffee and some form of normality. Wiping away tears, she checked herself in the mirror; still thankful she was not old.

Grabbing her bag, she merged with shoppers into the busy Arndale Centre. The old feelings started to return. She remembered she liked clothes shopping, something Fruma didn't care about. She never wore trousers like Fruma, but then she never walked for a hobby either. But she didn't feel like looking at clothes.

Coffee, keep to the plan of having that coffee.

She rode the escalator upstairs, almost breaking down again when she saw a couple sitting on chairs outside 'MuchRooms' vegetarian restaurant. The man reminded her of Mackey; it was the hat and the way he sat. She realised she was staring. She went into a card shop and checked the date on some cheesy dog calendar. It started to come back to her; today was her day off, and she'd had her usual appointment with Janis. That made sense to her. She arrived at the coffee shop and was greeted by a familiar waitress who recognised her. She checked the time: 3.30pm. She ordered a double espresso and sat in her usual seat. The coffee was good, hot, and just what she needed. Proper thoughts and feelings were coming back, so she decided to ring a work friend.

'Oh, hi Tamsin, it's only Fru—err—Laura. Do you fancy coming round my place tonight? Could do with the company—OK—chow!'

Chow? Really? Since when did I say that?

She then realised she did. In fact, it was one of her top words. Irritated with herself, she finished her coffee and decided some light browsing in the clothes shops might be just what she needed; something that *Laura* enjoyed doing. Ignoring all doubts, and filled with purpose, she walked galleon like, passing Eschalons Bookshop on the way. Doubling back, she looked in the shop window; reading was not something she did, being more of a magazine person. In fact, the last time she visited a bookshop was when she bought a shorthand typing manual for her secretary course. A passing thought came to her, to look at the travel section, that maybe there would be a book about Shetland, and she could put her mind to rest that Fetlar didn't exist. Then she could laugh about it all and cancel her classes with Janis. She wondered if therapy was one of those things that just becomes a habit in the end. Tentatively she walked in, the place was virtually empty as most people were at work. She found the travel section and glanced across the book spines. There were one or two 'Walks in Shetland' books—she eased the book from its place and checked the index. 'Fetlar—Circular Walk—The Lamb Hoga'

The photo confirmed it was exactly as she remembered it. Papil Water and Lamb Hoga stared back at her.

No. No. No way was that possible. What the hell is going on? So it's true then? How can this happen?

Yet a part of her felt strangely elated at seeing it. She even posited the idea that Mackey could exist. She availed herself of a seat and flicked through the book.

But how could I have lived it? Did I dream it? I've never been to Fetlar before, never visited the Shetland Islands—never even thought about the Shetland Islands; this is ridiculous! But there it is, no different.

She wondered if she'd seen a documentary about Fetlar, or maybe someone had described it, and she simply filled in the gaps. Walking over to put it back on the shelf, part of an image caught her eye. Disconcerted, she peered closer; the book was half obscured by a larger tome. She struggled to remove it as it had been really wedged in. As she yanked it out, she saw a picture of the Papil Stone; it couldn't have been anything else but the Papil Stone—but then, she realised; that would be too much of a coincidence. The title screamed at her. It tugged cruelly at a woman hanging over the edge of a precipice.

'The AdderStane'

Her coffee rose to her throat in acidic objection—she gulped it back down. She looked around, fully expecting someone to jump out from the Religious section, show their Candid Camera credentials, while laughing and pointing at a camera hidden behind a leather bound bible. There were four people milling around in the store and no cameras.

So? Just walk away. Walk away from this illusion. It's a trick. God's having a bit of a laugh at my expense. Maybe it's because I didn't go to Uncle Lionel's funeral last year. You see? Your life is coming back. Of course, I have to buy it—because Fetlar was—is—real. Lamb Hoga is real. How can I ignore the facts?

She didn't dare look inside the book. Annoyed with the Universe, and feeling like she had no other choice, she walked over to the pay counter and slammed the book down. Sensing her irritation, the assistant watched her warily as he scanned the back cover. He coughed nervously, and then checked the front cover saying,

'There doesn't appear to be a listing for this. Would you mind waiting for a minute?' She nodded grimly, but sincerely considered walking out, leaving it all behind, going home, having a glass of wine and forgetting the whole thing. The assistant returned and said sheepishly,

'This isn't a book we stock, so I'm sorry, but I can't sell it to you.' All the aggression and tension left her, she felt it waft away like the ethereal delusion it really was. She chuckled lightly.

'That's OK, it doesn't matter—really—it was only an impulse buy. I'll leave it then,' she smiled, relieved to be free of the burden. She was about to leave when a manager appeared.

'Excuse me—sorry—could I have a quick word?' Hesitantly, she turned around. As far as she was concerned, anything could happen: any minute now he'd call her Fruma, she'd collapse and be carted off to the mental ward. Flooded with endorphins, she was ready for a fight; ready for anything.

'I'm the store manager, obviously, I can't sell this book to you, but after looking up the title, we can't order another copy because the book is out of print— so Eschalons Bookshop have decided to give it to you.' Both the assistant and the manager beamed at the store's wonderfully magnanimous attitude. She shifted around uncomfortably.

'It's yours if you still want it, how does that sound?' The manager saw her looking bemused and tried to explain the situation,

'It's a little unorthodox I know and not something that we normally do as a company, but because it's an unusual situation, we'd—' She felt a giggle, deep in the bowels of her belly; felt it rise up, and before she could contain herself, it erupted, leaving him and the assistant looking somewhat shocked. She held up her hand,

'I'm so sorry—unusual, yes, you could say that! It's been one of those weird days where things don't make sense—you wouldn't believe it—you just wouldn't!' The manager smiled knowingly and leaned forward.

'Is it—shall we say—the icing on the cake?' She glanced at his name tag:

H. Finn

She burst out laughing again, doubled over in hysterics. Puzzled, the manager looked at the assistant. Recovering, and wiping tears from her eyes, she said:

'Your name—is this some sort of joke? Where's Janis then—she must be in on this?'

'I'm sorry, I don't know any Janis, shall I put it into a bag for you?' he said, no longer smiling, 'It looks like an interesting read.'

She stepped back, knowing she was out of her depth. Fear is a strange emotion. At first it tells you it's not possible that such a thing can happen, then it switches to being *so* possible, that how could it ever have not been possible? Before she could agree, her legs were carrying her from the bookshop, past startled shoppers, her shoes slapping against the marble-like surface. Shop names whizzed by, and all heads turned in her direction; even children in prams peered at her. She took the stairs to the car-park and didn't rest until she was safely in her car. Now she understood the expression: fear lends you wings. Frantic, she checked her mobile phone for messages, but none had been left. It became real—everything—there are no coincidences, she reminded herself over and over again She tried to ring Janis, but now there wasn't even an answer message—just a continuous tone; she racked her brains for what that meant.

She paid her parking ticket and screeched out of the car-park. Driving home she realised her trousers were damp where she'd peed herself. This was another shock, to not have noticed such a thing. Arriving home, she threw the book onto the sofa and rushed to the bathroom to take a shower. She turned the heat up and let the pinpoints of water massage her for an hour until she felt able to cope again. Glad she didn't have to to see anyone, she wrapped herself in a heavy, cotton bathrobe, and went to the kitchen to pour herself a large glass of red wine. She drank one glass straight down and poured another. Now she was glad to be at home and in her own space. Grappling with the carrier bag, she pulled out the book and read the back cover:

Something is unearthed that should have stayed buried . . .

When a retired schoolteacher visits the remote island of Fetlar in the Shetland Islands, she becomes obsessed with the story of a local man who went missing in 1965. While the island is plagued by strange events, she uncovers more than she bargained for. What is the true meaning of The Adder-Stane Prophecy? Who are The Papar, and why are they linked to Fetlar?

Stunned, she could do nothing but turn to the first page and start reading.

CHAPTER NINETEEN

'What's this book you've been carrying around with you?' Tamsin asked Laura while at lunch-break; they both worked for a Solicitor's firm: 'Mannons & Frederick'. Although they'd worked together for five years, it wasn't a close relationship; it was more like 'we're in the same boat, might as well get on with it kind of relationship.' Laura attempted to bury the book deeper into her handbag.

'Oh nothing, just some book someone loaned me, can't put it down, you know how it is!' she replied cheerily. Tamsin made a face. Tamsin knew how it was for most people, but not Laura; Laura never read books. She decided to ignore it, she didn't really care about her anyway. She considered Laura to be a shallow, gossipy person, but it was better than eating lunch on your own, and occasionally she was good company in the evening if no-one else was available. She noticed that Laura had been more subdued over the past few days; not talking about the usual television programmes, or the latest gossip, so she knew something was up.

'Sorry I couldn't get to you that day you rang, only Steve decided to take me out on some adventure trip, I wasn't sure at first, you know me, I don't even own a pair of trainers! But I had a great time and most of the gear I managed to borrow from Anna, she's about my size, although I did double-sock her trainers, we all know she's got terrible Athletes Foot . . . . ' Tamsin droned on; however, Laura was still obsessed with

Fruma's life. The day she found The AdderStane, she had read it assiduously, the chain of events, thus far, had turned out to be exactly as she experienced them. This sent her into a spiral of doubt about everything in her everyday existence. Her working day was completed in a robotic manner, in fact, she was more attentive than normal; much to the delight of her boss who was used to a somewhat *giddy* Laura, whose interests didn't go beyond the latest fashion or the latest 'in' actress. She found herself asking Tamsin more about her holiday, just to be polite and to pass the time before she could go home and read the next part of the book. But Tamsin knew when Laura was being disingenuous; she was a terrible liar, there was no real engagement in Tamsin's story. Laura's body language gave her away, and her eyes betrayed her; not bright and sparkling at the latest bit of gleaned information, but belonging elsewhere—to another. Tamsin was surprised when she felt a pang of jealousy that she was not the centre of Laura's world.

The day dragged on before Laura could settle down again on her sofa and read more about Fruma's journey. She tucked into a Chinese takeaway, fork in one hand, book in the other, shovelling noodles without taking her eyes off the page. She'd got as far as Frater Alick and Frater Niven having the private meeting and had an overwhelming desire to rush to see how it ends. Then a certain sense of decency seemed to overtake her; that the author would be upset if the reader missed a piece of the jigsaw, so she dutifully continued reading in the conventional, linear fashion. Then she was hit again with shock. In the written version, it turned out that Mackey had really been double-dealing with Lily all along, to get the Shamir, and they were using Fruma to bring the Shamir to them. Lily was a witch, and they had no intention of following

Frater Alick's instructions. She hurriedly read on, horrified to find out that they'd killed Frater Alick.

But this was not how the story went. So I—Fruma had been played like a fiddle. Everything else was the same, the Haby story, and the fact that he was my brother—but Mackey and Lily betraying me?

Indignant, she threw the book onto the floor in disgust. But then, she realised she didn't know how it really ended in her version. The last thing she remembered was the foggy car journey while on the way to retrieving the Shamir. Finishing the noodles, she picked up the book and smoothed down a couple of creased pages. She looked again at the author's name on the cover of the book: Avalina Kreska. An idea came to her, maybe she could meet the author and tell her what happened? She cussed at not thinking of this before, she decided to look up the author's name on the internet. She typed in her name. Lots of entries sprang forth, but at the top was the author's website. She clicked on the link; the cover of The AdderStane cover graced the front page. Finding a 'Contact' page, she suddenly became self-conscious.

What shall I write? She'll think I'm some sort of nut-job fan. But what if she's as intrigued as I am? I won't know unless I try.

"Dear Avalina,
I hope this message finds you well. I wanted to tell you about a strange experience I had, you will probably think I'm nuts, but I was in a life regression therapy session where I was someone called Fruma, then I found your book and couldn't believe it, your book was almost exactly the same as my dream! How is that

possible as I have never been to the Shetland Islands? I would really like you to write back. I don't know what to expect, but nonetheless, I felt I should share my experience with you. I'm not crazy; I work in a Solicitors office and have never had a history of mental illness. I was surprised when the book took a different turn to my dream. I'm so intrigued! I would like to talk about this if at all possible or maybe visit you sometime; if you live in Britain.

Laura Harrison, Sussex, UK."

'Have a good time visiting your distant cousin,' Tamsin commented sarcastically, as Laura grabbed her coat and bag at exactly five o'clock. Tamsin was seething that Laura had never mentioned this trip before; knowing the 'normal' Laura would've spoken of nothing else for weeks, especially if it was something as newsworthy as a cousin she'd never met. Laura couldn't wait to get out of the oppressive office atmosphere. The more time went by, the more she felt a longing for the clean air of Shetland, and to step in Fruma's shoes. She'd still not told anyone about her experience except the AdderStane author, and no-one knew where she was going.

She'd finished reading the book. At the end, the Shamir had filled Fruma with great power, allowing her to overcome Mackey and Lily. The Shamir didn't need to be buried. The black wooden box opened of its own accord. The little, green worm inside seemed to have some sort of mind control, it made Fruma pick it up, and she laid it on the centre of the birthmark where it was assimilated into Fruma's body. It then telepathically asked Fruma one question:

'Who is your Master?' To which Fruma replied,

'It will bear evidence of its own Truth within itself.'

She thought it had a strange ending, but at least it had an ending; not just disappearing into white fog. The following day, she was just about to leave for the airport when she had a sudden pressing thought; and grabbing an envelope from a recent gas bill, she hurriedly scrawled on the back:

To whoever finds this, I'm visiting the Shetland Islands, heading to an island called Fetlar to meet an author called Avalina Kreska. I aim to be gone for seven days. Laura.

She then undertook the long and arduous journey to the Shetland Islands. She travelled by train to Gatwick Airport, flew to Aberdeen, and then booked on the overnight ferry to Lerwick—the capital of Shetland. Fortunately for her, it was a calm crossing, so she slept peacefully in the cabin, arriving in Lerwick a little earlier than the scheduled eight o'clock in the morning. Unusually, she travelled light; no face cream, make-up or jewellery. The day before she'd shopped at Millett's for casual trousers, walking boots, cotton t-shirts, two warm sweaters and a waterproof coat. It was exciting trying on Fruma-style clothes, in fact, she felt unfettered by this one act, it being a welcome change from her incessant desire to colour match clothes with shoes.

When she woke that morning in the ferry cabin, she showered and briefly ran a hairdryer through her hair, just to take the wetness from it without styling it. Not using a brush, she felt as if her hands belonged to someone else. She looked in the mirror, feeling naked at wearing no make-up—no 'social paint'—but she was not known here, so no-one could criticise her facial emptiness. Here, Laura could become Fruma, exploring these islands for the first time.

She was surprised how comfortable trousers and trainers were, and how she still felt feminine without wearing a blouse or jewellery. The previous night she'd scrubbed away all traces of nail polish, there was no way she could keep up that regime, and anyway, a part of her was tired of dressing up; did she have more men because of it? No. She worked out that she spent a total of thirty-six hours a week to make herself look as good as she did, and even after all that, she realised she looked entirely average. The previous week she'd made an internet booking into the same bed and breakfast that Fruma had stayed at, although it wasn't run by Mary and Peter Smith. On the website it looked exactly the same as she remembered it, but then she was beginning to wonder about all things seemingly 'going about their normal business', and what did it mean that she'd experienced being Fruma? How could she know Fetlar, yet she'd never visited the place before? Did it mean that somehow she was linked to Avalina Kreska's thoughts?

She briefly walked out on deck and espied what she presumed to be Lerwick in the distance, bathed in a propitious weather. The mellow northern sun was not so hot that she felt the need to strip off, just comfortably warm. She ate a hearty breakfast on board before exiting the ferry terminal. With a rucksack on her back, she thought of Tamsin, and how shocked she'd be, seeing her in hiking togs; she resisted the urge to take a selfie—that wouldn't be Fruma's style. It was a couple of miles walk to the town to pick up the rental car; the main road, she recognised. The road was relatively quiet as the shops had not yet opened, giving her the feeling that Shetland's alarm clock had not yet gone off. The gulls screeched and wheeled around the harbour in the distance. Of the few people that walked around, everybody searched everyone else's face as if they were a computer equipped with facial recognition software.

It was the beginning of September, the tourist season hadn't ended in Shetland; in fact the tourist season never really ends on Shetland as people also visit to experience the reported wild weather across the various islands in autumn and winter. She took possession of the car, and set off for the North Isles, double checking her map along the way. She thought it curious, seeing the Shetland scenery exactly how she remembered it; the craggy coastline, miles of peat and grassland, freshwater lochs, and rolling hills that were once the tops of the Caledonian mountain range. She followed the A970 all the way up before turning off at the North Isles Rd junction on the A968, to reach the first inter-island ferry crossing at Toft. She was waved into position on the Yell ferry, and was just about to venture upstairs, remembering Fruma's interaction with the Tait Sisters when she heard a woman shouting,

'Fruma! FRUMA!' She turned around, the name like an arrow piercing deep into her psyche. Something rushed by her, something small, a woman followed in pursuit.

'Shona! SHONA! COME HERE! COME HERE!!!' The woman shouted, in pursuit, finally grabbing hold of the toddler by the hood of her jacket. As the woman scolded the girl, the girl stopped and looked straight at Fruma. Inserting a thumb into her mouth, she smiled shyly before being dragged off. Fruma stood there, wrestling with her thoughts.

I'm sure she shouted Fruma, I did hear Fruma but then Shona does sound like . . . Jesus—you've got to calm down.

Finally, she shrugged it off, remembering Mackey's idea of seeing and hearing what you wanted to see and hear. Repeating Fruma's actions, she went upstairs, and paid for a tea at the vending machine. She turned around; nobody offered her a plastic cup holder, there were no Tait sisters. She clucked at her naivety and sauntered over to the pull-down seats to enjoy the view over the Yell Sound. The occasional miniscule seabird bobbed by on tiny waves, reminding her of how she felt; at the mercy of the something else far bigger than yourself, and you can either fight it and lose, or be guided by it and become stronger. A woman sitting on a seat across from her smiled. She immediately smiled back, overjoyed to make human contact.

'Visiting someone?' The woman enquired, in a thick Shetland accent.

'No—yes—but not a relative, it's an unusual situation I guess you could call it. I've never been to Shetland before, but it's looks exactly as I remember it—I —I mean—as I remember it from the photo—brochure —from the brochure,' she stammered. The woman nodded and returned to her magazine. Returning to the view, she became embarrassed at being flustered, and feeling self-conscious, she decided to take a look around the ferry. Pretending to take an interest in the notice board with the various local fundraising events, she suddenly felt an overwhelming, crushing loneliness; as if the reality of the situation meant she *had* to be alone from now on—the woman who just spoke to her confirmed it—who would want to talk to someone who doesn't make sense? Who wants to speak to a mad woman? Here she was, following some stupid dream, thinking people are calling her by her 'other' name—yet how could she deny the weirdness of the reality of living Fruma's life?

She looked down at the thin, plastic cup that reflected her situation. The cup itself, just a paper skin barrier of existence shielding her from the scalding contents. She had *truly lived* Fruma's visit to Fetlar— at least in her mind—yet it seemed as real as the ship that was moving her closer to meet Avalina, who was also *real*—the book she had in her coat pocket proved that, in fact it was the only proof she had of anything. She calmed her distressed mind by recalling Avalina's enigmatic reply to her on-line message:

"Interesting. This book seems to have a life of its

own. It would be great to talk in person, is there any way you can visit Fetlar? I have something interesting to show you. Let me know. Avalina."

At first she laughed at the thought that the author lived on Fetlar, that maybe it was one big joke. It was a long trip to make, only to find out the whole thing was a hoax; but she considered that the book wasn't a hoax, that it had mirrored the events, therefore it must be true. She thought of nothing else for a week before she decided to take the plunge and visit. She wrote back to Avalina saying:

"I shall be arriving Tuesday week, shall I pop round sometime in the afternoon? Can't wait to talk."

To which Avalina wrote back a simple message.

"We'll be here waiting. Safe journey."

She thought about the message, perhaps Avalina included her husband, as spouses or partners often do. For the first time in her life she realised there was nothing more she could do but go with the flow, take a leap in the dark, live a little, be adventurous. Laura Harrison, the woman who normally couldn't leave the house without looking perfectly coiffured didn't have a choice. The ferry docked at Ulsta on Yell, in antici-pation of spitting out current passengers and swallow-ing new ones. She double checked her map; nothing had changed. She raced across Yell to catch the 10.30am Fetlar ferry from Gutcher. She just arrived as they were boarding the ferry, she found herself check-ing all the faces, hoping to see someone recognisable; then laughed at her stupidity. Emerging from the car, and standing on the deck filled her with a sudden burst of optimism; she felt travel weary, but strangely contented to be finally on her way to Fetlar. She checked over the map she'd been studying assiduously since she knew she was coming to Shetland, remembering how Fruma felt, learning she was not who she thought she was. She wanted this desperately too, but knew this was too much to expect. An unexpected gust of wind ripped the map from her hands, the map flew end over end before landing flat on the sea. A seagull flew over it, investigating its possible edibility. At first she felt lost, as if her Linus' blanket has been taken from her, before realising she didn't need it anyway. She watched the map float until it was no longer visible to her.

Then she felt a surge of exhilaration, as if the map being ripped away, ripped away all doubt that she was doing the right thing. Not only that—but she was doing it all on her own, with no girlfriend to egg her on, no dominant boyfriend giving her directions. It was all 'her'—she totally owned the experience. She leaned over the side of the boat, gazing at the churning water that mesmerised her with its synergy. She was the only passenger out on deck, everyone else sat in their cars; reading or sleeping, seemingly bored with the scene. She looked back at Yell getting smaller. As the boat head out to deeper, open water, the wind picked up, so she retrieved her new waterproof coat, and zipped it up, relishing how windproof it was. Her black, silk jacket would have been useless here. The twenty minute journey flew by, and a ferry man squeezed by the cars to reach the controls for docking the ferry, he smiled and waved before shouting something. She made hand movements to indicate that she couldn't hear, the ferry man beckoned her forward.

'You here on holiday?' he shouted, his sharp features and beady eyes scrutinising her.

'I'm here to see Avalina Kreska,' she found herself saying. She thought it was probably wise that someone knew why she was here, just in case anything happened. The ferryman turned away, and then, thinking better of it turned to her and said,

'Have you got an exit strategy?' He looked deadly serious. Her expression changed to one of shock. The man's face softened, he shouted again above the noise.

'I bet it's about the book—yes?' She nodded, the adventure was already starting and yet somehow, she was still not quite ready for it. The man nodded knowingly; then his thin lips formed a one-sided smile.

'I'm just kidding—we've had so many people in the past wanting to speak to Avalina, I like to have my own fun,' he stated, smiling broadly now. She relaxed, realising she'd been holding her breath.

'You really had me going there,' she replied, half liking his stepping over a boundary, and half terrified that she might have travelled all this way to be let down. Disembarking the ferry, she had a mixture of feelings—fear mixed with joy, like oil and water. Driving along, she thought about the ferry man's joke, he was unaware he'd done her a great favour; it confirmed that Avalina actually lived on the island. All the buildings were in the same place and were precise copies as she remembered from being Fruma—she could only presume that different people inhabited them. She took the Tresta turning, driving slowly past what would have been Mackey's house. She visualised his dogs running around in the garden; Quincy, the odd, brown, scruffy dog, loving being the only male dog among Mackey's 'girls'—causing trouble. She didn't feel as heartbroken as she once did about Mackey, but being on Fetlar made her feel as if she were entering a familiar film set. She turned another corner and

Tresta Bay came into view. She drove to the kirk and parked the car, relishing the chance to stretch her legs like Fruma had done when she first arrived. She paused at the gate, her conscience pricking her; she'd told the B+B owner she would be arriving at a certain time, so she decided to stick to it. Relishing the silence, she got back into the car and drove the short distance to her base.

CHAPTER TWENTY

The room was adequate, with plenty of supplies. She glanced at the view over Tresta Bay; it was just how Fruma originally saw it, with no black water, and no fog, which was a relief. She felt strange seeing it again; looking at it with a different pair of eyes. Remembering her time with Mackey, she made herself a cup of tea, unpacked the few possessions she'd bought, drew back the net curtains and sat at the table, gazing at the sea. While she was reminiscing, she mulled over the ferry man's comments again, wondering how many people had visited Avalina; had they experienced being Fruma, like she had? Planning to visit Avalina that afternoon, she had approximately three hours to kill. Shoving her key into her coat pocket, she ventured out to Tresta Beach, retracing Fruma's footsteps.

Everything was as she remembered it; the light and the dark water, the sea, bringing fresh news, life and rhythm. Papil Water still looked dark and sullen, the sun had retreated, making the black water look blacker still, but she didn't experience a sense of foreboding, only peace; in fact, an overwhelming peace. For a short time, she stood on the banks of Papil Water, remembering when Quincy swam out to pick up the wood. She felt calm and still, and for the first time in her life, she enjoyed her own company. She realised she'd only ever holidayed in cities; never in the countryside, and never on her own. The remoteness had frightened Fruma, but not Laura—and she wondered if the reason it didn't frighten her, was because she had been through so much with Fruma. There was nothing to be afraid of anymore; Fetlar was not bathed in fog, people were not scared, Da wasn't waiting on the corner for her. She checked her watch: 2.30pm, she realised she'd been walking and standing far longer than she thought; surely she hadn't stood there for two hours?

Walking back to the car, she picked up a pristine, white seagull feather on the way. She gazed at it as she walked. It was from the body of the bird, a curling contour feather; gently bowed, not straight or taut like a wing feather. It, in its dry lightness, appeared to weigh no more than a breath. She lifted it gently, allowing it to fall back to her palm, closely inspecting the barbs that linked it to the rachis stem, so evenly spaced, seamlessly connected, pure perfection. A small breath of wind caught the feather, lifting it above her head where it stayed momentarily, like a bird hovering on a thermal, before being blown away. The feather never touched the ground again—rising, falling; lilting its way along the shoreline.

She contemplated its journey and her brief moment with it, and realised it was so much more beautiful than anything she'd ever cared to take notice of, which wasn't very much until today. She contemplated the fragility of life, how it can be swept along by the vagaries of innovation or changing tides.

Driving past Avalina's house, she decided to park near the other cars, not knowing the rules for parking, or whether she might be inconveniencing someone by parking right outside Avalina's house. Her copy of The AdderStane was safely tucked in her inside coat pocket; she touched it through the cloth before opening the gate, to remind herself of why she was here. It was the only proof of her connection to The Adder-

Stane—to her *other* life—to Fruma's life. The author's garden was overshadowed by an enormous fuchsia tree that still had flowers that hung like drowsy chandeliers. Dozens of bees attended them, their staccato buzzing a welcome relief from to the black house flies that provided a constant middle note; like bowed strings. She noticed a seven-fold labyrinth of life had been cemented into the door frame, just under the number of the house; she smiled, recognising the symbol—there was no doubt she was at the right place. Pausing at the door, the realisation hit her; that she'd made it, she was now closer to understanding Fruma than she'd ever imagined—the author of Fruma was behind this door. She was also excited that Avalina had something to show her, or so she said in her message.

Filled with nervous expectation, she knocked loudly on the outer door; not a timid knock that would mean that she was unsure of knocking; as she had never been surer of something before. She desperately wanted to meet Avalina; to immerse herself in this reality before she went back to her life in a town where feathers never settle on busy people. She heard movement, an inner door first, then the outer. A woman, on the shorter side of five feet tall, bright-faced with mesmerising green eyes, scrutinised her, like a curious bird.

'I presume I'm at the right house—are you Avalina?' Avalina nodded. Her short stature shocked Laura, as if the unseen image of her had metamorphosed, and grown in her mind to godlike proportions, only to be knocked back by the reality of this small, ordinary stranger.

'Laura?' Avalina asked, with a wry smile. Laura nodded. They stood silently staring at each other before Avalina swung open the front door, inviting her in. She accepted, amazed to be stepping over another threshold. She patted the book in her inside pocket like a person would feel for a wallet. Avalina offered her a seat and sat opposite her. Breaking the silence, which Laura didn't feel was apposite to break first, Avalina offered her a drink.

'Thank-you. I've just come back from visiting Tresta, the first time for me, but of course, I remember it from being Fruma,' she admitted shyly. Avalina smiled warmly and trotted out to the kitchen. Fruma looked at the surroundings. The wall facing her was filled with strange, ethereal pictures, with titles such as: 'The Snake has the Lion Inside' and 'Spirit of the Night'. Plastic geometric shapes hung from hooks, and behind the door, almost hidden, was a white board filled with scribbles and equations. She noticed there wasn't an ounce of the original underlying wall colour visible. She fixated on one picture which reminded her of a psychedelic sentinel, shining a bright, yellow beam across still, black water; she saw no attribution to an artist.

Avalina brought back a tray—on it a clear, glass teapot, narrow glasses with handles, and a tiny, white jug of milk. The sugar was neatly cut into amber cubes, the tongs for which sat beside. It reminded her of Da's careful tea making ritual. She smiled knowingly. Avalina looked up and caught her expression

'Reminds me of Da, and his tea-making ritual,' she offered. Avalina blushed and nodded, beaming back at her.

'I guess some things spill over from real life,' she replied, almost wearily. The clear teapot showed the swirling tea leaves; their brownness eking out as if artist brushes had been dipped in and stirred. This mesmerised Laura until she realised she was taking up Avalina's time.

'Sorry, I seem to be finding everything fascinating since I arrived.'

'It's a rare thing these days, most people don't have time to stop, to allow themselves to be moulded and shaped by the Creation. A feather falls from a bird and starts its journey alone; once it was attached, part of the whole, then it becomes an uncomplaining hobo, drifting with no agenda, changed by its separation— who knows where it ends up or what it becomes?' Laura sat upright, her eyes accusing Avalina of spying on her; this didn't go unnoticed.

'The feather is a good example and a common one.' Then in sudden realisation Avalina said,

'Don't tell me you've just . . . . ' Then she made a clucking sound, and shook her head gently, as if reprimanding herself. Laura looked on in amazement.

'How did you know I found a feather at Tresta? Ah —but then I guess that's what makes you an author— you see things,' Laura said, with sudden wisdom. Avalina nodded, pleased with her reply.

'I see too much, that's why I'm here, I can get swamped by the smallest emotion sometimes,' Avalina offered quietly. Then pulling herself together, she asked Laura,

'So you say that you experienced being Fruma during regression therapy is that correct?' Laura felt herself blush although no outward sign was evident.

'I was Fruma for three weeks. It felt like it was a dream. One minute I *was* Fruma—can you believe it? Then I was thrown back into being Laura, having lived through Fruma's entire experience on Fetlar—everything—the black water, the cup, Mackey, Quincy . . . . I have to say, it was the weirdest thing I'd ever experienced. I had a hard time adjusting, I didn't feel I could tell anyone—I mean—I'm just an ordinary person, but then to live someone else's life? It's a wonder I'm not in a mental hospital!' She felt good talking to someone who would understand; who'd take her seriously. Avalina listened avidly.

'I think the worst thing was missing Mackey, but really, I missed—oh, I don't know, I missed Fruma's life, even though it was torture at times.' She knew she was near to tears talking about it. Avalina nodded and poured the tea, saying nothing. She picked up a sugar cube and offered it to Laura's cup; Laura indicated two lumps with her fingers. She poured with reverence, the brown clear liquid first, followed by a dash of milk, the tea was carefully stirred again. Laura watched the liquid swirling clockwise, the white milk disappearing into the brown liquid. She handed her a glass cup, saying,

'It all ends up going around in circles until completion. You're not the first person to say they've *lived* the book; about twenty people a year visit. I had more people visit in 2009. Originally I published The Adderstane with a small publishing firm, I sold the whole print run within two weeks, then a commercial publisher approached me and it was re-published.' Laura pulled out her own copy from her coat, it was a little tattered around the edges. Avalina eyed it, but said nothing.

'People started ringing the publisher, asking for my contact details. I started talking to some folk, the same way as I replied to you, and it became apparent that something unusual was happening. Like I said, people started visiting the island. The trouble was, the odd one or two people went missing, and they were never found—the police got involved of course, but had nothing to go on, you might have heard about it on the news?' Laura shook her head.

'It was their choice of course to pursue the course.' She leaned forward as if others would overhear,

'Listen Laura, this island is special, it's like a kind of conduit. It seems as if you've already experienced something—a connection—and only certain people find this from reading the AdderStane. But—I mean—the Police would never believe this, when people went missing—who would believe it? They investigate and find nothing.' Avalina seemed to deflate at first, then as if a whole different character had entered her body, she smiled brightly, sipped her tea and looked off into the distance. Laura looked at the cover of the book, then back at Avalina who appeared to be trying to avoid it. As if the cover would reveal some truth of the situation.

'Look, enough of what happened to me, tell me more about what happened to you.'

'After I'd had my—my—anyway, I was in a book-shop trying to see if Fetlar existed. I found it in a Shetland travel book. I was curious to see if it looked the same as what I saw—which of course it did—anyway—right next to it, almost covered by an over-sized book was your book, with the Papil Stone peering back at me. Well, you could've knocked me for six! Anyway, I thought it was too much of a coincidence to leave behind so I tried to purchase it, but it wasn't one of the bookshop's listings. I was about to leave when the manager called me back and offered it to me as a gift. But—get this—his name badge said: H. Finn. I mean, can you imagine? I—I didn't know how to feel—apart from being scared,' she paused, not wanting to mention wetting herself.

'I haven't told anyone else about this—' Avalina interrupted her.

'Yes, others found this too,' she said quietly. Laura sat back in the chair as if moving away from her would have changed her words. Avalina sighed.

'Time slippages. It's more common than you think,

but some places amplify this effect, Fetlar is one of those special places. Sometimes people get stuck inside, it depends on what happens,' she offered matter-of-factly. Although Laura was glad to hear the truth, it didn't make it easier to accept.

'I honestly don't know what to say—I don't—are you saying that's what happened to me? But I was— I *am* Laura Harrison before I was Fruma—damn it— you know what I mean!!' Avalina nodded and looked as if the whole Universe was on her shoulders.

'Do you remember what was different in my book compared to your—to Fruma's experience?'

'Well, in your book—as you know—it turns out that Mackey was in league with Lily all along, and they tried to take the Shamir from me. The Shamir was put onto my birthmark and became part of me. Whereas in *my* experience, Fruma didn't get to retrieve the Shamir. She's had the conversation with Frater Alick, and was in the car with Mackey going to pick up the Shamir from Liam's house when it all went white, and I was suddenly back to being Laura. It was a shock reading in your version that Mackey and Lily had been plotting all along to get it.'

'Mm . . . interesting, not too departed from the truth, so which one is the right one I wonder . . . . ' she said, half to herself. Annoyed, Laura stood up.

'What? What are you talking about?' The diminutive Avalina looked up at her and shrugged.

'One of these stories may be true, one is not. Others have come to me, saying they were different characters in the book, also with a different course of events. Someone met Liam, he was homeless and living in London, begging for money, I even had someone who thought he'd lived Quincy's experience, can you believe?' Avalina beseeched her. Then, as if the craziness of the whole situation crashed in on her, Laura couldn't help but burst out laughing, real deep belly chuckles, the whole confusing mess erupted into the air, then descended like confetti; covering the two of them. Avalina found herself laughing too.

'Someone thought they were Quincy?' Laura said, chortling. Avalina nodded enthusiastically, before a kind of seriousness slipped over her like a veil, she said.

'Laughing and crying, it's the same release.' Avalina's sudden seriousness stopped Laura's laughter.

'What happened to the person who dreamt of being Quincy?'

'Oh, he passed through, it's complicated,' Avalina explained, then seeing Laura's horrified face, she waved the whole notion away like a Jedi mind trick.

'Look, you're the first who's come to me saying they'd been Fruma—most people have been Mackey, or Liam, Mary, Lucy, Ted—or as I said, even Quincy,' Avalina offered, somewhat sadly. Laura smiled weakly, hearing she'd been the only Fruma placated her ego. Avalina took the cups and refilled them with the same care as before. Laura was beginning to wish she'd told someone about what happened—she was starting to feel there were no up or down, that it was all shifting sand, yet strangely, she felt that the author was somehow telling her the truth.

'I wrote The AdderStane story because of what I experienced, much like you, it was so real, I thought it would make a good novel—I really was just trying to understand what was happening, it was my way of exorcising the whole thing—by writing it down. But when people started arriving on Fetlar—I mean—I couldn't turn them away could I? Neither could I have turned you away Laura—I couldn't leave people floundering,' she said sadly. Laura felt an overwhelming compassion for her, realising how difficult it must be, talking to strangers about such weird events, not knowing how they'd take it.

'You could've drawn a line in the sand, you could've stopped me coming, eventually I would've forgotten. Why did you tell me you had something to show me? You could've just ignored the message, or tried some other way to warn me off,' Laura suggested. Avalina looked down briefly before returning the gaze.

'Because, as I said, I've never had *Fruma* return—I had to try . . . . ' She implored.

'Try what?'

'Try to understand something. Too many people had disappeared, I've been trying to do so ever since I published the book and folk started turning up. Listen, what happened to you has happened to me five times already, each one different.' Her green eyes flashed with the truth of it.

'Five?' Laura echoed incredulously.

'Yes, always as someone else, but not from regression therapy like you experienced, this happens as if I dream their lives and then wake up—the latest one I wrote about in the AdderStane. It can make you feel very alone. In fact, in the beginning, you have to be alone to cope with it.' Laura suddenly felt very sad for her; figuring that she must be mad. A part of her had already decided that she'd be leaving soon, so it didn't really matter about whether it was true or not, it was all too crazy, Avalina was crazy, she was sure of it—yet part of her wasn't sure, otherwise that meant she was crazy too.

'Are you alone in all this? I got the impression you were married?' she probed. Avalina nodded.

'Yes, but he's on a research project and away most of the time, that's why it was so hard when I had the latest experience, and he wasn't there to support me. But I had another experience where I was married to someone else—the one where I had children.' She saw Laura's expression, her distrust.

'Look, you might look at me as if I'm mad, but you only remember being Fruma for a few weeks—well, get this, I had an experience that lasted for seven years!' Laura gasped.

'Boy oh boy, that was the hardest thing—waking up from that! I was this different person from about the age of seven to fourteen. Like what happened to you—it was sheer panic at first—oh, it was sheer agony Laura—in some ways, you got off lightly!' Laura sat there, open mouthed.

'I lived being a child again and going through all those teenage years. I was about fourteen when I woke up back here. It was hard to cope.' Laura felt Avalina believed what she was saying, but it all seemed so far fetched.

'So, when did you originally come to Fetlar? When did all this start?'

'It started happening before I came to Fetlar. I call them flashbacks, but the real name is Delusion—it's to do with the seven-fold labyrinth, anyway, they happened before I came here in 2009. I was working down south, some menial job when the first one happened. It didn't last very long, I lived through someone who'd had a car crash. I remembered everything; not paying attention on the road, then the car flying in the air—I felt the pain, the recovery in hospital . . . then I was suddenly back to being me.'

'How long did that one last?'

'Seven days.' Avalina looked at her sheepishly.

'Geeze. That must've been awful.'

'It was. But not as bad as the seven year experience. I hope I never have to go through that again. '

'You said there was five—'

'Yes. In another flashback I was a man. I'd rather

not talk about that one. So many regrets and such a bitterness ... it wasn't very pleasant, but mercifully it was short—but I learned a great deal from it. That's the other thing—we're supposed to learn from our experiences. So anyway, experiencing the AdderStane was the last flashback, that's why I wrote about it.' Laura's open mouth could've caught the whole bunch of black flies from the fuchsia tree outside.

'But, I know now that it all happened because I was being shown something, I was getting closer to the truth—this special place helped. Maybe it's true about the serpentine rock, it does make a person *see*. Writing about it helped somehow—but how could I know others were experiencing the same thing until people started coming to me? You see, not everyone came here because they'd lived through my book, some had just lived being someone different—nothing to do with the AdderStane.' Avalina sighed with the weight of it all.

'To cut a long story short, as far as I know, for me, there are two more flashbacks to come,' she paused.

'There are seven flashbacks until the completion, it's known as The Seven Delusions; remember the sevenfold labyrinth?' Laura nodded, but was feeling overwhelmed and numb.

'The seven-fold labyrinth is in operation everywhere in the Universe ... but not everyone is 'open' enough to understand. Not everyone is a seeker. Some folks just live ordinary lives. Listen—I only know this is my fifth delusion because I touched on something—some knowledge. You may be on your last, or your first—who knows? Anyway, enough about me, who knows what you will find out if you go through—if you want to know, that is ....' Laura put down her tea in total disbelief; a dark negativity crossed her face; Avalina could tell that she was losing her.

'Please bear with me Laura, I promised I had something to show you, and so I have. I've got someone for you to meet—do I have your permission? You'll stay to see it?' Avalina asked getting up.

'I—I—err—I don't know really—well I guess—I mean—to an extent I'm at your mercy,' Laura floundered, then correcting herself,

'Well, I know I'm not a prisoner here—but look—I'm having a hard time believing all this, but a part of me thinks you're being truthful—how I know this I don't know,' she said sincerely, 'as long as I'm not in any danger, I guess I'll just have to trust you.' Avalina bent over and patted her arm. She smiled, feeling her job was much easier now.

'Just hang on one moment then, I'm just going next door. I'll literally be two seconds,' she said and left the room. The front door closed. It would've been so easy to just get up and go, she could run to the car and back to the bed and breakfast, but somewhere inside, she knew she'd probably have difficulty going back to her life as Laura—a line had been crossed. The thought that this might happen again scared her. Especially Avalina's story about the seven year delusion. She heard Avalina's voice, and then she heard something odd, a tapping or clicking sound on the floor. The door opened and Laura shot up in the air.

'I don't believe it—MACKEY!! AND QUINCY!!' she screeched. Quincy leapt into Laura's arms, licking her face, licking her tears—she sat back down heavily. She couldn't stop the tears flowing while she hugged and kissed Quincy who was beside himself at seeing her. Mackey looked at her with tears in his eyes.

'Hello Fruma. We really missed you.'

Avalina and Mackey waited for her to finish petting Quincy. Mackey was wearing a huge smile at seeing them both reunite. Quincy, knowing the petting had reached a natural end, walked happily back to Mackey, his tail wagging. He looked at his Master as if to say—*well, I wasn't expecting that!* Laura stood up slowly to face Mackey, she flapped her arms up and down, unsure whether to hug him or not.

'My goodness Mackey! I don't—I mean, how can—?' Mackey stepped forward and pulled her to himself. She didn't struggle, she just sobbed in his arms. Embarrassed, and a little shocked, she was the first to pull away, Mackey held her hands at arm's length, smiling.

'But you're exactly as I remember you, you're the same . . . yet I'm different—if that makes sense! I was much older then—when I was Fruma,' she explained, turning to Avalina.

'This is where you are special. It was a risk I had to take.' Avalina explained.

'What do you mean?' Mackey took over the explanation.

'You're the first one to recognise me.' They all stood in silence.

'I don't understand.' Laura felt she was swirling into madness. She felt a little sick.

'Look, let's sit down, let me explain.' Quincy nudged her hand, making her bend down and stroke him again, as if dealing with animals seemed a whole lot easier than working out what was going on with humans. In fact, at this moment, she felt she would've been happy just taking Quincy and walking away. She said to Mackey:

'How did you know I was Fruma? Did you have a flashback, I mean *Delusion* about me too? It seems strange calling it a Delusion! I mean, I look totally different than Fruma, and I'm younger too.' She marvelled at how he looked *exactly* the same as she remembered him.

'It's complicated. I know you—you as you are now—from a *different* life—Delusion. In America. We had an affair that lasted for five years.' Laura gasped. She couldn't believe it.

'We had an affair? In another life? What—so I looked exactly the same as me—as Laura Harrison?'

'That's right. As you are now. In this other life, I had an affair with you—but calling you Laura didn't seem appropriate somehow—you are Fruma to me, but not like in Avalina's book—you are the Fruma I remember in that *other life*. Are you with me?' Laura could see that he was sincere, even if the situation seemed totally insane, and she still trusted him, despite the craziness. Laura made sure of her facts before voicing them out loud.

'OK—let me try and work this out. I'm Laura now, but woke up one day feeling like I had lived being Fruma from Avalina's book, but Mackey knew me as Fruma but in Mackey's other life—or—flashback.' Avalina and Mackey both clapped their hands briefly.

'That's it! You got it!'

'My turn.' Mackey said. 'So you dreamed I was Mackey the Minister, like in the book?' Laura nodded.

'Yup. You look exactly the same—exactly—which is *so damned weird,* considering I'd never read the book before I was Fruma—I mean—how is that possible?'

'I had my Delusion years ago. I couldn't believe it either—one minute I was there with you, with you as Fruma—the next minute I was back here. Like your experience, it felt very real, the other life. When I was with you, I was younger of course—I was a cop, and you, as Fruma, had to report a break-in. You turned up at the police station and we then realised that we

were virtually neighbours—and you had kids . . . . '
Mackey recalled. They all fell silent. Laura felt as if the
world was turning inside out, but was compelled to
get to the bottom of it all.

'So, me and you are connected in a previous flashback, err—Delusion, and I only know you from my
past life regression thing—I don't remember *your*
Delusion, I mean, I don't remember sharing it with
you, I don't remember reporting a break-in or having
kids!'

'No, that's right, because it was *mine* you see . . .
not yours, you were just part of it. I know, it all sounds
so unbelievable—but it's what happened,' Mackey
said, knowing it sounded totally unfeasible.

'So what are you now then, in this life, if you're not
a Minister from the AdderStane?' Laura asked.

'I've retired from the Civil Service—as far as I
know!' Laura shook her head and called Quincy over
to her, she fondled his ears. She looked down at
Quincy saying,

'And you—you are the same too—yes—you are the
same too Quincy!' she said in that silly voice people
reserve for pets, before looking up to Avalina with a
bemused look on her face.

'So what's the story with Quincy? How did I recognise him?'

'The same way you recognised Mackey. I can't tell
you—the book reaches out somehow—'

'Has Quincy always been your dog?'

'Yes, I've always had Quincy—in this life—even I
can't get used to calling it by the proper name. Delusion sounds so harsh, but it's really what it is.' Laura
turned to Avalina.

'But how does Quincy recognise me if I've never
met him before?' The whole room fell silent. Avalina
said quietly,

'Maybe he's had a previous Delusion too.' Nobody spoke. Laura felt a welling up, a bubble of laughter in her stomach. She looked at Mackey, who looked at Avalina, and then slowly each one of them started laughing. Laura remembered Avalina's words:

"Laughing and crying, it's the same release."

Eventually recovering their composure, Laura continued questioning Avalina.

'Tell me again—so you woke up from your latest . . . but what about Mackey?'

'I hadn't told anyone about my experience until I'd read the AdderStane. I was so glad I'd read it, I didn't think it was possible to have happened, that it was simply a dream. I couldn't share it with anyone, until I spoke with Avalina.'

'That's right.'

'We became friends after that, and he helped with people coming to visit me.'

'So, as you said, not everyone experiences this . . . . '

'That's right. Only certain individuals.'

'Lots of people wake up having lived another life, all the time—but most people dismiss it, as you say— as if it's just a strange dream. It's like six degrees of separation, you may have heard the term before—'

'But lots of people have come to you because they experienced the same thing as me, they dreamt of being a character in **your** book.' Laura explained. Avalina looked down and sighed.

'Like I said, I didn't expect it to happen. There is something special about this place. I found it drew people, just like the book does.' Laura was beside herself to ask another question before she lost her train of thought.

'So what is The AdderStane then? It was never really clear from my experience as Fruma, nor in the book.' Avalina and Mackey looked at each other.

'The AdderStane is Fetlar—the island itself. Do you remember from the book that an adder stone is a stone with a hole in it? It's considered lucky?' Laura tried to recall the idea.

'That's right, Mackey explained it, to Da—that's what I read.'

'The island—Fetlar itself is that stone, it's one piece of rock—there's a hole in the rock, and this is a gateway, can you guess where the gateway is?' Avalina quizzed her. Laura thought about it before blurting out:

'At Tresta somewhere?' Avalina and Mackey nodded.

'Papil Water actually,' Mackey announced proudly, Avalina nodded in agreement.

'It could be thought of as a gateway to another dimension, but it's more than that—it's time slippages—there are many dimensions or planes of existence, these events have already come to pass—you can go back in time or forward.' Avalina said, her eyes shining with excitement.

'Like a time machine?' Laura asserted.

'No—not really—because it's more than that . . . . '

'Then why are you encouraging people to come?' Laura asked,

'Because people are *still* trying to get hold of the Shamir. Laura—*the Shamir is real*,' Avalina whispered desperately. Laura shook her head, her mouth open.

'So there really is a worm that can cut stone?'

'Absolutely.'

'So, is the story of the Papar real too?'

'It's even more complicated than that! When I wrote the book and published it, people came out of the woodwork. I had visits from all sorts of people, trying to find out if I knew anything about the Shamir.

But one day, I had a visit from the real Fraters. That changed everything. They knew about my other lives, and they knew about Mackey's too.'

'It's as if they were some kind of Time-Lords. That's when they told me they'd been looking—watching all along. The difference was, they didn't know where the Shamir had been buried. Don't forget, my version of The AdderStane book was different to your version you experienced. This is the same for everyone. The Fraters told me to question everyone who came, find out their story, to ascertain their intention. If I thought they were only here to capture the Shamir, I called in the Fraters, who—err—dealt with them.'

'Dealt with them?' Laura said quietly.

'I—we didn't ask.'

'Why do these people want the Shamir?'

'To change the world beyond measure. If the wrong people get hold of the Shamir . . . . ' Avalina paused, and lowered her tone, leaning forward.

'If the wrong people get hold of the Shamir they could use it as a terrible weapon.'

'What would happen, what can it do?' Laura asked, now totally caught up in the story.

'It could cut through time and space—no—not just time and space—we're talking about a weapon that could be used against the Universe—and maybe even reach the centre of everything. The Singularity.'

'The Singularity—do you mean—God?' Laura asked, looking shocked. Mackey and Avalina looked at one another.

'Yes, well, you could say that. Don't get me wrong, nothing of this Earth can harm God, but remember, the Shamir is not of this Earth. It was made *for* the Earth, but like anything, its use can be corrupted.' Avalina said quietly, Mackey interrupted her,

'Avalina means—that God made this creature for a

specific purpose here, that much is true, but it can't usurp God's power, but in the right hands it can be used to disrupt the Universe in trying to reach him,' Mackey repeated. Avalina nodded in agreement.

'So, the First temple story is true then?' Avalina nodded.

'And then there was the second temple . . . after the first one was destroyed.'

'They built the second temple with the Shamir too?'

'Absolutely. But then the Second Temple was destroyed. The people who are looking for the Shamir now want to build the Third Temple. But we mustn't let them find it Laura. They must be stopped. It's why the Fraters are desperate to reclaim it so it can't be used for the wrong purposes.'

'So, the third temple shouldn't be built? Why not? If the Shamir was used for the first two temples?' Mackey and Avalina looked at one another. Mackey continued explaining.

'Because the men who want it are—how can I put it? Let's just say they have their own agenda, it's not necessarily in alignment with Truth. They are trying to force *Time,* even prolong it for their own ends. You see, time has been played with—manipulated. It's too complicated to go into now.' Avalina leaned further forward in her seat and concentrated on Laura.

'Is it making some sense now? Can you see why the Shamir must be found and kept safe? I'll go one stage further Laura, OK?' Laura nodded, her mouth set in a grimace, balancing between belief and non-belief.

'You've probably heard it said of Fetlar, that it's the Garden of Shetland—it's true meaning has been lost over time, this is The Garden—the Second Garden— this is the direct connection—this island from the beginning of time—this is the place of The Great Fall from Paradise, this is the direct connection to —'

Suddenly, as if the spell had been broken, Laura turned to Avalina and said:

'No—no—oh no—come on—I think this has all gone too far. I mean really—really. This has all gone too far. You're playing games with me, just like the ferryman, you get people to come here and then you mess with their heads don't you—well, that's enough, that's quite enough—I think I'm going to go back home now. Adam and Eve? Really! The Great Fall from Paradise? You must think I'm some kind of idiot! My name is Laura Harrison and I live in Sussex. Now, you've had your fun both of you—I spent quite a lot of money to get here too—and for what? Some unbelievable story! You've both just crossed the line. Well, it's been some kind of crazy fun!' Laura spat out, she stood up, determined to leave. Quincy urgently nudged her hand. Mackey stood up too, concern all over his face.

Avalina smiled awkwardly at Mackey and rose from her seat. Laura noticed something like a veil slipping over Avalina's face, and a change in the room, as if disturbed by an unknown wind. Avalina looked down as if gathering energy from somewhere; Laura noticed she was shaking. Avalina muttered something briefly before slowly looking up, she took a step towards Laura. Mackey quickly grabbed Laura from behind. Silently, she struggled in his grip. Avalina's visage slowly changed. Her eyebrows disappeared as her eyes widened into crude holes. The holes were deep and something moved within them. Laura gasped.

'Oh dear,' Mackey whispered in Laura's ear, 'what you said—that wasn't wise.'

A male voice came out of Avalina that shocked Laura so badly, she almost passed out.

'You IDIOT!!!' Avalina shouted. 'You think that your existence means anything?? You think that time is linear—you are born, live and die? What do you know of anything? Laura Harrison, the shallow creature who delights in gossip and fancy clothes—do you think you can turn your back on ME?' Mackey gripped her tightly, she fought against him but he was stronger. She tried to avoid Avalina's eyes by thrashing her head from side to side.

'I thought you'd realise if you came here, that you knew *nothing* and you would have some *humility*, but then you smirk in disbelief and think you are right? Such arrogance! That your existence is the Truth? I tell you—you have no idea, not even remotely an idea of the Truth! And then you think can just leave? Walk away? That you can laugh at me? Mock ME?' Avalina took one step towards Laura, who was still desperately struggling.

'Do you think you cannot be rewritten when it is required? Are you so arrogant to think that the story you live is that important? You are what is dictated, you have never felt, seen or experienced who you *really* are! This is only *one* story!' Avalina's mouth now started widening unnaturally.

'Look! Look out of the window—there's your TRUTH!!' Laura looked. The whole landscape on the horizon was disintegrating as if eaten away by acid, the headland in the distance was gone, she realised that soon, Fetlar would be no more. She couldn't bear to look; she couldn't think straight—flashes of her own childhood had become mixed up with Fruma's childhood.

'Time is not linear. It's all an illusion Fruma! Now you can't tell where you are—you are lost—lost to everyone!' Avalina started laughing, it was such an evil laugh, and so loud.

'YOU THINK YOU ARE LAURA HARRISON??' Mackey laughed—this shocked Laura. She couldn't bear that he was being unkind to her.

'I am Laura Harrison—I am Laura Harrison!' she weakly shouted back; like a prey animal whimpering before the predator tears out its throat. Avalina moved closer, now she had no recognisable features, her face had become a vacant black void that seemed to pull and consume Laura; now even her name eluded her. In the blackness, she saw a hovering luminescent letter; it was a four-pronged shin. As she felt it, she experienced regret—a terrible regret—the letter was the only light in the darkness. She heard a voice in the distance, the same voice who once asked her, *who is your Master?*

'She is given one saving grace, one letter—you cannot touch her.'

CHAPTER TWENTY ONE

As she fell into the blackness, there were forms in the dark that she couldn't quite make out. They weaved in and out, indistinctly, yet somehow she had felt their presence before—like crab creatures, their limbs falling into hideous shapes before her. The falling slowed, she saw something in the distance, but it was encased in a light mist. Then the mist gradually cleared, and she slowed to a stop. The building in front of her was surrounded by scaffolding.

Where am I? Am I Laura or Fruma?

She noticed an open door. As she looked around, she saw there was no sky, no floor and no other buildings; only blackness surrounding her.

How do I walk here?

She heard someone calling her name. It seemed familiar. She recognised it from somewhere.

'We're in here!'

The voice sounded urgent. Feeling what she thought was herself move forward, she wondered what was next. But she was able to walk quite normally even though no floor existed. The doorway was dark. Steeling herself and holding her breath, she walked through and found herself in a room. It was completely empty except for a spiral staircase leading into an unknown void.

'Come, Come quickly.'

Now she recognised it—it was Mary's voice! Elated at hearing a friendly voice again, she climbed her way up the stairs that seemed to go on forever. She felt a little dizzy and paused. Another distant voice. It sounded like Da.

'You're almost there!'

With this new affirmation, she quickened her pace. She looked down at the tight, spiral staircase; it reminded her of a snake, it wound itself around a central point. She looked up but saw only mist.

'Hurry up!'

This was Peter's voice, kindly. Faster still she turned. No sense of height filled her, her eyes remained on the goal, towards the voice she knew. She was surprised that she felt no tiredness, yet felt as if she had been rapidly climbing for at least half an hour. She continued, realising that she wasn't gasping for air; in fact, there was no air to breathe at all. Panic momentarily consumed her; and then she focused on a small girl in the distance, it calmed her anguish, it was something human, something that made sense. She continued turning, her body becoming the serpentine staircase, she saw and felt her backbone twisting; a double helix made of naked bone. The girl was close, she was holding out something, Laura's mind reached out, she was climbing faster, it all became a blur. Suddenly, it was clear what the girl was showing her—it was the seven-fold labyrinth pendant, she felt her consciousness almost touch it.

'Hang on to something, you must HANG ON TO SOMETHING!' said the small girl who she felt was Lucy. She reached for the pendant, but missed, then was whisked off of the staircase into . . . .

Blackness . . . a clawing aching, tangible abyss tore the fabric from her body and mind, leaving only bare soul to cope with sensory deficiency at all levels. Internally she knew she was suffocating, but she had no mouth or nose to receive the satisfaction of breath. Logic told her she was dying, but the panic rose and lasted, lasted . . . with no time, no place, No! No! Nothing. The dark took on a tangibility, it was the *ALL*, the only *THING*, the only *HOW*—the only way to anchor in the abyss of infinity, of loneliness so acrid that it stripped even the notion of an 'other'.

Fruma; if that name meant anything anymore, was encased in suffocating black amber that preserved a husk that had no memory or possibility; it was, and is, and will remain. And then she felt, she *perceived*, somehow . . . structure. It was caught like crystallised sediment. Both internally and externally. A movement of linearity, from form to form that vibrated like a note that hung in the air without a discernible instrument of production. It moved closer, and its form forced her own—the structural posture—forced her reality into mimicry, as if she were *created* in *its* image and until now had been formless; a non-existence, in infinite lack and loss.

'Fruma!!!'

The voice echoed as if the black had walls, or as if her own structure could resonate with sound—it disturbed the fabric of whatever she must now understand on such a fundamental level that she needed to scream in answer . . . needed something . . . wanted . . . but she had no ability to 'do' anything, she was formed by something she no longer had any means to understand. She had run out of mathematics long before emotionality, and now she wanted to stop, just stop; as if she now knew what that meant. There was no time here, no before—no after—how can things stop when there is no form or movement?

'I know.'

She winced with the pain of her vacuous emptiness being filled. No real sensation, just a movement that she longed for, so that she could hang on to something —anything. This was rapture, this was *a* truth, but even that thinking did not make sense. Any thought had faded to truncation—to *a* singularity—this occupancy was filled with neither true nor false, just a wondrous . . . IS! An orgasmic, indescribable ecstasy hung in the air between tick and tock. It described moment as eternity hovering through music.

'I know!' It seemed to say to her. 'You are!'

The full stop hovered at the gap fearing to fall over, it barred completion and creation, it walled her in worse than the black, it was, a moment hewn from endlessness, the 'white fire' on the black that structured the book of time. She saw the Shamir carve the letters on the stone tablets; at that moment, Fruma ceased to be, and fell. How? She could not tell; there was no *down*. She hit the sentence so hard that her consciousness descended further than the full stop, and she could see only one thing that carved into her a movement that caught the dance in her. It provided form in the formless, the letter, one Hebrew letter, *the four-pronged shin*. It was there, in her mind of no known existence, and something in her concentrated to behold it, to grasp, to encounter—then she heard Lucy saying:
'Hang on to something!'

The sentence faded; it was no longer needed, no string of words could convey meaning like this encounter. It was the completion of the symphony, the return to the fundamental tonic key, exalting and simultaneously completing, and destroying all that preceded it with such joy, she felt torn apart. But it ended her with such love that it provided structure that formed a 'staircase' of vaporous non-existence that ascended to yet another non-physical door. The door slammed. She heard this.

'Who are you, that you should be *that*?'

This was now a different voice that questioned her. She 'felt', she now could form an 'I' that could create a sentence, at first she thought she needed no judge, she knew no judge.

'Who are you, that you should be *that*?' The voice asked.

'I will, we are, we are the night that day has to part, temporarily, so that the blind may believe they can see!'

A different voice proclaimed.

'We are the Creation itself that stands alone in separateness from *the Truth* in a wondrous logic of our own making, and in our own image—we write the story that people can fill their vacuousness with, reason that they laughingly call sense, we are '*The Creation*', we are the only way that that mathematics can maintain your existence, we are the balancer of equations, if we do not have existence neither do you.' The voice faded. The same voice asked her the question, the voice from her dream.

'And so I ask again—who are you, that you should be *that*?'

Suddenly she saw herself 'nailed' to the black in the coalescence of Christian remembrances and gasped her first air as if reborn. This was negation, and it was conceived and born of herself, she had engendered it by the experience of entanglement. The Seven-fold Labyrinth had closed a loop, she had gone through to the other side.

'I AM . . . I AM.'

She stammered, she gasped this air, how good just to breathe again, this was life—this breath was needed —this was a want—she had been where want had no meaning, and now she knew, in stark contrast, the lust for life, and the appetite for more. She knew its danger, she could see consumption in front of her, and it was tangible, realer than truth itself. She cried, her first cry and was lifted away from her mother. She was manipulated, and wrapped up, she felt the pain of separation from the womb. She felt the cord cut. Then it all stopped. There lay before her a thousand-fold silence.

This was Nothing.
This was 237.
But this was not the place of Death.

Sighing, Avalina picked up Laura's book and sauntered over to an enormous cupboard that spanned the
entire back wall. She opened the door and found one
small, free space among all the other AdderStane
books that were ever in existence. Mackey watched
her while stroking Quincy.

'That was the last one, it was my last chance, there
was only ever one Fruma,' she said, sadly. He looked
at her with compassion.

'Something may yet come of it, she may come
through, we don't know everything yet,' he replied
encouragingly. She looked at the approaching fog out
of the window.

'Mistress, look, I must be going. Dinner in one
hour?'

'Thank-you, I feel famished, I don't know why!' She
saw him to the door, and with reverence, he bowed
deeply, before walking down the garden path, Quincy
gambolling along beside him. She was then distracted
by the phone ringing; she took her time answering it.

'Hello?'

'Hi Avalina, how's it coming along?'

'Just fine, in fact, I can have a final draft to you by
next week.' Avalina's editor was relieved, it had been
two years since the first book.

'Oh, that's fab—you know—everyone's saying they
can't wait to read this AdderStane sequel.'

'Oh come on—you flatter me! I must admit, it feels
like it's been a long road, writing this second book, I
almost gave up at one point, but this afternoon I had a
breakthrough.'

'Looking forward to it—I'll be in touch, bye.'

'OK—bye—take care!'

She put down the phone and decided to do the
washing up, the image of the floating four-pronged

shin clear in her mind. She was so close—then it had been ripped away. In a tumultuous frenzy, she grabbed a large kitchen knife and started crazily slashing at the water, foam sticking onto the kitchen blinds, water soaking her blouse, her eyelashes dripping. She stopped, the swaying, foamy water calmed from the violence, and under her breath she muttered a prayer:

'Open to me, my sister, for the opening is within you. My children shall enter only through you. If you do not open your opening—I am closed; and I can't be found, so open to me—open to me. Open the gates of righteousness. I will go in, and I will praise HaShem. This is the gate of HaShem. To find and cleave to Him.'

Then, as if the moment had passed, she pulled on some rubber gloves, and fumbling with the knob she switched on the radio. An Annie Lennox song rang out, and Avalina sang along as the bowl filled with hot water; about sweet dreams and travelling the world; because everybody is looking for something.

EPILOGUE

Frater Alick closed the pale, blue folder and carefully placed it in the open safe on the wall. He closed the door, turning the lock several times before placing the picture over it. He checked the time on his watch against the clock on the wall; he was behind by seven seconds.

'And the AdderStane Prophecy?' Frater Alick enquired.

'They never saw the missing section, they were not ready. There is time yet.' Frater Niven replied.

Nothing and Something.' Frater Alick uttered solemnly.

'And the eagle?'

'Thwarted—for now.'

THE END.

BIBLIOGRAPHY

A History of Norway and the Passion and Miracles of the Blessed Óláfr -
Trans. Kunin, Devra & Edited by Phelpstead, Carl,
Published by Viking Society for Northern Research
2001; Page 8

For all things Papar -
The Papar Project: www.paparproject.org.uk

Frumentius, *founder of the Ethiopian church* -
Smith, William & Wace, Henry (Editors):
*A Dictionary of Christian Biography, Literature,
Sects and Doctrines; Volume 2, Page 575* , Published
John Murray, 1880.

Solomon's Shamir -
http://www.jewishencyclopedia.com/articles/13497-
shamir
https://en.wikipedia.org/wiki/Solomon' s_shamir

The Demon: Asmodeus -
Schwartz, H. *Tree of Souls: The Mythology of
Judaism.* Oxford University Press, USA, 2004.
p.77- 96.

The Ebionites -
*Marjanen, Antti & Luomanen, Petri.
A Companion to Second-Century Christian
"Heretics", Vol 76.* Published Brill NV, Leiden, 2005:
Ebionites (Häkkinen, Sakari) Page 247.

The Modern Fetlar Prophecy -
Grydehøj, Adam:
". . . *Local tradition holds that in the 19th Century a now-unidentified elderly woman predicted a series of events that would precede the island's depopulation. One version of this prophecy goes as follows:*

There will be a mansion on the Ripples
Soldiers on Vord Hill
A harbour in Papil Water
And nothing but a shepherd and his dog."

http://shimajournal.org/issues/v2n2/f.-Grydeho-j-Shima-v2n2-56-72.pdf

The number: 237 -
Coleman, W. *Sepher Sapphires: A Treatise on Gematria; Volume 2.* Fraternity of the Hidden Light Edition, 2008.

The Papil Stone -
(Front Cover Illustration by Avalina Kreska)
The original stone was found in West Burra, Papil, one of the Scalloway Islands within the Shetland Island Group.

The Prayer uttered by Haby and Avalina -
(p. 171 & 370) Fm. *The Sefer ha Zohar, Emor, Verse 1295* (interpolated from various English translation).

ABOUT THE AUTHOR

I live on a remote island in the Shetland Islands with my husband, a handful of folk, and plenty of sheep. I regularly write flash fiction, short stories, poetry and various musings.

www.avalinakreska.blogspot.com

I wrote this book because both me and my husband have experienced some of the weirdness that is in the The AdderStane. Other strange happenings have occurred too, such as receiving a legitimate phone-call from the year 2049. Seriously.

Thank-you for reading my debut novel!

I value your feedback; please consider leaving a book review on the site or shop where you purchased it, or you can leave a review on my website.

'The AdderStane (Prophecy)' song can be found on my website or on YouTube.

www.avalinakreska.uk

The Flashdogs

I write with, and support a worldwide group of flash fiction writers. I'm proud to say—I cut my 'writing' teeth with them. All profits from selling their anthologies go to worthy causes:

www.thebookbus.org

Improving children's lives one book at a time. The Book bus operates in Africa, Asia and South America

www.ibby.org

IBBY (The International Board on Books for Young People) Bringing Books and Children Together.

. . .

I have two stories in their 1ˢᵗ Flash Fiction Anthology.

Visit their website: http://theflashdogs.com

Buy their Flash Fiction Anthologies on Amazon.

Printed in Great Britain
by Amazon